I. Town

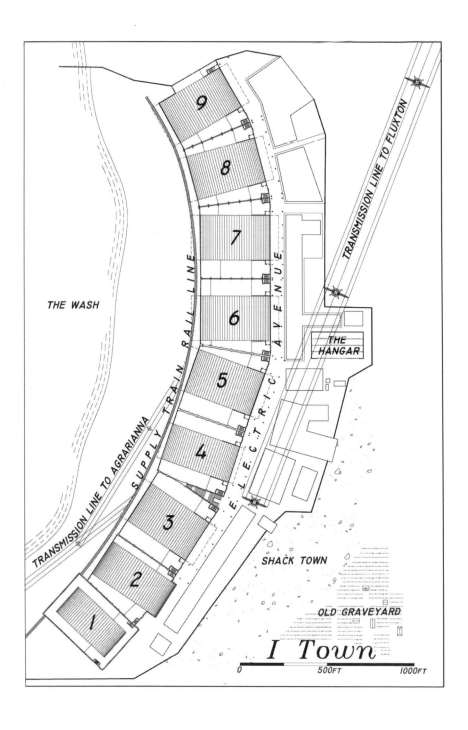

THE WASH

TRANSMISSION LINE TO AGRARIANNA

SUPPLY TRAIN RAIL LINE

ELECTRIC AVENUE

TRANSMISSION LINE TO FLUXTON

THE HANGAR

SHACK TOWN

OLD GRAVEYARD

9

8

7

6

5

4

3

2

1

I Town

0   500FT   1000FT

I. Town

Timothy Koch

[signature]

Author Published

I Town

www.inductiontown.com

P.O. Box 1524
Fayetteville, AR 72702

This book is a work of fiction. Any similarity of characters, settings, or events to real persons, either in physical appearance or behavior, either living or dead, to actual places, or to historical events is purely coincidental.

ISBN: 978-0-9910201-0-2 (e-book)

ISBN: 978-0-9910201-1-9 (hc)

ISBN: 978-0-9910201-2-6 (pbk)

Printed in USA

For Sonja,

always.

Society as a whole is more and more splitting up into two great hostile camps, into two great classes directly facing each other . . .

from The Communist Manifesto
by Karl Marx and Friedrich Engels

Chapter One

Jackson led the way through a forest of rustic stone piers into the cellars within. His little sister Ava followed. Above, a latticework of timber trusses supported one of I Town's nine induction generator treadwheels. Wheel Three was five hundred feet in diameter, half that in width, one hundred tons. In a football stadium it would cover the field, end zones, sidelines, and the seats around them. The weight of thousands of walkers inside the treadwheel drove it. Copper coils overlaid its outer surface, revolving within an electromagnetic sheath to induce voltage into the power grid of the Trintico Corporate Society.

When he found the man who had summoned him, Jackson took Ava's hand, wishing that he hadn't had to bring her. But Dad had gone from unloading the train to diaper duty, and their mother was out of their lives, or at least they were out of hers. Mr. Myrtle leaned against a stone pier. His scarlet pants and clashing vermillion jacket draped over his small frame, shimmering in the dim cellar. "Some light utility work," he had said. In exchange, Jackson would get some books and a five-by-five place on the weigh-in platform. There he would peddle the books to the walkers who strolled inside the giant treadwheel, especially the smaller ones toward the back who risked losing their place as the weight requirements increased. Of course, he hoped the Ironclad walkers up on the front lines would be interested too, because they had money to spend—the weight of their armor and chainmail made them rich.

A crate sat in the shadows behind Mr. Myrtle. Jackson hoped it had the books in it. He hoped the books would be big ones. The bigger they were, the more they would be worth to the walkers who were paid by the pound for their time in the wheel. In the aftermath of the collapse of the Carbon Nation, the Global Power Authority banned the conversion of resources, renewable or not, into energy, so geniuses like Secretary of Electricity Michael Faraday built treadwheels that converted human effort into useful watts of electricity.

Mr. Myrtle tipped his tall purple hat to them and offered a little bow. Thin black hair wafted from his shoulders. Green eyes twinkled at Ava in the dim light. She was the fortunate child, having come out of the gene pool at their mother's end with a healthy, hefty body. Jackson had been cursed with their dad's thinness and weighed barely over a hundred pounds.

With his huge hat back on his head, Mr. Myrtle gestured into the recesses of the cellars. An electric panel hung on a frame of scrap lumber. A big service wire draped from it and coiled on the floor like the tail of a monkey. All had been salvaged from abandoned Carbon Nation buildings out in the Wilds. "Hook that to something up there." Now his knobby finger pointed upward at Wheel Three.

Jackson was about to ask, to clarify, what the man was suggesting—vamping a connection to the induction generator? Vamping an unmetered connection to any point on the Trintico power grid was a felony. He could get life on the jail wheel for it, or, more likely considering his slight build, farmed out. Getting sent to Agrarianna to work the farmlands was the same as a capital sentence—they either worked you to death or they ate you. Nobody who had ever gone behind its Iron Curtain ever came back.

If the legal risk was high, the threat of electrocution was off the charts. Even though Mr. Myrtle had picked a time when only about two thousand walkers were inside the wheel, before the shareholder citizens of Fluxton were out of bed and putting demand on the power grid, the output was probably a thousand kilovolt-amps. But before Jackson could question or protest the idea, Mr. Myrtle reached behind him and brought out an object that caused Jackson to tighten his grip on Ava's hand.

She wriggled free. Hugging her Ironclad Heavie doll against her round middle, she glared up at him. She was six, the look said, and would not be babied.

Mr. Myrtle toggled the head of a walking stick from hand to hand, a gentleman's cane, sleek and black, but not just a cane. The round rubber handle concealed two blunt prongs, electrodes attached to the leads of a hefty capacitor hidden in its handle. The cane's shaft held magnets salvaged from old speakers sheathed in coils of fine copper wire. The device was called a knocker rod, the only weapon Trintico's bylaws allowed. The name either came from the knocking sound the magnets made inside the coils, or from the way their charge would knock a guy off his feet.

Along with the restriction of energy conversion, the GPA had also banned the storage of energy in every form from explosives to batteries. Jackson couldn't understand how the knocker rod didn't violate that ban: a capacitor was an essential component and was an energy storage device. Likewise, the Wireless out in the Wilds argued that growing food to fuel walkers on a treadwheel was no different from burning a tree to make steam. But the treadwheels of Induction Town provided Trintico with electricity and the people of I Town with jobs and incomes, so Jackson wasn't going to argue against it, just like he wasn't going to raise any disputes with Mr. Myrtle.

Ava darted toward the odd little man, revving Jackson's heart, paralyzing his lungs. She brushed past the knocker rod, the broad body of her Heavie doll actually thumping against it, setting chainmail and armor rattling, as she skipped to the crate. "Is this the books?"

"Why, yes it is, princess." Mr. Myrtle's eyes traced her movement like the needle of a compass following a magnet. He twirled the cane, rattling its guts. "And when your big brother finishes this little favor for me, it and a four-foot square on the weigh-in platform upstairs will be all yours."

Again, Jackson wanted to protest. This was no 'light utility work' and now the man had reduced the offered space. But, again, the walking stick came out, this time its business end pointing right at Jackson. He resisted the strong urge to flinch, despite the insulating rubber ball, but did lean back, watching the black ball hover in front of his face, hearing the powerful little magnets clack inside.

Mr. Myrtle's green eyes twinkled again. "Up you go." His smile was simultaneously cunning and cordial, devious and gracious.

Jackson followed the cane's rise and fall. The knocker rod was perfectly legal as long as it was registered. Possessing an unregistered knocker rod carried a fine of a hundred dollars, a year's income to the average walker. Jackson doubted its current owner had taken it up to Civic Level to register it, considering that the man was daring enough to hire a vamper. And carrying a concealed knocker rod was a thing robbers and thugs did; it would get a person several thousand kilowatt-hours on the jail wheel. But constructing and then selling a concealed knocker rod was a crime proportional to vamping an unmetered electric connection. This was the problem the device posed for Jackson—he had made and sold it to earn the deposit and rent for the little apartment he and his dad and sister now called home. That's how he knew the source of the magnets clacking to and fro inside it. He had padded the magnets with bits of fabric to soften the sound. He guessed now that it should have been more. Or maybe, now that his sin had come to light, only his conscience was hearing the ticking, like the beating of the telltale heart.

He immediately thought of Sir Isaac Newton's First Law of Motion: a body at rest tends to stay at rest; a body in motion tends to stay in motion. A body earning an honest living would likely go on doing it, and a body committing crime would probably have to do it again. But this was it, Jackson promised himself as he looked up at the enormous treadwheel. Maybe he would fry up there like bacon in a skillet. But if he came down alive, he'd shake off the yoke of crime and walk the straight and narrow the remainder of his days.

All this must have shone from Jackson's face because Mr. Myrtle's smile changed to one of pure satisfaction as he tossed the walking stick playfully into the air, caught it by its handle and leaned on it with the confidence of a big game hunter leaning on his rifle beside the carcass of his kill.

Jackson backed away. The odor of foods in the pantries and breakfast preparation in the kitchens swept through the cellar. His stomach twisted with a spasm of hunger and made a sound like the rumble of the wheel and the feet of the walkers inside it.

Ava opened the crate. "Ooh, Jackson, can we read one?"

"Yeah, Ava. Just let me get this job done."

Mr. Myrtle nodded. His grin went all toothy.

Jackson turned to the awaiting electric panel and coil of wire but then paused. "Listen. My . . . our dad—"

"Levine Koss," Mr. Myrtle said. "I know. He's at the laundry right now."

"You'll . . . I mean, if I—"

"*You'll* do fine. What are you, thirteen, fourteen years old?"

"Sixteen, sir."

"Older than I thought. Well into manhood. And I trust you, or I wouldn't have hired you."

Jackson nodded reluctantly and turned to a pile of scrap at the base of one of the fat concrete columns. As he picked through the debris he kept an eye on Ava. Their host had joined her at the crate and she immediately set into telling how their mother had gotten sick and they needed to leave her alone until she could get better. This was a myth to comfort a child. Hearing her repeat the lie made him regret fabricating it, and seeing the small man stare hungrily down at Ava and Heavie spurred Jackson to get the job done and get them out of here. It didn't take him long digging through the salvage from old Carbon Nation buildings to find the components of a hotstick, a tool to hopefully help him make the connection without getting fried. A long piece of pipe with a jagged broken end would do for the handle, and a length of flexible cord would secure the service wire to it.

Ava stood by the crate, swinging the expensive doll around, the solitary symbol of the well-to-do family they had once been part of. Jackson gave her a quick wave. On the one hand he wished Mr. Myrtle would take her away in case something went wrong, so she wouldn't hear and then smell her brother's body as it took amperage. On the other hand, the way Mr. Myrtle gawked at her, almost drooling over the admirable bulk of her promisingly substantial young body, made Jackson want to keep her close. Ava flung Heavie into the air, returning his wave without breaking stride in her conversation.

She was fine without him. Maybe she would be better off without him. Maybe it had been his growing so tall and thin that had cursed them with expulsion from their mother's family—the Piedmonts had the stout build necessary to turn the big treadwheels of I Town. Maybe if he didn't come down alive they would take her back.

He was being dramatic again—had read too many stories, Uncle Blaine would say. Ava would be fine and so would he. He just had to focus and get the job over with, get on with their new life.

Jackson took the free end of the service wire and ascended a ladder of bars sticking from the mortar joints of one of the piers. The bowels of I Town hung like a girth beneath the belly of Wheel Three, a lattice of pipework and conduits.

He gathered the full length of the ropy service wire up to the lowest beam. This close to the wheel, he felt like a bug sitting on Atlas's shoulder, the weight of the world pressing down on him. The high-voltage bus ribs of the wheel were just above his head— too close, each one carrying enough electricity to kill. He could smell the metallic aggravation of ionized air around the excited coils. Suddenly doubting the potential of his plan, he paused and considered going back. What if he did all this and nobody wanted the books? It seemed perfectly logical to him that walkers would enjoy reading while they trod up the curving inner tread of the wheel. He'd been wrong before, though, thinking Uncle Blaine liked him. But he was damned either way; Mr. Myrtle would turn him in for the walking stick if he didn't vamp the connection.

Mr. Myrtle's voice drifted up. "How's it going, boy?"

Jackson crawled across a stone arch that spanned between piers like the bows of great trees and gave a thumbs-up through the gap in the structure. He was thirty feet up now and just at the first stage of his climb. No turning back. He would get the books and make the plan work or die trying. He sidled up a timber truss supporting axles of old railcars, wheels rolling opposite the constant revolution of the treadwheel. Wheels Three and Five were two of the biggest of I Town's nine wheels because they had aft feeds above the cellars to send power to Agrarianna on the plateau to the south. Jackson moved toward the aft side of the wheel, away from the walk zone.

Each time Jackson passed an opening in the lattice of timbers he checked on Ava, and each time she was talking contentedly to their host and he was gawking attentively and hungrily down at her, absorbing her.

At the next stone arch, a massive pipe, probably sewer, tried to bar his way, but Jackson pulled his thin body through the gap between pipe and stone. Gathering the service wire to his new purchase, he realized that he had arrived. It was a bittersweet situation: the climb was over, but a garden of deadly bare connections surrounded him. Bus bars, transfer brushes, lugs on transformers—gray metal appeared cool and benign, but oh the power hidden within. Big wires plunged from transformers to the loading docks below where they serviced the rail line that brought food down from Agrarianna. Scant morning twilight marked the rails and the power lines along their curving ascent until they disappeared into the dark sky of the western horizon.

Tempering himself for the task at hand, telling himself again that it would be worth it, he took a deep breath and wiped sweat from his palms onto the legs of his baggy chinos. Moisture was a conductor, and he didn't want to aid conductance where he stood. The electric charge in the components around him was a bulging bicep, ready to strike out. The earth below and the mass of the stone structure were a punching bag, ready to take that charge with ignorant bliss. All they needed was a connection point, and he didn't want to be the place where the fist hit the bag. He inventoried the bare metal conductors. All were spaced well apart to prevent arcing. He needed to maintain that distance.

Below, Ava had arranged a pair of the books into a sofa for Heavie. The doll sat contentedly and stared at the girl who went on chatting with Mr. Myrtle while he watched her with lustful delight—an obvious Ironclad child. Did their mother wonder right now where they were? If she saw them now, or if she had seen them scavenging in the huts and tents and gravemarkers of shack town would she stand up to her brother and insist he let her husband and children back into the family? Or would she at least join them, putting her weight to work on a wheel to help support them? Jackson snorted the distraction away. It didn't matter; they were here now, and he was two steps away from finishing.

He spied a pair of fuses. Big things. Tubes several inches long and held in place by stout metal jaws at each end. That would do it. He untwined and spread apart the two conductors of the service wire, making a Y as long as the plastic pipe handle of his hotstick, then twisted a hook into the end of each branch. With a quick slip knot, he cinched one of the branches of the service wire to the broken end of the plastic pipe. He gritted his teeth and walked his hands along the pipe handle of the hotstick, booming it out toward the fuse connection, feeling sweat on his hands again, trickling down his arms.

Maybe his idea would work and he'd make a good living, at least for a small person, renting books to walkers. Maybe he'd show Uncle Blaine and Grandma Piedmont that he and Dad and Ava didn't need their wealth to survive.

The hotstick bent under the weight of the heavy-gauge wire. Jackson grabbed up the wire and held it high, using it to lift and straighten the pipe, each supporting the other. The free end quaked as he guided the trussed couple of pipe and wire toward the target. The fuse connector seemed smaller now that the end of the fat wire was near it. The fit was going to be tight, which was good and bad: it would insure the connection held if Jackson could manage to make it. He could do it. He had to. Hate swelled in him, for the people inside the wheel who were big enough to walk for a living, for round-bellied Mr. Myrtle with his wrong red suit and his ridiculous purple hat and his long stringy hair and the way he salivated when he looked at Ava's healthy build and expensive Heavie doll.

Jackson stabbed the wire into the connector and held his breath.

Mr. Myrtle's voice pierced the moment and seared Jackson's mind. "You about done up there, boy?"

Jackson didn't answer. He tugged the cord that tied the stubborn service wire to the pipe. The end of the pipe fell away and the wire held its place in the fuse connector. Jackson sucked in a huge breath. He leaned back until he could see the curious face of his host, gave a quick nod and then scooped up the other branch of the service wire.

Just this. Just one more thing. Then he would be free to launch his new life. He swiped sweat from his forehead with the baggy sleeve of his shirt, and tied the free end of the service wire to his hotstick. One down, one to go. If he'd managed the first, then why not the second too? He had this in the bag, he hoped. He boomed the pipe out again. Palms sweating, thin arms shaking, a tremor moved down his body, not born of anxiety or exertion but of pure fear.

Shevi's rotor wasn't where she had left it the night before. It was her engagement token, the disk part of the brakes of an old Carbon Nation car, the symbol of the Turney family she would marry into. Because of her name, her fiancé had special ordered a brake rotor from a Chevrolet Chevelle from the scavengers who pilfered the scrap heaps of the Wilds. "Just the sweetest thing," her friend Tasha had said the first time she wore it onto the treadwheel while her other friend Stacey had been too envious to say a word. Shevi had proudly worn the twenty-two pound hat-shape steel disk on a chain around her neck for several months before the minimum weight limit had gone up. Since then she'd worn it out of pure necessity. It and Dad's two ten-pound struts just got her from one-sixty up to the two hundred pounds she needed to get on the last row of Wheel Three.

The load warning horn made its buzzing blat in the hall outside the apartment. Demand was up earlier every day. The weight standards would be going up again soon; maybe they already had overnight and Shevi wouldn't know about it till she got down to weigh-in and found herself out of a job.

"Perry, have you seen my rotor?" she shouted.

Perry strutted out of his bedroom. His perpetual smirk bunched his fat cheeks. "Last time I saw it, Mom was wearing it."

Shevi groaned. "I hate the nightshift."

Perry giggled maliciously and pulled their dad's chain vest onto his shoulders.

"Can I borrow some?" she asked.

Perry outweighed his big sister by thirty pounds—he was one of the biggest fourteen year olds on Wheel Three. His vest was made of a set of tire chains. Weighing forty pounds all by itself, it was more than enough to get him on the wheel. Then he had another twenty pounds of accessorizing bolts and parts hooked through and dangling from the crisscross of chains. It wasn't a set of Stendahl custom armor, but they weren't high class like the Turneys. The Lilbourns were somewhere at the lower end of the middle class since the random killer thrombosis had taken her dad.

Perry laughed again, this time disgusted or disbelieving or both, and shook his head.

"Come on," Shevi coaxed. She knew she wouldn't get anywhere with the punk until she came right out and begged. "You can get on the wheel easy."

"Nope."

"You take the struts. That'll be enough for you."

"I'm not walking back there with you. Wait for Mom."

"I could miss a spot altogether if she's too late."

"Too bad."

"I'll tell Cole."

Cole Turney was her fiancé, and Perry followed him around like a second shadow.

"Tell him what? That your mommy wears his engagement rotor to walk the nightshift?"

Shevi froze. Her jaw tightened.

Perry swaggered past her. "Sorry, sis, but Kyle's bringing his new scepter today—it's a gear-ended axle—and I want to see it."

"So you can see it. Doesn't mean you have to walk beside him."

"We're the Titanics," Perry said with sarcastic slowness. Then his tone went teasingly apologetic. "We walk together."

"You're selfish. That's what you are. Dad would want both of us walking."

"Maybe. But he also might want *me* walking with *my* gang."

"You didn't know him very well if that's what you really think."

He leaned back and gave her a long up-and-down look. "How low are you willing to go with this?"

"If I can't walk . . ." Shevi began, but that was as far as she could get. She shouldn't have brought Dad into it.

"Rent something from one of those crazy Dims that beg on the weigh-in platform."

"If we could afford that, Mom would have done it."

"Maybe the both of you ought to eat a little more. Maybe that's really what Dad would say."

"You're an ass."

"Yup, a big one. Big belly, too." His shirt stretched over the rolls of fat around his middle. He grabbed them and shook them proudly.

The apartment door opened before him. Their mother's tall frame filled the opening, and for the first time Shevi realized that she was getting thin—too thin. Her face was long and gaunt and covered with worry.

"Better get up there," Mom said. "Weird heavy demand this morning. Like something's shorted out."

"Cool," Perry said and pulled his lunch pack onto his back.

"Maybe a vamper's gettin fried somewhere."

Then Shevi noticed what was missing about Mom's wardrobe. The shoulder straps and girth of the saddle Dad had carried her and then Perry in were there, crossing the thin and delicate scalemail Mom had worn when she and Dad had been married. Her dashboard was there across the front of her waist with a big cup in its cupholder. But not the brake rotor. Nor the heavy chain that passed through the big center hole of the rotor. Neither was around Mom's neck.

"What happened?" Shevi asked as Mom stepped inside.

"Roll on," Perry sang as he charged through the open doorway.

"Perry!" Shevi barked.

She knew Mom would make him share with her. And she knew he knew it too. The sound of chains rattling down the long hall faded as he made his escape.

"I bet it," Mom said.

"What?!" Shevi would not accept it. The first thing she'd been afraid of when she saw the rotor was gone. The one thing she knew had happened, and at the same time knew never would or could, had actually happened. The cost of having a parent who played the gambling tables. Oh, Shevi hated the night shift. "You lost it?"

"I'll win it back."

"No!"

The implications piled up in Shevi's mind like Ironclads pressing through a peak demand surge. She wouldn't get on the wheel. She'd miss a whole day's wages. Cole would find out. Mr. and Mrs. Turney would find out. *He* would shrug and shake his head, but *she*, Mrs. Turney, had a way of putting her hands on her hips and glaring at you that was more forceful than the entire family of nine, twenty-eight counting in-laws and grandkids, piling on you.

"We'll pool our money. Perry, too. I'll get it back." She shrugged like this wasn't the stupidest thing anyone had ever done.

"How could you?" Shevi asked.

"I'm getting us out of the Gut," Mom replied, matter-of-factly.

"By throwing all my stuff away?"

"I didn't *throw* it away," Mom corrected.

Shevi snarled and pushed past her, pulling the straps of her lunch pack onto her shoulders. "Get back on days and put on some weight," she said, just wanting to hurt her. "That's what Dad would want," she gibed as she charged out the door, slamming it behind her.

Down the long hall of the Gut the yellow light in the middle of the red, yellow and green demand indicator flashed and the load warning horn sounded again. Shevi cursed Perry, him and his selfishness. She suddenly sensed Mom coming to the door, either hearing her footsteps or just tapping that mother-daughter link they sometimes shared. Shevi ran down the hall to the stairs. She'd had the last word and wanted to keep it as long as she could, but she didn't. The door opened and her mother called out behind her.

"Shevi! Shevi, don't be stupid. Take the saddle."

Shevi stopped, stared at the floor for a second, humiliated. "It won't be enough."

"Maybe not by itself," Mom said sensibly, holding out the leather seat and straps, "but it won't hurt to take it."

It would hurt plenty, but Shevi grabbed it and turned away. Her earliest and best memories were of riding on Dad's back as he walked way up in the front lines. Mom tried to get him to sell it when Perry grew too big and went off to school, but he refused. She'd tried again when they moved up to the Terraces, but he insisted that Shevi would carry his first grandbaby in that saddle. And then he was gone. Now that they were back in the Gut Mom wore the saddle every night.

Shevi wrestled her pack off her shoulders and put it back on over the saddle. Maybe if she took some extra lunch she'd have enough weight to get on the wheel.

Chapter
Two

On their third trip carrying books up from the cellars, a black-and-white had taken up post at the door to Electric Avenue, the spine along which Induction Town's nine treadwheels were arranged. The corporate security guard's uniform shirt was black and white done in wide horizontal stripes and padded to make him look bigger than he really was. The white stripe across his chest held the Scott—three engaging circles representing I Town, Agrarianna, and Fluxton, the capitol—the logo of the Trintico Corporate Society. A knocker rod in his right hand was almost as long as he was tall. Its brass prongs curved toward one another like a beetle's pincers, crowning a bulging fat capacitor like the horns on a goat's head. The man shook the rod vigorously up and down. Rows of magnets inside it knocked loudly. No padding on them, no need to muffle their presence; on the contrary—*the better to shock you with, my dear.* It packed enough amperage to make you evacuate your bladder and bowels *and* bite off your tongue, if you caused any trouble. The black-and-white narrowed his eyes at the load of books stretching Jackson's arms.

Mr. Myrtle had warned him about the black-and-whites. The company president, CEO, and Board of Directors were making a visit and the place would be crawling with security. "Let's keep this discreet," he'd said.

"What you got there?" the black-and-white asked.

"Kahn and Hugo and Tolstoy," Jackson replied.

The man's eyebrows twitched. "What?"

"*The Great God, Mann*, sir. *Les Miserables. War and Peace.*"

"I have Beak *House*," Ava declared proudly as she cradled the book that served as a bed for her doll.

"*Bleak House*," Jackson corrected. "Dickens. The verge of the Carbon Nation, perhaps even prophetic of it. And—"

"That's a nice doll," the black-and-white said to Ava.

"Her name is Heavie," Ava explained.

Jackson stifled a groan. Someday when she had outgrown the stupid Ironclad doll, he would take it to the Upper Crust and dropkick it over the side, just to watch it hurl down onto Shack Town. No, that wasn't true at all. He or Dad would sell it because it was worth more than they could make unloading the train and washing out diapers for six months.

The guard picked up the doll and examined it. "She's a *real* Heavie doll." His expression changed from impressed to suspicious as he eyed Jackson's skinny frame. He placed it carefully back on the book and asked Ava, "Why are you only carrying one?"

"That's one I don't have to carry," Jackson said.

The man laughed at this. "What'll you do with 'em?"

"Rent them, sir. These'll bring a penny a day or more. Five cents a week."

The guard took *The Great God, Mann* off the top of Jackson's pile. Jackson's shoulders lifted with the relief of the seven and a half pounds. He thumbed through the book then checked the stack from the side.

"Where you headed with them?"

"Wheel Three, beside the Bartlett's fob booth."

"Just these?"

"No, sir. I've got Tolkien and Gabaldon, too—all writers of nice big volumes," Jackson said proudly. "And there's a Bible. That thing's huge, a fifteen-pounder if it's an ounce."

"How many more?" the man asked flatly. Jackson had obviously bored him with extraneous information.

"A dozen, give or take, and the crate."

"Jackson climbed up in the pipes for them," Ava offered.

The man's eyebrows did their little dance again.

"They were down in the cellars," Jackson said, trying to laugh and be casual while perspiration dampened his skin again.

The guard stared long and hard at Jackson, glanced at Ava again, who beamed up at him. He was likely wondering where a diminutive kid would get that much merchandise without doing something illegal. Jackson's heartbeat thudded in his ears.

"All right," the officer said finally. "Go ahead. You don't look like a lawbreaker." This judgment was aimed much more at hefty little Ava than at Jackson's thin self. The black-and-white dropped the book onto the pile and waved them toward the onramp of Wheel Three.

"Thank you," Jackson said and walked on.

Behind him, Ava said, "Thank you, sir."

They went on with their hauling, like a couple of ants in a massive colony. Electric Avenue came to life. The yellow light on Wheel Three's demand indicator flashed as dayshift walkers hurried to weigh in. Time was short. Jackson was missing opportunities with every walker that boarded the wheel before he opened for business. If Mr. Myrtle's pirating was pulling that much extra power from the feed Jackson had vamped, he'd better wise up and pull the plug on whatever he had going on. But there was no way he could be using enough power through a 200-amp service to push up the demand on a two-megawatt wheel.

Christopher Bartlett was already hard at work peddling the concrete and metal fobs he and his mother sold, debris from the dam up the valley that the Winders blew up in W3, the Wind and Water War. The man was another diminutive trying to make a living in the tough economy of I Town. He wasn't short but was very thin, might have been bigger on a good diet. He didn't dress the part though; his clothes fit close and his sandy blond hair was cut short. It contrasted with skin tanned dark from spending time outside. He must have trekked to and from the old dam site to get his wares himself.

"Fobs!" He gripped each end of a metal bar kabobbed through a gnarly chunk of concrete and shouted into the cavernous expanse of the wheel's onramp. His voice faded into the drone of walkers on the revolving tread beyond. "Buy 'em or rent 'em! Move up a row and make more money!"

While Jackson listened to the barker he reconstructed his motives and intentions. He was a small one, a diminutive, and this was one way a skinny kid could help his family make ends meet. He squared his shoulders and hoisted *Bleak House* into the air. "Books!" he shouted, but his voice sounded like a rodent's squeak. He took a deeper breath and heaved his diaphragm upward as he shouted. "Read while you walk! Penny a day or five cents a week! They'll pay for themselves! Novels! Bibles! Dictionaries! Encyclopedias! Old World charms! Carbon Nation curiosities! Books! Books! Books!"

A large, broad shouldered woman came over and studied the pile of books that Ava sat beside on the crate.

"In this one," Jackson said, offering up *Bleak House*, "a big fat guy spontaneously combusts."

The woman turned to him and drew back. "That's disgusting, young man."

She turned and walked away before Jackson could defend Mr. Dickens's text. Jackson glanced back at Ava who shrugged.

He put down *Bleak House* and debated between an old apocalypse classic and *The Great God, Mann.* Had the energy apocalypse turned people off from a story about a disease that kills as many people? He chose the latter, about the valet of a globalist, and hoisted it into the air.

Christopher eased over to him and whispered, "Don't set your price, kid. Leave the chance to haggle."

"Okay," Jackson said.

"Some of the big ones are softies and will take our stuff just to keep us from starving. And two hands. Use both hands and act like it's killing you just to hold it up. Makes it look heavier."

Jackson nodded as he slumped his shoulders and hunched over the book. Christopher winked approvingly.

"Books!" Jackson shouted, already much more confident. "Each one a hefty addition to your weigh-in. Old World charms and Carbon Nation curiosities!"

◎

Shevi presented her weigh-in card to Matilda Pruitt. Matilda served breakfast and lunch to the walkers who lived in the Gut, corridors of apartments that wound through the center of Wheel Three. She was a Dim, a tiny thing that would surely get carried away by the breeze if she ever went up to the Terraces or the Upper Crust. As the woman studied the figures and inventoried her stock the load warning horn sounded again. This time it was three long blats, meaning that the demand was in full yellow already.

Matilda looked up, seeming to ponder the very air around them, as if it had magically produced the sound of the horn. "Oh, my. Big day—in more ways than one."

"How's that?" Shevi asked, truly just wanting to get her servings and get down to the wheel before it filled up.

"Big demand *and* . . ." Her eyes grew large and rolled theatrically. "All those dignitaries."

"What dignitaries?"

"President Burgess is here to give the Sunday convocation, and the royal family. They're showing us off to folks from out past the

23

Wilds."

"What royal family?"

"Haven't you heard? Vice President Tyler has taken the title of Lord for himself. And so Jasper and Sophia and Hugh are Prince and Princess and, well, Prince, respectfully."

"Respect-*ive*-ly?" Shevi suggested.

Matilda plowed ahead. "When Tyler Burgess takes his father's place as president, he'll be King and Trintico will be a kingdom instead of just a corporation."

Shevi shook her head. "Okay. Whatever."

"And the Secretary of Electricity. And some foreigners, too."

"Oh, yeah?" Shevi said carelessly. The woman's drawl was a waste of time. She'd get the news from Tasha and Stacey same as she always did, if she managed to get on the wheel.

"Okay," Matilda said, fumbling with her slide rule. "Let's see now."

Shevi glanced left and right at the other servers and their lines. No chitchat or bother in any of them. Was the whole day going to be one catastrophe after another? Why had she picked Matilda's line on the day when the Dim was really being dim?

"Okay," Matilda repeated, but this time with enough pep and certainty to give Shevi some hope. "I recommend three biscuits with gravy and a double chocolate milk for breakfast and a steak sandwich, large chips, large drink, and a couple of cookies for lunch—plus veggies, of course, and snacks. How does that sound?"

"Fine," Shevi said. "Extra veggies, please."

"It is *so* good to hear you say that. People just don't appreciate their vegetables the way they should. The dietitians have just had a seminar on the importance of vegetables in the diet."

Shevi wouldn't eat the things; she'd have enough to do just eating the steak sandwich and chips, but she needed every pound she could get.

"That'll be sixteen cents," the server said. "No extra charge for the veggies."

She paid the woman a big part of the money she had left—money that was supposed to win her rotor back over the nightshift—loaded the lunch into her pack and set off for the stairs, stuffing forkfuls of breakfast in her mouth as she went.

Electric Avenue was busy as a hive. Ironclads strutted around, the biggest in fine Stendahl chainmail and armor, others with Carbon Nation iron machine components hanging from home-made vestments like Perry's. Shevi saw a few people with rotors and ducked low, hoping none of them would recognize her and ask about her engagement token. She didn't know all of the people on the various branches of the Turney family, but she didn't want to take the chance that they'd know the newest upcoming member.

A pair of black-and-whites stopped her at the entrance to the Wheel Three weigh-in. They checked her bag while she waited as patiently as she could to get out of the mingling crowd and in to the scales. When they cleared her to enter, she charged through the doors and into another cacophony. She'd never seen so much activity at morning weigh-in. Huge steel girders spanned the 250-foot width of the treadwheel to support administrative and housing levels. A flag draped at the center of the great structure this morning bearing the three circles of the Trintico Corporation logo. She'd never seen the corporate logo on a flag before. The yellow lights of the demand signals on either side of the flag glowed steady on and the red light at the top already flashed on and off, another sight Shevi had never seen so early in the morning.

Shevi cut a bite from her second biscuit, a third of the way through with her breakfast and already beginning to feel full. A cluster of black-and-whites blocked her path to the weigh-in stations. She approached them, intending to skirt them and move along, but one of the guards rattled his knocker rod vigorously and said, "Distance, please."

The guards hovered around a young Ironclad man about Shevi's own age. At least she assumed he was an Ironclad by the elegantly ribbed breastplate and helmet he wore. But he also had a long cape draped from the bronze pauldrons that cupped his shoulders. A cape would be very impractical on the wheel, fluttering in the faces of walkers in the next row. And no Ironclad would have so much security around. Then Shevi recognized the soft round face with its paunchy lips that seemed to hang open all the time. This was Jasper Burgess, grandson of Merwin Burgess the president of Trintico. Jasper was something like the junior vice-president of the corporation. What had Matilda said about them? He looked at her and she thought she heard him say, "More like *Cow* Town." She gave a polite nod and backed away as best she could without dumping the breakfast from her plate.

She turned away and almost plastered her biscuits and gravy into the chest of a small man with the biggest mass of hair she had ever seen even on a Dim. His skin was pale, his lips unnaturally red. The blue of his irises was accentuated by an ample amount of blue shading around them. He wore a frayed but shiny bright green tie and baggy magenta jacket over a pink shirt and held a camera in his hands. A wide smile and bright twinkle broke out across his red lips and blue eyes as he studied Shevi up and down. His inventory settled on her broad and soft middle.

"What a lovely specimen," he said smoothly, his flamboyant eyes drifting upward to meet hers. "Have you ever considered modeling?"

Shevi shook her head.

"Take my card," he said. "Richard Philbrook. Official photographer for His Honor, Mayor Van Asche." The card affirmed this with a location somewhere along the edge of Level 5, the Civic Level of Wheel Three. He gazed at her. "Mmm, how I would love to capture your wonderful voluptuousness with my camera."

She stared at him through the vee made by her fork and his card.

"Please think about it. I compensate my models richly."

"I will," she said and retreated toward the weigh-in stations.

At one of the scales a big man dressed in ring-mail and carrying a square iron axle staff with a gear on one end snatched his card from the Dim who had weighed him in. "Row Nineteen?" the Iron-clad shouted. "I always walk on Eighteen."

"Sorry, sir," the Dim said, a tremor in his voice. "Row Eighteen is all full, with the high demand and all." He ducked his head as if fearing a strike from the big man's scepter. "You'll have to walk on Nineteen today, sir. Very sorry, sir."

There was no way Shevi was getting on the wheel. She craned her neck to see down at the last row. Tasha and Stacey were there, waving to her. She offered a reluctant wave, turning to get in line to weigh in. Then, out of the confusion of vendor Dims hawking snacks and armor and accessories, she heard a strangely high and sweet voice. Down at the end of the flat area of the platform, just before it fell into the sweeping curve of a halfpipe where the onramp followed the shape of the wheel's tread, a little girl held up a book and shouted, "Books! Read 'em while you walk."

The girl was plump and healthy and clutched what looked to be an authentic Heavie doll in her arms, but she stood with a boy who was undoubtedly a Dim, with skinny arms, baggy clothes to hide the small body beneath and shaggy blond curls left to grow, as most Dims did—their long hair and long names.

He shouted, "Day and week rental rates! Read while you walk. Old World charms and Carbon Nation curiosities in every one."

Shevi stepped out of line. Mom would die if she found out she was throwing her money away on the stuff of peddler Dims when they needed to get the engagement rotor back. It was fashionable, if you walked the front lines, to let a bit of your money trickle down to these lowest classes. But if you were still living in the Gut, with some of the higher members of the lower classes, then taking their wares would only look like an act of desperation, which actually was the case with her this morning. And why should she worry about what Mom would think? If she hadn't tossed out the rotor on a bad hand of Spades or Gin, Shevi would already be on the wheel with her friends. She wandered slowly and carefully past the other peddlers, approaching the girl and boy reluctantly, knowing she'd be in plain sight of Tasha and Stacey out here on the edge of the flat.

She studied the odd and cheap looking fobs that a little old woman and a much younger man were selling. The man rushed over to her.

"Concrete and steel debris," he said excitedly.

Steel bars caked with broken concrete didn't look safe. Shevi could see herself accidentally bumping the jagged shard against someone while she walked. She wrinkled her nose and shook her head.

"Ah, I see you're the discriminating walker. Looking for something special." He stepped behind the little table and beckoned her closer, pulling out a tiny axle. "A scepter for the beautiful lady." It was deeply pitted with rust and no more than a foot long. Beside her, the boy and girl with the books had stopped their shouting and stared at the Piedmont family symbol, or more correctly, a miniature version of one.

"No," Shevi said quickly, shaking her head and stepping back from the contraband.

"Oh, come on," the man said. "Stick it to the big guys." His voice dropped to a whisper. "Balance the power. Equate yourself." Then he raised his fist and shouted, "Rise up."

This Dim was a crazy revolutionary and stupid enough to campaign right out in the open with corporate security all around. Shevi backed away, shaking her head. She took a last half step backward and froze midstride as she noticed a small hat-shaped disk in the pile of debris the man and old woman were selling. Tiny, the same scale as the little scepter axle. A rotor—the symbol of the Turney family. But something small enough for a school boy to carry. Annoyed now, she put her foot down, ready to take a stand for the family she was betrothed into, to defend the family symbol and rebuke this nutcase Dim who would dare try to profit in that name. But there was nothing behind her. She had backed herself past the boy and girl and their books and right off the edge of the flat weigh-in platform. Before she could tumble headlong down the onramp, the book boy reached out and grabbed her hand. He was small but not too small to keep her on the deck. He tugged her to him.

Shevi jumped back quickly, struggling to regain her balance and not to look down toward her friends on the wheel.

"Want a book?" the boy asked. "Read while you walk?"

Shevi recovered her posture and rounded her shoulders to re-center her pack.

"I highly recommend this one," he said, offering her a substantial volume. "It's late Carbon Nation. *Very* interesting look at life during that period."

He was just another helpless Dim pushing himself at her. She'd probably find the same kind of crazy revolutionary propaganda the fob guy had dished out hidden in the pages of the book. But the book was big and heavy and she needed the weight. She handed him her breakfast plate and bounced the book in her hands, guessing the weight at close to eight pounds, not quite what she needed to get to the minimum, which would go up if walkers kept getting bumped from higher rows.

"Seven and a half pounds," he said. "Go ahead. Have a look."

"You have a Heavie doll," Shevi said, opening the book and trying not to look too suspicious that a little girl hanging around with a Dim would have such an expensive toy.

"My mommy gave her to me," the little girl said. "She's sick right now."

"Your dolly's sick today?" Shevi asked.

"No. My mommy."

"Oh, I'm sorry." Shevi glanced at the boy who was rolling his eyes. No sympathy there. How sad. She introduced herself to the girl. "My name is Shevi."

"That rhymes with Heavie," the little girl said. "I like your name. My name is Ava."

"That's a very nice name," Shevi said, glancing at the text. The opening line was: "The sun did not set on the great god Mann." People were flying in a powered aircraft, definitely a Carbon Nation story. That could be fun. Then the pages parted at a place near the center where some pages had been cut out. A quick thumbing through it showed other pages gone and lots of places where text had been blacked out. "Hey! Parts are missing."

"Well, yeah. It's been censored," he said, bothered at having to explain the obvious. "That's the stuff about their electric power generators—*carbon* powered generators—you know."

"You can read?"

"Yes, as a matter of fact I can. I—" He stopped short at some idea that must have deeply annoyed him because his gaze drifted away for a second and his eyes narrowed. "You want it?"

Shevi took another look at the beginning. A monkey sat on a boy's shoulder and studied Mr. Mann intently, examing his round purple face. The boy, his valet, must have been from the Wilds or the farmlands of the Carbon Nation to have such a creature with him. "I like it but I don't think so," Shevi replied, returning the book. "Anything else?" She took a deep breath and glanced around, feeling suddenly diminished by what she had to ask. "Got anything bigger?"

"Oh!" he said excitedly. "I have got the *mother* of all books. Wait till you see this." He whirled, deposited Shevi's breakfast onto his crate, and returned with a massive volume.

It was as big as a boot box and strained the Dim boy to carry it. Shevi's heart fluttered at the sight of it. The binding was tattered but she could just make out the title in gold script.

Holy Bible.

It fell into her hands like the burden she was looking for.

"Has this one been censored?"

"Depends on who you ask."

"What's that supposed to mean?"

"It's a Protestant Bible."

"Does it have King Ludd?"

"No. That's a whole different mythology."

"King Ludd isn't a myth."

"Oh, that Ludd. No. There's another from . . . Never mind. You want it or not?"

"How much?" she asked.

"Five cents," he said, "a day."

"A *day*?"

"Hey, that thing's like fifteen pounds. Five cents a day, and a quarter for a week."

"A quarter for *seven* days?"

"There are still seven days in a week as far as I know." He crossed his arms as if closing the bargaining.

"Well, I don't have that much," Shevi said.

He leaned forward and said, "You know, Christopher over there was telling me about a movement to get equal pay for all walkers."

"That's ridiculous. Not all walkers weigh the same. Not all walkers contribute the same. And your source is peddling contraband—controlled items—and should be very careful what he says."

The boy shrugged. "I know what contraband is, but equal pay would sure help you out this morning. Wouldn't it?"

"Not if all the Dims around town were already on the wheel." She'd heard all this nonsense long ago.

"I guess you'd have to get up a little earlier and maybe stand in line like *we* do to get something to eat. And just so you know, some of us take offense at being called *that*."

"Duh! Diminutive just says you're small. It's a fact. Get over yourself. And, here, keep your stupid book." She tossed it back to him and relished the way it strained his scrawny arms when he caught it.

"Hey! Okay." He chased after her. "I'm sorry. Four cents a day. You got that much?"

She ignored him and walked on, head held high past the crazy man with his illegal merchandise.

"Three cents for the day," the boy said, sounding apologetic and desperate at the same time.

Shevi stopped, turned, took the change from her pocket and counted out three pennies. The boy looked down at the three pennies that were left, then back up at her. His face showed anger and hunger and confusion, all at once.

"I don't have that much to *spare*," she declared. "A girl's gotta eat, too."

The words were still hanging between them as the little girl looked up from the plate of biscuits and gravy, eyes hollow with want. Shevi's insides tightened. She wouldn't be able to eat another bite. She handed the plate to the girl and took the book.

"No," the boy said stubbornly.

Turning away with plenty of weight in paper to insure a spot on the wheel, wanting to sting him somehow, Shevi called over her shoulder, "You should let her do your dealing. She's good."

Chapter Three

The wheel was full. Even the front rows were completely populated. All the biggest Ironclads were already on duty, and a good thing too. The middle yellow and top red lights of the load indicators were on steady.

Jackson took the empty plate from Ava. She'd seemed happy and content for a moment with the rich food filling her stomach, but now her eyes glistened with the onset of tears.

"When will Mommy be better?" she asked.

Jackson looked away. That's why he hadn't taken even a bite of the high society food: it would only remind him of their old life. And Mommy—their *mother*, he corrected his thoughts—wasn't ever going to get better. There was nothing wrong with her other than the shameful choice she'd made hooking up with a Dim.

Jackson sighed. That's what he and his dad were. Diminutives. Offended by the label or not. It's what they were. By some genetic accident or curse.

"Look at them." Christopher Bartlett had stepped up beside Jackson, offering a blessed interruption to his pondering. Of course, it would come at a price. Jackson could tell by his tone that Christopher was about to dispense more of his social and political philosophy. The girl had been right about him.

To steer the conversation another way Jackson said, "High demand today. What's up?"

"Probably some big harvest going on up in Agrarianna or something. Same thing's going on in Wheel Five, you know."

Jackson nodded while thinking of what to say next to divert his politically restless neighbor, but his conscience pulled him back to the crime he had committed that morning, vamping the power output of Wheel Three. Maybe all this high demand was his fault. It couldn't be though. Again, he reminded himself that the line he hooked into the hardware of the wheel couldn't pull that much energy without melting down and catching on fire. Christopher had to be right: the Agrarians had to be doing something up there, maybe with refrigeration. Heat exchange put big demand on power production. He was about to share this to keep the philosopher at bay, but he was too slow.

"Since its conception," Christopher said dramatically, "our species has been reaching toward the state of the self-willed individual. And look at them. Rats racing on a wheel, trying to get a piece of cheese. And for what? Nothing but to keep the Fluxtonians comfortable. To support the corporation."

"But if the Fluxtonians don't buy our electricity, what will we do?"

"We buy it ourselves," Christopher said, stabbing his chest with his thumb.

"But we couldn't afford it."

"Oh, we could. With a simple shift in the economic paradigm."

Jackson shook his head. There were rumors of an old society in which walkers and consumers lived and worked in the same economic system, but it had failed—completely collapsed. People like Christopher didn't take into account the careful balance of the corporation. The girl had been right about that, too. Even equalizing pay among walkers was absurd and ridiculous and could never work.

He wondered about the girl. Would she have taken the book he'd offered first if it hadn't been censored? If it had been the copy he'd read? The copy that sat uselessly in his grandfather's library.

He could see her down there, on the last row, walking with her friends. But she wasn't talking to them. He couldn't see her shining dark eyes, only the top of her flowing brown hair; her eyes were down, looking at the book she'd rented from him.

Something stirred inside him, something dangerous. He fought it. He would *not* be attracted to her that way, the way his dad had been to a bigger, high class woman who turned on him. Instead, Jackson would spite her. Do good to those who wrong you, the book she had rented advised. Of course, it also advised against stealing.

A crowd of black-and-whites flooded onto the weigh-in

platform from Electric Avenue. Finely dressed dignitaries filed in behind them.

"Speak of the devil," Christopher said.

Jackson hadn't mentioned a word about the devil. "Nice talking to you," he said and took his little sister's hand. "Come on, Ava. I don't think any of those guys are going to want any books from us."

Jackson crouched at his crate of books, snapped a tiny lock through the hasp of its lid and looked Ava right in the eyes. Smiling, he said, "We're going to go check on Mommy."

⟨◯◯⟩

When Shevi boarded the wheel and sidled along the rolling tread to her friends, they were in the middle of a momentous debate.

"What's it matter how you spell it? It sounds the same," Tasha said.

"But the e makes it longer," Stacey said. "And I feel like some Dim trying to make myself bigger with a longer name." This was Stacey's thing. She despised Dims, probably because some of the kids had teased her about being one when they all walked together on the school wheel. Kids could be mean that way. Now Stacey wore her black hair almost shaved in opposition to Dims' long hair. The lack of hair made her green eyes seem extra big.

Her parents were on board, of course. They were hard walkers and solidly built members of the middle class. The upwardly curving inside of the wheel gave the back row a clear view of all the other walkers. Stacey's mom was up a dozen rows. Her dad was way up at Row 10, where Shevi's dad had walked before he died. Wishing he was still up there to turn and wave to her as she took

38

her spot on the wheel, Shevi fell in beside her two friends and hoped the debate would be a good cover for her missing engagement token.

But Tasha's first words to her were breathy and panicked. "Where's your rotor?"

Stacey pushed Tasha down the tread and out of the way to get good and close to Shevi. "Oh my god," she said. "The engagement isn't off, is it?"

"No," Shevi said. "Mom borrowed it."

"Doesn't your mom walk nights?" Tasha asked.

"Yeah," Shevi began, "but—"

Thankfully Stacey interrupted. "We saw you up there talking to that Dim boy and not wearing your rotor. He attacked you."

"He did not attack me."

Stacey speculated, "It looked like either you were hugging or he tried to grab you. One or the other."

"Sweetie, that's a good way to get some bad rumors started," Tasha said.

"It's no big deal," Shevi said.

"It is a *very* big deal," Stacey corrected.

"What were you talking about just now?" Shevi asked, trying to divert.

"You're engaged to a *Turney*," Stacey said. "You are such a lucky girl. Isn't she, Tasha?"

Tasha nodded.

Stacey grabbed Tasha and swapped places with her again. She elbowed her, shoving her toward Shevi. "Tell her, Tasha. Tell her how lucky she is to be marrying into the Turney family. Go ahead."

She made a shooing motion toward Shevi, as if to reroute the steady, forward current of the walkers.

Looking quite bored, Tasha crossed her arms over her custom Stendahl chainmail vest—Tasha was a Worthen and Worthens could afford to finance such things, especially to get their daughters on the wheel and get them noticed. Dryly she said, "Shevi you are very fortunate to be marrying into one of the biggest families in I Town. But we know you'd never be dumb enough to throw that away for a Dim."

"Right," Stacey said. "My mom says Dims can be a fun distraction, but other than that they're totally useless."

Tasha gave Stacey an appraising glance then pleased Shevi by changing the subject. "Now tell this girl it won't matter in the least if she drops the e from her name."

Shevi smiled. Save an awkward tummy bulge, Stacey couldn't put on weight like she and Tasha could. To compensate for her modest body size and middle class status, she wore dense padding under her armor and clothes, which were a bit too loose to stylishly show off a big body. A Dim had made the bodysuit, and even at Dim wages the thing still cost a fortune, or so Stacey had bragged discreetly to her two friends. Only to her close friends, though. The bodysuit wasn't discussed outside their circle of three. When the weight minimum had gone up, Stacey stayed hidden for the week it took the little tailor to upgrade the suit. Shevi wondered if Stacey would be able to hide her true size right up to her wedding night then shock the boy with the sight of ribs and narrow hips. All the women said that girls would gain nicely after having a baby or two and maybe Stacey could find someone to love her enough to wait for that, but at sixteen she still hadn't had more than a few dates.

Thoughtfully, Shevi said, "No. No, I don't see the spelling mattering at all. It won't make it sound any shorter."

"But it's unnecessary," Stacey said. "Like a Dim. Just *there* and doing nothing."

"Dims contribute," Tasha shot back.

Stacey spewed theatrically. "Oh, please."

Clutching the big book in her arms, Shevi realized she wouldn't have made it on the wheel today if that Dim boy hadn't been there with his big, cheap books and his desperation. Up on the platform he was following a walker, holding out a book and giving his pitch. There was something . . . about him. He could read. Apparently he could read very well and had read a lot. Either that or he was a good actor. But that just couldn't be because he seemed smart. He had a confidence Shevi hadn't seen in most other Dims. And he was obviously very ambitious. She was sure that if he were bigger he'd be on the front lines.

She shook her head in frustration, resolved to stop thinking about him, and looked away from him before her friends caught her staring. "You could drop the y."

Tasha and Stacey had fallen back into their own little debate while Shevi's mind had been wandering. They halted their chatter and stared at her.

"Then you'd be just Stace," Shevi said. "One syllable."

Stacey's eyes swelled to bulging. "Yes! Oh, yes. That's perfect. Just Stace. Shevi, you're a genius."

Tasha beamed. "Way to go. Why didn't we think of that?"

Shevi hugged her rented book. Carrying it made her feel

smarter. Her talk with the Dim had been thought provoking, like a duel of minds. Maybe he wasn't like the others. Maybe he deserved respect rather than being taken advantage of. She shouldn't have been so hard on him. She would make it up to him. For starters, she would stop thinking of him as a Dim, since the label seemed to offend him. She would think of him simply as the book boy.

She opened his book and browsed its contents, settling on a section in about its middle, and began to read a section she assumed was about work. The page heading was "Job". She turned to the beginning and discovered that the section wasn't about work at all but about a guy named Job—long o. He needed the e Stacey had wanted to get rid of before she became Stace at Shevi's insight.

Shevi had a hard time with the text, but according to the commentary at the bottom of each page, the story went that a bad angel named Satan put a very good man named Job through a really bad time. Satan believed Job would turn from his good ways if his life wasn't so good. He did terrible things to Job, but Job wouldn't turn away from God.

Shevi wondered why more walkers didn't read while they walked. It was a great way to pass the time once she'd gotten tired of the monotony of her friends' conversation. She'd really have to find something to do for the book boy. Like Job, the book boy needed a break.

Chapter

Four

Jackson and Ava walked the length of Electric Avenue. Wheel Four dining halls they couldn't afford were filled with Ironclads fueling up for the day's walk, but the businesses along Wheel Five were empty, all its Ironclads already walking. Wheel Five had the same problem with massive demand that plagued Wheel Three this morning.

A huge contingency of Ironclads blocked Electric Avenue at Wheel Six. They all were craning their necks to see the front windows of the Stendahl armor dealership. Jackson put Ava on his shoulders—man, she was growing fast. As they approached a group of large women Jackson felt the weight of Heavie plop onto the top of his head.

"May we pass?" he said.

The heels of Heavie's big, booted feet stuck out above his eyes. He was sure he looked like a complete idiot, but Ava was his ticket, after all.

One of the women looked down at him. "Needing some new armor for the first family's visit, are you?"

All of them laughed grandly at this except one clad in a shawl of massive chains over a suit of heavy leather ringmail. She glared suspiciously at the pair and asked, "Where did you get that child?"

"She's my sister," Jackson said.

"Is that true, girl?" the woman asked.

"Yes, ma'am," Ava said. Her body rocked on his shoulders as she nodded vigorously.

They'd had problems before with Ironclads thinking he had snatched one of their little ones and was taking off to—who knows?—roast her and eat her perhaps. He was a Dim after all.

The woman ruffled her shawl, the links of chain jangling furiously, and returned to the conversations with her companions.

"May we pass?" Ava asked.

Trying their best to ignore the Dim rabble that had interrupted their morning, they made a narrow gap with no other acknowledgement.

At Wheel Eight Jackson lifted Ava down. He led the way to the offramp side of the wheel because the other way would be busy with the morning rush of walkers coming down to weigh in. Unfortunately, he couldn't afford the fare of the express lift they'd ridden with Grandma and Grandpa. Getting to the Upper Crust of Wheel Eight where the Piedmont family had its grand nest was more than twice the ascent of going to the Gut of Wheel Three.

After a few days in the older wheel on the south end of town, Wheel Eight's stairs were notably wider, the treads less worn. Jackson and Ava climbed past the Admin Level, then the Civic Level, then the housing levels for the lowest classes—the butt of Wheel Eight's Gut. Four hundred feet of stairs, around and around, past level after level of the Gut, rising through the classes. At the landing where a small window looked out across a wedge of roof between Wheels Seven and Eight, they would be passing the lower middle class where the common bathrooms had stalls for privacy. The adults would weigh-in at three-hundred pounds with their armor, and the biggest could afford the occasional blessed window. Next above, the four-hundred-pound middle class were more likely to have windows with views and live around a clean and spacious dining hall.

When they reached the Terraces of the upper middle class Jackson said, "Let's get out of here."

Ava agreed.

The Terraces followed the shape of the upper half of the wheel and provided airy homes for the walkers on the front lines. Jackson was wary; the people who lived up here brought more than five hundred pounds each to the treadwheel and didn't walk the long ten- and twelve-hour days of the lessers down below. They could stroll onto the wheel midmorning when demand climbed to its highest level, so they could be lingering around home now and catch little trespassers who didn't belong in this part of town. But the streets that ran the width of the wheel below, connected by narrow alleys of steep stairs, were vacant and quiet. Good thing everybody was down on the wheel to see the first family. Otherwise a skinny kid wouldn't have made it this far without getting arrested. The ascent was slower as they zigzagged through the empty streets, but the air was fresh. The sun's light was unobstructed out here, too. Its energy seemed to lift Jackson's soles off the pavement. He and Ava ran up the alley stairs and past the nice houses, each with a whole front door all to itself, while Heavie flailed at Ava's side.

The gates to the Upper Crust stood wide open, but old Mr. Lambert was there keeping his watch. Though he only sat on a stool by the gate, he wore a suit of ringmail. Its leather was cracked and its iron rings were tarnished, but it glistened with a fresh coat of oil. When he saw the pair he smiled brightly.

"How've you been?" he shouted.

They ran up to him at his post and stopped.

"Doing fine, sir," Jackson said. "How are you?"

"Well," the old man began, and his gaze drifted off into another place and time. "Used to be I was a walker on Wheel Four, back when a hundred and eighty pound feller could make a difference. Only six wheels back when I started. I was a packer. Back then, it was the littler folks who wore the diapers. Couldn't've afforded to get docked every time we had to take a dump. We added on and the big guys, well, some of 'em didn't wear more than a loincloth to show how big they were. Skinners, they called themselves, back before they started loadin themselves up and became the Ironclads."

Jackson patiently interjected, "Our grandfather was a Skinner." It would be counterproductive to seem too eager, and rude to deny the old man their audience.

"So he was, right up till he passed away. Sorry. He was a good man."

"Yes, sir, he was," Jackson said, wondering if Uncle Blaine would have ever been able to kick them out if Grandpa was still alive.

"Those were the days," he said. "But now I just sit around up here and watch and wait."

"That's very important work," Jackson said. "You're lucky to have it."

"Yes. Maintaining the order is very important. Keeping the old days from coming back around. Did I ever tell you about the old Carbon Nation days?"

Jackson stepped in front of Ava to keep her quiet and lied. "No, sir."

"My granddaddy was a banker and my daddy was a developer. Men used to walk all over one another to satisfy their own lusts. My daddy was barely in his thirties when everything fell apart. He was in the process of suing his own daddy, my granddaddy, over some bad investment or other. Father and son going at one another like mad dogs. That's what caused the wars. Not running out of resources or hotter weather. It was tit for tat. It was backstabbing and nobody caring about nobody else. This is an important job I have here—keeping the order."

"Yes, sir, it is," Jackson said. "And we all appreciate it very much. I hope I can get such an important job someday."

"Stay in there," Mr. Lambert said, gently swinging a fist toward Jackson's shoulder but pulling it short of bumping him. "Stay in there and show yourself a man of order and the corporate good and you'll find your place."

"Yes, sir."

"Now what brings you all the way up here today?"

Jackson gave a meaningful glance over his shoulder toward Ava. "Just wanted to visit Mom."

"Ahh," the old man said. "Well I doubt you'll find her up here this late in the morning."

Ava popped out from behind Jackson and said, "Oh, I hope we do, sir."

The old man smiled down at her. "That's a fine doll you've got there. May I?"

Ava handed him the doll, as she always did when they passed by, and he gave it the same sentimental appraisal he always did.

"My Lucinda had a Heavie when she was a little girl. She got farmed out to pay off her debts," he told them again, sadly. He sighed and handed the doll back. "You just hang in there, little lassie, and one of these days you'll be walking right alongside your momma." He looked Jackson in the eye and said in a choked whisper, "She's got a good build to her, a regular Heavie doll. Be a fine walker one day."

"I hope so, sir," Jackson said.

"Well, I hope you find Momma still at home. Demand is still low, but everybody's all abuzz about the President visiting. Any sign of them?"

Jackson wanted to lie and say no just to squelch the conversation, but Ava said, "Oh, yes, sir. We saw Sophia. She's so beautiful."

"Not as beautiful as you," Mr. Lambert said.

Ava giggled and hugged Heavie against her, hiding her face behind its broad middle. Jackson led her through the gate with a gracious final wave to Mr. Lambert.

The Upper Crust was a grand place. Its streets were lined with flowerboxes. Trees hugged the walls and reached for the sky between homes. Mayor Van Ashe's mansion occupied the center block. At night its spires were lit extravagantly. Now, the mid-morning sunlight glistened off their silver edges. The mansions of the frontline Ironclads enwreathed the top of Wheel Eight and respectfully faced the mayor's estate. Jackson and Ava crossed the square and trotted down the street that ended at the front steps of the Piedmont house.

A pair of geared axles crossed above the door as the Piedmont Family crest, an ornamental waste of weight that could be serving a walker right now, but Ironclads had plenty—enough to show off.

Jackson stepped onto the pedal to the right of the massive set of doors, but the stiff lever didn't give enough to ring the bell. He jumped up and down on it while Ava giggled.

"Well, come over here and help me then," Jackson said. You and your stupid Heavie doll, he thought but did not say.

Ava crawled up into his arms and he lept onto the pedal again. This time it sank far enough and fast enough to push a magnet piston through a wire coil and induce a charge that rang the bell. Not a hearty toll. More like the sound of a penny hitting the sidewalk. But it was enough to bring a servant to the door.

Mrs. Burge pulled open the door and smiled out at them. She was a tiny woman with hollow cheeks and lots of lines that echoed her small features. "Hello, dears. I thought it might be you by the ring."

"Is Mommy here?" Ava asked.

Jackson felt a tinge of guilt at the hopefulness in her voice. He was using his little sister, and for what? To get something to impress a girl who was too much like the woman who wasn't here and wouldn't be here for them even if they'd made an appointment.

"No, dear," Mrs. Burge said. "I'm sorry. They've all gone out to walk."

"Do you think she might come back soon?" Jackson asked.

"Well, no. Not until the evening when the peak is over. And what with the President visiting, there was talk of a—" She looked uncomfortable for a moment then said, "Come in and have a drink and a snack. You must be tired and hungry after coming all this way."

"Thank you, Mrs. Burge," Jackson said. "That's very kind of you. Are you sure it's all right?"

The maid gave a tiny uncertain nod. She led them straight to a servant's passage and into the dark kitchen where she glanced at the unlit bulb hanging from the center of the ceiling.

"It's okay," Jackson said. "We can see just fine. Can't we, Ava?"

Ava nodded and they took seats at the worktable. Mrs. Burge brought out shards of an old cracker and filled a tin with water. Jackson and Ava exchanged a glance. They wouldn't dare take her ration.

"Just a drink will be fine," Jackson said.

"Are you sure?" the maid asked.

Jackson handed the tin cup to Ava and let her drink. "Yes, ma'am. We've had a nice breakfast this morning. Haven't we?"

"Shevi gave me her biscuits and gravy," Ava said.

"Shevi?" Mrs. Burge asked. "Who might Shevi be?" She eyed Jackson with a look of concern.

Ava didn't give Jackson a chance to speak. "Her name rhymes with Heavie and she took one of Jackson's books and we like her a lot."

Mrs. Burge's voice quivered. "Oh?"

"She's a walker," Jackson explained with as much indifference as he could. "I'm renting books to walkers. She came to the booth and rented one and had some extra breakfast." He shrugged.

"That sounds like a very good business," Mrs. Burge said with a sigh. "Not here on Wheel Eight, though, I hope."

"No. Dad found an apartment over on Wheel Three. We're working there."

"Good. Very good."

Jackson's heart twisted in his chest as he prepared to ask the next question. He didn't want to get this kind old woman in any trouble. And that decided it for him. The mission was off. He was going to abort and be satisfied with the books he'd nearly killed himself to get. If nobody wanted them, then his business plan was a failure and his time had been wasted. He could live with that. But he'd brought poor Ava all this way and should try to make it worth her time, at least. So the question changed and his heart softened.

"While we're here, do you think it would be okay for Ava to play with her Heavie Dream House?"

This was the tiniest request and should have been no problem at all. But even at that the little old woman hesitated, making Jackson glad he hadn't posed his intended question that they take the thing with them—with a book from the library tucked inside.

With a relenting sigh that seemed to tear the woman's soul, she gave a consenting nod.

Excited, Ava jumped up and ran from the room. Jackson offered the maid a grateful smile to hide the relief he felt at changing his mind, though he didn't understand why letting Ava play with one of her own toys should be such a problem.

He was almost out of the kitchen, following in Ava's swift wake, when Mrs. Burge called his name softly. He turned and found her wringing her hands.

"What's the matter?"

"You just be careful, Jackson," she said. "Don't go getting yourself hurt or in any trouble."

"You mean like my dad did?"

She didn't reply but bowed her head shamefully. He turned away, shamefully. There was plenty of shame to go around.

Ava was already out of sight up the grand stair when Jackson emerged from the kitchen. He had his hand on the rail and his foot on the bottom tread when he noticed the card standing, like a tent in Shack Town, on the coffee table. It had the overlapping circles of the corporation logo and at first he thought it must be an invitation to a party for the visiting dignitaries. But the color wasn't the black of the Trintico Scott. Instead, the circles were gold. Gold rings on a white card. A wedding invitation? Was another of the Piedmont youth getting married? None of the boys were turning eighteen soon, but he supposed one of the girls could—

Then he saw her out of the corner of his eye. Mrs. Burge was gliding stealthily—and far too quickly for a woman of her age—toward the coffee table. Jackson shot across the great room and snatched up the proud card.

"Penny *Piedmont*?" he read aloud and couldn't help but cut his eyes at the maid. "Isn't her name still Koss? They're not officially divorced yet. Are they?"

"It was annulled," Mrs. Burge said, wringing her hands again.

"Annulled? How can that be?"

"Big people can do whatever they want."

He read on and wailed, "She's marrying *Ward Stendahl*? *WARD*?! He's barely older than I am. That can't be!"

"He's old enough to marry," the maid whispered. "And she's, well . . . available."

He glared at her and threw the invitation down on the table.

She called after him as he took the stairs three at a time. "Perhaps you should go now."

"We're taking the Dream House with us," he shouted back.

"Oh, no, Jackson. Don't do that."

No way was Ward Stendahl's kid playing with Ava's Heavie Dream House. And that wasn't all they were taking.

⟨◎⟩

Shevi adjusted the saddle on her back and suddenly felt like a complete idiot. Why hadn't she taken the smaller book with the valet and the monkey and offered to take the girl, too? The idea hit her with such force that she stopped walking and drifted back and down with the great tread underneath her feet. She coasted away from her friends and back toward the sweep and gutter at the back

53

of the walk zone that caught loose objects that had been lost on the wheel. Up on the platform the book boy and the girl were gone. She was a chunk and might have even put Shevi up a row. That would have been fine. Tasha and Stacey were especially annoying today, with their lectures and silly issues.

The governor *was* up there on the platform, however. He was there doing his job: watching the wheel and its walkers. His responsibility was to make sure the walkers' pace kept the wheel synchronized with the corporation's power gird. And at that moment he was looking at a walker who had fallen out of ranks and out of the array. He was staring intently at Shevi. And the expression on his face said he was not happy. She hustled forward, into the empty gap she'd left beside her friends, and got doubtful looks from them, too, so she turned her attention back to her book to avoid Tasha's questioning eyes.

Now God had shown up to talk to Job directly. The story was almost at an end and something big was bound to happen. Shevi was curious to see if God would save Job or finish him off when a squeal from Stacey interrupted her.

"It's Princess Sophia!"

"Princess?" Shevi looked up as a wave of applause and cheering burst from the army of Ironclads in the front rows. During her reading, the community theater stage had been lowered from the structure of girders that spanned the inside of the treadwheel. The weigh-in platform above the onramp was filled with black-and-whites. Mayor Van Ashe, wearing polished black armor, stood in front of a group of people everyone in I Town knew but rarely saw. The entire first family wore beautiful massive armor of golden chainmail and plating. Helmets shrouded all but their faces. Sophia, the Golden Girl of the corporate society, waved from the far right of the line. The wheel shook as the walkers reveled in return.

The governor waved a yellow warning flag and the walkers slowed their excited pace. The wheel continued its steady tumble. Even the president be damned if he caused a wheel getting out of phase with the other eight. Of all the lessons they'd had on the school wheel, reading and writing and math, Shevi remembered the repeated lessons about phase the best. The teachers of the two wheels had made the students of one wheel then the other speed up then slow down to put the wheels out of phase and show how they cancelled one another out of production. Nothing was more important than phase.

The president, his son and three grandkids followed the mayor onto the stage along with a man dressed in silvery-white armor. He was familiar, too—the Secretary of Electricity.

Mayor Van Ashe spoke first. "Walkers of Wheel Three, we are honored to have President Merwin Burgess and his beloved family with us, as well as Secretary of Electricity Michael Faraday. Please show them how much we appreciate their leadership here in Induction Town." The crowd roared and the wheel shook, but the walkers' cadence did not vary under the governor's watch. "I am delighted, as always, to have members of the Global Power Authority here to witness our success at maintaining a modern, electrified society generated in accordance with the Authority's prudent guidelines." He turned and offered a slight bow toward a group of dark-skinned people dressed in brightly colored robes and tunics standing together on the weigh-in platform. They returned a gentle wave and received moderate applause. "Also, we have visitors from other regions, here to investigate the possibility of obtaining a Trintico franchise for their own settlements." Another group waved from the weigh-in platform. They were a mixed bunch, varying ages and sizes, but all looked tired and as if they'd tried to clean themselves with too little water. The walkers gave a hesitant welcome. "And now I give you Secretary Faraday."

To a wild clamor of armor, scepters, and miscellaneous Ironclad gear, Sec Elec stepped forward and addressed them. "What a delight it is to see such a beautiful system in motion. All of you, from the greatest walkers on the front lines to the fine entrepreneurs offering goods and services along the platforms, contribute to the soul of our fine corporation."

More political talk. Shevi went back to her reading. God was asking Job some questions:

Where were you when I laid the earth's foundation?

Tell me, if you understand.

Who marked off its dimensions? Surely you know!

Who stretched a measuring line across it?

Wow! It looked like God was just going to rough Job up some more after everything he'd already been through. Shevi looked up again. The secretary had stopped for a moment as a commotion broke out on the weigh-in platform. The radical fob seller was in the clutches of a team of black-and-whites. He pulled against their hold and shouted something, but he was small and his voice was small and only incoherent squeaks and squawks made it to the back row of the wheel. The Ironclads in the front lines on the right must have understood what he was saying. They roared and beat their breastplates in response, which drowned out his voice all the more. He shouted back at them until a guard prodded him with a knocker rod. The Dim squealed as his back tightened, arching his body backward. A dark stain spread across the front of his threadbare trousers. Now the walkers roared with delight.

The secretary smiled politely, waving a soothing hand of acknowledgement toward the little disturbance, and went on.

"The society of Trintico is built firstly and foremost on the power of the human will and the spirit of corporate effort." He paused to give his own bow to the GPA inspectors. "Alone we are weak and vulnerable. We are in the Wilds, fighting for our very lives with ruthless abandon. We fight our fellow human for daily existence and fear everything, even our own minds and the atrocities we are capable of committing in order to survive." He smiled toward the visitors who offered vigorous nods in agreement, sharing comments among themselves. "But together, corporately, we build civilization and monuments to civilization and we power these monuments with pure and renewable resources.

"Again, I say thank you for your efforts—all of your efforts. You are the power and the source of life. And now I give you the brain to our nervous system, the reason of our doing and for our being. Walkers of Wheel Three, your leader and mine, President Merwin Burgess."

The secretary stepped back, presenting President Burgess who raised his arms over the crowd and spoke. His voice filled the great volume of Wheel Three.

"My brothers and sisters in power, we are here today to offer you our deepest gratitude for the essential service you provide the Trintico Corporation. You are the core, the very foundation upon which our society rests. And our society," he said, raising his right hand emphatically, "*is* the *greatest society* in existence today. We are the model all others look to and are looking to this day. We have brought leaders from other regions and nations here to Induction Town to see *you*, the source of our great corporate society."

Far ahead and above, Perry and the Titanics roared. His friend Kyle shook his new axle scepter high overhead. It was enormous. Its geared end looked like a king's crown except that it was the dark color of oiled rust. Why couldn't the Dims—or the smaller people, she corrected her thoughts—be just as proud of their situation and contribution?

◎

A feast of tangled wire spaghetti and beads for pretend meatballs was spread before Heavie in the dining room of her Dream House. Each of the eight rooms had a light bulb of its own—lavishness that rivaled some of the mansions of the Upper Crust and shamed the middle class houses on the Terraces. Ava cranked the handle on the generator wheel to light the bulbs when Jackson passed the nursery door. He locked himself in the library. Mrs. Burge pounded on the door and called in to him. He hoped the commotion didn't make Ava abandon the Dream House. She would have to enjoy it for the few minutes of their malign visitation because, with as much as he would love to scavenge it from Ward Stendahl's offspring, there was no way they could take that thing with them. Jackson had forgotten how big it was, bigger than the crate the books were in, a full quarter of the size of their apartment in the Gut of Wheel Three.

Jackson had no problem finding the uncensored copy of *The Great God, Mann*. He ripped off his shirt as he ran to it, then grabbed the heavy volume off the shelf and wrapped it securely. He ran to the balcony and leaned over the rail. The package fell straight down and landed with a soft thud on the roof between Wheels Eight and Nine. Jackson relaxed and breathed in the warm morning air. He took in the view from the high balcony one last time.

A single heavy cable spanned the space between the Wheels' Upper Crusts. It ran the full length of I Town connecting all the highest societies of the town together. A cable car at the dock on Wheel Nine across the way would run up and down its length, providing a convenient transit between the Upper Crusts, but with the majority of Ironclads doing their corporate duty of walking on the wheels below it sat idle now. In the distance, the remains of shanties and tents smoldered at the edge of Shack Town. A small band of King Ludd's Wireless from the Wilds had raided during the night. The damage was minimal, so the party had been small. Jackson had stood on the balcony more than once with Grandpa, the big man wearing only the loincloth he'd walked in all day, and watched the vandalism from the safe vantage. When the torches appeared and came out of the woods or swamp like a flood, the damage could cover acres and reach almost all the way to the base of town. But when only a handful of Wireless appeared, only a few families and lives along the outskirts would suffer being sold into slavery in Agrarianna. Life in I Town wasn't perfect, but it beat

Shack Town or the Wilds.

He closed the balcony door and unlocked the door to the hall. Mrs. Burge gasped and put a hand over her mouth.

"What have you done, child? Where is your shirt?"

"Come on, Ava," Jackson called past her. "Time to go."

Ava made a disappointed groan.

"Jackson," Mrs. Burge scolded, "you can't go out like that, with that rack of bones showing. It's indecent."

"Everybody knows I'm a Dim," he hissed, eliciting another gasp from the maid.

"Don't let your sister hear you say that."

"Why not? She'll be calling both of us that in a few years when she's an Ironclad."

"Calling you what?" Ava asked, coming out of the nursery with Heavie clutched in front of her.

Jackson grabbed her by the arm and towed her down the grand staircase.

"Take care of yourself, Mrs. Burge," he called back as they scuttled across the great room and out the front door.

Chapter

Five

The instant the door slammed behind Perry, Shevi's heart began to beat wildly. It had taken only the mention of her borrowing some weight to push him into high gear, claiming it was the warning horn blatting in the hall; he wasn't about to admit he knew Mom would make him share this time. But Shevi didn't want his weight. She had bigger plans than walking the back row with her friends. She could help herself and help somebody else, too—also—at the same time. There was a word for that. She'd learned it in school, but she couldn't remember it right now. Now she had to wait and hope Mom would come back without the engagement rotor. She should just bail, leave without the brake disk. She bolted for the door, sure that Perry was far enough ahead of her not to get in her way, but then she froze. She needed the saddle off her mother's back. She cursed and pounded the door with her fist. It swung open and she screamed. Mom stood in the open door, staring at her, startled and confused.

"I'm sorry," Mom said, holding out empty hands.

A relieving breath passed through Shevi like a cool breeze across the Terraces. She fought back the blossom of a smile but lost and had to cover her mouth. Mom interpreted this and the sparkle in her eye as the exact opposite of what they were.

"Shevi, I am so sorry. I didn't have enough money to get in a game with Murray. He's doing it on purpose. I hate that man. I'm so sorry I ever put it on the table." She worked the shoulder straps of the saddle off her arms. "I got paid this morning. You need lunch money? Of course you do. Silly me. When you're married you won't be broke every payday." She took out her pay and separated out some coins. "And you and Perry will get paid this evening and I'll get it back tonight. Okay?"

Shevi composed herself. "Just give me the saddle, please."

"This is all just so irresponsible of me. I am so sorry. My goodness, what would your father say?"

Shevi didn't bother with a comeback, just grabbed the money and the saddle, pocketing the one and loading the other onto her back while she ran out the door and down the hall. She couldn't help but laugh out loud, and a mean-spirited, rebellious monster inside her knew and hoped at the same time that Mom would hear it as weeping. She'd have to collect herself before she reached the weigh-in platform but until then she was celebrating.

At the food bar, Matilda Pruitt smiled her tiny smile and took

Shevi's weigh-in card. "Scrambled and hash this morning."

"I'm not very hungry this morning," Shevi said.

"But you must eat. If you don't take your ration of calories I'll have to file a report."

"Okay. Just . . . whatever."

"Are you well? You look very well, Shevi. As a matter of fact you look radiant this morning."

"I'm not radiant," Shevi declared, suddenly irritated by the demand warning alarms, braying and coughing out motivation.

"Well, you look radiant to me. Is there a new fella in your life?"

"Just give me my damn food and let me get on with my life."

"Well," the little woman breathed and began filling Shevi's breakfast plate. Pouting a little, she asked, "Do you want wheat or oat toast?"

"Wheat, please. I'm sorry. I didn't mean to snap at you."

"And I didn't mean to pry." The woman handed Shevi her breakfast plate and lunch sack, eyeing her suspiciously. "I mean with things between you and the Turney boy over and done with, it's only natural that a good looking girl big as you would just take the next one in line."

"Why would you say that?"

"Well, you are a very attractive girl, what with the thickness of your waist and—"

"Not that. The other. That Cole and I aren't . . ."

"Well, I just assumed, since you're not wearing his rotor." She shrugged.

Shevi said, "Have a nice day," and turned away.

"Yes, ma'am. Same to you."

Shevi's nerves were back. The plate of scrambled eggs and hash browns and toast shook in her hands. This was going to be too weird, leaving her two best friends behind to help a Dim—a smaller person, she corrected herself again—that she had just met.

It was for the girl, she told herself firmly, hoping she could convince herself before she boarded Wheel Three. It was to encourage a fine young citizen of Induction Town. What was wrong with that? It was a hand up, not a hand out, and all that. Ironclads did it all the time. It was her social and civic responsibility.

Then she pushed through the double doors from Electric Avenue into the weigh-in platform of Wheel Three and her resolve wavered near the point of fainting. The platform was full. Demand was exceptionally high again today. Walkers waited in long lines. The support staff of smaller people worked feverishly to check weights, assign rows and mark cards. Tasha and Stace motioned her to cut in with them.

Shevi heaved a labored sigh and all her joy and excitement evacuated with it. Her stride, which had been long and meaningful through the corridors and stairwells of Wheel Three, now became the tiny steps of a person in shackles. She waved back to the pair of girls then gave them a "one-minute" sign. Going over there would only add an unnecessary and painful step to the process.

The armor polisher and the snack vendors were busy with customers, but the old woman at the fob booth sat quietly, a sad lonely expression on her narrow and wrinkled face. The man with the crazy ideas wasn't with her this morning.

The book boy was showing off the big Bible to an Ironclad

woman while the little girl played beside the crate with her Heavie doll. "Five cents a day," he said. "Twenty-five for a week. That's two days free."

He blanched when he saw Shevi. His glance flashed from her back to the big book then nervously up at the woman.

"It's very good," Shevi said. "Definitely worth the money."

"Oh, you've read it?" the woman asked.

"Yes, ma'am," Shevi said. "Well, not all the way through. If you don't take it, I want it again. After all, it's worth another row. I could go thirty cents."

The book boy's eyes went wide. The big woman gave Shevi a mean look and said desperately, "I'll take it. I can give you forty."

"Forty-five," Shevi said, using the tone Dad had used at the gambling tables.

"Fifty," the Ironclad woman said and sealed the deal by pressing two quarters into the book boy's palm.

He stared at the dull silver coins. "Thank you. Thank you very much."

The big woman hefted her book into her arms and strutted past Shevi with her nose in the air and a triumphant smile compressing her plump cheeks. Shevi hid what she could of her own smile.

When the woman was gone the book boy said, "Thank you."

"No problem."

"You could have told her how much you paid for it."

Shevi shrugged. "Market prices should be fair."

The book boy plunged behind his crate and pulled out a cloth-wrapped bundle. "I have something else for you anyway. I hope you like it," he said, unwrapping it. He dropped his voice to a whisper. "It's an uncensored copy of the one you looked at yesterday."

Shevi took the book and opened it. She let the pages flow left then right then left again. No sign of missing pages or blacked out text.

"Where did you get it?"

"I have my sources."

Shevi wanted to say that it was a very sweet gesture, but the idea that he'd gotten it just for her made her suddenly very self-conscious. She glanced back at the line Tasha and Stace waited in. They seemed preoccupied, at least for the moment. But then Stace's eyes flashed Shevi's way and Tasha gave her a kick in the ankle. Yes, they were extremely preoccupied—with every little detail of what Shevi was doing.

"It's okay," the book boy said.

"What?" Shevi snorted.

She was sweating. She had to get herself under control.

The book boy whispered, "Nobody will notice."

"Notice what?"

"That it's uncensored."

"Oh. Right. I suppose not. How much?"

"Penny a day," he said cautiously. "Five cents a week."

He almost sounded as though he were asking rather than telling. Shevi found this very cute.

"I'll take it for the week," she said.

"Great," he said with a gush of relief.

As they made the exchange, the little girl looked up from her doll. She offered Shevi a smile and a tiny wave.

Shevi asked the book boy, "What's it called when two things help one another?"

"Cooperation?" he suggested, staring at the money in his hand.

"No. It's not that. It's when the two things rely on one another to get what they need and help one another—"

"Symbiosis?"

"That's it. Symbiosis."

Shevi asked the little girl, "Do you remember my name?"

"Shevi rhymes with Heavie," the little girl chortled.

"That's right," Shevi said. "And you're Ava."

The little girl nodded and giggled.

Shevi said, "Ava, would you and your Heavie doll like to walk with me?" She glanced at the book boy. His eyes were wide. "Would that be okay?"

Ava jumped up. "With Heavie?"

"Of course," Shevi said.

"Are you sure?" the book boy said.

Ava already had taken hold of Shevi's hand.

Shevi said, "I'm a bit light on weight. Without that big book, I might not get on."

"She's pretty big," he said. "And our dad . . ." He trailed off.

"You're brother and sister?"

The question snapped him out of his distraction. "Yeah."

"I'm sorry," Shevi said, but the idea was too surprising not to follow through with another obvious question. "Same mother?"

"Yes," the boy snapped. He grabbed Ava's hand and pulled her away from Shevi's side to his own.

"I'm sorry," Shevi said. "I just—"

"It's called genetics," the boy said.

"I'm sorry."

The little girl tugged on her brother's arm like pulling a rope to ring a bell. "Can I, Jackson? Please!" He looked down at her with a little snort. "I've never even been on this wheel before," she whined.

"I'm sorry," Shevi offered again, and pleading she added, "I'll give her her share."

"Yeah, whatever," the boy said. "It's just that Dad works nights and won't get to see her after work." He looked down at his little sister and shrugged. "If you want to, go ahead."

"Thank you, Jackson." She hugged him, gathering his baggy clothes around his waist, exposing its narrowness.

He patted her back and looked everywhere but at Shevi. "Whatever. Make sure she lets you weigh in on your own."

"I know how it works," Shevi said to the side of his face, beginning to shake with a rising fury. "I used to ride."

"Good for you." Still no eye contact.

"Thank you—Jackson," Shevi said, sternly and businesslike. She put out her hand. "It's been nice doing *business* with you."

His reply was a choked whisper. "She's not inventory." He continued to stare away, not accepting her hand.

Shevi kept her reply cool and soft. Typical Dim: unappreciative, a chip on his shoulder, and thinking everybody owes him because he got shortchanged by his own DNA. "I didn't mean that she was. And I didn't mean to offend your . . . genetics."

He turned to her then and reluctantly reached for her hand. She retracted the offer of a shake from a silly, whiny Dim.

He said, "It's not your fault."

"It's not like it matters."

"It wouldn't to you," he mumbled.

"Would it mattering to me matter to you? We don't have time for this. I'll bring her back here at the end of the shift. Come on." Shevi took Ava's hand and turned away. "Let's weigh in."

The little girl bounced along beside, her hand warm and soft inside Shevi's. Tasha and Stace were descending the onramp, ready to take their places in the back row. Stace grabbed Tasha's arm and tugged and pointed. Tasha watched Shevi and her new companion but didn't stop, towing Stace along with her, whispering to her and tugging back to keep her moving.

Ava weighed in at sixty pounds. With the novel's seven and a half pounds, Shevi was able to get a place six rows ahead of Tasha and Stace. That was fine with her; they could talk about her behind her back all day. She entered her row without even glancing their way. But facing forward she couldn't miss the look she got from Perry and the way he whispered to Kyle and the other Titanics. It wasn't any of their business what row she walked in or whom she carried in her dad's saddle. If she'd left her fate up to Perry she'd be sitting at home letting him make the rent.

⟨⟨⟩⟩

Jackson had done well, thanks to the help from the Ironclad girl. Was she an Ironclad? No. She only had a pair of rusty old car struts hanging at her sides, and a saddle, and the obligatory feedbag. Definitely not iron *clad*. Maybe iron *accessorized*. He grinned at that. She had been so uppity and snobby and acted like she had descended from Mount Olympus to bestow upon him some wonderful blessing; she wasn't but a wrung above him on the social

69

ladder. He latched his crate and set the flap in the lid to allow returns for the two single-day rentals he'd made. He had sixty-two cents in his hand but stranger was the feeling of being alone, of not having Ava by his side.

As he crossed the weigh-in platform he looked down across the sea of walkers to where Ava and the girl were. While Heavie sat on one of Shevi's shoulders, Ava perched in the saddle and looked over the other shoulder at the book he'd stolen from Grandpa's library. Ava looked up suddenly and found him. She gave him a big smile and a fanatic wave. Shevi looked up, too, and waved. His heart skipped a beat, magnifying the feeling growing there. He offered a quick flick of his hand in reply. "Bye, sis," he said. "Good luck." That was her life, down there on the wheel, making a real living. He knew it would happen eventually; he just hadn't expected it so soon. It was bittersweet to look at the two of them. He'd been watching out for Ava forever it seemed, and now she was finally and already going somewhere he never could. And this Wheel Three girl? Well, she stirred something inside him, and there was no good way that could ever turn out. Maybe she was only a wrung above him, but what a gap between—talking space flight to span the gulf. Best? A torn up heart. Worst? She could dump him for a Stendahl.

He peeled his eyes from them and gritted his teeth against the feeling raging down inside him. He needed to go down in the cellars or up to the Gut or out to Shack Town and find a Dim girl to hang around with. Maybe he'd do something totally selfish and take her out on a date—just blow his money on a good time while his dad unloaded the supply train and washed out diapers.

Chapter

Six

Jackson jogged the long narrow hallways of Level 6, the lowest residential level of Wheel Three. The passages snaked and twisted inside the great void middle of the wheel like intestines in a huge Ironclad's belly. Below the roofs that connected each wheel to the next, even the units on the ends of the level didn't have windows. It was no joke that everyone called it the butt of the Gut. As the saying goes, the sun didn't shine there. It was also the first level above the wheel's civic and administration levels, so the walking tread of the jail wheel was just below—one of several wheels inside the great one. The separation between rectilinear hallways and apartments and the curve of the embedded wheel was poor enough that Jackson could catch glimpses of the inmates once he learned where to look. Seeing those poor souls was the only redemption of his being cast from the heavenly Upper Crust down into this level of hell, but along with seeing them, he could hear them and smell them as well. The smell of a thousand walkers with bad hygiene was like old mustard and bad meat. But Jackson had already learned to tune the odor out after just a few seconds on the floor. By the time he reached the food service, he already couldn't smell the jail.

The food service was stocked with hand-me-down veggies higher classes had been offered and had rejected. With Shevi's nickel, Jackson bought a nice big loaf of bread, one with no mold to pick off and not brick hard, and some broccoli and carrots that weren't too rubbery. He carried them deep into the intestinal maze of apartments.

His dad sat on a cot in the corner of the one-room apartment. He had already made significant headway on a mural of big muscular figures on the wall behind him—myths and legends, Ironclads and interesting people from around I Town. They'd lose their deposit when they moved out.

Dad angled the pages of a graphic novel to catch the light of the single dim bulb in the middle of the ceiling. Dad loved The Mighty Deeds of Gargantua and The Grand Advetures of Pantagruel, father and son giants that CorpPress had resurrected from French literature in a comic book format. Jackson wasn't as calloused to the comics and the light bulb burning away as he was to the smells of the jail wheel; he had to actively make himself ignore Dad's foolishness.

"Where's Ava?"

"On the wheel." Jackson thumbed over his shoulder as he dug the coins out of his pocket.

Dad's face fell, his eyes widened, and his hands crumpled the little rag of a magazine. Jackson wished he'd brought a real book for the man to read, but Dad had a short attention span and bad eyes, so he didn't do well with long stories or with prose. Short with lots of pictures was more his speed.

"Your mother took her?"

"No. A girl on Wheel Three."

"You just gave your sister to the first person who came along?"

"No, Dad. She's rented a couple of books from me and she had an empty saddle."

"Oh my God." Dad ran his fingers through the sparse strands of his long hair. The poor man was a shadow of Jackson's future: even his hair was scant, and Jackson would likely lose his bushy mane of blond curls by the time he was thirty. "We don't know the people on this wheel. Someone puts on a saddle but doesn't have a kid in it. She's probably abducted Ava and will sell her to—"

"She's a regular walker on this wheel. People know her. She's running a bit light for some reason."

"Because she sold the last kid that rode in her saddle. Geez, Jackson, Ava is a nice healthy girl. We need to go down there and check on her."

"You need to eat something and get some rest before the afternoon train."

"I can't. Ava might be in danger. Oh, why didn't Penny keep her?"

Jackson rolled his eyes and sighed. "Because letting you have her stopped you from crying, at least till we got down to Electric Avenue." Jackson had roamed the maze of halls and levels of Wheel Eight since he'd gotten too big to ride Dad and nobody had worried about whether or not he was safe. Of course, a skinny kid in I Town had less than no value. "You eat and sleep and I'll go back down and check on her."

He held up the remainder of the money he'd made, two pennies and two quarters. Dad studied the coins with amazement.

"She helped me get this."

"Ava?"

"No. Shevi. The girl Ava's riding."

Dad reached out and took one of the quarters. He stared down at it in the cup of his open hand. "How?"

"The books."

"You made this from the books?"

"Most of it from just one. A big old Bible. Shevi helped talk this huge Ironclad woman into taking it." He dropped the rest of the money into Dad's palm.

"Yeah?" Dad looked at the coins and shook his head. He offered the two pennies back. "You keep that. Do something fun. This is great, Jackson." He put his arm around Jackson's neck and pulled him over to kiss his forehead.

Jackson allowed the kiss but pulled quickly away. "Gee, Dad. Give me a break."

"You don't need a break. You don't even need to be big enough to get on a wheel. You're going to do just fine."

"We're going to do just fine."

Jackson hefted the loaf of bread under his father's nose. The thin man took it appreciatively.

"Still—you'll go check on Ava right away?"

"Right away."

The two ate a good part of the loaf, then Dad lay down on his cot. He was asleep in minutes.

Jackson opened a thin sketchbook Grandpa Piedmont had given him. He thumbed past drawings of induction treadwheels and their components, plans of the Piedmont mansion, and sketches of parts of washing machines and clothes dryers to a series of pages dedicated to the walking stick Mr. Myrtle had acquired. In the bottom corner of the last page, he did a quick sketch of a reading lamp that used the same induction system for power. The things he would need to make it were basically the same as for the knocker rod, with the addition of a base to make it stand up and a socket and light bulb. He'd have to remember to keep an eye out for parts as he wondered around town. They wouldn't have to use the expensive ceiling light at all after he finished it.

He picked up the comic book from Dad's bed, smoothed it flat, and thumbed through its pages. Gargantua and Pantagruel were huge. Jackson's eyes traced their bulging bodies. His mind conjured images of himself being so big. But that was as likely as equal pay and first-come initiatives becoming the way of the wheels.

Jackson tossed the tattered little rag of a storybook onto the floor and jumped up to turn out the burning light bulb. He had two cents in his pocket and didn't want to blow it on useless light. But what could he do?

The answer to that question came as soon as he got back down to the weigh-in platform to check on Ava, who was fine, as he knew she would be. He returned her wave but acted as though he had some other reason for being back in the middle of a shift. Mrs. Bartlett was still sitting at her fob booth, staring blankly at the odd collection of debris she and her son tried to rent or sell to walkers.

"Mrs. Bartlett? Are you okay?"

The old woman turned her gaunt and lined face up toward him. She took a few seconds recognizing him, or making the journey from wherever her mind had roamed to the reality her body occupied.

"They've taken him."

"Who? Chris? I mean Christopher. Where?"

She shrugged. Her bottom lip quivered. Her eyes glistened with tears.

"I don't know where he is. Nobody will tell me anything. Nobody will buy my things. Oh, he should have shut up about all his ideas and opinions." Her face drew up into an angry mask. "Stupid, *stupid*."

Jackson pulled the two pennies out of his pocket. "Here, take this and get out of here. Get something to eat. I'll see what I can find out about Christopher."

She stared at the coins, shaking her head, a look of disgust on her face. "I couldn't."

Jackson plopped them down on the little counter in front of her between a twisted and rusty old scrap of metal and a chunk of concrete with a bolt sticking out of it. "Better take it or somebody else will. I'll have Christopher reimburse me when I find him."

He turned and hurried away but checked over his shoulder to make sure she took the money. He was almost out the door to

Electric Avenue before she gave up her pride.

Every wheel had a ground-level office of the Guard, usually behind the shops on the main avenue, along the barrier between civilization and Shack Town. The big wheel had a skirt of structure that protected it from the elements. The shops along Electric Avenue snuggled underneath the apron like chicks under the wings of a mother hen. One building, The Hangar, a single remnant of the Carbon Nation, stood boldly between the structure above and a rugged wall that defended the town against the dread of the Wilds. Jackson hurried along the side of the old building in glittering sunlight that shone between the hem of the skirt and the wall. The Guard would be the best place to start looking for someone who had offended the rule of order. Likely, Chris was just doing some time in jail, pumping out some amperage for the magnetic field of the main wheel.

⊕

Shevi didn't go the whole twelve hour shift even though demand was incredibly high. The red light of the demand indicator finally flashed off for the first time well after six o'clock; it usually did this by five when the schools and businesses of Fluxton had closed for the day. When the managers asked for first exits, she took the option. Her legs were tired from the extra weight and the greater incline of the higher row.

Ava had become a bit wiggly, too. Together they had read the first chapter of *The Great God, Mann*—Shevi was impressed at how well the girl could read—but once the monkey's narration had come to an end Ava lost interest and started playing with Heavie and eating. They ate the lunch and snacks Mrs. Pruitt had packed, a thick sandwich stuffed full of sliced meats. Shevi was glad to have someone to help her with it. And there would be even more tomorrow after Shevi's higher weight; it had been a challenge for the two of them to eat all of today's calories.

Shevi and Ava sidled left through the ranks across the tumbling tread of the wheel to the gentle curve of the offramp that mimicked the wheel's inner radius. Ava had been walking beside Shevi for the last hour and the stillness of the offramp made them stagger after walking in place on the wheel. Ava fell over and giggled as Shevi helped her up.

"Walking is fun," the little girl chirped as she squeezed Shevi's finger and followed her up the ramp.

"You liked it?" Shevi asked, a bit surprised.

The little girl nodded then pinched her nose and giggled. "But it's smelly down there."

"That's all the diapers," Shevi said.

"Yeah, I know. Walkers pee and poop in them while they're walking."

"That's right," Shevi said.

"Did you pee and poop in yours?"

Shevi's face warmed. She held up a finger to admit that she had performed the number one activity.

Ava covered her mouth and giggled. "Me, too. Just pee. No poop."

Shevi felt both free and self-conscious in the presence of the child's honesty and openness. Across the wheel, on the weigh-in platform at the top of the onramp, Jackson's crate stood unattended. Shevi kept her uncensored novel hugged tight against her body now that she was off the wheel and mingling with management, but the controller who marked their time on Shevi's card and sent them to the pay window didn't give it a glance as tired walkers trudged up the ramp toward him.

They got into line at the payout window behind a mammoth Ironclad man. Ava waved her hand in front of her face. She pointed at his broad, kilted backside and held up two fingers. Shevi tried not to laugh while grabbing the girl's hand. A second later they were both doubled over, laughing. The large man turned around and looked down at them. Shevi's face went blistering hot, which only made her laugh harder.

The skinny little teller behind the barred window—Shevi tried hard not to think of him as a Dim despite Jackson's rude hypersensitivity that morning—bumped the beads of his abacus to and fro to figure Shevi's daily pay while she dried her eyes and tried to compose herself.

On the back row she had made thirty-two cents a day but today Ava's weight moved her up six rows and gave her fifty cents for the day, even with it being a bit short of ten hours. But the more she weighed, the higher she could walk, which gave her more leverage and made her weight worth even more. That's the way things worked in a world governed by physics and economics: more earned more; less earned less. The eighteen cents difference was Ava's rightful share, of course, but Shevi gave her a full twenty-five cents, half of their total for the day, because without Ava Shevi wouldn't have gotten on the wheel at all and wouldn't have made a penny. It was only fair.

The little girl looked at the quarter with sparkling eyes. "Thank you," she said as she took it from Shevi's fingers.

"Thank *you*," Shevi replied.

She glanced back at the teller and saw the lust in his eyes as the little girl probably had just been paid more for riding in a saddle than he would for a week of clerical work. Shevi hurried Ava away.

"Put that in your pocket, okay?"

Ava obeyed.

Shevi wasn't sure how to handle the diaper receptacle with a child, but Ava seemed to know exactly what to do. She took her own stall and, while Shevi waited and listened next door, Ava went through the motions so quickly that the sound of water swishing in the bidet startled Shevi and made her realize she had her own diaper to take care of. She unfastened it, dropped it in the chute and rinsed herself faster than she ever had. Ava was waiting outside the stall, Heavie dangling at her side, a proud smile on her face.

They exited Wheel Three and checked for Jackson on Electric Avenue but he wasn't waiting there. Shevi waited outside while Ava went back into the boarding side to see if Jackson had slipped in while they were getting paid. When Shevi went in, Ava was sitting on the crate alone—even the little old lady who sold the fobs was gone.

Several walkers were arguing with the manager. They weren't dressed in heavy armor; they were nightshift walkers—gamblers and gamers. Each held a large square of board under their arms that would become tables for playing cards, rolling dice, and other risks and chances. The four sides of the boards had long straps to go over players' shoulders.

"You can't cut the number of tables," one said.

"I can and I will if demand stays this high," the manager said.

"I'm puttin in a transfer to another wheel then," another said. "The other wheels welcome gaming on the nightshift."

The manager said, "You do what you need to do, but I've got to satisfy demand."

"There you are," Shevi's mother's crystal voice rang from the group. "I need the saddle."

Shevi undid the girth and took it to her.

"Give me your pay so I can get the rotor back."

"Mom, don't worry about it. Let's make sure we have money for the rent and the electric meter and food first."

"Who's this?"

Shevi felt Ava's soft hand slip into hers. When she looked down, the girl's big eyes were fixed on Shevi's mother.

"This is Ava. Ava, this is my mom, Jo Ann Lilbourn."

"My mommy is sick and we had to leave her alone so she could get better," Ava gushed.

"Ava has just moved here from Wheel Eight and her brother rents books to walkers." Shevi held out the novel he'd gotten for her. "And she rode with me today. We had a great day, didn't we?"

Shevi and Ava exchanged a smile.

"Well, girls, that's just wonderful."

"I made this," Ava said, pulling the quarter from her pocket. She held it high in the air.

The nightshift gaming walkers turned suspicious and wanting eyes on the coin.

Shevi said, "Put that away, Ava. You don't want to lose it."

Mom's expression turned skeptical. "How did she manage to

make that much?"

"Well," Shevi began. "I made fifty cents."

"So you gave her *half* of it?" She leaned close and whispered, "Is she from a Dim family?"

"It's rude to call them that and I wouldn't have gotten on the wheel at all without her."

"You don't just give some stranger's child half your wages."

Shevi's voice went a little higher than she intended. "You'd just throw it all away on the tables."

Several of the gamers craned their necks to hear the conversation about their card tables.

Mom's face went stony. "Give me your pay, get rid of *that* girl and go home. We'll talk about this in the morning—when I come back with your engagement rotor." When Shevi held her ground, she held out her hand and barked, "Now!"

She shoved her hand into her pocket and grabbed the coins, but she didn't pull all of them out. She let a few drop into the bottom of her pocket and surrendered the rest. Mom studied it then looked ruefully back into Shevi's eyes.

"Do I look like an idiot?"

"I'm keeping the rest."

Shevi grabbed Ava's hand and towed her toward the door where they met Perry and a few of his gang members. Kyle was right behind Perry. He carried his new scepter axle like a club.

"Where's Mom?"

Shevi thumbed over her shoulder.

"Whose kid is that?" Perry called after her as she pushed her way out onto Electric Avenue.

Shevi didn't answer. She stopped in the crowd of day walkers leaving the wheel and night walkers coming to weigh in, feeling completely lost.

Ava said, "Daddy unloads the afternoon train."

Shevi looked down at the girl. "That's no place for you."

"I went one time before."

"Would Jackson be down there?"

"Maybe."

"Okay. It's at least a place to start."

Chapter

Seven

Jackson hurried through the crowd until he reached the doors to the weigh-in platform of Wheel Three. A cluster of night walkers bottlenecked the passage trying to get in. Another obstacle.

His search for Christopher Bartlett had been a complete waste of time—too much time. The chief's secretary at the guardhouse of Wheel Three had sent him up to the jail. The warden's assistant had forwarded him to City Hall. City Hall had sent him to the Port Authority customs house at the station where the cable cars traversed the Wash to and from Fluxton. The officers there had only laughed at him and suggested he double check with the guardhouse at Wheel Three. All of this had taken a bit too long, and now that he had made the girl wait for him she would have something else to hold against him besides just his bad genes.

He squeezed his way in and ran to his book crate, but no one was there waiting for him. He looked around frantically, all the things his dad had said about Ava being sold rushing back through his mind. He ran toward the door, but it was impassable again.

Behind him a voice asked, "Looking for somebody?"

He turned to meet a group of very large boys. The one at the front wore a vest of chains cluttered with a conglomeration of random metal parts. Underneath, a shirt strained skintight over a huge belly. A froggy grin stretched across his face. He was big, more than twice Jackson's size, standing over Jackson with the confidence of a full grown Ironclad.

"My little sister," Jackson said. "She walked today with—"

"Shevi," the boy interrupted, knowingly but polite.

"Yes!" Jackson said. "Shevi. Do you know where she is?"

"I'm Perry, her brother. Of course I know where she is." He glanced left and right at his companions.

A silent exchange wove among them. Jackson didn't care what they thought of him; he just wanted to get Ava back in his sight.

"Come on," Perry said. "We were just going to meet her. You can come with us."

"Great," Jackson said, not even trying to hide his relief or downplay his appreciation. He fell in behind the team of massive boys and followed them to the door.

"Coming through," Perry shouted. "Make a hole. Make some room for the Titanics and our new friend."

A hole did in fact appear almost magically through the cluster blocking the door. Size was power.

As soon as they were outside, one of the boys peeled away from the gang and ran off without saying goodbye or giving a wave. It was as if things happened this way all the time.

One of the boys was wearing a rotor on his chest. He looked down at Jackson and said, "Shevi's quite a girl, ain't she?"

"Yeah," Jackson agreed.

"Everybody knows Shevi," another boy said.

Perry gave them disapproving looks as the gang moved down Electric Avenue several blocks and crossed into a back alley beneath the structure of Wheel Six.

Jackson asked, "Where are we going?"

The boys exchanged glances again, then Perry said, "There's a Dim has a saddle repair place just up here. Shevi wanted to get some work done to the saddle, now that she has someone to ride in it."

"Oh," Jackson said and followed along.

One of the boys was carrying a scepter axle. He asked, "Hey, you don't mind us calling you little guys Dims, do you?"

"Nah," Jackson lied and waved the question away—might made right. "Are you a Piedmont?"

"Yeah," the boy said and smacked the axle into his open palm. He pulled open the door of a small shed and led them inside.

"So is my mom," Jackson said, squinting into the darkness to find the workings of a saddle shop. The place was empty. Dirty glass strained the sunlight. Millions of dust motes swam in its orange shafts.

"I know," the boy said. He spun the axle on his palm and the gears that crowned it vanished into a blur.

Jackson studied the boy's face and said, "I guess we're cousins or something."

The boy stepped forward, popping his palm harder with the axle.

The one wearing the rotor stepped forward and said, "Wait for Cole."

"Who's Cole?" Jackson asked.

"Never mind," the Piedmont boy said.

Perry said, "He's the saddle maker."

Jackson caught the sly smile that flashed on Perry's face. The bad feeling that had started when they turned down the alley—no, it had actually started when the customs officers had laughed at him and it had redoubled when Ava wasn't at the crate—broke fully through to his consciousness as a wave of self-preserving panic. He flung himself toward the door. As he did, one of the gang slid the door closed. It caught him halfway through, its sharp metal edge biting his middle. He wriggled out while fat hands grabbed at him.

"Stupid Dim," one of them said.

"Just get him." That was Perry; Jackson would have bet on it.

He was free then, wondering what had gotten them so out of round. He turned to run for the clear open alley, back under the protective structure of I Town, away from the wall that mediated between it and Shack Town and the Wilds, caring less right then where Ava was or if she was safe, knowing for sure that he wasn't. But the alley wasn't clear. It wasn't open. Something big was blocking it. Several very big somethings. The only thing that was clear in Jackson's vision was the hat-shaped disk of a rotor. It was the biggest rotor Jackson had ever seen.

⟪⟫

"There's Mr. Myrtle," Ava cried, pointing at a small man with a round belly sticking out the open front of a shiny green jacket.

The evening supply train had just rumbled away, starting its ascent from the docks of Induction Town up to the Wash port where the remaining goods would be sent to Fluxton. I Town's massive underbelly smelled of fresh meats and breads and vegetables that had just come off the train. A few workers moved crates within the foundations. Mr. Myrtle eyed the little girl with what looked maybe like concern. Then he cast hungry eyes on Shevi.

"What about your dad?" Shevi whispered, a chill sliding up her back. "Is he still here?"

"Ask him." Ava pulled Shevi toward Mr. Myrtle with Ironclad Heavie dangling from her other hand.

"Can I help you?" he asked, swinging his hips as he strolled to meet them.

Shevi said, "We're looking for Jackson. Have you seen him?"

"I know him," the man said, a tinge of defensiveness in his voice but a twinkle in his green eyes. There was something familiar about him; he reminded Shevi of someone. "But I haven't seen him."

"Of course you know him. He climbed up there for you." Ava's words came out in a kind of singsong chide.

The man's offense at this was obvious on his face before he opened his mouth. "You need to be out of here. This is no place for a couple of girls—unless there's something I can do for you." His eyes traveled up and down Shevi's body.

"No. We'll just go," Shevi said. "Thanks." Now she tugged Ava away from the little man. When they were out of earshot she said, "He's a bit creepy."

Ava nodded. "He's a Dim."

Shevi looked down at her trying to figure out if she should scold her, ask her where she heard that word, or just agree. She decided to ignore it and ushered the girl back to Electric Avenue.

Families of Ironclads drifted from exit doors of wheels across the avenue to feasts where they would refuel for tomorrow's walk. They crossed and Shevi had the funny feeling she should crouch to try to see through the crowd's legs to find someone as small as Jackson among them. But he wasn't short, really, just thin—tall even, but very thin. In an instant, she found herself on a collision course with Perry. He wasn't alone. Cole was with him. Two of Cole's brothers and a few of the Titanics were there, too. They were laughing and carrying on, enjoying carefree life like typical teens. Shevi's first impulse was to change course and avoid them, but one of them spotted her, said something, and the whole assembly halted, crashing into one another. Their mood fell from fizzy to flat just as suddenly. There was an exchange of glances, shuffling about and grunting.

Finally, Cole said, "Hello, Shevi." His attention fell quickly to the little girl at Shevi's side then back up again. "How are you?"

"Fine, thanks. How are you?"

Cole responded with a simple nod. He was being unusually cool toward her. "Where's your rotor?"

"Oh," Shevi said, patting her middle where she wore it then pointing over her shoulder toward the entrance to Wheel Three. "My mother has it."

Perry gave a grunt. Shevi turned a reprimanding glare his way. He laughed. "Come on, guys. Let's let the lovers talk."

As the Titanics peeled away, Cole's brother said, "Perry, thanks."

Perry turned quickly, jostling his gang members. "Glad to help out," he said, giving a put-on smile.

No one had acknowledged Ava yet, not openly at least until she pointed at Kyle and said, "I know you."

Kyle gave her a hard look.

Tugging on Shevi's arm, Ava said, "He came to Grandma and Grandpa's house one time."

"Okay," Shevi said and turned her attention back to her fiancé.

Cole asked, "Does she need some weight? We can get her some weight." He glanced over his shoulder at his older brothers who quickly agreed.

"I think she just wanted to show it off," Shevi lied, hoping Perry hadn't already told them what had really happened. "And I have Ava to ride with me."

Cole gave another single nod but didn't look down at the girl.

"For now," Shevi said.

"Right," Cole said without enthusiasm. "For now."

"Yeah. It's helping me and it's helping them."

Luke was the shortest but heaviest of the Turney brothers. His body was big and soft, and his speech was usually sparse and just as soft as his cheeks and neck, which now blossomed with red blotches. He spoke up gruffly. "You need any help, the Turneys will give you all the help you need."

"That's right," Blake said.

"Yeah," Cole said. "Just let us know what you need. We'll get

90

your mom her own rotor. She'll be part of the family too, after all."

"That's right," Blake said again.

"Yeah, okay," Shevi said. "Well, we're looking for her brother—so I can get her back where she belongs."

The three Turneys exchanged a look.

Cole said, "Okay. See you tomorrow night."

"What's happening tomorrow night?"

"The wedding," Cole said, his tone scolding.

"Yes," she said. "Of course. Slipped my mind for a minute. It's been a crazy couple of days."

"Yeah," Cole said. Now he looked long and hard at Ava. "You haven't forgotten bid day, too, have you?"

"No." Shevi laughed although the upcoming prenuptial event actually had gotten lost in her mind along with the Stendahl wedding.

"Okay," Cole said, speaking with sarcastic slowness. "See you tomorrow."

Shevi walked away more rattled than she had felt through missing her rotor, struggling to get on the wheel, and making her debut with a stranger's child in her saddle. Cole was nice. He'd be a good husband and walker. She often felt talked down to, like a lesser class, when she was around his family, but now, for the first time, she felt that way coming away from him. If seeing him once in a week had left her feeling that way, what would marriage be like?

She had suddenly almost completely lost Ava in her mind too, until she felt the squeeze of her hand. She looked down and mustered a smile. "Can I just take you home? Will there be someone there? Will you be okay?"

Ava nodded vigorously, but her face said she wasn't so sure. Maybe what she wasn't sure about was Shevi.

Chapter Eight

Shevi took Ava to the nearest stair, just wanting to get away from Electric Avenue and the crowds and the chance of another strange situation. She didn't know why her life was unraveling around her, but she knew she had to pull things back together right away. She needed to get that freaking rotor back and get back on track with her friends and everything she knew and trusted.

Ava pointed out the blood; Shevi had been too lost in emotional vertigo to notice the bright red trail of spots on the stair treads.

"Ketchup?" Ava asked.

Shevi shook her head. "I don't think so."

A long smear coated the dull gray handrail of the next flight. Ava danced up the steps, dodging the droplet as if playing hopscotch. Shevi wanted to ask the girl to be careful. Instead, she asked which level they lived on.

"Six," Ava chirped over her shoulder.

The butt of the Gut, Shevi thought. Lots of Dims lived there. And when they arrived at the door to Level 6, they found blood on the handle. The hallway smelled dank and musty. The food service area was sparse. A single old man sat behind a table piled with overcooked or moldy loaves of bread. Farther in, the bouquet of odors became thicker—sweat and dirty diapers. The rhythmic sound of walkers and the trundle of a wheel filled the corridor. They were near the jail wheel.

The trail of blood went on ahead of Ava, as if leading her home, and it was smeared on the knob of the door she stopped at. She craned her head back from the knob and studied it with disgust, then she carefully pinched it between finger and thumb and turned it.

Shevi looked in over Ava's head. The single small room was dark except for the sleeve of wan light from the hall. Shevi pushed the door open all the way. Piles of bedding filled each corner, little nests. A big spatter of blood spotted the center of the small room. Shevi pulled the string that dangled from the center of the ceiling to turn on the light. A snuffling sound from the nest in the darkest corner behind the door startled her; she couldn't even scream, could only draw in a sharp breath and hold it.

"Turn it off." The words were throaty and raspy, sounding like a very old man's attempt to start a story he couldn't quite remember. A figure on a roll of dingy bedding turned his face to the wall but not before Shevi saw the disfigurement and swelling of Jackson's once fine and elegant features. "Turn it off and get out," he said, his voice muffled by the tattered blanket, blood, swelling and tears.

Shevi knelt beside him. "What happened?"

Ava was close beside her, holding onto her arm with both hands. Jackson burrowed his face into the corner and began to shake.

"Jackson, what happened?"

His face whipped out of hiding like a striking snake— monstrous, fiendish, and ugly. "You," he bellowed hoarsely. "You did this. *Get out!*" He slapped at her and curled back into his reclusive ball, shoulders heaving as he sobbed.

Shevi glanced at Ava. Crouching, she was eye to eye with the girl. Ava studied her suspiciously. Shevi reached out and touched Jackson's arm. He flinched and lashed out again, this time knocking her backward. She put down a hand to steady herself and felt the warm stickiness of blood.

Jackson was up now, out of his hiding, fully exposed. His clothes were torn. Every inch of exposed skin was purple with bruises. He had a perfectly curved scar across his forehead. It looked like a wide, frowning mouth. Blood beaded and dripped from it like little teeth. His right arm dangled by his side. His body shook, partly with rage, but partly from the strain of standing upright. His right eye was swollen shut.

"You—you and your kind," he wailed. "You're a bunch of bullies." Blood sprayed from his mouth.

Shevi pushed herself up and backed away from him. She'd landed in the pool of blood. Now it was just another dark stain on the dirty floor. Confused, she could only check her hand and the leg of her pants for bloodstains she already knew were there. But seeing them made them real. Behind her, Ava cried. She looked around to find the girl standing in the middle of the pallet of rags, clutching her Heavie doll, her bottom lip jutting out, her eyes sparkling with tears.

Shevi turned back to Jackson and found him holding his fierce wrestler's stance, his right arm turned away protectively.

"Jackson, let me help you."

"Oh, yeah." He swiped his left arm across his mouth and nose, dragging a string of saliva, snot and blood from them. "You've been a big help. A real big help. You're crazy. All of you are freaking mad. *Rabid!*"

Ava let out a terrified howl. Shevi turned and put out her bloody hand to comfort the girl, but that only made Ava shake her head wildly.

Back to Jackson, as calmly as she could, Shevi said, "We need to get you some help."

"Help?" he cried. "Help? Girl, you've done way too much for me already."

"We need to get you cleaned up."

"We?" Jackson said. His voice was low now, dangerous. "We? *You* need to GET OUT!" He pointed to the open door. "*You* need to go away and leave *me* alone."

Shevi agreed absolutely. She started toward the open door then spun quickly and grabbed Ava off her little nest.

"Yeah, take her," Jackson howled. "She's one of you anyway. And I hate all of you. I hate you, you big, fat freaks."

Shevi coddled Ava against her shoulder with one arm while she slammed the door shut with the other. Inside the little one-room apartment Jackson went on raving while Ava shook violently and howled and blubbered against Shevi's shoulder.

"Sh-sh-sh-sh-sh-sh," she whispered into Ava's ear and bounced her up and down. "Sh-sh-sh-sh-sh-sh."

She started back the way they had come but immediately found her bearings in the structure and system of the Gut and realized that another stair was closer to where she was and where she needed to go. Passing by the bloodstained door to the other stair she felt the strain of the day and Ava's extra weight on her legs.

Despite the steady, noisy and odorous traffic of lower class walkers and middle management heading to their homes in the Gut, the inside of the stairwell was a sweet solace after the bedlam of dealing with Jackson. Shevi squatted in the corner of the landing and sat Ava on her knee so she could talk to her. The girl's face was a mess of mucus and tears. Shevi did what she could to wipe her off. She took Heavie and cleaned her a little.

"Is Heavie okay?" she asked Ava as her sobs abated.

Ava threw her head back and howled, "Jackson!" and her crying escalated again.

Shevi pulled her close and hugged her and shushed her again. "It's okay," she lied. "It's all going to be okay."

A short but stout couple with saddles on their backs and children walking along beside them eyed Shevi and her ward as they passed. The worry and discomfort of seeing a girl and child broken down in the corner of the stair showed plainly on their faces, along with the strain of their day's walk. Shevi offered them a smile as she went on consoling Ava, but they just hurried by. In a few years the kids would be too big for them to carry, then the whole family would be off the wheel, especially if the weight limits kept going up. For now, though, they could go home and enjoy their evening meal knowing they were better off than what they'd seen in the stairwell.

Shevi gathered Ava up into her arms again and began her ascent homeward, away from the blood and the tears, and was comforted to find that Perry wasn't home. She sat Ava down on the couch and drew her a drink from the water bottle. While the girl sipped, Shevi took some rags down the hall to the bathrooms to wet them. She waited in line for a sink behind other tired walkers while stall doors squeaked open and clacked closed as other lower middle class walkers disposed of their soiled diapers and got ready for the evening meal. Back in the apartment, a luxury suite compared to what Jackson was in below, Ava sat with the cup in both hands, Heavie sitting in her lap, both staring at nothing. Shevi didn't speak, just went to work cleaning the girl up.

Finally, in the curious and quizzical but simple and straightforward way of a child, Ava asked, "Does Jackson hate me?"

"No," Shevi bayed. "No, ma'am. He's just hurt and when people are hurt they can say things they don't mean."

"Why is he hurt?"

"I don't know."

"Why did he say you did it?"

"Sweetie, I don't know."

"What should we do?"

"Well, I'm not really sure. But I think probably we should give him some time to rest and we should eat and get our strength, then we should try to find some ice for Jackson."

Ava studied Shevi carefully. "Ice? What for?"

"For the swelling."

"Where're we going to get any ice?"

"I don't know. But we'll just have to see what we can do."

Shevi sat down beside Ava and put her arm around her. The little girl was smart. She knew how expensive and rare ice was and how hard it would be to find enough to help her brother. Images of Jackson's face flashed through her mind, alternating between the hopeful and ambitious book dealer who had been on the weigh-in platform that morning and the crazed beast downstairs right now. The blue and swollen nose and lips and eyes had burned themselves thoroughly into Shevi's memory, but the most disturbing of his injuries was the curved scar across his forehead. She shivered at the thought of how it might have happened.

Chapter
Nine

The food court of Level 10 was absolutely luxurious after the food service area at the lowest level of the Gut. Middle class families laughed and talked together while they ate at long tables. Dietitians policed buffet lines stocked with steaming pastas and golden loaves of bread and reminded walkers to partake of salads slathered with thick creamy dressings. Suddenly, being middle class didn't look so bad, even if Shevi was on the lower end.

Ava squeezed Shevi's hand tightly. Shevi now understood it as a signal that the girl was uncomfortable in yet another strange place.

Shevi asked, "Where did you live before you came to Wheel Three?"

"Eight."

"What level of Wheel Eight did you live on?"

"The butt," Ava said, sighing. "After we moved down."

"What level did you move down from?"

"The top."

"Just below the Mall?"

"No. Outside."

"Outside?" Shevi laughed at this, but played along and offered, "Like the Terraces?" It was an outrageous idea.

"No," Ava confirmed, then shocked Shevi with an even more outrageous suggestion, "the *very* top."

Shevi stopped and gave her a downward judgmental glance. "You didn't live on the Upper Crust of Wheel Eight."

Ava nodded enthusiastically. "With Grandma and Grandpa Piedmont—in their big house. Until Grandpa died and Uncle Blaine got his picture on the wall. Daddy said that's what made Mommy sick. Could that have made Mommy sick?"

Shevi shrugged and led Ava to the buffet and away from the whole confusing conversation. She handed the chief dietitian their weight card, pondering the life of a family that had made such a dramatic class shift. Whatever had happened to Jackson, Shevi understood how he would blame anybody and everybody from all the upper classes.

She chose a penne and chicken dish for her main course and plain white bread. The dessert of the evening was cheesecake—chocolate cream or plain with blueberry or cherry topping. The server checked Shevi's card and began weighing the courses on a big tray. She watched the woman scoop up large helpings while checking Shevi for approval.

"Is there a problem?" the little server woman asked.

"I don't know if I can eat that much."

The chief dietitian stepped over. "The buttered wheat bread will reduce the other helping sizes."

Shevi knew this but knew it would lay in her stomach a lot heavier than the plain white bread.

"Walkers need their strength," the server placated. "And girls need to grow."

The dietitian was less accommodating. "You don't want to fall out."

Shevi smiled and nodded, thinking she could just share with Ava until the server filled another plate. It was smaller than Shevi's tray, but still seemed large for little Ava. The meal for the two of them cost nineteen cents.

Shevi turned from the buffet and found Tasha and Stace sitting with some boys from several rows ahead. One of them was a Titanic. The whole group was looking at her; the instant she turned to them they all looked down to their trays of food and began eating with theatrical enthusiasm.

Shevi led Ava to their table. When she and Ava took seats, the others scooted their chairs about as if needing to make special room for them. Shevi felt like an intruder in company she'd been keeping for years now.

No one spoke. The sounds of their chewing grated in Shevi's ears. Ava looked up from her plate.

"This is Ava," Shevi said.

Her words jarred the others. They looked at one another, as if not sure of the etiquette of dealing with a stranger.

"She walked with me today. Didn't you?"

Ava nodded. "And now we need ice for my brother." Utensils rattled on trays and trays rattled on the table as the little clan reacted. "He's hurt."

The Titanic snickered at this.

"Where're you going to get ice?" Stace asked. Shevi heard a tinge of something in her tone. There was something very unsettling about Stace this evening. Was she bothered by the presence of a child at the teens' table? Or was she confused by the idea of needing ice? Or was it something else altogether?

"I don't know," Shevi said. "Maybe we can buy some from the kitchen." The other teens reacted with head shakes and exchanged whispers while Shevi studied Ava across the table. "Would your grandparents have any ice?"

Ava dipped her sausage in its sauce and popped it in her mouth. Matter-of-factly she said, "Only for special occasions."

The clan was staring at them now. Shevi took the opportunity to say, "She's a Piedmont." Another wave of energy cycled around the table.

The Titanic boy said, "Her daddy isn't."

"What do you know about her or her dad?" Shevi asked.

The boy gobbled down the last of what had been a very big portion of lasagna and finished stuffing his great mouth with a wad of heavily buttered bread.

Stace said, "Her brother is the Dim with the books, right?"

"Yeah," Shevi said. "That's right."

The Titanic attacked his cheesecake.

"What's your name?" Shevi asked him.

"This is Les," Tasha said. "His friend Kyle is a Piedmont."

Shevi said, "I know Kyle. I didn't realize he was a Piedmont. So that axle isn't just a show?"

Les coughed, sending splatters of his dessert onto the table. "No," he said defensively. "It's not a show. He's a Piedmont."

"Well, then," Shevi said. "Ava, here, is one of his cousins, likely."

The big boy gave a low growl in response to this, accompanied by a sly smile, as if the implication reminded him of an inside joke.

"What?" Shevi asked.

Les's grin stretched until his face looked like the face of a menacing frog ready to devour a pathetic insect. He shook his head. "Nothing. Just funny."

"What's funny?"

Les stood with his tray in one hand and his fork in the other. Stace stood too, though she still had a load of food on her plate. She grabbed both their drinking cups.

Shevi looked up at her. "Where are you going—Stacey?"

"It's Stace—in case you forgot. With Les."

"I didn't forget."

Stace glared down at her and, flashing a hateful look at Ava, said, "Seems to me you've forgotten a lot of stuff." That look reminded Shevi of someone or something, but she couldn't remember what or who.

"Like what?"

Stace didn't answer. She turned her nose up as she took leave of the group.

Tasha asked, "You going to adopt her?"

Shevi stared down the table at her, unsure how to reply.

" 'Cause it seems she ought to be eating on her own level."

"She walked with me," Shevi said, hearing the defensiveness in her own voice.

"But she doesn't belong here," Tasha said coolly.

Shevi said, "Maybe I *will* adopt her."

The others exchanged glances.

Tasha asked, "What would Cole say about that?"

Looking across the table at Ava who was staring intently at her, anticipating her answer, Shevi said, "Hurry up and eat. We need to go."

Ava took another piece of sausage.

Someone at the table said, "Got to get that ice."

Someone else said, "Must be hurt bad if he needs ice."

"Yeah," another drawled sarcastically.

Shevi had a long way to go to finish her dinner, but her appetite was gone. She stood and took her plate. A look down at Ava was enough to get the girl to do the same. The little group of peers hushed. As she left the table, Shevi watched Tasha out of the corner of her eye. The expression on her face at least seemed to be genuine concern, which only fanned Shevi's anger and irritation. Why did there have to be such animosity among the classes? Why could one person not just lend a hand to another person in need without everyone else getting offended?

The server smiled as Shevi approached the buffet line. "More?" she asked.

"No. I need to take this to go." Shevi knew better than to admit she didn't want to eat it. "And I need to get some ice."

The little woman's smile waned as she reached to take the plates from Shevi. "I can cover that for you and let you take it out, but there's no ice here."

"There's none in the service pantry?"

"No." Now she laughed. "Whatever would we be doing with ice down here?"

The dietitian left her post by the waste disposal where she was watching to make sure at least most of the walkers were consuming their necessary calories. "What's the matter, Virginia?"

The server spoke to her superior without taking her eyes off Shevi. "Well, it seems this young lady has a taste for some ice."

"How extravagant," the dietitian said, studying Shevi and Ava critically.

"It isn't for me," Shevi said. "It's for a friend. Her brother." She looked down at Ava.

"I see," the dietitian said. "But he isn't here?"

"No, ma'am. He's hurt and needs an ice pack for the swelling."

"Then he should go to the clinic."

"He can't. He's not a walker."

The dietitian inventoried Ava again, her nose wrinkling up like she'd come across a bad smell. "There's a clinic in the wall for non-walkers and underprivileged."

Shevi had heard of the place. Walkers jokingly referred to it as the coffin clinic. She shook her head. "No, ma'am. He doesn't need a doctor, I think—I hope, anyway—just a cold pack to decrease the swelling."

"Good luck with that." The dietitian laughed. "And good luck with your *friend*." She exchanged a look with the server, watched her covering the plates and offered Shevi a threatening glare. As

Shevi took the covered plates from Virginia, the dietitian's eyebrows rose. "Do make sure you maintain your *own* diet, miss. The corporation is counting on its walkers."

"Yes, ma'am." Shevi gave the best reassuring nod and smile she could muster despite the way all the negativity around her was cinching her stomach into a tight knot and making it extremely unlikely that she would be able to eat anytime soon.

"Especially the vegetables, dear," Virginia chirped.

"Yes," the dietitian said. "Very important."

"Of course," Shevi said.

Chapter

Ten

The atmosphere on the wheel during the nightshift was as different as night is from day. Someone had just hit a jackpot at one of the gambling tables when Shevi and Ava came onto the platform. Somebody whooped and yelled while the collective groans of others matched the volume. Rowdy uproars from the tables made general conversations more chaotic than would be allowed during the vital load demand of the day.

The manager eyed Shevi's little companion as they crossed the desolate weigh-in platform. His small eyes narrowed and seemed to suck back into their sockets as the pair approached him. Nightshift generally was considered incompatible with kids, and vice versa.

"I need to talk to my mother," Shevi said.

"How long?" the little man asked.

"Just a quick minute," Shevi said.

"Sign in," he said, looking relieved.

Shevi bent over the registry to sign and casually added, "She might keep Ava while I run some errands."

"What'd you mean, keep her?"

"Just for a bit," Shevi said. "Not long."

The man issued a disgusted growl. "No kids on the nightshift."

Dismissively, Shevi said, "I used to come with my dad all the time when I was little. I'll be back before ten. Please weigh her in for Jo Ann Lilbourn." She felt the power she was exerting over this diminutive member of society, talking down to the man. It seemed a necessity but made Shevi wonder what she would be capable of as she moved up in society.

Shevi and Ava had dropped off their leftovers in the apartment and descended the stairs to Electric Avenue, and along the way they'd had a long talk about what to expect when they got down to the wheel. Shevi explained that it would be best for Jackson if Ava stayed with her mother so Shevi could track down some ice. The girl seemed okay with the idea. Shevi warned that the nightshift was different and that the manager might need some persuading. Now, when Shevi checked Ava, the little girl was looking up at her respectfully, like Shevi was the most knowledgeable authority figure she'd ever seen. Shevi smiled and squeezed her hand. Ava reciprocated.

The little manager obediently motioned for Ava to step onto the scale. When Ava did and he had recorded her weight, he smiled approvingly.

"Not bad," he said. "You're quite a little chunk."

"She's very solid," Shevi said.

"I didn't realize Jo Ann had a little one," the manager said.

"She's not my sister," Shevi said, but as she looked back down at Ava she could see enough of a resemblance in their builds to understand the mistake.

The little man checked his clipboard and smiled up at Shevi. "Tell your mom she can move up to Row 14—if she'd like."

"I will," Shevi said. "Thank you, sir."

"My pleasure. Ten o'clock, remember. The little ones need to be home in bed getting their rest so they can grow."

Shevi nodded and stepped off the edge of the weigh-in platform onto the curving slope of the onramp. Flavors of foods had replaced the odor of dirty diapers as many of the crowd of only about three thousand, half again more than usual, now enjoyed their breakfasts while they walked. They wore less armor and tended to be smaller than the Ironclads of the dayshift. They all watched Shevi and Ava make their way down to the back rows. A short but sufficiently round man carried a tub of omelet and potatoes in one hand and his fork in the other while a large milkshake perched in the cup holder on his dashboard. He offered Ava a wiggling wave of his fat pinky and ring finger from his fork hand along with a cheery grin. Others were less accepting. A younger man was doing tricks with a yoyo. He was tall with long skinny legs and a round paunch offset by an enormous homemade pack on his back. Ava watched him, looking quite impressed, but the man only scowled at her through the angles of string he'd made with his bobbing toy.

The gambling tables were at the rear of the wheel's walk zone; they took up too much space to be farther up. Walkers who signed up for spots at them walked at reduced weights, even when they were walking on rows farther up and waiting for a loop at one of the tables. But a few good hands or rolls of dice could make up for it, or so Shevi's mom insisted. The last time Shevi had visited Mom at work there had been twice as many tables. Unless Shevi remembered wrong, they'd taken up at least half the walk zone. Demand was up, the yellow light in the middle of the demand indicator still flashing at this late hour.

Shevi took Ava into her arms before stepping onto the revolving tread of the wheel and assuming the metronomic pace. Though demand was lower during the night, the wheel still turned at the same rate, producing the same frequency of alternating current and voltage.

They found Shevi's mom at one of the tables near the center of the tread. She was facing away from them, walking sideways on the wheel. Shevi fell in beside the player walking the low side of the table and walked several strides before Mom looked up from her fan of cards. Her eyebrows rose witht pleasure at the sight of Shevi but then furrowed as she studied the girl in her arms.

"What's she doing here?"

"I need you to take her for a while."

Mom's expression changed to surprise. She quickly checked the cards that had been played, checked her hand, and threw out a queen of diamonds. The next player, the one walking forward at the bottom of the table beside Shevi, tossed a king out and dragged the trick into his pile. Shevi's eyes followed the cards until she caught sight of the large steel disk hanging on the man's chest. It was her engagement rotor.

"Murray?" she asked the man.

"No," Mom said. "This is Ty. He won it from Murray in the first game tonight."

The man smiled over his shoulder at her. His ruddy cheeks drew up into big round balls on either side of a shiny red nose. Enormous, bushy eyebrows bobbed at her. He was quite proud of himself. He led the ace of diamonds.

"I'm Murray," the man across the table said. He was small for a walker, but he carried two big axles crisscrossed across his back, a necklace of five-holed bricks lay against his chest and the pointed shape of a bell housing crowned his head.

"Are you a Piedmont and a Rollston and a Stendahl?" Shevi asked, referring to the family symbols he sported.

The man threw his head back and laughed then stopped just as suddenly and glared at her. "No, my dear. I'm a collector—and I'll have that Turney rotor back if it's the last thing I ever do." He gave Shevi's mom a spiteful sideways glance and asked, "Jo Ann, do we need to stop play while you work this out?"

"I've already played," Ty whined. "And I'm keeping this rotor."

Murray said, "Perhaps Jo should make room for another player. Tables are getting scarce with demand going up."

The player facing Shevi's mom and sidling to the left on the wheel was a short stout woman. She placed the three of spades on Ty's ace and said in a gravelly voice, "The night shifts on the other wheels haven't lost any tables, so I've heard."

Mom cut harsh eyes at Shevi.

Shevi said, "Just for a couple of hours."

Mom motioned a hand toward the table that hung by loops from the four players' shoulders, as if Shevi didn't know what her mother was doing.

Ava said, "We played Spades before Mommy got sick."

The woman across from Mom said, "What happened to your mommy, dear?"

Murray said, "I hope you didn't bid that ace, Ty." He chuckled vengefully and played the four of diamonds.

"It's a long and very sad story," Shevi said. "And now her brother is hurt and her father is still working and she needs to stay here while I go take care of something."

"Jackson needs ice," Ava said. "He's swollen."

Mom rolled her eyes and cast a sardonic gaze across the great expanse of space inside the huge revolving wheel.

"I help him," Shevi explained. "He gets better. He takes her back."

"In a couple of hours?" Mom said doubtfully.

"Not to cure him. Just to help him out."

"You're a walker, Shevi, not a social worker."

Murray said, "Jo, dear, it's your turn and I would like to win my rotor back this evening."

Mom took in the cards on the table, scanned the ones in her hand and put down the four of spades. As she dragged the cards to her side of the table, she mumbled, "Oh, all right," then gave a beckoning rolling motion.

"Thank you," Shevi said, helping Ava into Mom's saddle. "Thank you so much. I'll be right back."

Mom grunted as the girl's weight settled into the saddle. "You're a big one," she said. "Reminds me of having Perry on my back."

Shevi leaned in close to her mother and whispered, "I need some of my money back, too."

Mom gave a restrained but appreciable sigh. The fight was gone out of her, that maternal instinct from having a child in her saddle taking over her mind—Shevi knew how it felt now. She took a random collection of coins from her pocket and discreetly slipped them to Shevi. But Shevi noticed Ty tip his head then grin subtly.

As she left he said, "Thanks for stopping by."

Shevi rushed off the moving tread back the way she'd come and signed out with the manager. She counted the coins as she descended into the cellars. A dollar eighty-five. Surely she could get at least a little bit of ice for that. As she crossed the docks on her way to the main kitchens she saw Mr. Myrtle and waved. He gave her that same suspicious glare and acted like he wanted her to stop and talk, but she ran on.

The expanse of the main kitchen was empty and silent except for a cloud of steam that drifted along the ceiling and the echo of a single rattling pot. Shevi followed the noise to a small man in a dingy white uniform and rubber boots. He sweated over a huge skillet big enough that he almost could've slept in it, mumbling as he scraped at a thick burned crust lining it. Shevi stopped behind him and cleared her throat to get his attention, but he continued his vigorous attack, seeming to recite a litany while he worked.

After standing patiently for several long seconds, Shevi said, "Excuse me."

The man jumped and shouted the words he'd been about to whisper, "And I told her not to!" He dropped the pot, whirled and glared at Shevi. They faced off for an unsettling moment, then he turned back to his work and growled, "Damned potatoes. Always sticking to the pan."

"Sir," she said.

"Sir?" he snapped over his shoulder. "You call me sir? What do you want?"

"Some ice."

"Ice? What for?"

"Swelling. A friend has been hurt and needs some ice."

The man slammed the pot down across the gaping mouth of the sink and turned the water on. He stood motionless while the pan filled. Shevi watched, completely confused about what she should do. Distant mumbling suggested Shevi should follow them and find someone else to help her, but when the water had covered the highest stains the man shut it off and dried his hands.

"Let it soak," he said, smiling and waving over his shoulder as he turned. "Easier anyway. But scrubbing helps me vent. You know? You ever just need to vent?"

She looked at him uncertainly.

"Nah. A big girl like you. You got no worries. You're a walker." He gave her an overt head-to-toe appraisal. "And a fine one, at that. What brings you to the lowly state of a working Dim? Ah, yes. Swelling. Ice. Expensive stuff, ice."

"I have money." She held out her hand.

His eyes grew wide and twinkled with delight. "That's a lot of money." He licked his lips and glanced around the kitchen toward the source of the conversation Shevi had picked up on. "You come in here looking so good and waving that kind of money around. You could give an old guy a heart attack." He fanned his face theatrically.

"I'm sorry."

He let out a big laugh. "Don't be. You made my night. But you don't need ice. You need veggies."

Shevi sighed. Why was everybody in I Town pushing vegetables all the time? "No, sir. It's swelling."

"Right. And you don't need to waste your money on ice that's just going to melt and be gone." He turned and beckoned her to follow.

She puffed out what frustration she could in a deep sigh and followed along. The book boy was turning out to be more trouble than she'd expected. He just better appreciate all this when he got over the injured animal phase of his pain.

The little kitchen worker led her to a massive door with a latch handle as big as his leg. But he didn't open it. Instead he popped open a small hatch down low and stooped to go through it. Cold air turned into fingers of fog and enwreathed him. It had a foreboding metallic odor. Again he invited her to follow. Her solitary situation dawned powerfully on her as she ducked into the dark space beyond. Inside the freezer, light was low and scarce. The chill in the air and the creepiness of the place brought a rash of gooseflesh up on her arms and excited the hairs on the back of her scalp. Her guide darted past several rows of crates then turned down a dark alley. Shevi crept slowly toward the gap he'd vanished into, but before she could reach it to see where he'd gone he jumped back into sight. His hands were raised high on either side and each held a ghastly, horrid object—heads with hair pulled up for handles, distorted and disfigured faces.

Shevi screamed and lost her footing as she tried to turn and flee. Her butt and hands landed hard on the cold floor. She sat helplessly, trying to make her brain recover enough to make even a single muscle move as her host stalked toward her.

"I'm sorry," the odd little man said. "I didn't mean to frighten you."

From her seat on the frosty floor, she saw the two objects he held in his hands from a different angle and in a different light. They weren't heads held by tufts of hair. They were big bags full of—

"Peas?" Shevi asked.

"The very best cold pack for swelling," the man said. "Here, let me help you." He set the bags down on the floor and offered his hands. When she was standing again, he hefted the big bags and led the way through the little portal to the light of the kitchen area. Back at his sink and his dirty pan, he turned and held out the bags of peas. "Here you go."

"How much?"

He made a sudden spewing noise that surprised Shevi again. "Don't be ridiculous. Veggies are free in I Town. Can't get the walkers to eat them fast as we get 'em from Agrarianna, so we have to freeze 'em."

"Thank you," she said and declined her head emphatically as she took the bags.

"Thank *you*, my dear, for gracing me with your divinely

beautiful presence. Come again, any time."

She smiled and felt the warmth of a blush rise in her cheeks. "You're too kind."

"And *you* are too beautiful."

Unable to bear any more of his flattery, Shevi darted away with her goods. She ran from the kitchen, up the stairs and out into Level 6. Breathless, she tapped the door of Jackson's apartment with the toe of her shoe. It creaked open.

"Jackson?" she said. "Hello?"

"Go away," he mumbled.

She stepped inside, proudly holding up her treasure and offering. He squinted up at her. She raised one hand high enough to grasp the string to turn on the light.

Jackson threw his hands over his face and screamed, "What are you doing?" When the light came on, he turned away from it and wriggled into the corner like a scared insect.

"It's peas," Shevi said.

"What?" he shrieked, glancing over his shoulder.

"Frozen peas—for your swelling. Here." She knelt beside him and gently laid one of the bags against his face.

He flinched and hissed at first, but then made several long sounds of relief, an mmmm and then a shhhhh . . .

"Better?" Shevi asked.

Jackson turned toward her and sat up. He reached out for the other bag and put it against his shoulder. He sucked in a sharp breath at its first touch but a second later let out a sigh and relaxed.

Finally he said, "Yes. Feels good. Thank you."

He rolled over and adjusted the bag against his face. His chest heaved as he took several cleansing breaths. Shevi sat back and took a moment to look around the tiny room. On another wall, above another little nest, was a collection of very nice colored drawings of big, hulking figures from some other world and Skinners and Iron-clads from I Town. She crept to the bed.

"What happened?" she asked.

He took one exceptionally long breath and cast an odd almost accusatory glance at her before turning and staring away, fumbling with the cold packs.

"Tell me," she said.

He shook his head.

She touched the figures on the wall. "These are good."

"That's stuff my dad does. He likes Gargantua and Pantagruel. The bald one is the Gargantua. You ever read CorpPress comics?"

Shevi shook her head. He was at least opening up to her.

"That one with the loincloth is my grandpa."

She pointed to a sketch of a man with big, round arms and legs, a big belly and a long narrow strip of cloth hanging beneath it. Jackson nodded.

"Hello?" The door creaked open a bit more. A small and very thin man with sparse strands of long brown hair stood in the doorway.

"What's going on here?" he said. "Who are you?"

Shevi stood and put out her hand, but the man turned to Jackson. "Who is this?" He gasped, finally seeing Jackson's condition. "What happened to you?" His face turned back toward Shevi. There was fear in his eyes.

Jackson said, "This is Shevi. She took Ava on the wheel today."

The man looked around the tiny single room. "Where is Ava? Where's my daughter?"

"This is my dad," Jackson said. "Levine Koss."

The man's voice was small and uncertain as he gave Shevi an indicting stare. "Jackson, what happened and where is Ava?"

"I don't know," Shevi pleaded. "I mean, Ava is fine. She's with my mom, but I don't know—"

"With your mother?" the man said accusingly. "Who *is* your mother? Where is she? What happened to Jackson?"

"Dad," Jackson said, sitting up a bit straighter. "It isn't her fault. Some of her . . ." He brushed at her with the back of his hand as if to shoo her away.

"Some of who?" Mr. Koss asked. "Some of her what?" His eyes bulged open. "Oh, Jackson." He looked from Jackson to Shevi and back again. His voice waxed with sadness, even mourning and sorrow, as if someone had died. "No, Jackson. No. Absolutely not. You know better. And you, please go. Stay away from my son and my daughter. Go now." He pointed to the door as Jackson started to rise. "You stay there," he said to Jackson. "I'll be right back."

His manner was terribly agreeable as he swept Shevi out the door and to the stairs. "Let's go. Take me to her." He never touched her; he kept his head bowed in subordination.

"I don't know—"

"My daughter," the man said. "Please."

Chapter
Eleven

Jackson migrated to his bunk with the bags of frozen peas. The cold was a blessing on his wounds. As he lay there letting it soak deep into the inflammation, only one image filled his mind. It was the image of Shevi when she looked up from the Kahn novel and said it sounded interesting. Her eyes had sparkled just then, caught the light in such a wonderful way that it would make Jackson go and steal Grandpa's copy. He smiled remembering the sound of Mrs. Burge pounding on the library door while he stood bare chested, proud for a moment despite his bony torso.

Then the deep soul-ringing sound of his head hitting the rotor passed through his mind, obliterating Shevi's gleaming eyes and shining face, like a porcelain doll dropped onto a stone floor. The boy—Cole, the others had called him—had reached around behind Jackson's head, palmed it and drawn it forward and down into the shiny hat-shaped metal disk. Oh, the sudden and total contact Jackson had made with it. His teeth snapped against one another. His brain seemed to thud inside his skull. After that, being dragged back into the shed, punched in the face, and kicked in the ribs seemed to be happening to somebody else.

"You Dims need to stay away from our women," one of them had said.

"They all need to be castrated so we don't have to keep on doing for them and us too," another of the big boys suggested.

"Let's castrate him."

"No, guys." It was the big one with the rotor that Jackson now wore an impression of on his forehead—the one they called Cole. "No weapons. We don't need that, because we're big enough. Just let them die off."

"Yeah." Perry had crouched beside him and smirked down at him then. "I hear that Dim mommas are so stupid they throw out the baby and put a diaper on the afterbirth. Is that what happened to you, Dim? Is your momma that stupid?"

Somebody told Perry to shut up.

"My dad says they're like roaches," somebody else said as they walked away and left him alone.

Jackson's mind replayed the scene of the herd of Ironclad boys sauntering carelessly out the shed door, into the light of day, and the changing currents of dust motes in the air. Not one of them glanced back at him. Nobody looked back to give him a smirk or see if he was alive or dead. What did it matter to them?

And what was he thinking? This girl's eyes sparkled when she found a book she liked. And he had let himself get all into her. They were right. He needed to stay away from *their* women. Didn't he know this? Hadn't he learned anything from *Mother*?

The door popped open and Ava trotted in, looking over her shoulder. Dad followed. He gave her a sad, sheepish look.

"I'm sorry, Ava. I didn't mean to push you." Then he looked at Jackson and his expression made a polar switch. "Interesting taste."

Jackson relocated one of the ice packs. Ava stared at him and moved toward Dad. She was afraid of the disfigured thing she saw and couldn't recognize as her brother and of the crazed person he'd acted like earlier. Jackson waved to her and tried to smile, but it made his face ache. He covered more of it with peas. "Did you have a good day?"

She let go of Dad's pants leg and asked, "What happened?"

"Some guys beat me up."

"Why?"

Dad made a huffing noise and sat himself down on his bedding. He opened a comic book and looked at it. When Jackson didn't answer, he said, "Yeah, Jackson. Why did they do that?"

Jackson lay down on his mattress and stared at the glowing light in the middle of the little ceiling. After some contemplation, he said, "Because I was stupid."

Out of the corner of his eye he saw his dad nod at a new figure as he brought it to life on the plaster surface. Jackson rolled over and faced the wall. He put one bag of peas under his head like a pillow. He hugged the other with his bad arm. Inches away, the dull and dingy wall seemed to pulse at him to the rhythm of his own heartbeat.

Behind him Dad said, "You want a story?"

His dad's mattress squeaked and the pages of a comic book rustled.

Ava asked, "What did Jackson do?"

"Nothing, sweetie," Dad whispered.

Jackson listened to the dull murmur of the Butt, the distant drone of the jail wheel and of other Dim families having end of day discussions. Had anybody else fallen for an Ironclad they couldn't have? Or was Jackson the only one that stupid?

Finally, Dad whispered, "He learned a very important lesson today." Then he began reading the exploits of the muscular Iron-clad Metalman. Jackson drifted off as the mighty hero commenced another battle against injustice in the confines of his fictitious world.

◯◯

Perry was being smug. He knew something Shevi didn't. She was relieved when he finally left for the morning and left her alone to wait for Mom and the saddle. But just seconds after he closed the door there was a knock. Shevi opened it and found Cole standing in the hall. He held a long loop of chain in his hand and a rotor dangling from it. But not any rotor—her rotor. She recognized the oiled patina and fine polish marks he had rubbed into it getting it ready to present to her.

"You got it back," she said.

"Yeah," he said, holding open the loop of chain to put over her head. She ducked and accepted it. Its weight felt strange and un-familiar already. Cole said, "Those two gambling addict geezers ought to know better."

"So should my mother." She ducked her head again and shook it ruefully.

Cole took her by the shoulders and lifted them until she looked up at him. His hazel eyes glinted in the living room light. "If you need *anything*, you have to come to us. You're practically a Turney now and your family too." He kissed her gently on the forehead.

"We don't *need* anything. We're doing fine. I don't know why she did it."

"Well, it's over now." He pulled her up some more and pressed his lips against hers. His mouth was firm and tense.

She pulled back. "Is everything okay?"

"Yeah," he said, giving his head a quick nod. "Yeah. Everything's fine."

She reached up and kissed him back. Still, he felt tense. "Did your parents find out?"

He made a little huffing sound. "Don't worry about them."

"I'm not," she lied. "Why should I?"

"You shouldn't." He kissed her.

Suddenly, in her mind, it wasn't Cole kissing her but Jackson, and not the injured animal down in the one-room apartment in the Butt of the Gut but the book boy who had so enthusiastically introduced her to the Holy Bible and *The Great God, Mann.* The mental flash made her breath catch. She looked down at the curve of the hub of Cole's rotor and drew back from him. The puffy roundness of his face conjured an image of Jackson's swollen features complete with the arc-shaped scar on his forehead. The thought confused her. She stepped back. Cole grabbed her shoulders with a desperately firm grip and stopped her.

"We're alone, aren't we?"

"Yeah," she said, shaking her head to clear all the confusing sketches from it. He pushed her backward. She looked around behind her and then back at him. His face was dull but grinning. "What?"

"We could get started."

"Started?"

"Started on our family." He stared hard into her eyes. "Kids."

"I have to go to work."

"No you don't."

She pulled out of his grasp. "Yes, I do."

"No you don't. Come on. My dad kind of expects it."

"I'm sorry, but—no. Not . . . not now. My mom will be home any minute."

"Maybe. Maybe not."

"Why wouldn't she be?"

"Maybe I already thought of that."

Shevi took another step back. "Does she know?"

"Well, duh. It's what people do. If she's smart, she probably expects it too. Everybody in Trintico expects it, Shevi. Hell, they need it. They're counting on us to have lots of kids. Big ones."

Shevi suddenly felt like she was being watched, like everybody else in I Town could see what she was doing and know what she was thinking. And what she was thinking was that she wanted to check on Jackson, to see how he was—to see him, which was ridiculous. And she knew it without a doubt.

"Are you sure I'm the one?"

Now it was Cole who stepped back. "What?!"

"The *one*, the only one you want to be with. Are you sure it's me?"

"Well, yeah," he said, and the yeah sounded a lot like the duh from a few seconds before.

"Yeah?"

"Yes!" he said. "Of course."

He took a step toward her and she countered with a step closer of her own but seized his arm and turned him toward the door.

"Walk me downstairs." When he only stood stubbornly, she gave a tug and said, "Come on."

He sighed. "Yeah, okay."

They descended to Electric Avenue where she was willing to relieve him of his obligation, but he insisted on joining her inside the weigh-in platform. She forced the last of a too big breakfast down while trying not to look in the direction of Jackson's crate of books. And in so doing she had the chance to see that Cole did look that way. He took a long look down at the end of the platform and grinned at what he saw. She thanked him for the walk and kissed him goodbye and when he was out the doors and back onto the avenue and had finally stopped looking back to check on her, she looked that way herself. The crate sat closed and alone—as did the fob booth beside it. There was nothing she could see that should have entertained Cole. As she joined a line to weigh in, she studied the area carefully and considered his little grin and wondered why he'd done it and why she cared.

The line moved quickly as the demand, high again to start with, soared. She stepped onto the scale confidently with the weight of her engagement token hanging around her neck, but the manager moved the smaller weight down and down and down until it hit zero. He looked up at her and cut his eyes around to see who was watching. Then he moved the larger weight to one-seventy-five and slid the smaller weight back across its track. It stopped at twenty-four.

The manager quickly slid the larger weight back to two hundred and cleared his throat. "Only a pound under," he whispered. "I'll allow it this time."

But when she took her weigh-in card back from him, she noticed that he wrote two hundred on it—he had lied about the pound. And it was a meaningful pound. It meant nothing to him but a whole day's wages to her. He could be farmed out for that. How could he take that risk? Why would he? When she thanked him she mustered all the graciousness she could, considering the confusion she felt, but he just shooed her way, admonishing her not to make a fuss.

Shevi wandered over the edge of the platform and down the onramp. More curious than the manager's unwarranted help was the fact that she needed it. The last time she had weighed in with the rotor she had been several pounds safe of the minimum. She hadn't fussed with the servers about the amount of food she was expected to eat because Cole was with her, and they had loaded her up with a massive pork sandwich, a huge serving of potato chips and tons of those persistent veggies. Then she remembered that Jackson's novel was in her pack and weighed almost eight pounds.

She was losing weight.

She came out of her quandary in time to see Tasha and Stace

cease a lively discussion they had kept hidden with the ironic subtlety of talking behind their hands. They cleared their throats and welcomed her back into the row, Stace trying too hard not to ask some obvious question like where's your little rider, and Tasha continually giving her glances that said they needed not to bring it up.

"There's a big wedding on Wheel Eight," Tasha said. "Did you hear about it?"

"Uh, I think I told you about it," Shevi said, daring them. If they wanted to play games she could certainly do her part.

"Oh, yeah," Stace said. "That's right. You and your betrothed have invitations."

"That's right, Sta*cey*," she said, defiantly calling the girl by her loathed longer name.

"What about the bachelorette party?" Tasha said, taking Stace completely by surprise. "Do you have an invitation to that?"

Shevi felt as surprised as Stace looked. "What bachelorette party?"

"I don't know," Tasha said, throwing the sarcastic tone Shevi had used back at her. "But there's a big *bachelor* party planned and Cole is going to it."

"How do you know?" Shevi asked.

Now Tasha put her shoulders back and strutted up the revolving tread. "Because I went on a date with Kyle and Kyle knows all about it and is going and says that Cole is going too."

Stace screeched, "You went out with *Kyle*?" Her high pitched voice carried up and across the heads of the walkers. Ten rows up, Kyle turned and looked to see if someone was calling to him. A couple other Titanics glanced back too. They turned back to their own goings-on but someone must have said something about Shevi because Perry glanced back, directly at her. He gave her the same sly grin he'd left with this morning.

"Hey," Tasha said suddenly, almost as if she'd been hit by an electric shock. "If Cole's going to a big party and you can't go with him, we should go out."

Stace was again overwhelmed. Her eyes bulged and her mouth gaped open. "Oh! Yes! Shevi, we have to!"

Sometimes Shevi got the feeling that everything Tasha did was premeditated and contrived, like every conversation was a game of chess. "Maybe," she said.

"Oh, Shevi," Stace said again, "we *have* to."

"If you don't mind I'm going to read now." She reached over her shoulder and pulled *The Great God, Mann* out of her pack, then said goodbye and sidled a few places down the row.

The text was great but she began to miss Ava's weight on her back and her sweet little voice in her ear, the Heavie doll. And she couldn't help glancing up as she turned each page to see if the book boy had come down to his crate. And each time she did, she caught her friends eyeing her and glancing quickly away. The sense of becoming a square peg in a round-hole world or a fish in a glass tank crept into her mind as she read the story of a valet trapped in a relentless cycle.

Chapter Twelve

Dad and Ava came back from the kitchens empty handed.

Dad shook his head. "Sorry. They wouldn't trade them for more frozen."

"Yeah," Ava said sourly. "They just grabbed them back."

"I feel a lot better anyway," Jackson said, putting the finishing touches on a sketch of the big fuses he'd seen when this whole business started. He blamed everything on Mr. Myrtle's vamping job, which led to the books, which led to him meeting Shevi, which led to her people beating him.

"You look better," Dad said. "A bit . . . less swollen."

"Colorful," Ava said, definite and honest. She pointed with her fat finger. "There's green and purple and—"

Dad grinned and mussed her hair. He looked back at Jackson and pulled out a shiny coin. It was one of the quarters Jackson had given him, one he'd earned with Shevi's help. Jackson's focus jumped between the silver disk and Dad's face, which broke into a wide grin.

"What?" Jackson asked.

"This is yours," he said.

"No," Jackson said, shaking his head. "That's for the rent."

"You paid the rent last week."

"You're working two jobs."

"So are you. Your sister made one of these riding that girl you met. I'm still not completely comfortable with it, but for now . . ." He sighed. "Jackson, for now I want you to take this and go have some fun. Because it's been a long hard time lately. And because you're a great son and the best a dad could ever hope for."

Jackson saw Dad's eyes begin to glisten with tears and felt his own throat tighten. He grabbed the quarter and jumped up—a bit too fast, in fact. He staggered. Dad caught him and helped him stand.

"Maybe you're not up to having some fun."

Jackson managed to laugh. "I probably look like a monster."

"Yeah," Ava muttered.

"Well, then," Dad said. "Go act like one. Just don't get arrested. Here," he said, pulling a long strip of fabric from their box of clothes. It was the sling Mom had carried Ava in. "Wrap up in this and nobody'll see your hideous disfigurement." He wrapped it around his head and peered out maniacally.

Jackson laughed again. "Wow. And no one will suspect I'm

hiding anything."

As Jackson went to the door, Dad tossed him a fresh pair of pants and shirt he'd slipped through the diaper laundry. "Showers are free because the visitors. Take advantage."

Jackson did, even though it meant crowds. And free didn't mean unlimited water either. Jackson waited in a line to get a token from the attendant while the guy behind him was already stripping off his clothes. Then he waited in another long line with more naked men and boys for a space in the shower, but he kept his clothes on until he was in the shower room. While Jackson washed himself, the guy at the next shower head struggled to wash his clothes and body at the same time. For this one thing, clean clothes, Jackson was glad his dad worked diaper duty, but he hoped that book renting would work out so well that Dad could quit.

When he was dressed again, he checked himself in the mirror and thought maybe he should just put his dirty clothes back on. The pants and shirt Dad had washed were things Uncle Blaine had given him as a mean joke. They fit tighter than the clothes most skinny people wore. The swelling didn't look as bad as it had felt that morning, but the bruising on his face made him look like a spotted cow. He wound the fabric Dad had given him around his head and shoulders like a cloak, ducked his head a bit and checked the mirror.

The guy behind him said, "Beautiful. Now can I have a turn?"

"Oh, sorry," Jackson said. "Sure."

He climbed the stairs up a dozen levels to the Mall. He could feel that he was making a mistake the instant he stepped out of the stairwell. It was all so clean and bright. Families from the Terraces and the Upper Crust browsed specialty armor and shoe shops and ate together at gourmet restaurants. But there were only two options on Wheel Three: the Mall or Electric Avenue. The avenue would be a mob scene now, especially with the dignitaries wandering about. And every wheel was basically the same—a Gut and a Mall and some administrative levels and a Club inside the wheels' void middles. Jackson wouldn't even be able to get out of the stairwell into a wheel's Club because it was for the highest classes only. So he ducked his head and strolled across the Mall toward the movie wheels as quickly as he could. Inside a dark movie wheel, no one would see his bruises and swelling.

There were two movie wheels in the Mall of Wheel Three. Jackson stood before the "Now Showing" posters and debated. One movie was another episode of *Crystal House*. Its billing showed a street in Fluxton lined with beautiful and spacious glass houses. The other was a Buckminster and Steve movie. Just the picture of the comic duo made Jackson smile so big his face hurt. Little Buckminster was always getting into some kind of trouble and his friend Big Steve always had to get him out of it. Normally there was no competition between any other movie and a Buckminster and Steve. But this one was called *Diaper Duty*. The billing showed Big Steve holding Bucky by one leg as he dangled over a heap of steaming, freshly soiled diapers. The problem was that Jackson would have to go home and report on what he'd done, how much fun he'd had and how much he'd enjoyed it. The other members of his family couldn't be expected to let him blow a whole quarter just because he let himself get beat up and not at least get the pleasure of hearing about how he'd spent it. Jackson wouldn't want to tell his dad he watched a show that made fun of little guys stuck with washing crap out of diapers.

So *Crystal House* it was to be. The daughter Madison was small but beautiful anyway.

Stace was still prying details out of Tasha about her date with Kyle when the trio arrived at the Mall. Tasha answered the question of whether or not they had kissed with a question of her own. "Dinner or movie first?"

Stace grunted and stomped her foot. "Come on, Tasha. Tell us."

Shevi declared, "Movie." She had already tuned her friends out, though, because she recognized a figure standing in front of the posters at the twin cinema. The act of recognition was startling. She couldn't see any part of him. He was dressed in snug fitting clothes she'd never seen before. What was the book boy up to now with his pride and intellect? Defying style and custom to proudly present his true build to the world despite what the world thought of it? And he had the strangest cloak wrapped around his head. It made her smile. Shevi was so sure she knew exactly who he was that she would bet enough to make Murray himself fold. She knew his frame and his stance, that unusually confident uprightness that separated him from others of the lower classes who slumped and looked uncertainly around them. She led the way and her two friends followed along. Not far beneath the surface, she wished they'd just go away.

She stopped beside and a little behind him. Stace and Tasha caught up. One of them grabbed her and tugged her along.

Stace said, "That's a no-brainer."

Shevi looked over her shoulder and the boy turned and looked in their direction. She would have won that bet. His face was purple and green with bruises but his features were returning to a fineness that resonated inside her somehow. The sight of him attacked and defeated her resolution to make good decisions for a healthy future.

When he turned away and left the cinema complex, Shevi crashed into Stace at the box office line. She tried to fix her attention on her companions, but her eyes cut and her head swiveled toward Jackson like metal to a magnet. And when she found him again in the crowd, he was staring back. She beckoned to him as subtly as she could, but he turned away again.

"I'll be right back," she said and ran from the cinema.

Stace called out after her, but Shevi didn't turn around. She marched after Jackson, tracking that funny getup he had over his head. She caught up with him at the newsstand, looking through a collection of CorpPress comics.

"How are you?" she asked before he looked over at her.

"Oh. Hi. I'm okay. Thanks for the peas."

"No problem." She watched him thumb through a *Metalman* comic. "Are you going to see a movie?"

"Nah." With a quick glance in her direction, he put down the Metalman and picked up a Gargantua and Pantagruel.

"That sounds more like, 'nah, I was going to but decided against it,' than a, 'no, I don't want to see a movie'."

"Yeah—well—I thought maybe, but I think I'll just take a couple of comics and go back home."

"Really? Because I'm going to see a movie and if you wanted to see a movie too, then we could see it together."

136

"Nah."

"That sounds more like yeah, I want to but . . ."

He looked at her now, turning his bruised but intriguingly beautiful face toward her. "You're not here alone." His gaze fell to the rotor on her chest.

"Never mind them."

He turned back to the pictures and stories of the giants. "I can't."

"I'll buy."

"I can pay my own way," he snapped.

"Don't get out of round."

A smile flickering across his face. "Don't try to hold me back when I'm on a roll."

"I'd never do that." She stood beside him while he thumbed through the comic. After a couple of pages she broke the silence. "I'm not offering you charity. I just want to repay you for helping me out."

He dropped the comic back onto its stack and turned to face her straight on. "For what, exactly?"

"For the book. If I hadn't had it, I wouldn't have gotten on the wheel today."

"You paid me for the book. Remember? And if I go to see a movie, it will be because you did."

"Yeah, but it was worth so much more to me."

"You made a wise investment. Good for you."

"So, you do want to see a movie and you can because you rented a book to me. And I can pay for my ticket because I rented a book from you. So, see there."

"Ah! Symmetry." He picked up another comic.

"Come on," she said, and got a bit angry at how much she sounded like whiny little Stace. "Okay. Fine. Whatever." She turned and walked away.

He was stubborn and arrogant, but oh how that made her tingle inside. She was being silly, just looking for a distraction—like Stace's mom. But when she weighed in, paid her five-cent admission and rejoined her friends, brushing off their questions about what she'd been doing, she noticed a quick dark look flash on Stace's face and turned to find him coming up the ramp with a ticket in his hands.

When she turned back to her friends, Stace was glaring at her. "What?"

Stace whispered, "Isn't that that Dim with the books?"

"Uh, yeah," she said without turning around. "I guess so."

While they waited for the usher to check their tickets, Tasha leaned over to see around her then covered her mouth but snickered and spoke loudly. "Oh my god, look at his face."

Shevi felt suddenly compressed between her old friends and her new one as Stace said, "Yeah. They really worked him over."

"What must it cost for a Dim to get in?" Tasha whispered. "A whole quarter?"

Shevi stepped aside to give the three full view of one another. "Jackson, do you know Tasha and Stace?"

Jackson ducked his head at first and acted like he was going to turn around and go, but instead he tossed off his hood and put out his hand. "No. Jackson Koss. Nice to meet you."

"Tasha Worthen," she said.

"Stace Prathers."

Jackson looked doubtfully at her. "Stace? Is that short for Stacey?"

"No," she snapped. "It's just Stace."

"Okay," he said. "That's a new one." A big smile spread across his face, then he winced and ducked his head.

The two expressions together made Shevi's heart race and skip. His face was so wonderful and the pain must have been just as intense.

Stace asked, "What movie are you going to see?"

He seemed a bit reluctant with his answer but finally admitted, "Diaper Duty."

"Us, too," Tasha said sharply. "What a coincidence."

"Yeah," Stace said, her tone cool and dry. "Bucky is such a ditzy little Dim."

Tasha laughed and said, "That's just part of the show, Stace."

"Right." Again, Stace's tone was nothing less than inhospitable.

She and Tasha exchanged a look that worried Shevi. She knew she was taking a risk here. She just hoped it wasn't too much of a gamble. The four of them followed the usher's direction through double doors to the right, but when they got to the onramp inside the cinema and were ready to board its small wheel, there were only three.

Shevi asked, "Where's Stace?"

"Oh, she decided she had to get back home after all," Tasha said.

"What? This was her idea."

"Yeah, well, she changed her mind." Tasha's eyes made a quick involuntary flick toward Jackson.

Shevi shook her head and sighed. "Her loss. I don't care."

Jackson said, "I don't want to interfere."

"You haven't," Shevi said. "Has he, Tasha?"

"Noooo." She waved her hands in surrender or indifference. Tasha was gifted at dishing out sarcasm and covering it thinly but thoroughly.

"Good," Shevi said. "Then let's watch the movie."

They stepped from the onramp onto the motionless tread of the cinema wheel, and Shevi thought that the only thing stranger than Stace's behavior was the sight and feel of a treadwheel sitting still.

Chapter
Thirteen

The wheel was idle but not perfectly still. As the audience of about two hundred boarded it from the onramp, their added and unbalanced weight caused the small drum, only about forty feet wide and eighty feet in diameter, to shift and rock on its undercarriage. Jackson's stomach tumbled with it. The tread curved up and behind the big white screen. Everyone turned to face it. At the manager's command, they all began to walk. He ordered and organized their positions on the wheel, inviting some to come forward and others to move toward the back. Jackson got only a dark, contemptuous glare, too insignificant to bother with. As they reached the pace the projector needed, it shone flickering light into the cinema wheel.

Moving images canvassed the screen and sound broke the air inside the revolving drum. A dot in the middle of the screen became a head of broccoli that whizzed toward them then out of the frame. A carrot shot past. A cucumber and a tomato. Squash. A head of lettuce. Then a frontline of walkers strutted proudly on a treadwheel. Feedbags across their broad stomachs were filled to overflowing with vegetables. They munched, smiling satisfyingly. A caption flashed: *Get out front with Veggies.* The letters of the last word were leafy and green. They sparkled and twinkled for several seconds—a bit too long, Jackson estimated, based on the little murmur that drifted across the audience. Finally the message blinked away, leaving the screen dark but its image floating in his retinas.

The gray turned into the back of a uniform of a man navigating a small two-seat tram through a bustling crowd, a ladder strapped to the side of the tram, a single shiny white light bulb sitting in the unoccupied seat. Jackson knew this one. Seeing it again reminded him of the many times he and Grandpa Piedmont had come to the movies. Men and women around the man worked feverishly on electric calculating machines, processing information from big books that sat open on desks in front of them. One man in a fine gray suit hunched over his book beneath a dark ceiling light. The man on the tram halted it beside the darkened desk and quickly put up his ladder. He took the bulb from the seat, climbed the ladder and replaced the burned out bulb. The man in the suit offered praise and thanks to the new bulb. The glowing bulb became the center of view and soon it filled the screen, sending a blinding light into Jackson's eyes. Then the light faded and the bulb turned into a loaf of bread. The background slid slowly into focus: the smiling round face of an Ironclad boy. A voice boomed across the open volume of the cinema wheel. "Fluxton: their light is our life."

The screen went dark then, and in the nothingness Jackson felt a surge of pride that he was walking on a wheel and that his weight and effort were contributing to something outside himself, if only providing power to the projector behind him. When new light shone on the screen again it was scant gray light. Rays of gray were cast from the center of the screen like the blurred rays of light Jackson had first seen when he came around after the beating in the shed. Similarly, the blurred rays of light took on transverse angles that turned into corners and planes of objects in a landscape—a row of glowing glass houses. The words *Crystal House* appeared in the center of the screen in brilliant white letters. The letters burst forth in rays of white light that engulfed the screen before fading into a scene of a boy and a girl standing in opposite corners of a glass-walled room sparsely set with boxy furniture. They glanced self-consciously toward Jackson. Jackson knew that every member of the audience saw the same trick of perspective, seeing the characters' eyes look directly at them, but a chill came over him anyway and the little hairs on the back of his neck stood up.

Tasha leaned around Shevi. "That's Madison," she whispered to Jackson. "She's the middle child of the Baker family. The Bakers are this Fluxtonian family who have to try to live their private lives in a house of glass."

The people walking in front of them looked back, first at Tasha then at the strange specimen who needed the storyline of the longest running series explained to him. Jackson acknowledged with a nod rather than explain that he knew all about the Bakers and *Crystal House* and that he didn't need anyone to explain it or to keep breaking the magic spell of cinematography.

At least the other girl had decided to pass on the movie. Something about her made him very uncomfortable. It wasn't that she was a skinner; some of the Ironclad kids were shaving their heads these days. Jackson wasn't going to judge her because of the way she chose to wear her hair. He knew she despised him, but he got that all the time. It was something else, something he couldn't quite declare.

The next preview was for a movie called *Ten Rows Up*. It was about a really big guy who made a heavy jacket and belt for a girl so they could walk in the same row.

After it was over, Tasha said, "How romantic."

Jackson felt the almost overwhelming urge to reach around Shevi and punch the girl. But wouldn't it be just like a little Dim boy to hit a girl.

Wild and playful music filled the wheel and lifted Jackson up. A little guy in baggy and ragged brown clothes meandered across the screen. Buckminster! Jackson glanced over at Shevi and the two shared explosive smiles. Jackson couldn't care less what this scrawny guy implied about people like him and his dad. In his awkward way, Bucky sauntered up to a door and yanked it open. The space beyond was filled with dirty diapers that tumbled out toward elfish Bucky. A big man in exquisite bronze chainmail and studded leather ran in and grabbed Bucky to keep him from being buried alive by the disgusting mess. The audience screamed wildly, "*Big Steve!*"

144

Chapter

Fourteen

Jackson wanted to kick himself the instant he stepped out of the cinema. *Stace* was back, her bare scalp peppered with stubble of black hair, her green eyes lit with anger. She wasn't alone. Now Jackson had a great reason to dislike her. Some of the crew of Ironclad boys who had beaten him were with her. Not exactly with her but milling about behind her. Enough distance for she and Tasha to distract Shevi or coax her away.

"I'm starving," Tasha said. "Let's eat."

And Jackson could hear the melodrama in her voice. He wondered why Shevi couldn't hear it. Instead, Shevi had the numbness to turn to him and ask if he wanted to join them. He laughed at her and gestured at the army of thugs, but Tasha whirled

Shevi and tugged her.

"Nice to meet you, Jason," she said. "Oh, look. Stace is back."

Shevi glanced over her shoulder at Jackson, completely confused. Jackson just shook his head at how stupid she could be and turned and ran back into the cinema. The thugs didn't run after him, figuring they had him cornered and didn't need to make a fuss, but Jackson was a little guy and little guys didn't spend their days plodding inside a wheel like rodents. This little guy spent his time crawling around in the rafters and pipeworks of I Town trying to scrape together an existence. They knew about the gaps and interstices that resulted from fitting a round wheel into an orthogonal environment—some of them did, the ones who had accidentally learned to read and to think outside the wheel. Jackson was smart enough to know how to get out of a cinema wheel without using the door as surely as he was smart enough to know a second beating when he saw it coming.

The manager shouted at him as he plunged down the onramp and up the stairs to the projection room. The projection room wasn't his goal, though. It sat upon a structure that spanned the inside of the wheel, the same way the Gut and the Mall and the admin levels filled the space inside Wheel Three. That structure attached to the framework of the Mall level and somewhere up there would be a gap for conduits or plumbing big enough for Jackson to slip through. And even if there wasn't a passage there was plenty of space for Jackson to hide in. Maybe the manager would come up with a knocker rod to prod Jackson out, but as he scaled the concrete frame and pulled himself up onto the first layer of pipes Jackson became more confident that no one would get to him. Beat him once, shame on them. Beat him twice? Not today! Below, the manager shouted up at him as he scurried along a run of pipes.

Jackson looked back. He couldn't see the manager, so the manager couldn't see him. He slowed his pace to be quieter. Down below, the manager was talking to someone now, perhaps sending someone up into the maze of pipes to retrieve the pesky little Dim—another Dim following orders. Jackson sped up. There was light up ahead, a bit of hope. He pulled himself up onto the next level, then the next. He was right underneath the floor structure of the Club and at the edge of the demising wall for the cinema complex. All the amenities for the Club required lots of pipes, and the demising wall had lots of penetrations to allow sewer plumbing to flow as it needed. The penetrations weren't huge, but neither was Jackson. He flattened himself onto a pipe and pushed his head through. A coupling caught his shirt and tore it. He was glad of this. If the gap was almost too tight for him to get through, there was a slim chance anyone would be able to follow. The chance of anyone being slimmer was very slim. He chuckled, first at the play on words then at the manager's helpers whom he could hear now—he could hear how big and heavy they were and how much trouble they were having just navigating the lower runs. He laughed at the fat Ironclad boys who would be so disappointed that they'd let the chance to pummel a Dim slip from their grasp.

Then he thought of Shevi, how her friends had manipulated her: the one with the weird name slipping away to gather some thugs, the other distracting her. Like poles reversing in the power grid, his mirth waned and anger rushed in to fill its place. He stopped and lay down on the pipes, letting the worst of the dark feelings pass. Water babbled through one of them, probably carrying some Ironclad fat man's crap to the Wash. Behind him, through the penetrations in the demising wall, the voices of the ones the manager sent after him were low and indistinct but had the tone of someone satisfied or ready to give up.

Jackson lowered himself down onto the next run of pipes just in case they had the ambition to peek through the passage. The last of the evening shoppers and diners milled about the Mall some hundred feet below him. For someone so small of stature, heights had never bothered him. He rolled over on his back and watched the light and shadow play on the utility lines and structure above him like a fantastic code.

On the other side of the demising wall the cinema wheel resumed its steady revolution for the next showing. Sounds drifted through the pipe passages. He could clearly hear in his mind and could almost make out the voice saying, "Fluxton. Their light is our life." He closed his eyes and there was the happy, healthy and fat Ironclad boy holding the golden loaf of bread.

There was no going down from here; even plunging into the Mall's fountain pool would kill him. Going back would probably mean interrupting the movie and another run-in with the manager. Up was his only option. He couldn't get in the Club, but he was sure he could get thrown out. He rolled over again and crawled along the pipes to the glass wall that during the day flooded the Mall below and the Club above with sunlight. Here some of the pipes turned and followed the wall; three small silver conduits bent upward and passed between the glass and the floor structure.

Jackson wrapped his arms and legs around them and commenced climbing. Two of the conduits turned again when they had passed the depth of the structural floor system. Jackson followed these. The portion of the Club level he was on had a raised floor. Jackson could almost duck walk between the two floors. Crawling on all-fours was easier though. He crept into the darkness slowly to let his eyes adjust. Somewhere there had to be an access panel for workers to get down here and make repairs and changes. He just had to find it.

Above him the floor creaked. The sound of footsteps overhead flowed from the distance toward him, then over him. Voices, deep and booming, sifted through the floor. Jackson turned and darted away from the sounds, and as he did his forehead—precisely, the arc-shaped scar on his forehead—banged into a pipe. Jackson froze. His pulse doubled. He held his breath and waited, listening. The voices droned on without perceptible change. Someone crossed the space above him. Someone else scooted the legs of a chair. Jackson moved each arm and leg with survival caution. He found himself against a wall. He sat back against it as the voices from above broke into corporate laughter. Jackson took a calming breath.

Sitting against the wall gave him a better appraisal of the place he was in. There was just enough light from the night sky to highlight the amenities. The times he'd been sent to work on plumbing or electrical or heating and cooling systems in the Piedmont mansion had taught him how to see the layout of a place by its pipes and ducts. The crawlspace stretched greedily along the glass exterior wall. Wires turning up in a row indicated a wall above. A branch of pipe with limbs connecting to the floor above showed the location of a bathroom and its fixtures. A private bathroom. The thought of being able to enjoy a private shower conceived thoughts of living here in the crawlspace and sneaking out at night like a rodent. But he wasn't a rodent; he was a boy with a dad who would be expecting him home soon and would begin very soon to worry about him. He was a brother with a sister who needed to know that he was all right, who needed to learn her letters and words and numbers.

Jackson got back on his hands and knees and crawled beneath the shuffling, laughing convention happening on the floor above him. He navigated the pipes and ducts and little columns that held the one floor above the other until he found what he was looking for, almost exactly where he expected to find it. At the back corner of what must be an elaborate apartment, where plumbing pipes split and contorted for laundry and kitchen appliances, he felt along a header that interrupted the floor system. He waited for another eruption of joviality from the other end of the apartment and then popped the latch. He lifted the hatch door with the same reluctance that he'd poked the service wire into the fuse holder of the wheel to vamp the connection for Mr. Myrtle. He didn't mind, even expected to get caught somewhere in the Club and thrown out like garbage, but he didn't want it to happen in a private apartment—it would just be too personal that way.

But there were no surprises waiting for him. The space was empty, as he had hoped, and a laundry room, as he'd expected. A big washing machine and electricity-gobbling clothes dryer stood against the far wall, giving ignorant witness to his illegitimate entry. He eased the hatch open and crawled out onto a floor of marble tile far nicer than even the dining hall in Grandpa and Grandma's house. The room had shelves and rods for clothes and cabinets for storage. That was what he noticed first. Next he realized that it was bigger than the apartment he and his dad and sister now called home.

The room had two doors. One would lead down a path of increasing elegance through the kitchen and dining hall and finally to the big glass-walled room where fat cats were likely enjoying some tasty liquor and jokes about Dims. The other would take him out the service entrance and hopefully to a stair where a guard would try his best to zap him with a knocker rod. Jackson chose this door and tiptoed to it. He squeezed the knob and twisted it slowly and carefully. He pushed it open with the same caution but stopped when he heard the whispers.

"Come on. It'll just take a minute." Even at a whisper, Jackson knew the voice. It was Mr. Myrtle. "I made us a ton of money tonight, and if you want any of it you'll let me."

Jackson swallowed. Curiosity overwhelmed survival and escape. The possibility of blackmail wasn't the first notion to excite him, but it was at the top of the list. He eased the door open a bit more and adjusted his eye to see into the next room. Something blocked his line of sight, a cabinet or shelf. He squatted at the rate that a plant grows toward the sun until he could see under the barrier. Something familiar came into view on the counter just inside the door. It was the long and lean black walking stick, the illegal knocker rod. Mr. Myrtle, just beyond it, dressed in a shiny black suit, had a girl as skinny and not much bigger than Jackson pressed against the opposite wall. Her eyes were sunk in deep, dark sockets and her cheekbones were sharp and jutting enough to use as a bottle opener. When Mr. Myrtle took off his comically tall black hat and bent his head to press his face into the side of her neck, Jackson saw the rest of her face and knew who she was. She was the mayor's secretary—Miss Myrtle, by name—and Mr. Myrtle's sister.

Satisfied but disgusted, having seen enough and too much all at once, Jackson left the door ajar and backed away. If the mayor's assistant was at home enough to let her brother come on to her in the pantry then Jackson could only assume he had surfaced in the mayor's own apartment. He hustled into the kitchen, paused only to take in the aroma of fine cuisine, and crouched, ready to run the maze toward the main entrance. There was still a chance he could escape into the common area of the Club level, and the stakes if he didn't had just increased exponentially.

⟨⟨⟩⟩

The book boy was about the strangest little creature Shevi had ever come across. She never knew what he would do next. First he had been looking at the movie posters like he really wanted to watch one, then he'd run off to look at comic books. He finally conceded to honor her with his presence after she begged him, then acted completely strange about eating with them. He could say what he wanted about the label of Dim, but he wasn't doing anything to present a better image of the smaller class. If he'd just gone back into the Mall it wouldn't have been so bad, but he ran back into the cinema. You couldn't just go back in and watch another movie without buying another ticket. Shevi figured the manager would run him out soon enough and maybe she could get him to change his mind about eating with her. But Tasha kept tugging at her and hurrying her along. And then Stace was back, which was even more confusing, and with her was Perry and the other Titanics who apparently hadn't been invited to the bachelor party.

And, man, weirdness had taken over everyone's actions. Stace looked mad, like she always did when she got left out, but that had been her choice and no one else's. And Perry and his gang didn't look like they were coming to see a movie; they looked like they were here for a fight. Shevi laughed at him.

"What's the matter, little brother? Feeling all left out?" She raised an eyebrow at Stace. "Change your mind about a movie?"

"Yeah," Stace said. Her tone was smug.

"What is everybody's deal these days?" Shevi asked.

"Where's the Dim?" Stace asked coldly.

"I guess he went back in to try to watch the movie again. What's it matter?"

"You need to stay away from him, Shevi," Perry said. He and his gang had taken up positions behind Stace that made them look like the Trintico Guard.

"Butt out," Shevi said.

"Seriously, Shevi," Stace said, crossing her arms over her padded body suit. "What is *your* deal?"

"What do you mean?"

"You keep hanging out with that guy."

"He's a friend. He has good taste in books. What's the problem?"

"You're engaged."

"I don't want to marry him—Jackson, I mean. We're friends."

Tasha spoke up behind her. "Does he know that?"

Shevi turned and put on an are-you-kidding face. She backed it up with a little grunt. "That's just stupid."

"Why?" Tasha asked. "The way you're chasing after him."

Stace pecked at her now. "Yeah, he's just a poor little Dim."

"Don't call him that."

"Why not?" Perry asked.

"It's what he is," Stace said.

"He doesn't like it."

Stace said, "It's the truth."

"Let's just go eat," Tasha pleaded.

"I want to be able to make a new friend and not catch a bunch of crap from you," Shevi said, swiveling back and forth to stare both of them down. Then she fixed her glare on Perry. "And you, butt out of my life altogether."

"I'm not here for you," he said. "I'm here for Cole."

"Let Cole fight Cole's fights," Shevi said.

One of the other Titanics spoke up then. "We don't need Cole's permission to beat the little Dim again."

Tasha grabbed Shevi by the arm and yanked hard. "Come on. Let's go eat."

Shevi jerked her arm free and stepped up to the boy who'd spoken up. He wore thick leather armor studded with bolts and draped with chains. He was only a couple of inches taller than Shevi.

"You lay one finger on him and I find out about it, I'll tell Cole to—" Then what he said resounded in her mind. "Again?"

Tasha pulled at her. "Shevi, don't."

"Again?" Shevi repeated. She turned and looked at Tasha.

"Again?" She studied Stace. "What has . . . ? What have . . . ? *No!*" She put her hand over her mouth as Jackson's accusations came back to her, accusations that she thought had been mindless outbursts brought on by pain, the manic cries of a wounded animal.

Tasha said, "You're supposed to know better."

Shevi remembered how rude they had been to Ava at dinner. Everyone around her—her friends and family—were not the people she thought they were. *They* were the animals. They were threatened. And by what? A boy who rented books to help feed his family? She looked around at all of them and began to understand: he was a threat because he really was special: he was different. Smart. And not just smart. Intelligent, even intellectual. What could be worse than a Dim with ambition? She didn't chastise herself for thinking this way because she knew she was delving into *their* minds, *their* evil thoughts.

Stace said, "Now *he* knows better, too."

Shevi whirled on her. "You skinny slut." She grabbed Stace's padding and yanked it, but it wouldn't come off. "You're nothing but a Dim in a body suit."

Stace pulled free and backed away, gathering the neck of her armor up to protect her secret.

Tasha hissed, "Shevi, stop it."

But Shevi went right on. "You know the truth, don't you, Tasha? Her mother slept with a Dim and that's why Sta-*cey* is such a skinny ass."

Stacey threw herself at Shevi, but Shevi stepped back, letting the girl fall toward her. Her head fell forward and clanged against

Shevi's rotor. She stumbled back, hands raised to her forehead, but not before Shevi saw the familiar arc-shaped scar. Now she turned her fury toward Perry.

"Was Cole there?"

"What?"

"Was Cole there? When you beat Jackson."

Perry didn't have to answer. His face showed it. Shevi's fists clinched, not of any conscious want to strike out but of something deeper, more intuitive. She walked slowly away. Behind her Tasha called out, but Shevi didn't acknowledge. She had a bachelor party to crash.

Chapter

Fifteen

Of all the foods spread out on the buffet, Jackson was most impressed with the broccoli. Its buds sat perkily upright. He picked up one and loved how it held its shape. When he bit into it, the crunch made him flinch and hold his breath again. But, oh, the flavor—it wasn't the taste of dull brown but of a rainbow of colors. He grabbed handfuls of the foods laid out before him and piled them into a pouch he made from his cloak. Then he crept to the doorway opposite the pair of Myrtles trysting place.

But the doorway from the dining area opened directly into the room where the footsteps and chair scooting and laughter had been happening. Luckily Jackson realized this before anyone saw him. As he started to make his exit the raspy voice of an old man said,

"Now, where were we?"

Jackson ducked and went to his knees. A high-backed couch faced away. He thought just maybe he could crawl past the little congress and out to the foyer. And he could have, had one of the group not chosen to seat himself off from the rest. Jackson was blessed that he managed to poke his head out into the hall and get it pulled back in without the discrete member noticing him. A shock of white hair and thin feature: Michael Faraday, the Secretary of Electricity himself, barred the way.

Jackson was mere feet away from the man he idolized. He wished he had his sketchbook to show the man. He fought against the urge to run back to the utility room and grab Mr. Myrtle's walking stick and present it to Sec Elec and say, "See what I did, what I can do. Make me your apprentice." But why was a bruised little boy lurking in the mayor's apartment? How would he be received, especially after interrupting the Myrtles' mating?

And so he was stuck not only between the two groups of people but between the best and worst possible of situations. He'd weighed the consequences of getting caught when he climbed upward from the pipes, but he hadn't counted on ending up in the mayoral suite. Hiding was his best option, finding a place out of the way and hunkering down until one group or the other satisfied its hunger for union and dispersed. There was a large cabinet in the corner of the kitchen. It had big, wide doors and the way it cut the corner of the counters to either side made it look like a spacious place. Jackson grabbed some more food, actually assembling himself a plate and pouring himself a cup of a bright red drink, and fit himself into the bottom of the cabinet. The door snapped shut a bit louder than he anticipated. Jackson settled himself cautiously inside. He took a small cracker, adorned with cheese and meat and raised it to his mouth, but he stopped with surprise at the volume of sound that passed through the wall into his hiding place.

"Is your person safely preoccupied?" It was Secretary Faraday asking about Miss Myrtle.

"I'm sure." This was Mayor Van Ashe.

There were footsteps away and then back to Sec Elec's station by the wall in the hall, then he said. "All clear. I just thought I heard something."

"Oh, Michael, our man of caution and calculation."

" 'Tis my job, Mr. President."

"Indeed," replied the raspy old voice Jackson now recognized as President Burgess. "It has brought us to this place, and we thank you daily."

"And it is my daily honor, sir." Jackson took the chance while Sec Elec spoke to push the hors d'oeuvre into his mouth and commence chewing it as quietly as he could. "Which brings us back to the question of balance and how we shall maintain it."

"Isn't it actually a matter of imbalance?" This was a young voice, a boy, the youngest of the first family, Jackson was almost certain, Hugh.

"Very astute, my young friend," said Sec Elec. Wow! What a lucky kid, to have Sec Elec say *that* about his comment. Better than the richest food. "It is only when the wheel is imbalanced that it produces power. But imbalance above all else is to be carefully controlled. And we must determine how to manage our population here in Induction Town if we are to maintain that precious imbalance."

"I don't understand the problem." A female voice now, had to be the president's granddaughter Sophia. "They seem to be producing just fine. All the lights are on in Fluxton."

"For now," Sec Elec said. "For now. But we must always think of the future."

Mayor Van Asche hissed, "Yes. Too much of this. Not enough of that."

"Balance and imbalance," Secretary Faraday said. "Fat and fiber."

Jackson wallowed the bouquet of meat and dairy in his mouth and wondered if Sec Elec would approve of his choices.

"We continue to raise the weight limits on the wheels to get the required output," the mayor said, "which has dramatically increased of recent."

Silence followed and was finally broken when a young but mature male voice, Tyler Burgess, Senior Vice President of Trintico, said, "Yes, well," then cleared his throat, "Agrarianna has its needs, too, producing the fuel for the walkers."

"Fuel, yes," said Sec Elec. "Calories, to be specific. And fat calories are simply cheaper to produce per unit volume of food."

"And it's much easier to get them to eat," said the mayor, "but we have to consider sustainability. How long can it last, the way it is now? We've started campaigning for increased vegetable and fiber intake, but it just doesn't seem to be working."

"What methods are you employing?" Tyler asked.

"The servers and dietitians encourage it," the mayor said. "Posters and pamphlets."

"There's a new movie ad."

"Is Big Steve in it?"

"No."

"Why not?" This was Tyler. "They'll listen to him. And we need to get screens on the wheels so we don't have to rely on people going to the cinema to get the message."

"Yes," Sec Elec said. "I'm sure that would be a more efficient method of propagating our agenda."

Jackson considered the phrase and thought how much it sounded like an extended version of the word propaganda, which made him wonder about Christopher Bartlett and whatever had happened to him. He realized now that the beating had derailed his quest for the missing social agitator.

"As the weight limit increases, more people are pushed down into the lower classes putting a terrible strain on society here in my town, calling to question the sustainability of our system. This rabble around the edges—Shack Town, they call it."

Sophia said, "It isn't any bigger than the last time we visited."

"Thanks to crazy old Ludd," the mayor said. "But when the farmlands stop buying the ones he takes away, things will change quickly. Besides, it's an eyesore you can see from the top now. Dreadful."

President Burgess said, "What can we do about this sector of the population?"

"Discourage reproduction," Tyler said. "It's what we do in Fluxton."

"We already require sterilization for those receiving paid positions, Tyler," the mayor said.

Jackson stopped chewing. His brow wrinkled as he thought about the Ironclad teen thugs saying they should castrate him.

"Please use my title, Mayor."

"Excuse me. *Prince* Tyler. Forgive my lapse," the mayor said. "We call the initiative the Piedmont Protocol after one of our noble Ironclads who requested it."

Jackson's insides curdled. What kind of madness was this? Were people being neutered at Uncle Blaine's request?

"Let's just gas 'em, or mow 'em down." This was from someone new, and whoever it was elaborated with a rat-tat-tat imitating a sound Jackson recalled from one of Uncle Blaine's favorite old Carbon Nation movies—automatic gunfire.

"Jasper," President Burgess said sharply, "that isn't governing. We are a civilized people and civilized people do not *mow down* their own."

"Why not?" Jasper whined.

Sec Elec expanded upon this. "Jasper, governing is best done with more carrot and less stick."

The voices of reason, Jackson thought. These were the men who had resurrected society from the last apocalypse and would surely prevent the next one.

"Titles," the president's son said. "*Please.*"

Sec Elec said, "Forgive me, *Prince* Tyler. And *Prince* Jasper. Habits."

President Burgess said, "Really, son, we're in common company here."

"If it isn't important to us," *Prince* Tyler said, "then it will never be important to them."

162

"These people do not need to be slaughtered or sterilized," Sec Elec said, reining the conversation back on route. "They need hope. They need something to strive for. And they need an anthem and a champion to show them the way."

"*We* need an anthem, for the monarchy," Prince Tyler said.

Sec Elec voice dropped into a low growl. "We *need* a solution to these *problems*, Your Majesty. It must be real. At the end of the day it must be *real*."

The president, sounding very tired, said, "What on earth are you talking about, Michael?"

Sec Elec went on, softly now. "Gentlemen, and my esteemed lady, I have a formula." Silence followed this assertion. Jackson even stopped chewing his soft and delicious sandwich to hear the pronouncement to follow. "It is a drug to encourage development of the physique."

"Medicine?" The mayor sounded perplexed now. "Now you're a chemist? I thought you were an electrical engineer."

"My dear sir, I am an engineer of civilization—a civil engineer, if you will."

The mayor said, "I don't know if *I will* or not."

"I assure you," Sec Elec said smoothly, "you will."

"Please, Michael," President Burgess said, "tell us more about this formula. Is it a pill? Can we put it in the water? What is it?"

The Secretary of Electricity allowed a moment of silence. Jackson could see him basking in the moment as the world waited for his reply. He leaned over to put his ear closer to whatever crack transmitted the sound. When he did, the cup of red drink slipped from his lap, landed upside down beside him and oozed under him.

He flinched and knocked against something in the back corner.

"See, now I've heard something again."

"Oh, come on, Michael. He does this, milks every drop of drama from every possible situation."

The room went silent again and the footsteps made their journey to the doorway of the dining room. Then Jackson heard footsteps just outside the cabinet. They passed him, paused somewhere across the room, came back by again, and finally returned to the chair on the opposite side of the wall. Jackson continued to hold his breath as his drink soaked into the seat of his pants.

Sec Elec said, "I think your person is entertaining someone."

"She's sterile," Mayor Van Asche said. "It's quite all right."

A round of muffled laughter ensued.

"Michael, the formula, please, expound, elaborate."

"Yes, well, it is a dietary supplement to encourage the building of body mass, heavy substance—muscle, not just fat."

The mayor said, "Side effects?"

"Minimal."

"Sounds perfect," the president said. "When can we begin it?"

"Immediately," Sec Elec said.

The president said, "Excellent." He punctuated his proclamation with a clap. "Now let's get on with our evening. We can rejoin our visiting dignitaries with confidence that Secretary Faraday has everything worked out, as usual."

"There is an event," the mayor said. "It is quite important to some of our influential families that we attend."

Prince Hugh asked, "Do we have to wear the suits?"

"Actually, it may not be suitable for, eh, women and children."

"I'm not a child," Prince Hugh declared.

"You look like an idiot in a fat suit," the elder said.

"You don't even need a fat suit," the younger fired back.

"Shut up," Prince Jasper said.

"Boys! Please," President Burgess said. "Hugh, you will stay here with Sophia. You may go anywhere in the Club, but do not leave it. Do you understand?"

Prince Hugh whined, "Even if I take guards?"

"There is no need to make a spectacle," the president said.

Shuffling of shoes on the floor and the drone of adult male voices drowned out the youngest prince's rebuttal. Then the door Jackson needed to escape through slammed shut and Jackson braced himself for his chance.

"Where are you going?" Princess Sophia said.

"Outta here," Prince Hugh said.

"Don't leave the Club."

The door slammed again. Footsteps came into the dining room, then another set came from the other way.

"Anything I can get for you, ma'am?" Miss Myrtle asked. Her brother had apparently finished and left.

"No. I'll be in my room."

The princess left the dining hall and her footsteps hadn't traversed the living room when the door of the cabinet Jackson hid inside flung open. He looked up at Miss Myrtle who at first didn't see him. She seemed intent on finding something on a higher shelf. When she looked down at him, her eyes narrowed.

"What's this?" She grabbed a handful of his bushy hair and yanked him up.

"Hey, let go."

"Hiding in the mayor's pantry. Eating the mayor's food. Just what I need."

"I'm sorry. I'll go."

"Oh no you won't. Not until I'm done with you." She grabbed something off the shelf—a long stick—and swiped it across the side of Jackson's head.

He tried to pull away, but she managed to turn his own efforts into a movement that put him facedown bent over the table. She commenced to thrash his butt with the stick, frantic and angry, even possessed, until a voice behind them said, "Excuse me!"

Jackson looked back over his shoulder at the president's granddaughter standing in the doorway and staring at them.

Miss Myrtle said, "An interloper, Princess. I'll handle it."

"It's a boy," the princess said. "What are you doing?"

"I'll tell you what he was doing, Your Majesty. He was—"

"Not him. *You!* What do you think you're doing?"

"Punishing him," Miss Myrtle said confidently, but she let go of Jackson and stepped away from the table.

"This is unacceptable," Princess Sophia said. "Intolerable. I'll not have it in my presence."

"Fine. Come on, boy."

The princess said, "No. I'll not have it happen at all. Look at what you've done. Nothing he did could warrant this."

"He was trespassing in an official's premises and eating the mayor's food."

"You are dismissed."

Miss Myrtle stepped stiffly to the service entrance door. "Fine.

166

As you wish, *Your Majesty*."

"Thank you." When Miss Myrtle was gone, the girl rushed to Jackson as he stood up and tried to compose himself. He offered a quick bow of his head and thanked her. She came close to him. Her gaze ranged the marks and bruises on his face. "What a horrible person."

"She didn't do all this, just a few licks." He reached around and gently flapped the seat of his sticky wet pants to give the few stinging stripes some room to breathe.

"But you're bleeding," she said, leaning to suggest a look.

"No. That's just . . . I spilled my . . . I'll clean it up."

"I'll have a member of the staff clean it. You need a doctor."

"No, really, I'm fine."

"How can that be?"

Jackson could only shrug. "Really, it wasn't so bad."

"Well, you at least need fresh clothes." She apparently saw the apprehension on his face because she immediately offered her hand. "I insist. Do you think it's wise to refuse the insistence of a member of the *royal* family?"

Jackson did not, so he took her hand, which was very soft, and followed her out of the dining hall.

Shevi didn't have a problem finding the party. Kyle had told one of the Titanics all about the secret location and the whole gang had known all day. Once Shevi made it down to the cellars, she only had to follow the noise and the trail of happy Ironclad men and boys coming and going. Getting past the guards and bouncers wasn't so easy.

Holding up her engagement rotor, she shouted over the noise of music that was as loud as any movie she had ever been to. "I'm a member of the Turney family and need to speak to my husband."

"No guests without proper invitation." The guard was burly, likely an Ironclad making some extra money off the wheel.

Shevi let a tiny bit of the anger simmering down inside her seep into her voice. "It is very urgent."

The guard's face hardened for a second—Shevi could tell she was about to get her tone right back at her—but then the man's attention lifted to somewhere behind her. Someone came alongside her.

"Trouble, Hugo?" It was Mr. Myrtle dressed in a shiny, baggy black tuxedo and a tall black hat perched on his thin hair.

"No invitation," the guard said, pointing an accusing finger at Shevi. "Says she's a Turney."

"Turney? I assumed you were a Piedmont. But, lo and behold, a rotor. If you're still looking for Jackson, you won't find him in here." The words were greasy as his gaze licked up and down Shevi's body.

"I found Jackson."

"I hope he's well."

"He's fine," she said, her lips pursing with frustration.

"I didn't have a hand in the guest list," he said, taking off his hat and offering his elbow. "But I seem to be without a date. Would you do me the honor of adding Myrtle to your list of attachments?"

"Sir, I am betrothed to a member of the Turney family."

"Thought you said you were married," Hugo growled.

"Which is it, deary? Married or betrothed?"

"What's it matter?" she asked.

Hugo folded his arms across his broad chest.

Mr. Myrtle smiled slyly. "If it doesn't matter to you, I guess it doesn't matter at all. Are you coming in with me, or not?"

Shevi stepped back from the man's offered elbow. "No, sir. But could you please ask Cole Turney to come out?"

"Cole?" Mr. Myrtle turned to Hugo and laughed and the big guard joined in. "I don't think we'll be disturbing any of our guests. Glad to hear that Jackson is '*fine.*'" His green eyes narrowed as he hissed this last word, reminding Shevi of someone again. He put his tall hat back on his head, nodded it at Hugo and strolled into the cellar, his walking stick tapping the floor with every stride.

Shevi looked up at Hugo whose body shook with silent laughter.

"You ain't too bright, are you, girl?"

"What do you mean?"

"If you wanted to check up on your man, all you'd've had to do was take Mr. Myrtle's arm and go on inside. And now here you stand, still looking up at me like I'm the reason you can't."

"I don't want to 'check up' on him. I just need to talk to him about something."

"That can't wait till the morning?" Hugo said sarcastically.

"No."

"Well, then. I would suggest you suck in your pride and take the next offer that comes along." Hugo looked around then spoke behind his hand to her. "Actually, I don't think a delicate flower like yourself really wants to be a part of this particular event."

"Why not?"

He laughed again and waved his broad hand at her. "Get on

outta here."

"I need to talk to him now."

"Well, wait over there." He pointed to the big stone piers that reached up to support the undercarriage of Wheel Three.

Shevi marched to the base of one of the piers and leaned against it, crossing her arms over the engagement rotor and glaring at the guard. Hugo returned a satisfied smile.

High overhead, Wheel Three turned in its magnetic cradle. Shevi looked up and wondered how it all worked, how such a simple turning thing could make all that power. A small woman stormed past carrying a stick. At first Shevi thought she was a guard carrying a short knocker rod, but the rod was only the broken wooden handle of a mop or broom. When she reached Hugo's post he whispered something right into her ear and nodded toward Shevi, smiling. The little woman turned around and set a hard but curious look on her. Her eyes seemed to be empty, dark sockets above sharp cheek bones. Shevi pushed herself up off of the pier. The woman strolled over to her and looked up at her.

"You looking for a job?"

Shevi stiffened and glanced at Hugo who looked back as if to say, well, are you?

"I . . ." Shevi said. "I . . ."

"Are you, or not?" the woman asked. At the bottoms of the dark eye sockets were even darker eyes.

"I . . . Yes," Shevi finally made herself say. "Yes, I am wanting to go in."

"Well, let's go," the woman said and prodded her with the stick. Reluctantly, Shevi allowed the little woman to herd her forward.

"You got a name, girl?"

"Shevi Lilbourn."

"Speak up, girl," the woman said and poked Shevi in the back.

Shevi yelled her name over her shoulder as they reached Hugo's station. Through an enormous smile, the guard said, "Good evening, Miss Myrtle."

The woman nodded. "Hugo." She turned her face up at Shevi who stared straight ahead but could see the sadistic pleasure on the man's face. "Miss Lilbourn will be dancing this evening."

"Excellent," Hugo shouted, beaming. "Mr. Myrtle is already inside. Make sure he sees her."

"I've already had all the pleasure of my brother's company I want for the evening. I wouldn't be here if it weren't for the show he promised. If he sees her, he sees her. But I'm sure he will."

"I'm sure, too." Hugo gave a little bow as he stepped aside and motioned them toward the entrance. Miss Myrtle adjusted her composure, stretching her long skinny neck to its full length, and marched Shevi past him.

Inside the cellar behind a curtain that blocked the view, light pulsed from bright to blinding. Music pounded Shevi at unreal volumes. Big Ironclad girls danced on a raised platform. Some of them were naked under their armor, showing off seductive rolls of flesh. Miss Myrtle's face screwed into a hateful glare as she stared at them. Then she shot a glance over at Shevi, and Shevi knew that if looks could kill she'd have fallen dead right there in the middle of the party.

"Take off everything but the rotor and get up there and dance," the little woman said.

"*WHAT!?*" Shevi screamed.

"You heard me. You've got the body. Now get up there and show it off."

"I will *not!*"

"What are you, a prude? Oh well, get up there with your clothes on then. Look like a fool. See if I care. But I brought you in here to dance, and dance you will. Now *git!*"

Shevi opened her mouth to protest, but Miss Myrtle's face turned red and her dark eyes seemed to go even farther back into their deep sockets. Shevi staggered through the crowd of hooting men, looking back at her host who stood with her arms crossed on her tiny frame, the mop handle sticking out from her armpit. Her look dared Shevi not to mount the platform. When she did, several of the men shouted at her to "shake it" and "take it off". She recognized several of them from the wheel. A few were front-line Ironclads, but most were middle class men who walked closer to her row at the back of the walk zone. Their behavior fanned the flame of rage she'd kindled against Cole for what he'd done to Jackson. Class didn't justify cruelty, and Jackson was twice the person any of these pathetic men would ever be.

A light flashed in her face, sending blessed spots across her view of the obscene audience members and blocking at least a few of them from her mind. The face of the photographer Richard Philbrook popped up from behind a camera. His head of wild black curls framed his grin. His eyes were ringed with violet and his lips were painted blue. "I knew I'd get you to pose for me eventually," he said. He shook the knocker rod charger of his flash and shot again.

A man in an obvious bodysuit stumbled up to the stage holding a quarter out to Shevi. "Show me some skin, baby," he shouted. "Let me see your sexy body."

Shevi was about to kick him in the face when she glanced to the back of the crowd where Miss Myrtle stood watching. The woman raised an eyebrow as if to ask Shevi what she was waiting for. Shevi scanned the crowd. If she could find Cole and do what she came here to do, she'd tell the perverse little woman to go to hell and take the whole party with her. A sound behind her like the flapping of gigantic wings startled her and the other girls. Some of them screamed. Others ducked and covered their heads. The man with the quarter fell backward as the lights made one more blinding pulse then faded to a more natural dim. Shevi turned to see a huge canvas furling onto the platform. Behind it stood a small treadwheel, only about twenty feet in diameter. It sat on an undercarriage of wheels like the ones that supported Wheel Three high above them. But there were no coils on its curved surface and no field of magnets encasing it. It was simply a mesh of iron bars.

She and the other girls stumbled from the stage at Mr. Myrtle's dismissing hand. He took the center of the stage, took off his enormous hat and held it high in the air. A bright beam of light shone on him.

"And now, ladies and gentlemen." His voice boomed from high above, amplified as the music had been. "An event like no other. Like nothing you've ever seen before. The *Duel Wheel!*" He spread his arms wide and turned to showcase the thing behind him.

Shevi staggered to the side of the room where a buffet table held a banquet of fine foods. A man pushed past her with a big cup held out in front of him. He went to a machine with a dull red front panel. He shoved the cup against a lever and precious cubes of ice rattled into it. They piled into the cup and tumbled over the rim and onto the dirty floor while he watched with rapture. Shevi's hands gripped the edges of her rotor. She could clearly see herself slamming it down on his stupid head. Having a party was one thing, but even the lewd display on the stage didn't compare to this disgusting act. Who was paying for all this? How could even the richest Ironclad families afford such waste, or condone it? But the man wasn't alone. Several other men fell in behind him, each outdoing the previous in wasteful pleasure. Some of them added a drink to their ice, but some went away tossing back their cups to let the crunchy treats spill into their mouths and overflow where they were trod underfoot.

On the stage other men had joined Mr. Myrtle. Two Ironclads flanked a third much smaller man. Shevi left the drink fountain to get a better look at him. The crowd pushed her right up to the edge of the stage. The small man in the middle was almost naked, wearing nothing but a string around his waist holding up a swatch of fabric between his legs, a loincloth like the old Skinners used to wear. His neck and arms were very dark brown while the rest of his skin shone white in the harsh light. His limbs were sinewy and his middle was embarrassingly narrow. He tried to shield his eyes from the glare of the spotlight, but the other men grabbed his arms and pulled them down to his sides. He was the guy who sold fobs with the old woman beside Jackson's crate of books. Worry and the relative size of his flanking companions pressed him down into an even smaller man than he had seemed on the platform.

174

Mr. Myrtle spoke into his microphone. "This is Christopher Bartlett." His voice ramped up as he said the name. "Isn't that a nice, long name, folks? A big name for a little man?"

The crowd jeered and hooted. Fists pumped the air above them.

"May I call you Chris?" Mr. Myrtle asked, and the crowd laughed and hooted louder. The master of ceremonies turned wide eyes at them, encouraging them. He turned back to his guest. "Chris, is there anything you'd like to share with us?" He leaned in close to the man and waited for a response that didn't come. "Hmm. I heard that you were quite a talkative fellow. Anyway, here's a question. How many Dims does it take to screw in a light bulb?" He put the microphone close to Chris's face and waited, turning curious eyes to the crowd now and again.

Finally, his guest whispered something indistinct.

"What was that?" Mr. Myrtle said, flicking the mic back to his own mouth for a second. "I'm sorry. What was that?"

"I don't know," Chris said.

"Of course not!" Mr. Myrtle shouted. "You're a stupid Dim."

The crowd roared with laughter as the host slipped between Chris and one of the Ironclads. When he put his arm around the man, Shevi was surprised to see that, except for his big goofy hat, the host was actually smaller than his captive.

"Something you may know, Chris. You're dressed in the fashion of a previous generation of walkers. Did you know that? Some years ago it was fashionable for big men and women who were proud of their large statures and how much they contributed to the corporate society to show off how big they were by wearing just what you've got on. We figured it would be appropriate for you to dress the same way, since you're so proud of yourself. You see, Chris," Mr. Myrtle said softly, his words drifting through the air like gravy across a steak, "I've heard you say things like everybody ought to be paid the same."

Murmurs like feet on a wheel's tread shuffled across the cellar.

"Is this true?" He offered the mic again.

Chris ducked his head to get his mouth closer to it. He looked out across the crowd. "We ought to be treated more equitably."

"*Equitably!*" the host shouted. "What a big word. Do you need to sit down? How about a drink? Get this man a drink after such a workout." He pushed his guest forward and a cup full of ice hurled toward him.

Chris put up a hand to block it, but it struck him in the forehead. Cubes of ice showered onto the stage around his feet. He stumbled backward, back into the Ironclads' arms.

"Aw, that's a real shame you missed that chance, Chris, because I think you're going to get a bit thirsty before our little show is over. Gus, Bobby, would you two help Chris show us all a true example of *equitability*?"

The Ironclads nodded and took their guest to the wheel. One of them opened a door in its cage. The other shoved Chris inside. He turned and grabbed the bars and stared out at the crowd.

"Now, Chris, could you just give that wheel a quick spin?"

The man stood behind the bars and stared down at Mr. Myrtle.

"Go ahead, Chris. Let's see what you can do."

When Chris continued to stand, Mr. Myrtle gave the audience a surprised glance before stepping to the edge of the stage and pulling his walking stick into the beam of light. Some of the crowd laughed. A few shouted, "Yeah." Mr. Myrtle shook the stick, pulled off the handle to reveal the double-pronged end of a knocker rod and pushed the prongs through the bars. Chris leaped and screamed, making the wheel shake on its undercarriage. The crowd roared.

"Uh, yeah, just go ahead, Chris—like I said before—and give the wheel a little spin."

Inside the cage Chris began to walk. The wheel rolled on its supporting hubs.

"There you go, Chris. That's good. Very good." Mr. Myrtle looked at the crowd. "He just needed some motivation." They laughed in reply. "Go on, Chris. Let's see what you've got. Go!" he shouted, starting a chant.

"Go . . . go. . . go, go, go, go-go-go-go-go."

Chris responded by speeding up. Mr. Myrtle tucked his knocker rod walking stick under his arm and offered delicate applause. He nodded to the audience who followed suite, raising loud applause.

"Great job, Chris. Great job. You're doing great." The emcee stood back and watched the wheel turn, looking at the audience each time the speed perceptibly increased. Then he stepped back to the bars and said, "Whoa, Chris. Hold on. I don't want you to wear yourself out. That's only the first part of the show." The wheel slowed and Mr. Myrtle turned back to his audience. "Give him a big hand. Whew, he must be exhausted after that. Wow, what a performance. Yeah!" He waited for the wheel to come to a complete stop, then said, "Gus, will you do the honors?"

One of the Ironclads said, "Yes, sir, Mr. Myrtle." But Shevi only heard it because she was so close to the stage.

The other man—he would be Bobby—crossed the beam of the spotlight and disappeared into the darkness. Squeaking and rumbling shook the stage as he pushed a scaffold to the opposite side of the wheel. Gus climbed the scaffold and walked out onto the top of the wheel. Chris turned and watched. Bobby climbed into the cage with a long knocker rod. Chris backed up the inside curve of the wheel, but the wheel didn't turn because Gus shifted his weight above to counter the hostage. Bobby pulled himself into a seat that spanned the center of the wheel.

Mr. Myrtle raised the mic to his mouth and said, "Time to put your money where your mouth is, Chris. Here's the way it works. You and Gus walk against one another. Bobby is in there with you to make sure you don't turn around and join Gus. Go ahead, Gus. Give him the chance to prove how much *equitability* he deserves."

Gus took a step up the outside of the wheel. Inside, Chris staggered. He looked around like he was sizing up the new situation and not liking the direction it was going. Above, Gus broke into a run up the wheel. Chris rose with the revolving tread and turned to run against the Ironclad, but he was too late. A second later he was at the three o'clock point of the wheel. He grabbed its framework and rode it up, up, around and down the other side, the dangling ends of his loincloth flapping. The crowd roared. Mr. Myrtle gave them a silly, wrinkled-nose laugh, slapping his knee. As Chris passed the opposite vertical Bobby stuck him with the knocker rod. Chris howled, bringing louder cries of pleasure from the audience. His back arched. His feet lost their grip on the wheel and he tumbled down to the bottom.

Shevi checked the faces around her for sympathy or concern or even doubt about what was happening, but all she saw was excitement, thrill, and meanness—some men squeezing and groping rolls of bare skin beneath the armor of the otherwise naked dancers, but most laughing and jeering at Chris as the torment escalated.

"Whoa, Gus!" Mr. Myrtle said and the man on top halted the wheel. "Now that Chris knows the rules and how to play, let's let him try again. How about it, Christopher Bartlett of equitability? Want to take control of the second round?"

The man inside the wheel pulled himself to his feet and put his face to the bars. He said, "Please."

"Going once," the host said. "Going twice." Pain and confusion painted the hostage's face while the grid of bars framed it. He opened his mouth to speak but before he could, Mr. Myrtle said, "Gone! Go ahead, Gus. Take him for another spin."

The crowd clapped and shouted as Gus started the wheel spinning again. Chris's knuckles turned white as he gripped the iron mesh. His toes stuck through the bars where they met the radius of the wheel. He spun around and upward until he was hanging upside down. From inside the wheel came the rattle of Bobby recharging the knocker rod. Chris's eyes bulged and his mouth gaped open, but he didn't let out any sound, not until Bobby hit him again with the voltage. His bare body pushed itself hard against the cage. A dark spot spread across the front of the little cloth between his legs. Shevi cringed, her knuckles white too as she clenched her fist in a mixture of anger and fear. Laughter swelled from the audience. The hostage rode the cycle back to the bottom before falling onto the inner tread of the wheel.

"Gus, are you getting tired yet?" Mr. Myrtle asked.

"No, sir," the man on top shouted.

"Chris, Gus is ready to go again. Would you like to take us up on our offer to let you lead this time?"

Chris staggered to his feet. He walked up the tread, making the wheel shift and roll. Above him, Gus followed the emcee's direction and took a few steps down the ascending outer tread. He was down below the scaffold platform, the wheel slowly speeding up, when Mr. Myrtle flicked a finger up and around. The Ironclad turned and walked against the rotation. Chris rose on his side of the tread. He looked up at his opponent. The wheel slowed.

Mr. Myrtle turned to the audience but addressed the hostage. "What's the matter, Christopher? We need to see some of this equitability you're always running your mouth about. Come on, man, put that name into it." He made a wide-mouthed, theatrical laugh. The witnesses bellowed.

Chris climbed higher on the tread, bending his body against its curve to get all the leverage he could. Gus took a single step upward and countered Chris's effort. Chris took hold of the tread and pulled himself up it. Gus shifted his weight forward just enough to maintain balance; he was barely past the two o'clock point while Chris dangled opposite at ten o'clock. Mr. Myrtle made a spinning gesture with his finger and Gus charged up the wheel. Chris was flung upward again. This time his feet lost their hold and he hung straight until Bobby jabbed the knocker rod at him. Chris drew his feet up. Bobby turned in his suspended seat. Chris held on tight and dodged Bobby's next thrust, but as he did Gus stepped on the finger of one hand. Chris's mouth flew open again. A coughing cry came out as he let go and slid down the inner tread, bouncing

180

across the bars as he went. He curled up into a ball and covered his head as the motion of the wheel took him upward again and Bobby turned around to get a new angle.

Two big men jumped onto the stage beside Shevi. She gasped with relief, thinking they were going to stop this insanity. They climbed the scaffold and jumped onto the outside of the wheel, one on either side of Gus, and, instead of pulling him off, they matched his pace. He looked left and right and gave them big grins. The three began to run. The wheel sped up. Chris's body rose inside it, upward past nine o'clock to ten and almost to eleven before gravity overcame momentum and he tumbled down against the revolving tread, Bobby dodging his fall. He bounced and rolled and tumbled, almost reaching the bottom before being sent hurling upward again.

"Equitability, folks," Mr. Myrtle said. "Dims want to take your place on the wheel. They want to get paid the same as someone twice or three times their size. What do we say to that?"

The crowd shouted, "NO!" in unison.

Shevi pushed herself back into the crowd. A man grabbed her and kissed her, his armor rattling against her engagement rotor. She was tossed left and right, spun around one way then another. She looked up at the belly of Wheel Three, rolling along in its carriage. She tried to remember which way she had come in. Darts of cold peppered her skin—someone had dumped a glass of ice on her. She turned and saw that the wheel had stopped. The Ironclads had opened the cage and now Mr. Myrtle spread his arms to show-case their brutalized victim. He was so much worse than Jackson had been. The only sign that he was still alive was that his head lolled from side to side. His scalp was a patchwork of hair and bloody tissue. Blood mixed with snot and drool drained from his nose and mouth.

"Why did the Carbon Nation pass away?" the host asked. "Because too many people like this," he grabbed their victim's chin and shook his head from side to side, "concerned themselves too much with what *they* wanted, what was best for *them*, and not what was best for their society and their world."

Shevi pushed through the crowd, leaving behind the ranting crazy man in his queer tall hat and dangerous knocker-rod walking stick. People were not going to behave this way and get away with it. The woman who had escorted her in smiled from the place where she leaned against the base of the pier. Shevi remembered Cole and the reason she had bothered coming down to this pit in the first place. Miss Myrtle waved to her. Shevi marched past and out into the cool dim of the loading docks. Someone would hear about this.

Chapter

Sixteen

Jackson stood at the foot of a plush bed in an upstairs bedroom and watched Sophia—the princess, he reminded himself—browse through her clothing.

"Jasper is bigger than you," she said, "a lot bigger than you. And Hugh is a bit smaller. I think you'll come closest to fitting into my clothes. Do you mind?"

Jackson had to put a strain on his mind to calculate a response. "Uh, no. Not at all. I mean, within limits."

Her laugh made him tingle. Her beauty was extraordinary to the point of being scary. Jackson had seen amazing sunsets from his grandfather's library balcony. He had been in the innards of the greatest works of men's hands and minds. He'd read words that incited tears and outbursts of laughter. But standing here watching this girl—no, this woman—examine items in her wardrobe made him feel perfectly weightless, to the point that he looked down at his feet and shuffled them on the soft carpet to make sure he wasn't floating away. Her hair was silvery blond streaked with bronze. Her features were petite and composed with the delicate care of the leaves on the little tree that stood by the entrance to the Piedmont mansion. The one thing that surprised him the most was her small size.

"When you're out," he said, "you wear a body suit?"

She sighed. "Yes. I hate that thing. But Grandfather wants us to blend with the walkers here so he insists we wear them." She turned and held up a light gray sweater and a pair of denim pants. "How about this?"

He shrugged. "I guess."

"Go in and try them on." She tilted her head toward a door in the corner.

He obeyed and found that they fit almost perfectly, a bit too perfectly perhaps, showing his true small build. The clothes Uncle Blaine had given him weren't as baggy as was considered a good fit for a small person; the ones he wore now were tight. He went back in to her presence and she applauded, making him almost certain he would float right up to the ceiling.

"Perfect," she said, beaming. But her smile faded quickly away. "What?"

He shrugged. "I'm accustomed to more space in my clothes."

"Really? I thought tight was the fashion here in Induction Town."

"Well, yeah. With the bigger people. We smaller tend to wear things looser."

"Huh! This place is just so polar opposite from Fluxton. Maybe Jasper's would be better after all."

"No!" he blurted. "Yours are fine." Suddenly he had a newly found appreciation for tighter fitting clothing.

She looked intently at him and, as curious as serious, asked, "What happened to your face?"

Casually, he leaned against the door frame and said, "Some guys beat me up for wearing girl's clothes." She burst into laughter, and he felt bigger than a five hundred pound Ironclad. She put out her hand to him. "Come on, silly. Let's get you a proper meal."

As they ate, Jackson began to inventory and appraise the events of the evening to determine which he would most likely remember the longest. He'd watched a movie with a beautiful Ironclad girl, scaled the structure across the ceiling of the Mall, eavesdropped on a meeting of the royalty and power, been attacked by a crazy woman, and went with a princess to her bedchamber. Although this last one was only for a change of clean clothes, he preferred to think of it in more suggestively vague terms. But the sea scallops, the ravioli, and the fresh asparagus washed down with red wine threatened to eclipse all the other wild rides the day had taken him on.

Several times while he was eating, he caught her looking at him. Her expression seemed similar to the way he had felt watching her upstairs. He captured an idea of her falling in love with him and locked it securely in his mind. If he could dream of a relationship with an Ironclad girl, then why not a princess too? If he was going to fantasize, why not do it all the way? He glanced quickly up from a spoonful of rich broccoli cheddar soup and winked at her. She actually blushed, and again he had to assess which of the two sensations was worth more.

With his old clothes bundled into the cloth he'd worn as a cloak when he began his evening's adventures, he followed her out of the mayor's apartment. It turned out to be at the end of a picturesque little street at the center of the Club's west end. High above, the tread of Wheel Three revolved past like clouds sailing across the dome of the heavens. Seen from this perspective, the wheel seemed big enough to contain the whole universe. It was a dynamic monument to the species.

The street opened into a piazza ringed with cafes with brightly colored umbrellas and centered by a pool with fountains at each end.

Someone shouted to the princess, just her name without her royal title. A boy ran from an arcade across the piazza.

"Hugh will *have* to meet you," Sophia said. "He's just that way."

Hugh bounded up to them and said, "Who's this?" Then he leaned forward and pointedly examined Jackson's face. "Wow, that's some shiner you got there."

Sounding exasperated, the princess said, "This is Jackson. Jackson, this is my brother Hugh."

Jackson bowed. "It's a pleasure to meet you, Prince Hugh."

"Hey, you got the title," the prince said. "I think that's a first. Slap me some skin."

Jackson stood and looked at the prince who held out a hand flat rather than upright as if to shake.

Sophia said, "It's a Carbon Nation thing. Hugh is positively captivated by the Carbon Nation."

"*Give* me some skin," Jackson said. "With all do respect, Your Highness."

"Ooh, he did the bow and got the title right and gave me a 'Your Highness.' Dad would love this guy. And he knows about skin. Let's keep him."

Jackson looked around. Ironclads at tables around the piazza had turned their attention on them—perhaps on him most of all.

"Hugh," Princess Sophia said in a tone of mixed reprimand and boredom.

"Come on," the prince said. "Up here." He raised his palm to Jackson, and Jackson couldn't help but flinch before obliging. He went on to show Hugh the up-high-down-low-too-slow routine and the boy cackled with delight. "I can't wait to get Jasper with that one. Don't you ruin it." He pointed at Sophia. He leaned in close to Jackson and whispered, "Man, finally somebody around here who knows how to dress. All these fat bellies in tight shirts is enough to make me sick. And the skinny people look like kids playing dress-up."

"We should go," Princess Sophia said as she and Jackson exchanged knowing smiles.

"Wait. What happened to his face? And where'd you find a guy with style in this place?"

The princess sighed.

Jackson said the first thing that popped into his mind. "The clothes are hers and I'm a professional whipping boy."

The prince's eyes grew wide with surprise and he asked

dubiously, "They have those here?" When Jackson batted his eyes, the prince barked a laugh. "You're good." He pointed at Jackson. "He's good. Where did you find him?"

"On the buffet," Sophia said with such intense earnest that now Jackson laughed louder than the prince had. Prince Hugh chuckled uncertainly. Sophia pushed past him. "We really must be going."

"Hey, don't leave the Club without guards. You heard what Dad said."

"I'm escorting him to the exit," the princess said.

"I'll go with you."

She stopped and turned. "No, you won't."

He grunted a reproach.

She pointed to the arcade he'd come out of. "Go back to what you were doing. You're making a scene."

The prince looked around the piazza self-consciously.

Jackson offered a wave. "It was nice to meet you, Your Majesty."

Prince Hugh returned his wave. His face was long with disappointment. As they walked away, he said, "I'll catch you next time."

Jackson exchanged a glance with the princess that made them both laugh. The princess walked him to a lobby at the corner of the level beyond the sliding atmospheric curve of the wheel's tread. When she approached the driver of the elevator, Jackson cleared his throat and whispered, "I'll take the stairs."

"What level do you live on?" she asked, concerned.

"Uh—quite a ways down," he said. "This one may not even stop at that level."

The driver said, "I make stops at every level except six, seven and eight."

Jackson gave her a big shrug. "See. Besides, I don't exactly have the fare."

"Well, then. Take us to Level 5 or 9, whichever is closer. My treat." She returned his shrug with a spiteful little nod of her head that thrilled him.

"Us?" he said, achieving near ecstasy that their time together would be extended by another minute. "I thought you weren't supposed to leave the Club level without security."

"I'm sure I'll survive a ride in the elevator. Besides, if you get off on Level 5 that's the civic level. What could happen?"

"Never ask that," Jackson said, and the princess laughed again.

To hold himself back from skipping with joy Jackson put his hands in his pocket and marched stiffly through the elevator car's open doors. The driver checked their weight and the princess paid him sixty-five cents—Jackson didn't see how anyone could afford to take the elevator at all. The lights blinked on and off as they descended to Level 5. His stomach churned. When the car stopped, disappointment washed through him. As the doors opened he sighed and put out his hand. "Thank you."

She took his hand and smiled. "I hope to see you again soon."

Outside the elevator a woman shouted, "I'm sorry, you'll have to come back in the morning. I can't help you."

"But it's urgent," a familiar voice said. "A man has been injured badly."

Jackson glanced over to see Shevi standing at a window in the Civic Level lobby.

"I'm not a doctor," the woman said.

"Intentionally," Shevi yelled. "Doesn't anybody care what goes on in this town?"

The window slammed shut and Shevi turned and looked into the open elevator car. Jackson stared back for a second then glanced at Princess Sophia and down at their clasped hands.

Shevi said, "Well, don't you get around."

Chapter
Seventeen

When the cranky little woman at the Office of Civil Order slammed the window in Shevi's face, she turned away and found the elevator door standing open and Jackson, of all the people in I Town, standing inside in. One instant he'd bolted back into the movie wheel and the next he was riding the express. Shevi hadn't ridden the thing in a long time. Back when her dad was alive he liked to take them on it for a treat, but it was a luxury even when they were high enough in the middle class to move to the Terraces. And there Jackson was, in a close fitting gray sweater and a tight pair of jeans. The fine knit of the sweater made his bruises and that awful curved scar—Cole's scar—stand out even more than they had when he had that silly cloak over his head. The cloak wrapped a bundle that he carried under one arm. The other hand held the hand of a girl. Sophia Burgess seemed thin and small, even beside Jackson. Princess Sophia! How had he managed that?

Jackson pulled his hand from her, gave her a slight bow and thanked her. They seemed the oldest of friends. They actually looked sweet together, the princess watching after him intently. As the elevator door closed, she seemed to be creating a special place in her mind for the moment.

Jackson stepped forward, shoving his hands into the pockets of tight jeans. Shevi looked him over, but her eyes kept going back to the curved scar on his forehead.

"Where did you go?"

"When?"

"From the movie wheel."

"To the Club."

"They let *you* in the Club?"

"I went in through a utility entrance, sort of."

"There's a utility entrance from the movie wheel into the Club?"

"Sort of."

She stared into his eyes for a moment but the scar drew her focus again. "Cole did that to you."

"Yeah."

"Why didn't you tell me?"

"I did."

"No, you didn't."

"Yeah, I did."

"I'm sorry."

"Don't be."

"Well, I am."

"Well . . . okay, then."

"Okay, what?"

"What, okay, what?"

"Do you accept my apology?"

"Yeah, I guess."

"What do you mean, you guess?"

"It isn't necessary."

"I feel responsible."

"I don't think you are."

"It's how I feel."

"Fine. Yes. I accept your apology."

"Thank you."

They went on facing one another but neither would look at the other. Her eyes suddenly didn't want to look at the scar anymore. She looked left and right, glancing down between, while he looked right and left glancing up between. Shevi's focus fell on the closed doors of the elevator behind him. She blurted what was out front in her mind. "Did your date pay for the ride?"

"What?" Jackson glanced over his shoulder. "Oh, the princess?" He turned and studied her critically for a moment then said, "No. My fairy-frickin-godmother did."

"What?"

"It's a literary reference."

"I know." Shevi heard too much of Stacey in her tone. "I mean . . . I'm sorry."

"Oh, geez, let's not go through that again. What's the problem?" He pointed behind her.

She turned and looked back at the closed window. A sigh gushed out of her. "Oh, Jackson, it was horrible."

"What?"

"There was this party in the basement. Cole was there."

"Uh-huh."

"It was a bachelor party for one of his friends. There were lights and dancers and ice."

"Ice?"

"Yeah. Lots of it. On the floor and one guy spilled some on me."

"You were there? At a bachelor party *with* your fiancé?"

"No. I went in with . . . There was this little man there . . . I mean, not that he was little. He was—Mr. Myrtle."

"Down in the cellars?"

"Yes. And there was this wheel—"

"But they weren't using it to make their electricity."

"No. It was—"

"This party wasn't by chance for Stendahl, was it?"

"Yeah."

"And you didn't like what they were doing?"

"No!"

"And you want to do something about it?"

"Of course."

Jackson stepped around her to the closed window and hammered on it. He grinned at Shevi while he waited for it to open. When it did, he smiled at the woman and said, "My friend here was just trying to tell you that they're pirating electricity in the cellars. They've vamped a connection to the wheel."

The woman put on a suspicious look, turning it toward Shevi.

"Is that right?"

Confused, Shevi nodded.

"Well," the woman said indignantly, "we'll have to see about that." She turned to a wall of large tubes capped with round flaps, lifted the flap of one marked Main and shouted into it. "Captain Cato, please."

First a garbled, soft voice replied then a powerful voice boomed out. "This is Captain Cato. Go ahead."

She pushed her mouth into the tube and said, "We have a report of vamping and pirating in the cellars."

"Is that so?" the captain said. "I'll send someone to look into it."

"Thank you, captain."

"Thank *you*," he said.

The woman let the flap fall closed over the tube and turned back to them with a satisfied smile on her face. To Jackson she said, "Thank you for informing us of this." Then she looked over at Shevi and said, "You should have just said so in the first place." She slammed the window closed again.

Someone was on their way to help the poor man, so Shevi could relax. She thought of telling Jackson about what had happened but just didn't think she could rehash it without falling to pieces. Once again he had come to her rescue. He had a gift for it. He must have done something wonderfully heroic for the princess. Shevi considered asking him what it was, but she really didn't want to think about Jackson being with Princess Sophia. What did a middle class walker like herself have to compete with royalty? It was just too absurd to think about.

"It's late," Jackson said.

"Yeah."

"What time is it anyway?"

"Maybe midnight. Very late."

"Yeah. I guess I should be getting home."

"Me, too."

He gave her a quick wave and threaded his hands deep into his pockets. "Well, see you around."

"Yeah. See you." She let him turn toward the stairwell then realized she had to go that way too. She bolted to catch up. Inside the stair she said, "Wow. What a day. I probably won't be able to sleep—with all the adrenaline."

"Yeah. Same here. I thought I was going to . . ." He shook his head.

"What?"

"Well." He smiled slyly as they climbed the stairs. "I didn't exactly get into the Club through a *real* service entrance."

"I knew you didn't. What did you do?"

He laughed wickedly.

"Tell me."

"It's a long story."

"I have adrenaline."

"It might just make matters worse then." He stopped at the door to Level 6. His chest heaved with a sigh, and all of a sudden she knew he didn't want their time together to end either.

"There's an all-night coffee bar on Ten. Want to come up?"

"You think caffeine on top of adrenaline is a good idea?"

"Sometimes that's what it takes."

He nodded and smiled knowingly. "An overdose to reset the

system."

"Exactly."

"Exactly." He let go of the door handle and turned to the next flight.

As they walked he began his story of escaping the cinema wheel and crawling along the pipes above the Mall. While they sipped coffee he told about the hatch into the mayor's apartment, the food, the pantry, and finally the crazy woman and how the princess rescued him from her.

People came and went. Sometimes they seemed to be staring at Shevi and her date, but she didn't care, especially when she found out that he had not rescued the princess. She had rescued him and he was amazing enough to admit it. Could anyone be any more incredible than that?

Shevi told him about her dad dying. He listened carefully and asked lots of questions about him, things like how big he was and if he liked to read and what kinds of food he liked best. It was the most attention anybody had ever given the subject of her dad's life and death. Jackson told her about living on the Upper Crust and the disintegration of his parents' marriage after the weight limits started going up and his grandfather died, leaving his mother's younger brother to lead the family. It was sad to hear that Ava was so mistaken and had such a heartbreaking reality facing her down the road. Their eyes were streaked with bright red by the time they admitted defeat. Jackson was first. His dad might be worried, might be still reading by their single dim light bulb, or he might be sound asleep. Jackson didn't know but he should probably get back just to know for sure.

She went with him to the door to the stairwell and watched him hurry down the stairs as the door closed behind him. Then she turned around to go home and found herself facing a fortification of human bodies. Mrs. Turney stood shoulder to shoulder with Cole's younger sister Leah and his sister-in-law Hester. Mrs. Turney and Hester were each almost twice as big as Shevi. Leah wasn't as tall but made up for it in width. She had a rodent-like face that always looked angry even when she laughed.

Mrs. Turney's two auburn braids had strands of steel cable woven into them. She was almost completely armored with rotors, the emblem of the family she had married into when I Town was a town of only six induction wheels. She wore one on each shoulder. One over each breast and one in the middle made the three-circled Scott of the Trintico logo. She grabbed the rotor that hung from Shevi's neck and turned it up into Shevi's face. "Do you know what this means?"

Shevi took a step back. "Hello, Mrs. Turney."

"This means that you are a Mrs. Turney, too, and I expect you to start acting like it." She dropped the rotor. It swung down and smacked into Shevi's stomach as it clanged at the end of its chain.

Shevi took a recovering breath and another step backward. "I'm sorry ma'am, but I'm not sure what you mean."

"Not sure?" the robust woman said. "You're not sure? Well let me educate you. It means that you don't go around with little insect boys behind my son's back. And it definitely means that you don't go out with them right out in the open where everybody can see you. Good God, girl, are you really that stupid?"

"With . . ." Shevi started but faltered. "With Jackson? Jackson is a really good friend, Mrs. Turney. We weren't *going out*."

"I know what you were doing. I know exactly what you did. I sat right over there and watched you and you were so," she wiggled her big body and batted the eyelids, "so silly about him." Shevi opened her mouth to protest but the woman stuck a big threatening finger under her nose. "And I know what he is. He's just like his father, moving in and putting the moves on a fine young Ironclad girl and destroying her family's life—*wrecking it*." Mrs. Turney's face drew up. It wrinkled in new amazing ways. Her eyes glistened with tears and her voice trembled.

Shevi crossed her arms over her rotor and backed against the stairwell door. "Ma'am, I am terribly sorry if I've suggested that anything like that could happen."

"I am very glad to hear you want to make sure it doesn't happen, Shevi. So you won't protest what we believe is unavoidable at this time."

"What's that?"

"You're coming with us."

"Where?"

"To Wheel Six. To the Turney estate."

"Now?"

"Tonight."

"But I walk on Wheel Three."

"We've made arrangements for a position on our wheel for you and your mother and brother, effective immediately."

Shevi looked from angry face to angry face. This was all so ridiculous. Yes, she liked Jackson. She liked him a lot. He was amazing. But she was going to marry Cole and she knew it and she knew everybody else knew it, even Jackson—especially Jackson after the beating he'd taken over it.

"We are—" friends, she wanted to say. She wanted to talk them out of taking her away, away from the wheel she had walked on with her dad, the wheel she'd grown up on—and of course the wheel where Jackson was. But she wilted. It was true. She and Jackson weren't just friends. At least he wasn't just a friend to her. She had felt something special for him since the first time she'd seen him. Had she seduced him? If they went any further, what would it lead to? The same kind of mixed up life he and Ava were already stuck in? She couldn't do that to him. "We are . . . going, then," she said. "We should go ahead and go."

Mrs. Turney offered a glance laced with satisfaction to her co-horts. "You're all Turneys now, as it should be. We've got your mother off that ridiculous night shift."

Shevi swallowed hard. It was a big pill to take, and bittersweet. They turned away and she followed them to her apartment. Perry was there. He was packing. He glared at her when he saw her. She smiled in return, loving that he wasn't happy with the move. That made it almost worthwhile, considering that he was in on Jackson's beating.

⬭

Jackson eased the door open and found both his sister and his dad asleep, the latter under a Metalman comic and both beneath the waste of their dim bulb glowing overhead. When Jackson pulled the chain and turned it off, he heard his dad stir.

"What?" Dad mumbled. "Jackson, is that you?"

"Yeah. Go to sleep."

"How was your movie?"

"Okay."

"Just okay?"

"It was fun. I had a lot of fun. I'll tell you about it tomorrow."

"Okay." He was quiet after that.

Jackson lay still in the darkness and let the memories of the evening swim around in his head as it floated into the ethersphere of dreamland. It was hard to distinguish memory from dream, considering how weird the day had been. Then there was a loud booming sound all around him—around and around him. The light was on again. The door was open. Dad was up and talking to someone. They were coming into the apartment with big, growling voices. They grabbed Jackson up and slammed him against the wall. "Under arrest," they said, someone said, one of them said   or all of them said. Jackson wasn't even sure how many of them there were, not until Ava woke up and started crying. One of them picked her up. Dad retaliated. Another one slammed him against the wall. There were five of them. They marched Jackson and his family out into the hallway and down the corridor while other inhabitants of Level 6 peeked out their doors. They took them down to the Civic Level and shut Jackson in a small room.

Chapter
Eighteen

The click of the lock and the squeak of the door hinges woke Jackson. He sat back against the cold, hard back of a metal chair and tried to discreetly swipe at the drool on his check. The man in the doorway smiled and clucked his tongue. Mr. Myrtle.

"Jackson, my boy, you've got yourself into some real trouble now."

"Why am *I* in trouble?" Jackson asked. "Why aren't *we* in trouble?"

"Well," Mr. Myrtle said thoughtfully. His mint green suit sagged on his little frame. "*You* did something atrocious. *You* vamped an unmetered electrical draw on an Induction Town generator wheel."

"For you."

The man wagged his finger in corrective instruction. "*Pirating* electricity is nothing compared to vamping an illegal connection. *Pirating* is a passive accidental offense, punishable by a mere slap on the wrist compared to vamping. An act of treason. The worst kind of disloyalty to the corporate society. You went up alone. I have no idea what you did up there, and how was I supposed to know where all the electricity came from? I just plugged in to *your* connection and it worked."

"And you made—"

The knocker rod came out of nowhere, hidden under the sleeve of the baggy jacket. Jackson flinched before the two prongs touched his neck—he knew what was coming, had felt it once before when he tested it. The jarring slap of electricity pulled his head down to his shoulder. He would have screamed had all the muscles in his throat not been paralyzed for the instant and his teeth pulled hard together. He did manage to make a foamy, buzzing sound.

Mr. Myrtle smiled. "And you built this."

Jackson could only cough and wheeze a reply. The charge had been light, otherwise he'd be unconscious right now.

"Another atrocious act. You sold it to Ricky Hickman. How much did he give you for it?" When Jackson narrowed his eyes while he rubbed the side of his neck, Mr. Myrtle shook the rod vigorously to recharge it—the next hit would be harder. "Your cooperation *will* happen, young man."

"Fifty cents," Jackson said.

Mr. Myrtle whistled. "Big money. What did you do with it?"

Jackson rolled his shoulder and rubbed the knot the charge had made in it for as long as he reasonably could without making the little man any hotter. "Deposit on the apartment."

"Ah. What a good son you are. You should be as good a citizen."

Jackson couldn't help but glare at the imp.

Mr. Myrtle tilted his head skeptically. "You're not going to keep on trying to blame others for what you've done, are you?" He swept the pronged end of the knocker rod through the air between them. Jackson shook his head. "Good boy. Now I have a proposition for you that will just show you what a fair and . . ." he rolled his gaze round the room as if searching for something, ". . . equitable society we are. Despite the grievous crime of vamping you've committed against the corporate society of Trintico, we offer you an opportunity for reform. You understand we could farm you out for this, right? Trade you off to Agrarianna for a month's worth of food. They're always looking for a few good men to till and sow and reap. Or, we could even execute you—give you a ride in the induction chair. But we have a new program that has just become available and I think you and your father would be prime candidates for it."

He rhythmically thumped the knocker rod into his open palm while he stared down at Jackson, and although Jackson kept his eyes fixed on Mr. Myrtle's, he was ever aware of the two prongs sticking from the bobbing end of the rod. Mr. Myrtle whirled away from Jackson's unrelenting stare and danced around the room until he was out of Jackson's field of view. The little hairs on the back of Jackson's neck stood up. His ears itched with curiosity.

"Of course jail time goes without saying. Three to five megawatts at least. I'm a great man, but even my power has its limits. But the program offers the chance to become productive members of society. To be walkers."

The man came back into view on Jackson's far left. He had capped the pronged end of the knocker rod. Jackson took a relieved breath. "Where's my sister?"

"Where she belongs. With her mother. Built like her mother, you know."

"Yeah, I noticed that."

"Well, why she was with you and your skinny little father is, of course, none of my business. Even the best of families make the occasional bad decision."

Jackson left that baited hook dangling.

"So, you'll begin the program and you'll begin your sentence immediately. Members of the Guard will see to the details. Any questions?" He toyed with the cap that protected him from accidentally touching the prongs and shocking himself.

Jackson, lusting for the chance to see exactly that, shook his head.

Shevi and Perry were allowed the day off after their short night—it had been almost dawn when they finished moving into a four-room apartment on the third floor of the Turney mansion—plus they had to get ready for the Piedmont-Stendahl wedding. Shevi polished her rotor then did it again when Mrs. Turney disapproved. They all wore rented armor in silver and bronze, and all Stendahl designs.

The wedding was held in the Brighton Theater Wheel, a wheel that walked only about a thousand people but was richly constructed. Its tread was oak slats with brass spacers. It made a low rumble when the audience got it going. The president himself came onto the stage that spanned the inside of the wheel. The audience paid homage with a deep bow which they gave while continuing to walk up the tread.

On the left side of the wheel, the photographer Richard Philbrook in an orange jacket and green pants and a brighter green tie shook his knocker rod to charge his camera's flash. He looked through the camera and the flash blinked across the crowd.

Crowned in the pointed bell housing symbol of the Stendahl family, the groom and his attendants sidled across the moving tread from the right. Necks craned to see the groom bedecked in gold armor. Like Cole, he was a boy becoming a man by the act of marriage.

The bridesmaids filed up a middle aisle defined by two bands of solid bronze inlaid into the oak tread. They wore brass armor over purple gowns. Each carried a scepter, the symbol of the Piedmont family, a gear-tipped axle.

Mrs. Turney said, "Aren't they beautiful?" Her daughters and daughters-in-law murmured agreement while the Turney men marched along beside them. Mr. Turney's arm was out like a handle for his wife to hold. His great hand engulfed hers. He smiled his enduring smile—he was the happiest man Shevi had ever met, robust and jolly and ruddy faced. He looked down the row at her and gave her a hearty smile that made her glad to have a father again. She hoped Cole would grow to be exactly like his father.

Beyond the Turney patriarch, a little girl trod up the aisle scattering rose petals. Audience members leaned forward and back to get a look at the girl. Shevi caught a glimpse of her once and thought her eyes were teasing her. She pushed her way into the next row and then the next to get another look while behind her her future mother-in-law hissed her disapproval. Shevi had not seen wrong. The little flower girl was Ava. Her hair was done up beautifully with silver ribbons and gold flowers. Shevi stopped walking and rode the tread back down to the Turney rows.

The bride was next, escorted by a man too young to be her father. She was not a girl becoming a woman at marriage, but a woman as old as Shevi's mother—marrying the teen Ward Stendahl. Worse than the age difference was the resemblance to little Ava. Their faces were almost identical. Shevi stopped walking again, riding back into Hester's path. Hester shoved her forward and gave her a foul look. Shevi staggered while trying to digest the fact that this woman, the bride, wasn't some cousin of Jackson's, as she'd assumed, but his own mother—the young man escorting her was the uncle who had thrown Jackson and Ava and their dad out of the family. Shevi's brain was so completely filled with chaos that she had to consciously blink spots from her eyes. She had to force each breath. She did not, however, have to make her heart beat; it thundered beneath her bronze and silver chainmail.

From that moment on, Shevi marched forward, trapped in the circumstance, unable to exit without making a scene that would never be forgiven. She didn't hear President Burgess's blessing on the couple or his benediction to the crowd. She flowed with them as they slowed and let the theater wheel stop. In the Club of Wheel Eight for the reception, she smiled at introductions but didn't retain a single name. Then she found herself passing along the receiving line and coming up to the woman Jackson had just, the night before, talked about while trying to hide the tears welling in his eyes. A tremor took over her body as she shook the woman's hand, but she managed to contain herself. She shook the groom's hand and moved on—to Ava.

The little girl looked up and smiled at Shevi. She tugged on her mother's new husband's hand and said, "She's my brother's friend."

Ward Stendahl glanced over at her and beyond him Penny Piedmont-Koss-Stendahl looked at her, too. Shevi bent, trying to avoid their eyes. She shuffled around the girl to get out of the way of Cole and her new extended family.

"It's nice that you could be in your mother's wedding."

Ava said, "I came back to live with Mommy because Dad and Jackson are living in jail now."

"Jail?"

The little girl nodded.

"They were arrested?"

Another nod.

"What for?"

"Vamping," Ava said. "Down in the cellars."

"No," Shevi said, exhaling the word, and when she stood up quickly she found herself dizzy and crammed into a tight cluster of people—Cole and his mother and several other of the Turneys had gathered around her. "*No!*" she said again, her voice ramping up uncontrollably. "*He* didn't do it. *He* turned them in. *He* told the *Guard!*"

Hands grabbed her arms. A voice hissed in her ear. "Young lady, mind your tongue."

Shevi jerked and swung around. She pushed away from her

future mother-in-law's grasp. As she did, the gathering onlookers gasped. A light flashed behind her and she heard the rattle of Philbrook's knocker rod recharging his camera's flash.

"Let go of me," she screamed. "This is all wrong. Jackson didn't do anything wrong."

People were backing away and staring wide-eyed. She thought that was a good thing—she had an audience who needed to hear the truth about Jackson and how wonderful he was and how he would never do anything illegal—until she realized they weren't looking at her but at something behind her. She turned and found Ava being helped up by her new father, silver ribbons disheveled in her hair, gold flowers scattered across the floor. Shevi had knocked her down when she pulled herself away from Mrs. Turney. The bulb of Philbrook's camera flashed in Shevi's face and left black spots dancing over the faces around her as she looked from one to the next.

"Oh, Ava, I'm sorry," she said.

Ward Stendahl picked the girl up and pulled her against the gold plates of his armor. Shevi was pulled backward with such force that one of her boots came off. She looked over each shoulder to find Mr. Turney and his eldest son Blake holding her arms. The gentle giant's smile that had seemed indelible was gone now. The look on his face was the look of a man capable of committing murder.

Shevi was removed from Wheel Eight's Club level. She was taken backward, her feet dotting on the floor occasionally, to the cable car station and dropped inside the waiting cab. Hester and Leah slipped past the men and quietly took seats on either side of

Shevi while Mr. Turney slammed her with a look of such complete disappointment that it forced tears from her eyes. He didn't speak. His massive round torso heaved and his eyes offered suggestions of things he'd like to say if he weren't a kind and gentle man. When he paid the driver and turned away Shevi broke into panicked sobs.

The cable car driver closed the doors then opened them again. Shevi squirmed, afraid Mr. Turney had changed his mind and was coming back in to pour out his wrath upon her, but her mother climbed inside carrying Shevi's boot and took a seat without saying a word. The car squeaked along its cable past Wheel Seven and stopped at Wheel Six. Hester and Leah grabbed Shevi's arms and yanked her upright. Her mom stepped over to her.

"Ladies, let me."

Hester said, "We were told to put her in her room."

"Which is where she will go," Mom said. "But she doesn't have to be dragged. Do you, Shevi?"

Shevi shook her head, looking at the floor as she put her boot back on.

"She's a big embarrassment," Leah said.

As she helped Shevi from the car, Mom said, "The situation was awkward."

"Awkward?" Hester squawked. "I don't know how *she* wriggled her way into this family."

"I think that was Cole's doing," Mom said softly.

The four women walked up the street to the Turney mansion, two by two, Shevi and her mother leading and Leah and Hester following along behind. The two in front were silent; the two behind carried on a passive aggressive assault.

210

"Cole is too kind."

"Like Mr. Turney."

"Exactly. Just trying to help a lesser out and this is how he's repaid."

"Just another reason why the classes should be fixed and permanent. People should just stay what they really are rather than even be allowed to climb up the ladder."

Shevi felt an ember start to glow inside her. If her dad hadn't died, they wouldn't have lost their place on the Terraces. What would the two Upper Crust Ironclad girls say then? So really, these two were gnawing at her back simply because her dad had died, and when she tried to help Jackson she'd just been doing the same thing they were praising Cole for. But then she thought about it and decided it really wasn't the same. There were those other feelings, the ones everybody seemed to know about before she had. She wasn't sure herself what was going on inside her, but she knew Jackson was a great person and deserved better than the way people treated him.

Leah said, "All the Dims should be kicked out. They just complicate things for the rest of us."

Shevi whirled. With Mom tugging at her arm and offering little coaxing calls of her name, Shevi lunged at the two girls. She planted a hand in each of their chests and shoved them, shouting, "Don't call them that."

Hester and Leah recollected their stances and assumed smiles.

Hester asked, "Don't call who what?"

"The smaller classes," Shevi said. "Don't call them Dims. It's offensive."

"Shevi," Mom said softly.

"Offensive," Leah laughed, clapping her hands with mock joy.

Hester spoke matter-of-factly. "They are *diminutives*, shortened to 'Dims' for convenience. It is not slang or disrespectful, you stupid lug, it is just what they *are*."

"Well, they can't help it."

"Nobody can help anything, Shevi," Hester said. Now she sounded more like she was talking to a child, which fanned the ember inside Shevi. "Things *are* the way they *are*."

"What if things were different? What if they were better off than us?"

Leah huffed. "Well, that's just stupid. In what kind of world would that be the case?"

Mom tugged at her arm again. "Shevi, come on."

"No," Hester said. "Let her answer. I'm curious." She stepped forward until her rotor clanged against Shevi's. "What's she see in a squirrelly little Dim boy that makes her want to throw away this." She held up her hands to offer the narrow street around her and its twinkling streetlights as evidence for her side of the argument.

"There's more to him than his size." Shevi clenched her teeth and said, "So, don't call him that."

"Ladies," Mom said. "Let's all go inside like we were told."

"What?" Hester asked. "Squirrelly or little?"

"You know what."

"No," Hester said, smiling at Leah. "What's she talking about?"

"I have no idea. She should just say it so we all know what her problem is."

"Yeah, I mean, she must be having a problem with me calling

him squirrelly, because maybe he isn't. But he really, for sure is little and a *Dim*."

"Ladies," Mom said sternly but too late.

Shevi shoved Hester backward. She stumbled over a flowerpot, rolled over, struck a handrail and landed facedown on the street. Leah slapped Shevi. Shevi pulled back a fist and slammed it into Leah's face.

"*Ladies!*" Mom shouted and stepped forward.

Leah shoved her. The flame of anger inside Shevi exploded into an inferno. She grabbed Leah around the neck and tightened her hold. Hester was back up now, her bejeweled and claw-tipped fingers coming at Shevi's face. Shevi put all her weight into launching one girl at the other. They all went down together in a heap. Bronze and silver armor and chainmail clattered on the pavement. Shevi suddenly remember that all this gear was rented. All would have to be returned and damages paid for. A heartbeat later she felt a deep ringing in her head and her teeth clacking together as Hester slammed her with a rotor.

Chapter

Nineteen

Jackson and his dad walked side by side in a long row of inmates. They all wore tight second skins of dingy white clothing with numbers smeared in paint on their chests and backs. All but Jackson and his dad held beanie hats out in front of them. These were smeared with different numbers, two-digits-dash-two-digits, row and position in the row. The word newbie bounced from one inmate to another like a ball in a game.

A man walked down the row, slapping a clipboard against his palm, and stopped at Jackson who figured him to be the equivalent of a wheel manager. Two men flanked him. Each carried two knocker rods, one a long and fat staff that looked powerful enough to kill a man, the other about half again a forearm's length that could be touched to the throat or the groin to put an inmate back in line. A small man stood back a couple of paces and carried a big sack. The clipboard manager man scanned down the list while mumbling Jackson's number, 824973, over and over. His eyes locked on a place on the paper and became wide. "Koss, Jackson," he said. His gaze drifted up to meet Jackson's. "Vamper." Now a murmur drifted up and down the line. The man stepped close to Jackson, so close their noses almost touched, close enough that Jackson could smell beer and beef on his breath. He whispered, "How did you manage to get off with a sentence of only three thousand kilowatt-hours? Who do you know?" He shook his head and clucked, looking back at his list.

"I'm small, sir."

The man scowled at Jackson. "Are you proud of that?"

"No sir. But I just wanted to answer by pointing out that the length of a sentence is relative to the weight of the inmate, sir."

"Oh, an educated guy, huh? What else is it 'relative' to?"

"Position on the wheel, sir," Jackson said.

"So you know if I put you back with the feebs and gimps and the crips and give you no kind of pack, with you barely weighing a hundred pounds, you could be here for a while."

"Yes, sir," Jackson said.

The manager glanced up at Jackson's forehead. "Cute scar. How'd you get it?"

"Ran into an Ironclad, sir. My fault."

The manager laughed, nodded and took a step. Now he was in front of Jackson's dad. "Koss, Levine. Aiding and abetting a vamper. Hmm. Also a three thousand kilowatt-hour sentence.

Interesting. How much you think you can carry?"

Jackson's dad said, "I'd like to walk where my son walks."

The manager leaned back and studied him. "Even if it means doubling your sentence?"

Jackson looked up at his dad in time to see him nod. He elbowed him and whispered, "Don't."

The manager gave Jackson a reprimanding glance. "He's just trying to take care of his son."

"Yes, sir," Jackson said.

"You got that sir stuff down pretty good. That's odd for a vamper. Most of y'all are spiteful anarchists." He stood still and let his attention shift back and forth between them.

Dad leaned forward just slightly and whispered, "There was supposed to be a formula to help—"

"Sh!" the manager hissed. He leaned in close to them and spoke in a gruff whisper. "One more mention of that and you'll both be walking on solitary wheels." He stepped back and bellowed, "Row five, both of them." He flipped through the pages then added, "One and two." He walked on, making a note on the clipboard.

Down the line, the manager stopped and said, "Maddox, you're on row twelve."

A man whined, "That's gonna double my sentence."

Jackson cut his eyes to get a look down the row of inmates. The manager stood and stared for a moment. Maddox didn't say more. The manager grabbed the beanie from his hands and tossed it to the man with the sack. "Shack Town will have to survive a bit longer without you, I suppose. Another word about it and I'll put you on nights."

The man with the sack stepped forward and riffled its contents. He handed Maddox a new cap and moved on down the line. Ahead of him the manager said, "Phipps, row fourteen." The beanie distributor made another trade then hurried back to Jackson, handing him a cap with 05-02 on it, gave Jackson's dad one numbered 05-01, and ran back to the manager and guards without speaking or looking at them.

Jackson placed the cap on his head. As he did, he saw Maddox and Phipps lean out of line and look at him.

The manager took position at the far wall. His guards stood off to his left. He assumed a wide stance with hands behind his back. "Row four," he shouted, "shackle up."

The far end of the long line of inmates marched forward and centered themselves facing him. The little man responsible for the beanie caps had disappeared into a closet behind the manager and guards. He returned now with a handful of belts and dangling, rattling chains. With the guards following along, he distributed what turned out to be a continuous string of belts. Each inmate strapped a belt around his waist.

"Row five," the manager shouted.

Another segment of the long line stepped forward and formed a row, jostling Jackson and his dad along uncertainly. Behind them, someone said something low and gruff that Jackson couldn't quite understand, but it didn't sound like congratulations. The little man invited them to a precise point. He handed Jackson's dad the first belt and Jackson the second. The chains jingled as he slipped quickly down the row.

When all the rows were assembled and ganged together with the strings of belts and chains, the manager led them down the onramp. They fell in behind three rows of men dressed in the same tight fitting clothes, but theirs were stained dull red.

Load lights dangled along the front of the wheel's tread where it disappeared into Level 6 above. The lowest green light glowed; the yellow light above it flashed on.

"Hurry, gentlemen," the manager shouted. "Hurry along."

Slowly but precisely the nightshift walkers sidled off the far side of the wheel while the dayshift walkers boarded.

Someone nearby said, "Hell, look at the load light."

The yellow light had come on again and hadn't turned off.

Someone else said, "We'll be packing up right away."

"Especially with those skinny-assed newbies right up front," another voice said.

"Quiet in the ranks," the manager shouted. "File on quickly."

"Vamper," somebody behind Jackson whispered.

Jackson and his dad exchanged a look. They marched with the motion of the wheel. Something clunked and rattled overhead. Jackson's dad looked up nervously.

"It's the pack rack," Jackson whispered.

High above them, a framework moved forward and down. Three rows of legs dangled from its front—life-sized human dolls made of canvas. Behind them the rack was filled with rows of bulky canvas bags, one row for each row of walkers and one pack for each walker in a row.

"What are they?" Dad asked.

"Food and water," Jackson whispered. "And some extra weight."

The rack was curved to match the curve of the wheel. Its rear descended faster than its front until it echoed the shape of the tread underneath their feet.

"Why do the people up front wear red and get packs shaped like people?" Dad asked.

"Not sure," Jackson said.

An inmate in front of them looked over his shoulder and said, "Murderers."

The man on Jackson's other side said, "They destroyed a natural resource so they have to carry a pack that replaces what they destroyed. It's the ultimate crime—next to vamping, I suppose."

Snickers and laughs rippled around them as each inmate took the pack above him off the rack and slipped his head through its neck hole. Jackson figured his pack weighed about thirty pounds. It made the endless walk up the revolving tread a little harder, but it was loaded! Each of the two cup holders on its dashboard held a pouch of *fresh* water. The backpack had hunks of bread, cheese and cured meat. Jackson examined the goods and looked over at Dad. He raised his eyebrows and nodded. Jackson grinned back. Obviously the powers that be failed to understand that the small people of I Town would consider this punishment a reward. Life on the jail wheel had its advantages.

The breakfast buffet in the dining hall of the Turney mansion was enormous and aromatic. Steam rose from eggs and meats and biscuits. Cole's brothers, sisters, in-laws, and cousins had numbered twenty-eight at the engagement party. Two births had happened since then. The Lilbourns brought the number up to thirty-three, but there were thirty-five if you counted the ones on the way.

The clan attacked the setting with silverware for weapons and plates for shields. The youngest would be off to the school wheel, clad in chainmail and armor like their adult role models. Some wore their rotors like hats. Some wore them as breastplates.

Shevi found herself stalled near a corner of the big room while Cole joined in. And although he wouldn't look at her after her campaign for Jackson's honor, she did manage to make the mistake of catching Mr. Turney's eye. His gaze fixed first right into her eyes then it slid upward to the bandage on her forehead, the bandage that covered an arc-shaped scar Hester had given her with the edge of her rotor, the stroke that had ended their little street brawl. His buoyant expression fell and his attention returned to his plate. People were getting hurt: Jackson beaten, he and his dad jailed, and this great man stripped of his resilient spirit. The cost of her curious attraction to a Dim boy soared daily. At that moment a representative from the Stendahl dealership was upstairs surveying the damage her little skirmish with Leah and Hester had caused to the rented armor.

It was all her fault, all because she had wandered over to Jackson's little crate of books. And why had she done it? Maybe she was just nervous about getting married and had mistaken anxiety for curiosity, had just imagined the magnetism of her eyes to Jackson's. No. There had been something there. But it was forbidden, and she knew it. And it had led to Cole and his buddies beating up Jackson, which had sent her to the bachelor party where she saw the heinous little man and his awful "Duel Wheel", which had sent her to the Office of the Civil Order where Jackson had helped her by telling about the vamping, which had gotten him in trouble—somehow, that part still confused her. She knew beyond a doubt she had two things to do. She had to abandon her interest in him before it got somebody killed—that was actually the second thing—but first she had to do everything she could to get him out of jail. She had to harness every resource she could find. Then she saw it: she was marrying into a powerful family. There were reins of power right in front of her. She only had to reach out and grasp them. She had to win them over, show them that she was a faithful daughter who only wanted justice for a friend. No, not even a friend. Just justice. Who wouldn't agree to that?

Mr. Turney glanced across the buffet at Leah and bobbed his head toward Shevi. Leah nodded to her father, set down her plate and smirked. Shevi dashed for the stack of plates at the end of the buffet, but Leah joyously obeyed the patriarch's silent command and met her there.

"You need to put on some weight if you ever expect to pay for that armor," she said, taking the empty plate from Shevi's hand. "Here, let me. None of us want to see a repeat of dinner last night."

Before the wedding, the family had gathered for the supper feast and several members had commented on the small portions Shevi and her mom took. Perry, on the other hand, had showed his capacity for consuming and had pleased all.

Now Leah began heaping eggs and biscuits and meats and gravy on the big rectangular plate while other members of the Turney family encouraged her. She smiled across her masterpiece as she handed it to Shevi. The plate had to weigh ten pounds. Shevi looked it over and wondered how she would ever eat all of it, but she conjured the most gracious smile she could manage, thinking only of the moment when she convinced Mr. and Mrs. Turney to take up Jackson's cause, perhaps while being fitted into her bridal armor or during the bid day festivities. She caught her mother looking down on her. She looked at Shevi's plate and at her own with an odd sadness that made Shevi feel like she couldn't do anything right.

She took the plate to the long dining table where the other family members were gathering and taking seats. A cousin took the one empty seat to Cole's right. He glanced back at her, looked down at the ruddy boy beside him, and returned his attention to his food. Shevi submitted herself to the far end of the table where the younger mothers and their little ones sat. Mom followed her, and so did Leah.

Leah had been appointed Shevi's companion, a sort of chaperone to manage her and make sure she did what was expected, like eating all her food and staying away from the wrong sorts of people.

Shevi ate quietly and with all the ambition she could muster. Her mom picked at her plate. Around them the young mothers struggled to get their little ones to eat properly. A little girl about three years old fought with her mother about eating her eggs.

Leah called down the table to her. "Sue, you don't want to end up like Shevi, do you?" When the little girl looked at Shevi and opened her mouth for the bite, Leah said, "I didn't think so."

Sue chewed and glared at Shevi as if she were responsible not only for the ultimate leverage against her own freewill but all the things she didn't like about the eggs.

Shevi paced herself through breakfast, hoping that her food

would settle as she ate and make room for more of the bounty Leah had served her, or that she would run out of time and just have to leave some of it. Across the table Leah shoveled in eggs and biscuits and alternated drinks of milk and juice between bites. Her eyes regularly bobbed between Shevi's mouth and plate, offering a not so subtle message that Shevi's performance was under close observation. At Shevi's elbow Mom's plate was almost empty, until Mrs. Turney came by with a serving tray and heaped more food on it.

"You need to gain a few pounds too, dear," the matriarch said. "Set a good example for the next generation, hmm?"

"Perhaps," Mom said cordially.

"Perhaps?" Mrs. Turney reprimanded. "Of course!"

Mom put a small bite in her mouth, chewed carefully under their hostess's surveillance, and, when the woman didn't move on, said, "I wonder if the diet we eat is altogether a good idea."

Mrs. Turney's laugh began as a kind of cough and rose to a red-faced cackle. Shevi and Mom swapped looks of regret as the family members still at the table looked to see what was so funny.

The patriarch asked down the full length of the table, "What is it, dear?"

"Well," his wife replied, "Jo doubts the virtue of these, our many blessings."

The big man leaned on his elbows. "Really?" The hard look he put on Shevi's mom made Shevi wish the demand warning horn would sound. Where was it? On Wheel Three it would have blown an hour ago already. "Why is that, Jo?"

"Oh, I don't know," Mom said and shifted in her chair.

Mr. Turney's attitude turned as serious as death. "If we are going to produce energy, we must consume it in equal quantities. You understand that, don't you?"

"Yes. Yes, sir," Mom said. "But who has room for the suggested vegetables on top of all the other stuff. Right? What about a balanced diet?"

"Ha!" Mr. Turney bellowed. His progeny laughed, echoing their patriarch. "We need fuel, not roughage. We're not cattle. We are the very heart of the corporation, and the kingdom to come, like the president said at the wedding—in case you happened to hear." He pushed back his chair and rose, casting the factuality of his declaration into the air with his noble brow. He looked up and down the table. "Finish up, you hearts of the kingdom."

Affirmations rose from the mouths and hands between him and Shevi's mom. No one looked their way; it seemed that they had been rendered nonexistent by the speech. Perry managed to snort and shake his head. He gave them a rueful glance before pushing back his chair and standing. Across the table Leah smirked as she fed a stack of sausages onto the tines of her fork. Shevi fought the urge to give Mom back the look of disappointment, but she shortly failed. Shevi wasn't sure if it was good to have some of the heat off herself or if this was just a new source of scorn.

Mr. Turney marched down the table. Shevi hoped he would just ignore them as he left the dining hall, but he honored them with one last sidelong glance then exchanged a grunt of contempt with his wife. Shevi ate more heartily now, and, as if finally satisfied or perhaps offering a reward, Leah scraped the last of her gravy into her mouth and took leave of her ward. The table quickly cleared— even Perry left without a word to the women of his family—leaving

Shevi and her mother to finish their quotas alone. But the instant the last person was gone, Shevi rose and took her plate to the trashcan. She left her mother picking aimlessly at her food.

Shevi was on the way up the grand stairway to arm herself with chainmail and her rotor for the day's walk when one of the tiny maids answered the door. Shevi recognized the voice right away. It was the horrible little man with the awful Duel Wheel at the Stendahl bachelor party.

"The missus is preparing for her day," the maid said crossly. "She's a walking woman, you know."

"I have very good news, dearest."

"Give it to me. I have a breakfast mess to clean up."

"Tell her that the matter of the Dim boy has been taken care of."

"The matter of the Dim boy?" the maid asked. "And she'll know what matter that is?"

"Most likely," Mr. Myrtle said sarcastically. "Tell her he's been removed from the picture permanently. The Turney family'll have no more trouble with *him*."

"Thank you. I'll pass it along." She began to close the door.

"Tell them Mr. Myrtle took care of it."

"Yes. I'll do that." She pushed the door a few more inches.

"Be sure you do. Mr. Myrtle."

"Yes. Yes." The maid slammed the door and turned. She looked up at Shevi and sneered at her. "None of your business, I'm sure."

Shevi turned and kind of swam up the stairs, wondering what they had done to Jackson, sure what she heard was a mistake—if not, then how was she supposed to recruit their support? It couldn't be. It was just the one more thing she had to do: get

Jackson free. Not because she *loved* him, but because it was the right thing to do. And she'd have to have their help; if not theirs then whose? But if they were . . . responsible . . . Shevi pushed open the door to the third-floor apartment she and her mother and brother had been moved into, looking forward to a few minutes of quiet, alone time only to find herself facing Leah, her appointed companion. Armor was strewn across the couch and chair backs—breast plates, helmets, gauntlets, and chausses made of thick leather covered with steel rings, chainmail, and actual steel plates. All were rusty and worn, but they were actual shaped pieces of armor, not just scraps of Carbon Nation machines—the kind of stuff the Iron-clads in the front rows wore, the elite.

Leah glanced lovingly at the assortment and sighed. "Sorry about the condition of it. Can't let you tear up any more of the good stuff." She hoisted up a long-tailed shirt of the densest chainmail Shevi had ever seen. "Let's try this on you. Mother says your appetite will increase when you're carrying more weight. She says you could go two-fifty, three hundred if you took care of yourself."

"I need to use the restroom," Shevi said. She felt bloated after the breakfast Leah had forced on her.

"Aren't you diapered?"

"Not yet."

"Silly girl. I forget how middle class you are. We carry that weight on the wheel."

"You mean . . ."

"What's the point in eating if you're just going to leave it all in the toilet?"

Shevi offered an apologetic smile, not sure if the girl was trying to pay her back for the little brawl they'd had the night before or was actually that crazy. "Excuse me," she said and walked around her to the back of the apartment.

"Suit yourself," Leah called after her. In a mockingly quiet voice she said, "You can take the girl out of the Gut, but that doesn't give her class."

Shevi worked miserably at ignoring Leah who preached from the living room about the value to the *kingdom* of every ounce the Ironclads could bring to the wheel. When she had her diaper and clothes on, she stood in front of the mirror. Her focus reached back into the depths of the glass far beyond her own robust figure, searching for a clue how she could rescue Jackson. She had to find a way. She had to find out what the disgusting little man meant and whether or not her future in-laws were responsible for the injustice. If she didn't, it would eat a hole right through her. She was sure it would. She took a deep breath, refocused on herself for one second, then left the sanctity of the bathroom to return to her guardian peer.

Leah loaded her down with more than fifty extra pounds of armor. The hauberk, a chainmail shirt, that hung to Shevi's knees was only the beginning. The gauntlets she chose were leather with steel cable ribbing. The greaves she strapped around Shevi's calves almost matched but had fat steel rings on them that rattled with each step.

As she sashed the waist of the hauberk with a hefty steel chain that wrapped around Shevi about six times, she said, "This is so much fun." Her cheeks bunched into big round mounds as she smiled up at Shevi and clasped the belt with a twist of wire. She turned back to the couch. "Which breastplate do you think?"

"Do I have to wear one?"

Leah turned a hard look on her. "Do you have to be difficult about everything?" She grabbed the heaviest looking one off the couch and raised it high over Shevi's head.

Shevi's mom opened the apartment door and peered inside at the goings on. Shevi could only offer a pleading look.

Holding the great breastplate aloft as if offering it to a god, Leah said, "Oh, good. You're next, Jo. Get ready."

Shevi pointed to a lighter one. "How about that?"

Leah smiled, first at Mom as she slipped past to the back of the apartment and then at Shevi, the proud tutor who had finally seen the light of understanding dawn in her underling's eyes. She obliged and traded for Shevi's choice then again offered Shevi the chance to select from the four sets of pauldron for her shoulders. Shevi chose a set of cup-shaped metal that seemed to be made of the thinnest material. Leah smiled knowingly.

"You'll build up," she said. "Both of you will. Mother will see to it." She bellowed toward the back room, "Jo, are you ready?"

Mom stepped reluctantly from the back hall.

Leah said, "You're thin as a wire, but we'll fix that. For you I recommend this lovely segmentata." She hefted the top made of overlapping strips of leather and decorated with steel rings.

While Shevi watched, Mom allowed Leah to cinch the laces up its front. The thing was form fit to a woman's torso but a torso much larger than Mom's. She looked like a clapper dangling inside a bell.

Leah stood back to examine her and clucked her tongue. "It'll be better when Mother has put some weight on you. She's a supreme dietitian, you know, as is the duty of the Ironclad matriarch. She'll rid you of those silly notions of yours."

There were chains and straps and buckles. Leah stepped back and admired her work. She clapped and giggled, then turned back to Shevi.

"Where's your rotor?"

Shevi plodded to her bedroom and hung the thing around her neck. Filled with the enormous breakfast and now covered in heavy cladding, she staggered out the door between her mother and her appointed guardian. The family was in the great room and foyer. Children were off to school. Adults were suited up and ready to board the wheel. Mrs. Turney was giving each of them their daily provisions in backpacks. She looked at the trio coming down the stair.

"Wonderful," she said and initiated a round of applause. "Now here's your packs. I hope it's enough."

Shevi lifted the backpack onto her shoulders and fastened the dashboard in the front. Big bottles of drink dangled on each side of her rotor. She looked up at Mrs. Turney, wanting desperately to ask what part they'd had to do with Jackson's incarceration. The woman returned her curious glance.

"Something else you need, dear?"

"No," Shevi said.

Now wasn't the time and here wasn't the place. The matriarch looked at Cole and tilted her head toward Shevi. Cole forced a smile and came to Shevi's side. He offered his arm. She accepted.

Mr. Turney beamed at them and clapped his son on the shoulder as they passed him.

"Ah, the bidding will be ferocious," he said.

Chapter

Twenty

Thanks to all the weight Leah had loaded on her, Shevi walked higher on the wheel than she ever had. It just didn't seem that it should make that much difference. Walking was still putting one foot in front of the other and keeping pace with the moving tread. In the back rows where the tread's angle was shallow, it had seemed that the wheel moved of its own will, magically, like the earth spinning in space. But up higher, where every step was higher, and with all the armor pulling her down, gravity pressed on her while the wheel resisted.

Leah was right by her side, having resigned her right to a place three rows higher. She sighed and declared it another cost of grooming a girl from the Gutter for an Upper Crust family.

Glancing cautiously at the short, round girl, Shevi pulled the novel Jackson had rented to her out of her pack and with it some of the jerky and cheeses and bread Mrs. Turney packed—the exertion was eating at her breakfast like a pack of wolves on a fresh kill.

With the cheese and bread on her dashboard, she took a bite of jerky and opened *The Great God, Mann* to her bookmark, stealing another glance at her warden. But still Leah didn't seem to mind one way or the other about the book. She obviously didn't relate it to the problem of Shevi's "affair". Shevi ate a few bites while Mr. Mann's poor valet lit the burner on the propane stove to make west breakfast for his master. Mr. Mann was a scrammer, a trillionaire who lived two lives, one in Indonesia and the other in Venezuela. After dinner in one place, as the sun set, Randall Mann and his entourage would climb aboard his scramjet and fly it halfway around the planet to have breakfast in the other only two hours later.

Someone interrupted the valet's frying of eggs with a tap on Shevi's gauntlet. She looked up expecting to see Leah's naturally frowning face glaring up at her, but instead she found another round face, this one adorned with a smile as broad as it was honest—and it was a very broad smile, frog-like.

"Hi. I'm Alice," the girl said. "My brother is a friend of Cole's and I was just wondering if you wanted to come over to our spot." She pointed across the wheel.

Shevi found a group of girls her own age leaning forward, fanned out like a hand of cards, watching her. They gave her big waves and smiles. She examined them carefully. They reminded her of Stacey and Tasha. She didn't miss her old Wheel Three acquaintances—she'd never consider them friends again—not even the way they were before Mom lost her rotor at the gambling tables and Jackson showed up with his crate of books. She could see one of them being as hypocritical as Stacey and another as manipulative as Tasha. But she could also see one of them being a window she just might be able to escape through, the excuse to go out, a reason she could be gone for long periods of time.

Beside her, Leah cleared her throat but didn't look their way.

Shevi said, "What was that, Leah?"

Leah said, "What? Oh. Hi, Alice. How are you?"

"Fine," the girl said. "I just wanted to invite Shevi over to walk with us."

"You know my name," Shevi said.

"Of course," Alice said. "You're the one who landed Cole." She glanced back at her little posse.

Shevi followed her gaze again and found them all still staring and smiling excitedly. Back at Leah she said, "I think I will."

"Uh, yes," Leah said. "It's okay."

Leah was like cobwebs stretched across the darkness: she couldn't have held Shevi back but certainly had the power to annoy her. Without acknowledging Leah's approval, Shevi stepped out of line and sidled along after Alice down to where the other girls waited.

"Here she is," Alice said, presenting Shevi to them. "This is Bangle, Sally, Cleo, and Moxie." She pointed to each down the line.

Shevi walked half sideways in front of them, trying unsuccessfully to keep from banging her pack into the packs and children on the backs of walkers in the next row. A little girl with wispy brown hair frowned down at her. All the girls beamed brightly and offered handshakes, all except Cleo. Shevi hugged Jackson's book tightly against her engagement rotor and put the jerky down on her dashboard between the cupholders, freeing up a hand to shake with. At the end of the line, Cleo's smile was a tight draw of her lips and her bright blue eyes took no part in it. The other girls wore unfortunately obvious body suits; Moxie and Bangle had plenty of hips and thighs but were sadly lacking up top. Sally's suit was full-body. Shevi was impressed that she could manage walking this far up on the wheel, but she was tall and apparently strong boned, just unable to rack up any body mass. Alice was short and round like Leah, but Cleo was tall and evenly built like Shevi, a beautiful girl and excellent walking stock. Shevi wondered what family she was from.

"What are you reading?" Bangle asked, craning her neck to see the cover of the book.

Shevi handed it to her. "*The Great God, Mann.* I got it from a vender on Wheel Three. He had some great stuff. Reading is a great way to pass the time while you're walking." Bangle had already opened the book and she and Sally had their heads together reading it, so Shevi turned back to Alice. "I wouldn't have even gotten on the wheel one day if it hadn't been for him. And then there was this horrible wheel in the cellars and they put this man inside and spun him and I tried to tell the Guard about it but they wouldn't listen and then Jackson showed up and told them they were pirating power off the wheel so that got them—"

Shevi suddenly realized how fast and loud she was talking and that everyone around her was listening. The mother of the girl with the wispy brown hair had turned almost completely around, as had people two and three rows up. She'd come uncorked. She'd finally gotten more than ten feet from Leah and . . .

She leaned forward to check on her warden, but it wasn't necessary. The round girl's petulant frown was turned upon her like a crescent moon at midday.

"I'm sorry," she said to no one in particular and ducked into ranks.

The row began to shuffle, sending fear of Leah's approach coursing through Shevi's body. But the change was happening on her other side. Bangle and Sally were drifting away, taking Jackson's book with them. Moxie came up from the clan's far end and nestled in the row beside Shevi.

"Hi," she said. "Welcome to Wheel Six."

"Hi," Shevi said. "Thanks." In want of something beyond a mere reciprocal, Shevi said, "It's nice to be here," though that wasn't true at all; she was too far from Jackson and too useless to him on this wheel.

"That's nice," Moxie said. "Did you come over alone?"

"No. That's my mom right up there and my brother over there." Shevi pointed and Moxie glanced and nodded.

"Wow, your mom looks good," Moxie said, "like you. What about your dad?"

"Moxie," Alice scolded from Shevi's other side.

Shevi said, "It's okay. He died several years ago."

"I told you that," Alice said, leaning forward to glare at Moxie.

"My dad died, too," Moxie said, ignoring Alice. "Cleo's, too."

"I'm sorry," Shevi said while Alice ejected a long sigh.

"Me too," Moxie said, then she leaned forward and without drawing a breath said, "Well he did and I know you told us but you didn't tell her and it's something we have in common so just let us have it and stop keeping her all to yourself."

"I'm *sorry*," Alice said. "*I* went and got her."

"But you should share."

"Fine then. Take her."

"No. She's okay right here. Besides, Cleo doesn't want her down there anyway."

"*Moxie!*" Alice barked.

Bangle and Sally looked up from their reading.

Quickly, Shevi said, "So, what happened to your fathers?"

"The thrombosis, they said. Mine died six months ago right before he weighed in and Cleo's actually died on the wheel. Just fell right onto his face." She pointed over and up, somewhere between Perry's place on the wheel and Mr. Turney's. Then she swept her hand down and back behind them. "He went right like that. And up the back side."

Alice said, "Moxie, *please!*"

"Well, he did."

"When?" Shevi asked.

"Right after my dad."

"Is that why Cleo doesn't want to talk to me? Still too fresh, and I remind her of it?"

"No," Moxie said. "That's because of Cole."

"Moxie, put a loaf in it," Alice said.

Beyond Moxie and the two readers, Cleo leaned forward and stared at Shevi before breaking ranks and sidling across the rolling tread. She elbowed Moxie into Bangle as she passed.

"Hi. I'm Cleo Vanderbilt," she said, sticking a hand aggressively toward Shevi.

Shevi took it and shook it. "Shevi Lilbourn."

Cleo's expression changed to say, well, obviously. "I am in love with your fiancé." She stared into Shevi's eyes while the declaration soaked in.

"Oh," Shevi said, her gaze bouncing from Moxie to Bangle to Sally. Then she turned and checked Alice who only shrugged and nodded.

"But he, unfortunately," Cleo went on when Shevi turned back to her, "is my cousin."

"Oh," Shevi said. It seemed to be the only word left in her lexicon.

"Some number removed," Cleo said. She held up splayed finger and began ticking them off. "My mother is his mother's aunt—or something like that. I don't know. But the mayor refused to grant us our betrothal. So, there. Best wishes and all that."

Shevi swallowed hard and turned to Alice again. Alice only shrugged, holding out her hands in complete candor.

Moxie said, "There. We have all that behind us now and we can get on with other things."

"Thank you, Moxie," Cleo declared, "for *all* of your efforts."

"Not a problem," Moxie said cheerfully, either oblivious to or in spite of Cleo's sarcasm. Shevi honestly couldn't tell if she was dense or just that much of a genius.

"So," Cleo said, giving Moxie a long hard look before turning an appraising glare on Shevi, "you got any more books in there?"

"No. Just the one."

"So—this Jackson, guy—this is the Dim you fell for?"

"You know about that?"

"Honey, when one of us falls for one of them it's way more than just a scandal. It's legend."

"Yeah," Moxie said, leaning forward again to peer around Cleo's towering figure and unwrapping a large, juicy sandwich. "It's like that movie where the Dim tries to break up the Ironclad couple."

"Jackson didn't try—"

"Leave it alone, girls," Alice said. "I didn't bring her down here so you could walk all over her."

Cleo laid a hand on Shevi's arm. "Shevi, they're always trolling for us."

"They should show that movie again," Moxie said through a mouth full of bread and meat. "It was *really* good."

"Maybe I'll suggest that," Cleo said.

"Cleo's family owns eight cinema wheels," Moxie said.

Cleo unloaded a sandwich from her own pack but paused short of taking a bite. She looked over at Shevi. "You're lucky."

"How?"

"You learned your lesson about Dims *before* you got married."

Shevi wanted to say she didn't like calling them Dims or hearing others call them that. She wanted to say that Jackson was the most amazing person she'd ever met and that he had not been "trolling" for her. But she picked up her jerky and took a bite. How would she go against such a current? It would be like turning around and walking up the backside of the wheel and expecting to start it spinning the other way.

Shevi woke to an eerie silence. She knew right away she was alone. The apartment was never that quiet. If Perry was there he would either be snoring or stomping. If Mom was there—Shevi listened— well, Mom wouldn't be making a lot of noise but the place wouldn't be this dead. As she sat up the muscles in her legs complained about the day before. More weight and higher on the wheel was haunting her. She stood up and crept into the hall.

"Mom? Perry?"

Just in case . . .

But—sure enough—no answer. She was alone. She inhaled. It felt good. But it was laced with the fear that Leah or Mrs. Turney or Hester would come lurching out of any doorway at her, thrusting armor and food upon her. Then she realized how hungry she was. She had cleaned out her backpack the day before and had no problem pleasing the matriarch of the Turney family at dinner last night. The day's walk had turned out pleasant—after the issue of Jackson was behind them. A couple of boys from two rows back tried to wheedle into the group, mainly interested in Cleo and Shevi, of course, according to Alice. Then Moxie joined in reading with Bangle and Sally and made them let her start back at the beginning. Late in the day Sally asked right out loud what gasoline was. That started a discussion among the nearby adults. The grand-father of the wispy haired girl wanted to know just exactly what kind of trashy novel they were reading. It had been fun and Shevi looked forward to doing it again, to being back in a group of friends that she could have good times with.

She pulled on some clothes and went to the balcony that overlooked the great room and foyer. The scents of breakfast washed over her and with them the sounds of the family talking and clattering dishes. If she wasn't mistaken, these were the sounds of the meal well underway. There was just that bit more of silverware scraping plates than words exchanged. She hurried down the stairs, wondering why Mom hadn't roused her, figuring she was in a whole new flavor of deep trouble.

She rounded the corner into the dining hall and found the table full, as she had expected. Everyone was there, except Cole. Two chairs were empty, one to Mrs. Turney's right and one to her left.

"There she is," Mrs. Turney sang in a voice sweet with surprise. "Someone get Cole."

Two young boys from her end of the table jumped up, each shouting dibs on him. Laughter drifted around the table. The matriarch rose and came at Shevi with open arms. Shevi's mother sat beside one of the empty seats on Mrs. Turney's end of the table. Her expression was happy but ambivalent. Perry turned around and smirked at her, his mouth stuffed with breakfast. Mrs. Turney swept her arms around Shevi and hugged her. Shevi froze. The woman towed her to the buffet.

"We've made some special treats for you on your special day."

"Special day?" Shevi asked.

The woman handed her an empty plate and lost some of the joy from her face. "It's your bid day, dear. You know that."

"Oh," Shevi said. "Yes. Of course."

Shevi didn't know—hadn't thought about it, could remember it being mentioned, had managed to put it away somewhere in the back of her mind's closet. It wasn't something middle class people did. Some of the Terrace dwellers mentioned it, but it was more of a show than an actual bid between wheel bosses to secure the weight of a new couple for their wheel. As newcomers to the Terraces of Wheel Three, their short life there before Shevi's dad died, they had been invited to a bid day, but only Mr. Halsted the wheel boss of Three had been there; it wasn't like any actual bidding had taken place. The couple didn't move to a different wheel for better pay.

The matriarch smiled. "Of course." She laid the foundation of Shevi's special breakfast, two gigantic pancakes. A full layer of syrup went down on the cakes and sausage patties of equal diameter went on next like bricks on a bed of mortar. Disks of egg. Another layer of cake. Syrup. Sausage. She looked up from her architecture to give Shevi another smile before repeating the process twice more.

Around Shevi, members of the family gave their dirty dishes to maids and filtered out to make the last preparations for their day on the wheel. All except Leah. She took her place at Shevi's side, followed her back to the table and took the seat beside her. Shevi began her assault on the fortress Mrs. Turney had constructed for her. Leah watched, as if daring her not to eat every bite.

Mrs. Turney had just settled back into her chair when she rebounded and said, "There you are, dear. No, no. Let me." She hustled away.

Shevi watched her go and found Cole at the buffet with a plate in his hand. The matriarch snatched it away and set to work on another palatial construction to match Shevi's. She shooed him away toward Shevi and he complacently obeyed. Shevi watched him come to her. He watched her eyes as carefully as she watched his. He sat down across from her beside her mother and Shevi found herself concentrating on her mother whose eyes clicked left and right expectantly. Shevi drew in a breath, held it, and reached across the table to take her betrothed's hand. Cole seemed surprised by this. But he came around and did his part just in time for his mother to finish her work on his plate.

"You two are just the cutest," she said, setting the plate on the table in front of Cole. "Aren't they just the cutest couple, Jo?"

"Yes," Mom said dryly.

Mrs. Turney came back to the table with a large teacup for each of them. "What a day," she said. "What a big day." She wrinkled up her round cheeks, a smile disappearing behind her teacup as she raised it. She took a long sip.

Heavy footsteps sounded across the room. Mr. Turney came in dressed in full armor and ready to walk. He came up behind Shevi and put a hand on each of her shoulders. "Ladies, enjoy yourselves." He patted Shevi lovingly as he let out a great sigh. "Son, just go along with your mother. It's just for the day."

"Yes, Dad," Cole said.

The big man laughed. "It's a big day," he said. "For all of us. Bid day." He chuckled. "Goodbye, Mother. Go easy on him."

"He will be appointed properly and proudly," she declared.

Her husband laughed and leaned toward his wife who stood and did the same. Their large middles spanned the table's corner like storm clouds across the horizon. They kissed and he marched from the room.

Shevi sawed off a wedge from one of her stacks and forced her mouth around it. She chewed quickly and, when she had finally downed the bite, said, "Is it too late to invite more guests?"

Mrs. Turney had taken her seat and was about to take another sip of tea. She looked surprised. "To the wedding?" she asked.

"Well, yes," Shevi said. "And to the bidding."

"To the bidding?" Mrs. Turney sat her cup on the table. "That's a bit rushed. Who did you have in mind?"

"The girls I walked with yesterday. Alice and Moxie and Bangle and—"

"And Cleo," Leah interrupted, rousing wide eyes from the matriarch.

"And Sally," Shevi finished, pretending to ignore the exchange. Cole's attention plunged to his plate. Shevi's mother snatched up her teacup and nestled it against her lips, watching thoughtfully.

"Well," Mrs. Turney drawled, "we'll have to see about that. Leah, can you see about that?" Special instructions were implied in her eyes and tone.

"Yes," Leah said decisively.

Shevi heard in this the affirmation that she'd make sure not to invite the distant cousin, so she said, "Of course Cleo will be there. She's family, right?" Cole's face was frozen, a big wad of food bulging his cheek. Shevi chopped off another bite, stabbed it with the tines of her fork, lifted it to her mouth and said, "I think she'd make a lovely maid of honor." She shoved the bite triumphantly into her mouth and watched eyes widen and faces color as she chewed. She fought back a smile but lost when she saw the curiosity in her mother's eyes as she peeked over the rim of her cup.

Mrs. Turney lifted her cup now and commenced another long

and thoughtful sip. Cole was chewing again, slowly and carefully, more constructive than chewing ought to be. Leah stood up from her chair but didn't leave her place. She stared down at her mother who stared back over her cup.

Slowly, she pulled the cup away from her mouth and placed it on the table. "Actually, I assumed Leah would fill that position."

Mom sat her cup down. "Shevi should decide, though. I'm sure."

"What about a friend from Wheel Three?" Mrs. Turney asked diplomatically.

Shevi attacked the breakfast stack again, shaking her head. "I'm finished with that wheel," she said. "Moving on. Not looking back."

"But the Wheel Three boss could win the bid this evening. What then?" the matriarch pondered.

"We don't have to go with the highest bidder, do we?" Shevi asked. She looked at Cole who was in the process of overstuffing his mouth, even for a teen Ironclad.

"Well, no," Mrs. Turney said. "But you shouldn't burn your bridges like that."

"I'm not burning them," Shevi said, stuffing her own mouth full and speaking through the conglomeration. "I'm just not waving to anybody on the other side."

"Well, it's decided then," Mom said. "Cleo will be Shevi's maid of honor."

"And they'll all be at the bidding tonight," Shevi finished triumphantly. She managed to consume another bite of the matriarch's twin towers of breakfast.

The mood changed quickly after Shevi's breakfast triumph. Cole sat wide-eyed. His eyes gleamed with anticipation, as if a special treat might be brought in at any second. Mrs. Turney had resumed her sullenness toward Shevi. Her eyes flashed with accusation and suspicion. Shevi was glad she overheard strange little Mr. Myrtle's conversation with the maid. Had she not, she would have never crossed the woman, and, right now, as she was fit into her bid day outfit, would be lobbying on Jackson's behalf, not knowing the Turney's themselves were responsible for Jackson's situation. Shevi would be wheedling and begging and striving for something from these people, making a fool of herself and would probably still do nothing but make the woman angry. As it stood this morning, she managed that, but on her own terms and for her own end. She didn't have a clear picture of what that end was. Maybe Cole would decide he wanted too much to be with Cleo and would do something to take the heat off Shevi. Hopefully, Shevi's connection to the girls of Wheel Six would give her the cover she needed to help Jackson herself.

Mrs. Turney poked at Shevi's side. "Not enough meat on you. You'll never get a decent bid. We can just hope Mr. Stendahl will do the family a favor and make you a reasonable offer for Wheel Six."

The proper dress for a couple on their bid day was a snug fitting outfit that showed their true bodies. No body suits. No armor. They wore matching white, which Shevi believed looked better against her dark skin and hair than with Cole's complexion; it magnified the orange in his hair and paled his sand colored skin, bringing out his freckles. He'd definitely lost whatever luster she'd seen in him before. But it had been traded in for pity now that she knew he wasn't getting who he wanted in this marriage arrangement. He looked at her and smiled uncomfortably, and she knew now that it wasn't the apologetic smile she'd always thought it was, the one a high class guy gives his middle class girl when she's out in deeper water than she's accustomed to. She thought about every time he'd looked at her, with or without that uncomfortable smile, and understood that he was seeing consolation, not accomplishment. She would always be the one he got stuck with. Cleo would always be the one he really wanted. It explained a lot about the gap that had always been between them, the distance that Shevi always related to class differences. She appreciated her own value now that she knew about Cleo.

Mrs. Turney huffed and prodded some more, then she waved Shevi away disgustedly. "Oh, just go take it off. It makes you look like nothing but a rack of bones."

"Mom," Cole reprimanded. His mother shot him a sharp look. "She looks fine."

Who's his favorite person now? Shevi couldn't hold back a grin.

Mrs. Turney said, "You're the one who looks fine. My son." Her voice resonated with pride. Shevi glanced back and watched the woman lay her hands on his bulging waistline. "Look at you—the picture of health."

She turned away quickly and ran into the back room to peal the clinging fabric from her body. She changed out of her bid day suit and into a loose gown. She brought the suit back to Mrs. Turney who snatched it away and said, "Now just go and try not to get any skinnier today. We'll be going to Stendahl's for bridal armor fitting at two. Just go sit or something."

Out of the corner of her eye she saw Leah watching her, the way a predator sizes up its next meal. There'd be no saving Jackson today; running out and trying on her own would only lead to a tightened grip.

Mom looked devastated. "I'm sorry, dear," she whispered.

"Don't be," Shevi said. "It's fine. Let's go."

"Where?"

"Well, you can do whatever you want with our time off, since you don't have a companion," Shevi said. "But I know what I want to do."

Mom followed along as Shevi ran up the stairs to their apartment. She sprang open the door and ran to her bedroom where Jackson's big novel waited for her. She hadn't gotten it back until the end of the shift the day before and didn't want to wait to get back on the wheel to see what happened to the poor exhausted valet as he continued his daily circumnavigation of the world. Randall Mann, who would make a perfect Ironclad, just kept getting meaner. He had started out manipulating and controlling people on both sides of the planet but had turned to murder. And the pitiful little valet secretly knew all about it. Shevi lay down on her bed, conserving her energy as the matriarch had requested, and fell back into the story.

Mom came to the open bedroom door and looked inside. Shevi looked up from the open pages. The two studied one another for a moment. Mom broke the silence between them.

"I'm going out."

Shevi nodded.

"Anything I can get you?"

Shevi thought of asking her to check on Jackson but figured that would only make matters worse. Mom cocked her head, sensing her daughter did have a request. She figured that her mother might just humor her, out of pity if nothing else, but haste makes waste, slow is fast, and all that. Best to wait. Best to see what she could manage with her newfound girlfriends. She shook her head.

"Sure?" Mom inquired.

Shevi nodded. "I just want to read."

"Okay," Mom said. "It's going to be okay." They studied one another for another long moment. "You'll see."

"Yeah," Shevi said, and backed it up with a significant nod. "Yeah, I guess it will."

"Enjoy your book," Mom said.

"Yeah," Shevi said, but didn't look back down at the open pages until her mother yielded and turned away.

Then Shevi immersed herself back into the pages, into the hospital in Venezuela where the big bad man kept getting meaner as his health and control of his world deteriorated. But as she read his treachery, implications in the story began to tickle the back of her mind, causing bumps to rise on her skin and a troubling notion to swell inside her.

Chapter

Twenty-one

Tired and hungrier than he had ever been, Jackson moved with the flow of his row from the wheel's moving tread onto the offramp—the end of his first-ever day of walking. He was exhausted but invigorated. He might be in jail, but he was a contributor to society rather than a growth on it.

A team of guards unshackled the inmates one by one and sent them down to the showers. With the others, Jackson and his dad stripped down, washed off, and pulled on another tight body suit, sans diaper.

They ate dinner standing up, shoulder to shoulder as they had been on the wheel. The biscuits were dry but served with a thick brine that made them absolutely heavenly to eat—devour was a better word to describe the way they all went about it. Strands of meat in the brine were like icing on a cake. A bell rang indicating the end of dinner and again Jackson and his dad followed along to a too big room so full of cots it reminded Jackson of the tight winding of wire around the outside of an induction generator.

But the manager was there just inside the doorway. He pointed at Jackson and Dad. "You two. This way." He waved them to follow, turned and walked away with startling confidence—orders had been issued, orders would be followed, no need to verify.

Jackson looked around. No one seemed to care as long as it didn't keep them from their cots. Those cots looked as inviting now as the brine and biscuits had when his stomach had been empty.

The manager led them through a maze, first of wire fences then of narrow passages between dirty transparent walls, to a large tired looking door. When they passed through it the world abruptly changed. The sounds and smells of the jail were gone. The place was dark and solid and quiet with a subtle bitter smell. Jackson felt his dad's arm brush up against his. He glanced over his shoulder. Dad's eyes were wide.

The manager pushed open a door and light flooded out. "You, in there." He flicked a finger quickly from Jackson's dad to the space beyond the door.

It was a sick bay or a clinic. There were cots and carts and curtains. A group of men looked up from a huddle in the far corner. One of them smiled and stepped out of the cluster. It was the Secretary of Electricity. Jackson stared at the man with such overwhelming wonder that he jumped and almost squealed when the man spoke.

"Ah, there he is. Our first candidate."

"What is this?" Dad asked.

"You wanted the formula," the manager said. "Go get it." He waved toward the open door impatiently.

Jackson checked Dad but turned his attention immediately back to the group inside the room. He didn't recognize two of them, but only two of them. The others included President Burgess, Prince Tyler, Prince Jasper and Mr. Myrtle himself, arrayed today in pink and purple with a tall but soft hat that perched atilt on his head like some kind of poisonous mushroom. Jackson locked eyes with the imp until one of the two strangers said, "Is that our little vamper?" Jackson glanced away from Mr. Myrtle to look at who had spoken but not without seeing the concerned way Mr. Myrtle did the same.

"Yes, sir, Warden Kelso," Mr. Myrtle spewed. "That's him, sir. That's the one. But, sirs, with all due respect, if I may, I'd like to just say that the thing that he did isn't necessarily and completely the fault of Mr. Koss. Neither Mr. Koss. Neither the elder nor the younger Mr. Koss, sirs. But the problem is with their own overwhelming number who cannot walk for a living, who cannot make their own way and must feed off others and make their way as parasites to the great system you fine sirs have blessed us with. And I am certain that this new thing you're doing here today will alleviate much suffering and deter many others from following down this awful path." He had folded himself over into a bow as he spoke, holding his strange hat before him upside down, leaning upon the handle of the knocker rod Jackson had made for the deposit on the home they no longer needed. Jackson thought perhaps he intended to go ahead and give their butts a smooch while he was at it. "Thank you," he went on, "for your abundant blessings upon us." And he finished by giving Jackson a sidelong glance, which was a nonverbal yet perfectly conveyed admonition.

Jackson allowed the slightest hint of a smile to curl his lips while he lowered his eyelids the way a horse might do as it pins its ears back at some territorial violation. He wanted to ask him where he got that great walking stick. Was it perhaps a knocker rod? Oh, yes, he wanted to hear the man admit: this boy is quite talented at induction and invention. He'd make a great protégé for Sec Elec. And Jackson wouldn't be escorted to some special room for extra reformative discipline; he'd be off to Fluxton to begin a glorious internship under the great man. But that possibility would stop at the barred gates of Jackson's imagination.

The warden gave Mr. Myrtle a quick appraising glance as he walked past him. Jackson thought it might mean the warden didn't approve of the little man's brownnosing, but it also might have betrayed jealousy or envy. These management types were the greatest mysteries Jackson had ever come across. They almost always ended up seeming metaphysical in their behaviors.

"Come along, Jackson Koss, Vamper," the warden said. "Time for your debriefing."

Behind the approaching warden Jackson's dad had been about to hoist himself up onto one of the examination tables, but he stopped and called out to Jackson. Jackson waved him to go on then gave him a thumb's up and a grin, his eyes flashing toward Mr. Myrtle. Dad sat on edge of the table. He sighed and nodded to Jackson. He was content, for now.

Mr. Myrtle, however, wasn't feeling as good about Jackson's

"debriefing". He stumbled along behind the warden. "Perhaps I should accompany you, Warden Kelso."

"Not necessary," the warden tossed back over his shoulder.

"I'm somewhat of an expert with the Dims," Mr. Myrtle offered.

The warden didn't acknowledge but directed Jackson to go ahead of him farther down the hall. Jackson obeyed after giving Mr. Myrtle one quick lift of his eyebrows and a shrug. What could happen? They could torture him and make him tell them *who* had benefited the most from his vamping. He might not be able to help himself. Could he be blamed if they hung him upside down or threatened the soles of his feet with some hot instrument? Rumor had it that the warden had a solo backfeed wheel. If a prisoner didn't walk fast enough the current he produced was sent through his own body. Jackson wasn't sure how such a contraption would work, so he couldn't suppress the hope that he at least might see it.

He marched along in front of the warden, following the man's directions: right, then right again, then up the stairs, then the third door on the right, into a sparse office with a view out over the walking zone of the wheel, the on- and offramps, the eating area, and the dense glade of cots. The entire jail was visible from this location, and Jackson recognized the angle of view. He went to the glass and peered across the expanse to a narrow slot where the orthogonal structure clashed with the circularity of the wheel. That had been Jackson's vantage of the jailed inmates from Level 6. Had he gotten on his knees and tilted his head, he could have seen inside the warden's office. But then he stepped back and examined the glass and realized that it was a one-way mirror. He turned away from it to find Warden Kelso studying him in just the way he had been studying the glass.

"Sit, please," the warden said, offering him the chair that stood alone before a vast and uncluttered desk.

Jackson sat.

On the other side of the desk the warden did the same, never taking his eyes off Jackson. He settled into a chair much larger and more plush than the one Jackson occupied.

"It is an important part of our system to investigate ways and means of wrongdoing so we may deter such activity and thus reduce the numbers of the incarcerated," he said.

"But the jail wheel is the excitor generator, sir. Without the inmates, the main wheels wouldn't make any power because their fields wouldn't be charged." He watched the warden with anxious hope, still thinking that if he made a good impression he would be sent off to work for Sec Elec.

The warden sat back and eyed him. "You're not implying that we purposefully incarcerate people, are you?"

"Oh! No, sir."

"Good. That would not be a fair assessment of our methods."

"Yes, sir."

"Your crime is a very special crime. Do you understand this?"

"Yes, sir," Jackson said, thinking how it showed off his skills of handling electricity, the life force of Trintico Corporate Society, making him worthy of special training.

The warden narrowed his eyes. He looked hard across the desk at Jackson. His voice went deep and stern. "Your sentence is exceptionally light, young man. Do you understand this?"

Jackson pressed himself against the back of the chair. He

couldn't speak, could only nod in reply.

"Others have died for it, young man, either trying to do it or for getting caught afterward. Executed—by electrocution." The irony of that was not lost on Jackson. "The induction chair slides down a long shaft and collects current that goes through the convict's body. If he survives the first trip, they have to drag him back up to the top and send him down again. Ugly business. You're here only out of the gracious benevolence of our glorious president. You owe your very life to him henceforth, as all in the corporation do. You're too young to know anybody who lived through the hell before, the Wind-and-Water War, the chaos of the post-petro crash. Have you ever been to Shack Town or even looked down upon it?" Jackson nodded. "Well, young sir, that's heaven on earth compared to the apocalypse of the Crash. And all of this—" he offered the comforts of their immediate surrounding with upraised hands, "that we have a penal system and order of law, and food to eat, and fresh clean water—is the providence of His Majesty, *King* Merwin, a title he has yet to become comfortable with but so fully deserves. Now what I am telling you, boy, is that you will cooperate completely with me in every way as the benefactor of our leader's good grace. Now, you will tell me *how* you accomplished your act of vamping."

Jackson felt that the scale of reality had shifted between him and his surroundings, making his relative size to all other things around him terribly small. He pressed the soles of his feet against the carpet to prove that he hadn't shrunk so much that his little legs only dangled above the floor. The proof did nothing to reestablish him to his merely 'diminished' stature. He swallowed the hard lump in his throat and told himself that he still had a chance at showing his skills. He plunged into a full disclosure of what he had done and how he had done it, including a thorough description of his hot stick that kept him from getting fried when he'd prodded the wires into the fuse clamps. The warden sat and listened carefully and thoughtfully until Jackson mentioned the crate of books and sneaked toward an indictment of Mr. Myrtle. Here the warden cut him off with the cleanness of a razor's slice. None of that would go. Mr. Myrtle would not be named.

Jackson backed off, not letting himself become the fool angels would peer after, watching with morbid curiosity. He turned slightly and went about his conclusion from a different angle. "My friend found this party and my vamping—"

The warden cut him off again. "There was no such party discovered. Your *friend* was mistaken."

"There was ice." Jackson managed to lean forward in his chair, having regained his natural size with the telling of his skillfully executed albeit highly illegal accomplishment. Hope had sprouted new shoots that reached toward the light of the warden recognizing Jackson's potential beyond his diminutive class.

"Be a grateful beneficiary, young man. From whom have you received the most? From this *friend* who told you all these wild tales or from the Sovereignty?"

Jackson sighed and bowed his head. The wheels are turned step by step. Whatever Shevi had seen, whatever the Guard had found when they went to the cellars, whatever had happened, getting himself in deeper wouldn't help or change anything, not for the better anyway. Jackson stared down at the carpeted floor of the warden's office, wanting desperately to ask if the man had gleaned even a trace of Jackson's skills and abilities.

"You are dismissed," the warden said. "Go on back to the cots and get some sleep. You'll need it."

Jackson rose. "Yes, sir."

"We'll talk again soon."

"Yes, sir." Jackson turned away. And there it was again, his hope. Maybe then the warden would see beyond the thinness of his body and recognize the value of his mind. It was a malignancy, this hope. Uncle Blaine had been right. He had read too many books, stories that encouraged hope, stories in which some underdog or other rose above some challenge or other. Most of it was just made-up crap that could never happen.

His dad was waiting in the hall outside the sick bay or clinic or whatever it was. He turned to Jackson and met him halfway down the hall while a guard watched from the doors leading back into the jail proper. "What happened?" He took Jackson by the shoulders and forced eye contact. "What did he do?"

"We talked . . . about vamping." Jackson shrugged. "And about the graciousness of my sentence. And all that."

"That doesn't seem so bad then. What's wrong? You look like he gave you your death warrant."

"Nothing. It's just . . ." Jackson looked away from his father. It was just that the acrid truth of his gratuitous hope was dawning on him. He sidestepped his dad and they walked toward the exit of the Admin area. As they passed the sick bay door, Jackson's eyes were drawn to it like ball bearings to a magnet. He could hear the deep rumble of voices, the president and Sec Elec. At his core a spark ignited a flare of anger. It wasn't just that he hoped to rise above what he was for that sake in itself. It was *her*. "Nothing," he said. "What'd they do to you?"

"Gave me a shot," Dad said. "In and right back out again. They weighed me and checked some stuff. I think I was out here waiting for you longer than I was in there. I was worried sick."

"Sorry," Jackson said.

Dad put his arm around him. "Don't apologize. It wasn't your fault."

Wasn't it? Wasn't this whole mess the fault of Jackson's ambition? And why was he ambitious? What was he really striving for?

Her.

Maybe it was his mother, like his father before him. Or maybe it was Shevi. Or maybe it was just the dream of being worthy of someone like either of them. He looked at his father as they passed out of Admin. It had been different when he was young. Back then a small guy could still hope to get a decent place on a wheel and walk for a living to provide for a family, but not anymore.

They found their cots. Jackson's was fourth up right above his dad's. He climbed up into it. Whoever walked in his spot during the night must be big because the cot sagged and smelled of a body too big to get clean with the allotted time and water. Jackson flipped the pillow over and let his head drift down into it.

"Good night, Jackson," Dad said from the cot below.

"Good night," Jackson whispered.

He turned over and stared up at the sagging cot above him. The guy he had walked beside all day lay up there. Jackson figured he was probably already asleep. Most of the walkers were. But then the cot began to jiggle above him. The guy up there was doing something rhythmical, either having some kind of spasm or . . . Jackson cringed and rolled onto his side, pulling the pillow around his head. He tried not to think about *her*. Either of *them*. (Don't think about elephants. What are you thinking about? Elephants. Typical.)

He drifted toward sleep, thought he had made the journey completely, thought the sneering face looking down at him was Uncle Blaine—it had the same disgusted look about it. But then it spoke and what it said made too much sense for a face in a dream. "This is from Phipps."

As a hand reached down toward him, he understood that Uncle Blaine wasn't looking down on him in a dream. It was the man in the upper bunk. But it wasn't the man who had walked beside him on the wheel, who was supposed to be up there. It was somebody else. There was something in his hand. A knocker rod! It was one of the short ones the manager's sidekicks had carried. That's what the rhythmic motion had been, the charging of a knocker rod. The prongs jabbed toward Jackson. Opening his mouth to yell out, he flinched and drew back but not fast enough. The arc happened across the side of his neck, making it twist violently under the magic spell of electric current. His teeth bit down on the back of his tongue, sending a bolt of pain right behind the agony of electric shock.

The hand drew back but the face went on sneering. "There's more where that come from." The face disappeared beyond the edge of the bunk. The rhythmic shaking happened again, just long enough to recharge the knocker rod.

Jackson's body quivered in his cot. His neck ached. His tongue throbbed. He'd just made the first payment for displacing Phipps to a lower row on the jail wheel, even though that had been the manager's doing and not Jackson's own. Guys like Phipps weren't likely to be so rational when it came to revenge. And how many more payments would Jackson be looking at? Had Jackson's sentence just been bumped up to death? Had that been the manager's intent?

One sweet consolation soothed the pain of the heavy electric shock—he wasn't thinking about *her*. Or he hadn't been for a few seconds. But now that he'd realized he wasn't thinking about her, ironically, he was, by thinking about not thinking about her. An emotion rose from deep inside him. It sent a shudder through his body. He couldn't tell if he was laughing or crying. He just lay there and shook and made obscene little noises while tears came to his eyes and snot ran from his nose.

Chapter
Twenty-two

The only bid day event Shevi had ever been to was the little mock ball for the girl and boy from the Terraces of Wheel Three. The circumstance she found herself in now didn't relate in any way to that night. The venue was not a hall on the Club level, as it had been for the couple from the Terraces. Out of fairness to each of the wheel bosses, the event was held in a massive space a block off Electric Avenue opposite the entrance to Wheel Six behind the Stendahl armor dealership. It was called the Hangar and must have been five hundred feet in each direction. Strands of lights criss-crossed the space, the tiny bulbs making the ceiling look like the star-filled heavens.

Mrs. Turney responded to Shevi's awe at the space. "This is

where they made the windings for the wheels," she said.

"Oh," Shevi said, unable to manage more as she took in the grand stage. A long table for the wheel bosses took up the front middle of the stage. Nine chairs, one for each boss, faced a podium pressed against the back wall. A single scale with a platform large enough for two stood on the podium like a sentinel at the gates of Shevi's future.

The matriarch patted Shevi's hand. "You won't be up there alone, dear."

"No," Shevi said. "Of course not. Cole will be with me."

The big woman was beaming at Shevi one instant and then, after glancing beyond her, gave her a frightful glare. "Enjoy yourself. You only get one bid night." She whirled and went to her son, sliding her hand around his arm and guiding him away.

A second later Shevi wasn't surprised when someone grabbed her from behind. Mrs. Turney's agitated expression had been like a mirror telling her exactly who was behind her. She turned and found Alice, Moxie and Sally hovering expectantly behind Cleo.

"Oh, this is so exciting," Moxie squealed. "Thank you so much for inviting us."

"Of course," Shevi said. "You're my new best friends."

"That's sweet," Cleo said sardonically.

Shevi stared into the girl's big blue eyes, trying to see if all this actually offended Cleo or if she was enjoying the irony in any way. "Where's Bangle?"

Cleo rolled her eyes. "I'm sure she's still fretting herself into her padding. She's sure we'll all come away with engagements tonight."

"Why wouldn't you?" Shevi teased.

Cleo narrowed her eyes like an offended cat, but they sparkled with genuine entertainment and a smile took over her face.

"Well, I have an announcement to make and I wanted all of you to be here," Shevi said, "but I don't want to put it off any longer."

"Me either," Moxie said. "Go on. What is it?" She squirmed excitedly.

Shevi squared her shoulders and proceeded. "You've all taken me in and made me welcome here. And, Moxie, you're so honest and open about everything. I feel I could trust you with my life. So I hope you'll do me the honor of being my maid of honor."

"*What*?" Moxie howled. "Really—*me*?" When Shevi nodded emphatically Moxie charged her, grabbed her around the waist and hugged while swinging her to and fro with surprising strength.

Shevi laughed.

Moxie looked up. Big tears rolled down her cheeks. "Thank you, Shevi. Thank you so much. I never . . . I mean, I just never—"

Shevi pulled her into a hug and said, "Thank you, Moxie, for being—well, for being who you are."

The others stood staring with wide eyes. Shevi turned Moxie to face them and kept an arm around her.

"Oh, shoot," Shevi said as Bangle appeared out of a part in the crowd. "I should have waited two more minutes."

Bangle approached the group hesitantly, watching Moxie's red teary face with special concern.

"Moxie's Shevi's maid of honor," Alice explained.

"Oh," Bangle said, relaxing. "Okay."

"And," Shevi said, "I would like *all* of you to be bride's maids."

This announcement ignited a round of explosive celebration.

One by one they hugged her and thanked her, all except Cleo.

Shevi said, "I'm sorry, Cleo. I mean, you're welcome too, but I won't be offended if you decline."

Cleo stepped forward and hugged Shevi, holding on a bit longer than Shevi was comfortable with. She whispered into Shevi's ear, "I'd've already scratched your eyes out if I didn't know you know exactly how I feel." When she let go and stepped back, the serene smile on her face and the twinkle in her eye sent a chill up the back of Shevi's neck.

Moxie said, "But you have to throw the bouquet to *me*."

Shevi put an arm around Moxie. "Honey, as good as you look, you'll still be trying to decide which proposal you want to accept."

Moxie laughed and patted at her dripping eye liner.

"Yeah," Alice said. "Except for the makeup issue. Come here. I'll fix you."

"Then we eat," Moxie said.

"Yeah," Sally said. "Pack on some more weight for the scales." She thumbed toward the raised platform beyond the bosses' table.

This reminded Shevi of the other important thing she wanted to share with her new friends, especially Moxie and Cleo, about what she'd read in Jackson's novel. She wondered if she'd get a chance to talk seriously to them before the night ended, and if she dared risk spoiling the night with talk about the deaths of their fathers.

Cole watched the posse of girls. Every time Shevi looked up from her plate or turned aside from a conversation, he was staring at them. And she wasn't the center of his attention; each time she caught him he had to shift his gaze from Cleo to his 'beloved' wife-to-be. Shevi hid a smile when his mother latched onto his arm and towed him to a vacant bit of floor between dancing couples and posturing families. Her fire was lit and she was warming her son's ear with it. Shevi could feel her window of opportunity closing.

"I finished that novel," she said as loudly as she could without seeming abrupt.

"The one about the valet?" Bangle asked.

Shevi nodded. "There's an interesting idea in it."

The girls were open to a shift in mood. It seemed they had all exhausted their pleasure centers and were ready to embrace some serious conversation. They lept into adulthood proudly and bravely, at least for a short time. Moxie put on a stern expression and tilted her head to one side.

"I don't want to ruin it for any of you," Shevi said, "so I'll try to be careful, but Randall Mann is this really big guy who has these two lives he leads on opposite sides of the world."

"Yes," Sally said skeptically. "He's big enough to be an Ironclad, but he seems like he might be a bad guy."

"Yeah," Shevi said. "Anyway—let's see, how to do this without giving too much away. He eats two breakfasts and two lunches and two dinners every day and he gets this problem, with his heart, and the doctor tells him—"

There was a tap on Shevi's shoulder and she stopped. Cole had come up behind her. His face was flushed and his eyes were wide, darting wildly around to keep from fixing on his strongest point of interest. It was so sad that he'd fallen for Cleo and then couldn't have her. Shevi's life had become a box for the collection of unfortunate situations.

"Let's dance," he said.

"Uh," Shevi stammered. "O—okay."

"We'll read it," Cleo said.

Cole barked, "Read what?" He had frozen on the spot, in one instant simultaneously pulling Shevi out of the group and practically falling into it himself. Shevi bumped against him, but he didn't seem to notice.

"Yeah. We'll read it," Moxie said. "All of us. Then you can tell us easier."

"Okay," Shevi said. "I'll bring it tomorrow." She turned back to Cole and began the rather involved process of removing him from Cleo's company. Finally, when he seemed to have become completely paralyzed, she lied. "Your mother's coming."

Cole spun around and marched toward the dance floor, now dragging his betrothed along behind him. She settled against him and began to sway with him.

"What were you talking about?" he asked.

"I just finished a really good book."

"The one you got from that Dim kid?"

"That's the one."

As they slowly revolved around the dance floor she saw her mother watching from a table to the left of the stage. Cole's mother stood nearby like a wheel governor watching the flow of walkers. Mr. Turney stood at the center of a group of Ironclad men. His pride radiated with the power of the sun's warmth.

"Was it good?" Cole asked.

"What?" Shevi said. She had become entranced by all the eyes that were watching them. "Oh, the book. Yes. It was very good."

"I'll try to read it."

"You should. I don't know why more people don't read while they walk."

"I don't know."

"Have you ever pulled the wings off a bug?"

"Sure. Why?"

"Did it bother you?"

She felt his shoulders rise and fall with a shrug. "Why would it? They're just bugs."

"True."

The girls had dispersed now. Sally and Alice were dancing with boys she didn't know. Perry was with his new band of friends. She caught his eye and he stopped talking to watch her for a moment.

"Are we just bugs?" she asked.

"I'm not," Cole declared. "I'm an Ironclad, and so are you. No, we're not bugs. Why would you say that?"

"Have you ever heard of a heart attack?"

"No. What is it?"

"It's something that used to happen to people if they didn't eat right and get enough exercise."

"What? Like Carbon Nation people?"

"Yeah. I'm just wondering about the way we eat."

"We eat a carefully controlled diet, Shevi. And we get lots of exercise."

"Yeah, maybe."

"Those people had all kinds of problems—selfishness and laziness and all kinds of stuff. You can't even start to compare us to them."

Shevi was about to present the second facet of her argument, that the Ironclads were actually being overfed and thus were fatter than they ought to be for the sake of generating more electricity for the kingdom, when a girl somewhere across the hall screamed.

"What was that?" Shevi turned and peered in the direction of the sound.

"Just a proposal."

"Here?"

"Sure. It's our bid day, but it's not just about us. Lots of guys will propose to their girls tonight. Believe me, we're not the most nervous couple in the room. And all those couples that announce their engagement will go up there first to show themselves off to the wheel bosses. You and me going up there is just a formality."

The music died away and Shevi pulled away from Cole, ready to get back to her friends, but he held on. He tugged her arm and spun her around to face him. Looking deeply into her eyes, he said, "You need to get rid of that book."

"What?"

"Get rid of it."

"Why?"

"Because I said so. Come on, Shevi. You're marrying *me*. Get over that Dim kid already." She yanked her hand from his. He checked the crowd around them. "It's a stupid story. Sounds to me like it ought to be got rid of, like burned or something."

Without a word she turned and walked away. It wasn't until she was almost back to her group of friends, thinking about how Mrs. Turney had at least had something to do with Jackson's arrest, that a horrible idea struck her. What if they sent someone—Leah, of course it would have to be Leah—back to the mansion and into her room to find the book and destroy it?

"What's wrong?" Moxie asked, rushing to her, eyes wide with concern.

The air around them cracked with a loud voice. Shevi remembered it well. Hearing it made her skin shudder beneath her tight clothes. She whirled and found the little man from the bachelor party posing on the stage. "*Good evening, ladies and gentlemen.*"

"What's he doing here?" she whispered to Cleo who had come up beside her.

"He emcees all the bid night ceremonies. That's Mr—"

"I know who he is." Shevi looked up at the strands of light bulbs crisscrossing the space and wondered if the electricity for this event was being paid for or was pirated like Ward Stendahl's bachelor party. "I'm sorry," she said. Cleo was on her right and Moxie was on her left. Both were looking at her with concern.

"*It is my privilege and honor to welcome all of you to the prenuptial bid day ball for Shevi Lilbourn and Cole Turney.*"

"Are you all right?" Moxie asked. "You're not going to do something crazy, are you?"

A group had assembled on the main stage at one end of the long table. Couples stood together on the dance floor wherever they had been when the music stopped and watched the activities. Across the room, Cole was talking to his mother who was searching the crowd while she listened.

"No," Shevi declared. "I've just forgotten something." Mrs. Turney's gaze locked on Shevi but only for an instant before continuing around the room. The person she eyed next was exactly the person Shevi expected. The matriarch beckoned and Leah started toward her. Shevi grabbed Moxie's arm tightly enough to make the girl draw in a sharp breath. "Can you do something for me?"

"Yes, Shevi. What it is? What's wrong with you?"

"Here to offer their bids and best wishes for the happy new couple are . . ." The little man in his bright and ugly suit and hat paused dramatically. *"From Wheel One, Mr. Fletcher Asgood."*

"Excuse us," Shevi said over weedy applause to Cleo whose eyebrows had drawn into a tight furrow. She pulled Moxie back into the crowd as Leah joined her mother and brother across the room. "I need you to do something for me."

"From Wheel Two, the lovely Miss Georgia Phipps." More applause.

"Sure," Moxie said. "Anything."

"That book—I need you to go get it and put it somewhere safe."

"What book?"

"From Wheel Three, Mr. Jonathan Halsted."

"The one we were talking about." A greater cheer went up from the crowd for the boss of Shevi's home wheel. It seemed to come from the left rear of the hall. Shevi craned her neck to find Kyle and some of the other Titanics standing with Perry. "It's by my bed. Tell the maid—"

"You're worried about that book right now? This is your *bid day*, Shevi." Moxie appeared to be falling apart at the thought of such blasphemy.

"Mr. Lawrence Parson from Wheel Four." Light applause.

Shevi spoke slowly and very deliberately. "Moxie, do you want to read it?" She lowered her voice to a whisper, putting her face right beside Moxie's head. "Do you want to know what really happened to your dad?"

"*The lovely Miss Ginger Wardlaw from Wheel Five.*"

Moxie jerked back. Her eyes were even bigger now, saucer sized, in danger of coming right out of their sockets. "What in the world does that have to do with anything?"

Shevi grabbed the girl and pulled her close, turning her away from the stage where tiny Mr. Myrtle and the tall and very burly Miss Wardlaw were exchanging a rather passionate embrace and inciting catcalls from the audience. Face to face with Moxie, Shevi said, "If you don't go right now and get that book, you'll never know."

"*Indeed, very lovely,*" the emcee remarked as he watched her stroll to her seat at the table.

Moxie snorted a couple of times and her eyes tightened to little slits. Tears welled up in them. "Nobody's even asked me to dance yet."

"Please."

"It's *your* night, Shevi," Moxie whimpered. The girl was in the throes of deepest sorrow. She yanked her hands from Shevi's grasp and wiped her eyes.

Shevi glanced around and found Mrs. Turney in a similar debate with Leah who, as far as Shevi could tell, had not been asked to dance either.

"*Mr. Mark Stendahl from Wheel Six.*" The last was drown out by a flood of shouts, whistles and cheering. The Turney family had

271

pulled in most of the guests.

As she clapped for her wheel boss, Moxie hissed, "Tell the maid what?"

Shevi's head snapped back involuntarily with surprise. "You'll do it?"

"Like I said, it's *your* night."

Shevi laid a hand lovingly and appreciatively on Moxie's shoulder. "Tell them you're getting something I forgot."

"Even though that's just a lie." Moxie analyzed Shevi's hand on her shoulder with obvious dismay.

Shevi sighed and took the girl's hands again, focusing her, wanting to hug her for coming this far. "My old pack is under my bed. Put the book in it and take it someplace safe."

"Bring it back here?"

"No. Not back here. Take it . . . Hide it somewhere, someplace where no one will find it."

"Why is it so important?"

"Because it is." Cole's words, because I said so, echoed in her mind. "Trust me, please."

"You're the craziest girl I've ever met, Shevi. Really. This is just the craziest thing I've ever—"

Mrs. Turney was making progress with Leah now, as both were finished applauding their wheel boss. Shevi led Moxie through the crowd. "And if anyone comes—if you meet anyone, like Leah for instance."

"Why would I meet Leah? She's here at the party." Moxie's voice broke again.

"Moxie, you have to tell them—just go quickly. Go and hurry

and don't tell anybody what you're really doing." She pushed Moxie out the door.

Shevi watched her meander down the street toward Electric Avenue, encouraging her with little shooing motions each time she looked back. When she rounded the corner toward Wheel Six, Shevi turned back to the celebration, bracing herself for another skirmish with Leah. Inside, the applause continued for another wheel boss. Leah was making her way across the dance floor. She was alone. Moxie had been the best of the bunch for Shevi to send, but she knew the girl didn't stand a chance against the formidable Leah Turney. Even if Moxie was true to Shevi to the extent of fighting for her, which she had no reason to be, there wouldn't even be a contest. Shevi knotted her hands into fists, which brought to mind the beating Jackson had suffered, which made her think of the Titanics: Perry, and the rest of them, right over there. Kyle! She broke left and weaved through the crowd, wedging herself between her brother and Kyle.

"Hey, sis. Great party."

"Yes, it is. I need a favor."

The audience was clapping as the ninth and final wheel boss crossed the stage to take his seat. Leah entered the fringe of people at the edge of the dance floor, her face aflame with fury. Her course was the exit and ultimately an altercation with poor, faithful Moxie. The book Shevi had gotten from Jackson was now an obstacle in Leah's way and her actions to remove it, or anything or anyone who got in her way, would be vehement. The band began to play another song. The people on the floor paired up again and began to move to the sounds.

"Anything for you," Kyle said, "bride of the bid." He bowed to her.

She latched onto him and dragged him. "Thanks. Here it is. Dance with Leah Turney." His face drew into an expression concocted of shock, surprise, and revulsion. "Now, Kyle. *Now!*" She slung him around toward the exit door, but too late. The door swung closed behind the charging missile.

Kyle stumbled to it and looked out. He turned back to Shevi and offered an apologetic shrug. "Looks like she's already gone."

"Call to her," Shevi hissed.

Kyle turned to the outside, stopping the door with his hip. "Excuse me," he shouted while Shevi peered through the crack between hinges. To her surprise, Leah stopped and looked back. Kyle's voice broke as he asked, "Leaving so soon?"

Leah put her hands on her hips. Her nostrils flared as she drew in air to expand her great bosom to its extreme. "Why do you care?"

"I'd like to . . . to dance." His voice broke again.

She paled then flushed so quickly Shevi was sure she would fall over passed out right there in the street, which would be fine. By the time she came to and righted herself, Moxie might have enough of a head start.

"I—" She pointed behind her, down the street toward Electric Avenue, the way Moxie had gone.

"Beg her," Shevi said.

"Please."

"I'll be right back."

"You may not be here," Shevi growled.

"I may not be here," Kyle echoed, reluctantly.

Leah looked around, at first concerned but then suspicious.

"Play with her," Shevi hissed. "Hard to get."

Kyle half turned. His voice grew either in hope or in the pleasure of the game. "Sorry. Go ahead. Didn't mean to bother you." He slowly eased inside, letting the door swing shut. Just before the gap closed, Shevi saw Leah commence a charge at it that made her departure look timid. Kyle offered a triumphant yet apologetic smile.

"Brace yourself," Shevi said as the door flew open and slammed against him.

Chapter
Twenty-three

The throbbing in Jackson's tongue kept him focused on the goal of making a weapon for self-defense. The pain was an intense throb that blocked the rich prison diet of all its pleasure. The bite had turned into a nasty sore bump which he bit again every time he ate. He knew the ins and outs of laundry from all the time he'd spent helping his dad, so while Sheldon Murphy, the trustee in charge of laundry, explained the process of washing uniforms and diapers, Jackson pretended to listen but inventoried his new assets among the equipment. The tools amounted to nothing more than a pair of pliers and an adjustable wrench, but that was all he needed. A dozen big industrial washing machines and dryers stood along the back wall. Vats lined one side wall. These were for rinsing dirty diapers, the whiskery little man explained. A row of tables for folding and carts for delivery occupied the other side of the room. Beyond the tables along the other side of the dingy room several small washing machines and dryers leaned against the wall, piled with uniforms and stacks of diapers.

"What're you in for?" he asked his guide.

"Me? Nothing," Sheldon said, chuckling. "They jist needed somebody to walk on that jail wheel." He winked at Jackson and patted him on the shoulder. "Least I ain't no vamper."

"No. Of course not. Anybody ever use those for anything?" Jackson pointed to the old machines.

"Hell, no. Does it look like they ever get used?"

"Just wondering," Jackson said casually despite the incomparable value he saw in them and the pure good fortune he felt at the find. There would be enough raw material inside one of those machines to make ten wonderful self-defense weapons.

"Well, time's wastin. Let's get busy."

Jackson pushed his sleeves up and fell in beside the man, attacking the work. It was harder for him to hide his real intention than to deal with the mass of dirty diapers. He restrained the manic drive that swelled inside him each time he swallowed and his tongue throbbed again and each time he replayed the mental image of the sneering face looking down from the cot above.

"Hey, you're good at this," Sheldon said.

"Helped my dad. He did diaper duty down in the main. Pardon the alliteration."

"Huh?"

"Never mind," Jackson said, smiling across the room at the old machines. All he needed was a little time alone with them. He tore through the separation of the uniforms and diapers with such cyclonic vigor that Sheldon couldn't keep up loading the washing machines.

"You a go-gitter, boy," Sheldon laughed.

"Ain't nothin," Jackson said, wiping sweat from his brow with the tight sleeve he'd pushed up to his elbows. "Hell, I could do all this by myself."

"Think so, do ya?"

"Yep," Jackson declared. "So now I'm bettin we fold the stuff that the nightshift crew left in the dryers."

Sheldon looked at him with a mixture of surprise and joy. "You really think you could do this without me?"

Jackson spewed and yanked open the door of the first dryer. "Sure thing, but it ain't like you got anything else to do. Right?" He peered around the pile of uniforms at the baited supervisor.

"Nah," Sheldon said. "Well, come to think of it, I could run down to the women's laundry and just see how's things is goin down there."

"Indeed," Jackson said, whipping a uniform from a wrinkled ball into a crisp rectangle.

Sheldon clapped his hands and rubbed them together. "I think I'll just go and do that." He licked his lips and looked around nervously. "Don't do nothin stupid while I'm gone."

"Hey, I'm in jail. Why would you think I'd do something stupid?"

"Ha-ha-ha," Sheldon laughed nervously and pointed a finger at Jackson. "You a good'n. I knew I was doin the right thing pickin you."

Jackson nodded and winked. Sheldon turned tail and fled. Alone at last, Jackson attacked the pile of uniforms, folding them and stacking them up like sandbags into a protective wall around a small foxhole workspace. As he emptied the next dryer and continued folding, he watched the glass in the door opposite his stacks of uniforms.

A guard passed by and glanced inside. Jackson smiled and waved. The guard nodded in reply and walked on. Jackson ran to the hook where the tools hung and grabbed them. He tore the cowling off the first washing machine and unbolted the motor. A few seconds later the machine stood as it had before but without its heart which was now on Jackson's makeshift operating table.

His nimble fingers ate away at the motor's guts, transforming its windings into a gauntlet of what looked like Celtic knot-work along the inside of his left forearm. He sandwiched gauze from the infirmary and foil from the kitchen into a capacitor bracelet for his left wrist and a series of small magnets into a bracelet for his right wrist. The two layers of foil would hold the imbalanced charges the magnetic field of his right bracelet would create in the coils when he slid them past one another; the gauze was the dielectric, keeping the two conductors simultaneously close enough together and far enough apart to allow imbalanced ionization.

Jackson looked up from his work and saw the guard peering back at him again through the door. Jackson nodded and tried to smile. The guard pushed the door open and looked around.

"Where's Murphy?"

Jackson pulled a thin rubber belt around his wrist, lest the induction weapon he'd just created backfire on him, and shrugged from behind the wall of uniforms. "He went . . ." Jackson stared up at the ceiling, feigning an Atlantean effort to remember something while his fingers set the prongs of the induction gauntlet into the sleeve of his uniform. "I think he said something . . . about checking with the warden . . . about parts for a . . . for one of the machines."

"*Bull!*" the guard said and took a wide stance.

Jackson yanked his sleeves down over the bracelets and dragged an unfolded uniform over the remains of the washing machine's dismantled heart. He began briskly sweeping his right wrist up and down his left forearm to induce the flow of electrons through the coils and create the unbalanced charge in the capacitor bracelet. He would hate to get caught with his new weapon before he got a shot at the intended target, but if the guard wanted to dance, Jackson would teach him some new moves.

"I know exactly where he's gone," the guard said. "He talked you into doing all his work for him, didn't he?"

Jackson looked innocently around. "I don't mind."

The guard huffed, "Kid, you can't let people take advantage of you." He whirled and slammed through the door, leaving it swinging like the pendulum of Grandpa Piedmont's old clock. By the time he returned with Sheldon, Jackson had returned the motor to its place inside the washer and had folded all the rest of the uniforms and diapers. He was transferring wet clothes from the washers to the dryers when the door burst open again and Sheldon stumbled along ahead of the guard. Jackson glanced over his shoulder. The guard didn't linger.

"Sorry," Jackson said.

Sheldon waved off the need for apology. "Ah, it was fun while it lasted." He examined the stacks of folded uniforms and diapers, his eyes twinkling. "We're all done?"

"I suppose," Jackson said.

"We could get into a little mischief."

"Didn't you just get caught doin a little mischief?"

"Yeah." Sheldon raised his eyebrows. He stood and stared at Jackson, waiting, allowing his protégé time to arrive at the obvious conclusion.

"So, there's no way in hell you'd step out of line right now."

Sheldon nodded slowly, encouragingly.

"So, there's absolutely no time like the present."

"That's my boy. I knew I done good pickin you."

And so the two slinked out of the laundry room, the old man with mischief on his mind, the young one with a surprise up his sleeve.

Wherever Sheldon had intended for them to go to get into whatever intended mischief the trustee had in mind, they didn't make it. They went to the kitchen which was common to both the men's and women's jail wheels and came to a dead end. Had Sheldon been alone, as he had an hour before, he would have gotten through just fine again. But now, being accompanied by his little sidekick, in whom he was so well pleased, a condition that had been benign before was transformed into a major obstacle. Phipps tossed a towel over his shoulder and put his hands on his narrow hips, blocking the way along the long dishwashing counter.

" 'Scuse me there, Phipps. Just passin through again."

Phipps said, "Maybe you is, but he ain't."

"But he's with me," Sheldon whined. "Come on, man. Let it go." He made a feeble play on passing by the wiry little man but only got a sharp elbow in his ribs. Sheldon cried out and backed into Jackson.

"You go on, Mr. Murphy," Jackson said. "I'll just go to my bunk."

Sheldon went on whining. "No, kiddo. You're gonna meet my girl. I told her all about you and she wants to meet you." He turned back to Phipps. "Your beef is with the manager. Don't go gettin all outta round with Jacks 'cause you got bumped down."

Phipps shoved Sheldon hard. The old man bumped against a shelf of pots and spun past Jackson. Phipps stepped up toe to toe with Jackson and put his nose against Jackson's. "Vamp our 'lectricity then come in here like some kinda superstar. Turned yourself in's what I heard. What kind of idjit does that? You and your stupid old man're both a couple of idjits, if you ask me."

The man who had been in the upper bunk and used the knocker rod on Jackson strolled up behind Phipps, holding up a long serrated knife by its point. Jackson stepped back and began running his right wrist briskly up and down his left arm, making sure he had all the charge he could get in the capacitor. The man dangled the handle of the knife over Phipps's shoulder. "Be wantin this?"

Phipps's eyes shifted. His thin lips stretched into a smile.

"Do him quick, 'fore the cook notices it's missin."

Phipps reached up for the knife, but Jackson didn't give him the chance. He lunged forward and smacked Phipps in the side of the neck with the two contacts sticking through his cuff. The right side of Phipps's body tightened. His eyes bugged and instantly teared, the right one shooting bright red with blood.

The guy with the knife watched Phipps contort and collapse between them through wide eyes. Screeching like a scared girl, he backed away. "What'd you do to him? What was that?" He fumbled the knife around, trying to brandish it, but the effect was countered by his bulging eyes searching Jackson for the weapon that put his tough little comrade on the floor.

Jackson looked down at Phipps, amazed at the result of his creation. He'd hoped for enough output to make a distraction. Now he was afraid he'd killed the little man. Phipps's chest gave a couple of spastic heaves. He had two black dots on the side of his neck—the mark of the vamper. Jackson couldn't help but smile at this.

From the other end of the kitchen someone yelled, "What's all the ruckus about?" A small man with an outrageously bulbous belly strolled toward them shaking a significant knocker rod.

"He's done magic on Phipps," the knifebearer squealed.

The round-bellied cook saw the knife and stuck the double pronged end of his knocker rod against the back of the man's neck. The knife swept upward and wiggled in the air like the baton of a conductor taking his orchestra into a screaming fortissimo. His body arched forward. A dark stain spread across the front of his pants. His teeth snapped together but his lips wriggled apart as he issued the most dreadful of whinnies. He fell to his knees, the knife sailed through the air, and as the man toppled over backward Jackson managed to catch the handle before the other end could puncture Sheldon Murphy, who had curled into a fetal ball on the floor.

Jackson looked at the knife then at the cook. He turned the knife around and very carefully offered it. Shaking his knocker rod ambitiously, the cook crept forward and took it. He examined the two men, taking a special interest in Phipps.

Phipps opened his eyes and began to wallow around between the other man's splayed legs. When he realized he was shampooing his scalp in the soiling of the man's crotch he sprang to his knees and cried out.

The cook lowered the pronged end of his rod to within inches of Phipps's nose. "Now here's the way it happened," he growled. "Y'all two jumped them two and I broke it up with this. And nobody wound up with one of my knives. I don't know what really happened and I don't wanna know. But if any other story gets out, all o' y'all are gonna be on solitary wheels for the rest of your miserable lives. Any questions?"

He poked the knocker rod toward Phipps's nose. Phipps leaned back and shook his head carefully.

The cook's story was *not* the story that spread across the jail wheel. Instead, everyone in the jail now believed that Jackson was capable of creating enough static electricity with his own body to kill a man with the mere touch of his fingertips. The man who'd delivered the shock to Jackson in his cot and had brought out the knife in the kitchen was Jasper Wartman. Wartman had been unconscious and either hadn't grasped the gravity of the cook's threats as handed down to him by Phipps, or was just overwhelmed by the situation.

Either way, neither Phipps nor Wartman were on the wheel the following day. But Wartman's story of Jackson's amazing ability was there. It was alive and well and thriving.

Jackson's status increased to 'local hero and legend' and things just kept getting better. His dad was already bulking up from the formula. He'd put on five pounds as easy as picking up a rock. But when Jackson complimented him on his weight gain, Dad returned a strange and somewhat angry sidelong glance.

As they walked in the middle of the morning something was passed down the row. Jackson took it from the walker beside him and offered it to Dad. It was an Adventures of Pantagruel comic book with a scrap of paper sticking out of it. The note said, *Levine, I heard you like these.* It was unsigned. His dad eyed the book with a look that Jackson could only interpret as contempt.

"Don't you want it?" Jackson asked.

"I wish everybody would just leave us alone," his dad growled.

Jackson shrugged and opened the comic, figuring the colorful pages would bring Dad out whatever funk he was in. But his dad marched on without giving the comic another look.

About fifteen minutes later a walker in the next row back said, "Hey, vamper kid, good job with the two goons." He reached up and patted Jackson on the shoulder.

Jackson's dad slapped the man's hand away and snarled, "Leave us alone."

The man said, "Whatever, buddy."

Jackson closed the comic and took in his dad's angry glare, not back at the man behind him but right at Jackson himself. "Dad, what's up?"

"Why couldn't you just leave things alone?" Dad said. "Why do you have to *always* screw up *everything*?"

"Hey, buddy, easy on the kid," the man behind them said. "He's a good—"

Jackson's dad spun, dragging Jackson and the other walkers along as he attacked the next row. They fell back and knocked into four people in the next row. The effect was viral. The even grain of forward motion broke down. The violation spread across the walkers like ink in water: four to a dozen, the dozen to twenty, twenty to fifty. The ones not directly involved were distracted. They turned. Some stumbled, sending others knocking into them. Jackson took ad-vantage of his narrow hips and slithered out of the girth that hooked him to the others in his row. He stumbled to the offramp out of the vortex of bedlam.

Guards ran down the offramp, knocker rods rattling. The governor barked for order. The manager shouted to his guards.

Jackson's dad was plowing his way deeper into the wheel, attacking anyone he could get hold of and dragging his row mates along behind him. Jackson screamed at him to stop.

The wheel shuddered and then stuttered. Then it halted completely. Warning horns blared. The ambient hum of the main wheel, a sound that had always, all of his life, been present around him, ceased. Jackson halted and looked around. Had the main wheel just stopped? That was the last thought that he had before the prongs of a knocker rod got him in the back.

Chapter
Twenty-four

It happened in the middle of the morning just after Cleo gave the book back to Moxie. Moxie was an incredibly slow reader and Bangle and Cleo had shortly taken the book from her so they could go on through it without waiting every pair of pages for her to finally finish. Cleo had taken the book home with her and finished it sometime late in the night or early in the morning. Now Bangle had questions and issues she wanted to discuss, but Cleo's expression wavered from skeptical to suspicious as she stared at Shevi. Bangle had just asked what coal was and if Mr. Mann was the cause of what had happened to the Carbon Nation's weather. There are events in history that stand out: the sinking of a great ship, the two great bombs, the toppling of the two great towers. In

Trintico, for a wheel to stop, the whole big thing to completely cease turning, was equal to these great events.

"Well, coal is obviously some kind of fuel," Shevi had said right before it happened, wanting to cut through Bangle's frivoling to get right to the point she wanted to make.

The tread of Wheel Six shuddered beneath their feet. The governor shouted an alert. "*Forward! Forward! Up! Up! Up!*" His managers repeated his orders here and there across the wheel. "*Forward!*" and "*Up!*" and the walkers responded immediately, charging, moving their collective weight up the curved slope of the wheel's tread. The demand indicator lights did something Shevi had never seen. All three lights, red, yellow and green began t-o flash. Shevi had heard that if demand got really high, like when the weather was extremely hot or cold in Fluxton, the red light could go from steady-on to flashing. She had only seen that twice, both on very hot days.

And she'd never seen the Ironclads up so far on the wheel before, not even on Wheel Three when demand had peaked. They marched. Idle chitchat stopped. Munching ceased. Moxie and others who had been reading closed their books. A man making chainmail dropped his work into a bag on the front of his dashboard and pumped his arms. Everyone felt the sudden incline increase and began breathing just a little bit heavier as they lifted themselves that extra few inches with each step.

"What's going on?" Alice asked, her tone epitomizing the sobriety in the air. "What's happened?" She looked to Cleo and Shevi.

Cleo shook her head.

A murmur swept across the current of walkers. Glances were exchanged. Heads shook. Eyes were wide with disbelief. The three lights of the demand signal went on flashing. In a matter of minutes the old man dug into his bag and pulled his work back out. Talk went from concerned back to casual. Snacks came out again. Moxie reopened the book and trudged onward through the thick volume, glancing up one last time to make sure it was safe to do so. The walkers of Wheel Six adopted the new condition as the status quo because they had little other choice—whatever was going on out there was going on out there; their job remained the same, to walk.

"So the coal was in the ground," Bangle said, picking back up where she had been interrupted. "How did it get there?"

"I don't know," Shevi said firmly but patiently. "But what about what happened to Mr. Mann?"

"What about it?" Cleo said, narrowing her eyes at Shevi.

"Well, what if the way he ate caused it?" Shevi argued. "He wasn't that old."

"That could be, I guess," Bangle said absently.

"Yeah," Shevi said. "And so what if the way we eat is the reason so many of us are dying so young, like my dad and Moxie's dad and . . ." She offered Cleo apologetic but questioning wide eyes.

"It's just a story," Cleo countered. "It's fiction—make-believe. It's not like this guy, this Kahn, is some kind of dietary expert or something. It's just a little part of the story. An aside."

Shevi started again. "Yeah, but what if—"

"I can't believe you'd suggest this, Shevi," Cleo said. "I mean, this is how people make their living. My dad was doing the right thing for his family and for the corporate society. And you're saying it was wrong."

"Did he eat his vegetables?" Bangle offered. "The president himself encourages all of us to eat our proper portion of vegetables."

"Do you?" Shevi said, watching Cleo's face grow even harder with Bangle's accidental accusation. The sound of an *n* issued from Bangle's mouth. She needed to admit that she didn't, but didn't want to. Shevi said, "Who can? I mean, have you ever considered how much we would have to eat to eat *all* they want us to?"

A smirk came across Cleo's face. "Wait a minute. I know what this is about."

"What?" Shevi asked, trying to imagine what was going through the girl's mind.

"It's about your little fling."

Bangle's focus bounced back and forth between them.

"What fling?" Shevi asked.

Cleo laughed out loud. "What *fling*? Oh, for Scott's sake. You're trying to justify the Dims. You want your little friend to come out on top one way or the other."

Shevi shook her head, trying to process Cleo's surprise attack. She had worked through every angle she thought anybody would come up with, but this completely blindsided her. "No."

"You got the book from him," Cleo said. "Didn't you?"

"Yeah, but—"

"Yeah, but—*nothing*," Cleo laughed. "Shevi, that's just the funniest thing I've ever heard. Oh, Shevi." She wiped tears from her face and laughed harder. Down the way, Moxie looked up from the book. Nearer, Bangle nodded carefully with an uncertain smile. "Oh, Shevi, you are a mess," Cleo finished.

Shevi couldn't believe it. She turned and looked ahead. The little girl with the wispy hair stared back at her. Otherwise, no one seemed to notice or care what was going on around them. A fury swelled inside her. It was a righteous fury, but one with no future; Cleo was a goddess among the girls and her opinion would trump all others. Shevi marched out of rank and sideways through the collated and gauged array of walkers, snatching the book out of Moxie's hands as she passed.

"I'm sorry," Cleo called out behind her.

Shevi stepped off the rolling tread onto the onramp without looking back. A manager who had been coaxing the pace from low on the boarding side shouted to her, provoking the attention of walkers who turned to look at her. She marched up the ramp toward the weigh-in platform and the exit.

Another manager met her at the edge of the upper platform. "Young lady, why have you abandoned your post now, at the corporation's greatest time of need?"

"Screw the corporation," Shevi hissed.

The man gasped. His eyes flashed with surprise and anger. Passing some of her own inflammation on to someone else felt good.

"How dare you," he growled.

Shevi marched on, bursting out the entrance door onto a deserted Electric Avenue, void of humans but filled with the howl of warning sirens decreeing the extremely high demand. The book was under her arm. Hot coals festering in her heart instantly collapsed into cold blackness. Tears swelled in her eyes and a laugh burst from her mouth. It was a wet laugh, sticky with saliva and laced with hate. The laugh became a sob. She hugged the book against her breast the way she had put her arms around her dad's neck when she rode in his saddle. She needed him; she wanted to go home. Had this place killed him? A new banner draped on the wall between the entrance and exits of Wheel Four, a familiar face smiling down, large hands holding out a basket of leafy, green goods, a caption declaring *Big Steve loves his veggies.*

She pushed open the entrance door to Wheel Three and stopped, unable to believe what she saw. The wheel was still. Emergency walkers had been called in. Night walkers who had already retired to their beds wore pajamas or bathrobes. Ty and Murray, Mom's old gambling buddies, were there. Not far behind the middle of the crowd a hand popped up and waved. It was Tasha. Shevi's old companions had been pushed far up on the wheel by the infusion of extra walkers. Stacey grabbed Tasha's hand and yanked it down, thrusting a hateful glare at Shevi. There were more walkers on the wheel than she had ever seen. They were farther up on the tread than she thought possible. Then she saw how it was happening. Cables stretched down from the structure of the Civic Level, allowing them to climb the tread of the stalled wheel like a sheer cliff. Ironclads pressed themselves against the tread well above the line where the stage had been set for the president's speech. The walkers weren't arrayed in rows across the wheel but made a single corporate whole, each pressing against the next in front, pushing either with hands on shoulders or shoulder into back.

Shevi was grabbed and shoved. She turned to see the wheel's governor wild-eyed and red faced. "*Get on!*" He shoved her again. "But I'm—"

"*We've got to get a thousand tons of wheel moving again, you idiot! GET ON, NOW!*" He shoved her over the side of the weigh-in platform onto the steepest portion of the onramp. Her body went over well ahead of her feet. She plunged, landed, skidded, then began to roll. She felt the book slip in her grip. She wanted to stop herself or at least gain some control over her descent, but she could not let go of the book. All the way down the curving slope of the ramp she bounced and rolled, hugging the volume to her. She stopped near the bottom of the throng of walkers. An enormous man in blue and white striped pajamas stepped off the stalled wheel long enough to grab her and yank her aboard so she could join the efforts to save the sinking society.

Behind the last row of walkers, the tread was cluttered with helmets and scraps of food, games and books and hobbies, things that had been discarded or had fallen away in the flurry. A scepter lay at the top of the heap—she was almost certain it was Kyle's. She turned away to look up the wheel at the wall of walkers above her then realized she had seen something move in the mélange. Things continued to tumble out of the bottom of the horde, but she was sure she'd seen something moving in the opposite direction—up, unnaturally. She glanced back again and saw a small child crawling over a helmet. She gasped and fell out of ranks.

"Keep walking," the man who had dragged her onto the wheel shouted.

"There's a baby," she cried.

"Leave it," he hissed.

Shevi turned from him and ran to the infant. As she did, the wheel rocked beneath them. Shevi stumbled. The baby teetered as it struggled over a bag. It was a bag with someone's knitting supplies in it and the prong of a knitting needle probed toward the baby's face.

"Get up here," someone yelled.

Shevi ran, tripping over Kyle's scepter and a loaf of bread. She dropped the book and grabbed the baby as the wheel jerked again. The debris shifted around her feet and something snapped in her ankle. A sharp pain shot up her leg as the wheel began to move steadily again. A cheer exploded above her. She and the baby drifted away from the multitude.

"*FALL BACK!*" the governor shouted. "*Fall back! Last three rows, clear the tread immediately!*"

Shevi and the baby and all the stuff that had been ejected moved steadily back as the last three rows of walkers turned in retreat. They parted, half toward the onramp and half toward the offramp. The ones closest to the edge of the wheel grabbed the stuff at their feet and threw it onto the ramps. The others formed brigades to hand the stuff off. The enormous man in blue and white striped pajamas put out his arms toward Shevi. She took a step and the pain in her ankle flamed anew. She almost fell onto her face and onto the baby.

"*Throw it!*" the man screamed.

Shevi looked down at the infant. It was a boy, she realized now. He was looking up at her, wondering what could have happened to his world. They were drifting upward on the backside of the wheel, changing the position of Shevi's feet relative to the vertical, torquing her ankle and grinding a throbbing pain up her leg.

The governor's voice bellowed across the huge volume inside the wheel. "*The field will reengage in FIVE SECONDS!*"

"*THROW IT!*" the big man yelled again. His face was bright red, his eyes wide with panicked anger, his chest heaving methodically. He bent down and grabbed up the knitting bag and threw it to a man in a ragged bathrobe that hung open in the front, exposing his global middle and the ample festoons of his chest. He was at the back of the brigade line. He reached out to grab the hobby kit but missed it. The tread beneath then jerked and shuddered as the shell of magnets became charged again from the jail's feed. The man in striped pajamas bobbed back and forth, snarled, grabbed something else, and tossed it. The man in the bathrobe also missed this catch. Pajama Man doubled his left hand into a fist. He glanced up at Shevi. His face went suddenly pale. "Get off the wheel, you halfwit." The left side of his neck tightened. He grabbed his left arm.

The governor shouted, "*Returning contact to the power grid in FIVE SECONDS! REPEAT, FIVE SECONDS!*"

Pajama Man hoisted another hobby bag and a book high into the air and hurled them toward the edge of the wheel.

A manager barked, "Clear the aft tread."

Pajama Man grabbed two more handfuls of stuff, reached high over his head to toss them, but never got the chance. His eyes bulged, his face went yellow-gray. His mouth gaped open like a fish sucking for water, and he fell facedown on the cluttered tread of Wheel Three.

The manager shouted, "Walkers, clear the aft tread. The sweep will get it."

Shevi heard the sweep then, sliding up behind her. She turned to see the tread disappearing behind a massive rubber lip. Only a few inches separated the two. She fell with her back to the sweeping lip, protecting the baby inside the curve of her body. The massive rubber flap pressed her down hard into the unyielding tread then scraped over her shoulder, hip, arm and leg. The instant it was past, she checked the baby. He looked up at her, too terrified to cry.

Above the sweep, tiny Dim workers ran back and forth, ridding the wheel of its useless and counterproductive weight. One of them rolled Shevi into a gutter behind the rubber lip, crushing the baby beneath her. Shevi sat up, fighting the pain in her ankle, and checked the boy again. A second later two workers rolled Pajama Man onto the ledge. He splayed onto a pile of debris, his head lulled back, his mouth still agape, his eyes staring terrifically at Shevi. The boy shrieked, grabbed Shevi's chainmail with both hands and pulled himself tightly against her armor.

Jackson's book landed on the man's chest with a hollow thud.

Chapter

Twenty-five

A council had convened. It consisted of President Burgess, Their Majesties Prince Tyler and Prince Jasper, and the Honorable Mayor Van Asche. Jackson understood perfectly why he and his dad were there. They had, albeit inadvertently, wreaked havoc in I Town and now faced a council of men who each looked angry enough to personally execute somebody, perhaps even slowly. (Prince Tyler's thin tanned face was drawn tight and radiated pure outrage.) What Jackson couldn't figure out was why Shevi sat accused with him and his dad. When they had been brought down from the solitary wheels, where they had not walked but ran for what seemed like days, she had been there waiting.

Jackson leaned closer to Dad. Dad turned to him, a look of

serenity on his face. This was one of two expressions he had portrayed lately. "Ask Shevi . . ."

Instantly the other expression surfaced, a look of wild fury, a polar-opposite mood shift. "*Oh, will you stop!*" he hissed.

Shevi's head turned but only a bit. She cut her eyes to see Jackson. He whispered, "Why are you here?" Between them, Dad exploded upward the few inches his binding chains would allow. His fingers curled into talons and he made little scratching motions in the air.

From the stage Mayor Van Asche slowly and intentionally said, "Will the accused please cease . . . *everything.*" When Dad had melted back into his chair, the mayor cleared his throat. "I call this hearing to order. If it be the council's pleasure I will call for charges." He looked down the row of men seated with him at the long table.

The only one who spoke was President Burgess, one grumbled word, "Proceed."

The mayor pronounced the names slowly. "Levine and Jackson Koss."

A man jumped to his feet and rushed forward. "Mr. Jonathan Halsted, Boss of Wheel Three. If it please the council I'll declare the charges against them."

The president gave a little wave of acknowledgement.

Pointing in Jackson's general direction, he declared, "These two have committed an act of terrorism resulting in sedition and high treason against the kingdom."

Prince Tyler beamed brightly at the man then returned his vicious scowl on Jackson, a manifestation comparable to Jackson's dad's bad side.

The ambient drone of the audience in the hall exploded into bedlam. The men of the council allowed it to live its natural lifespan.

When it was past President Burgess almost dismissively said, "And the girl?"

A woman carrying a small boy came forward. "She kidnapped my child."

As a murmur swelled behind them, Jackson leaned forward to look at Shevi. She sat stiffly and stared wide-eyed at the woman.

Another woman, draped in black, was helped forward. "She murdered my husband," she said between soft sobs.

"I would submit," shouted Boss Halsted, pointing his finger now at Shevi, "that she was an accomplice in their act of terrorism."

Jackson rose up against his restraints and shouted, "You people are all crazy." The members of the council offered him a look intended to silence him, but what sat him back and sealed his lips was Shevi's sidelong glance, not just the glance but the horror in her eyes.

"If I may," someone called out. It was a voice familiar to Jackson and apparently to Shevi too because despite her fear, she jerked around at the sound of Mr. Myrtle's words. The little man strolled casually forward waving his walking stick, Jackson's illegitimate creation, carelessly. He smiled pleasantly beneath a tall lime green hat. He bowed low within his baggy black suit, and as he rose let the big jacket unrumple around him. He reminded everyone of exactly who he was. "Mr. Mulligan Myrtle, sirs, if you please." When the mayor smiled and nodded, the imp made a flourish with his hat and twirled himself about. "Sirs. Ladies and gentlemen. Citizens of Induction Town and the *kingdom* of Trintico. I beseech you. This girl must not be held accountable for her actions, for she is, as each one of us, every member of our noble and proud society, a victim. All the blame lies with these two." He pointed the removable handle of his walking stick toward Jackson. "Especially the younger. A boy, indeed, but a man, too. Well into manhood. Prodigiously a fiend, consorting with the most vile of seditionists."

Shevi's arms were locked stiffly by her sides, her knuckles white as she held herself down to the chair seat. The color was back in her face, growing, deepening. Now Jackson was afraid—afraid she wouldn't take the option Mr. Myrtle offered, afraid she would blow it with some stupid outburst.

"*YES!*" he shouted, leaping up against his bonds. "*YES! Since its conception,*" he repeated the words of Christopher Bartlett, "*our species has been reaching toward the state of the* SELF-WILLED INDIVIDUAL! *Not rats racing on a wheel—*"

The mayor was pounding on the table and Mr. Myrtle was coming at him, grasping the handle of his cane to remove it and give Jackson a jolt, but Jackson was set upon from behind. He was slammed back into his chair, he was slapped, he was hammered, he was spat upon. Beside him, his dad jumped against his chains, and he got the same treatment until someone strapped gags around each of their mouths and tied shirts over their heads. The last thing Jackson saw was Shevi staring at him with disgusted shock.

Muted, in the dark, Jackson sat and listened to Mr. Myrtle continue his dissertation. He could see in his mind the demon's grandiose gestures; he didn't mind missing it. But what he waited for, what he prayed he wouldn't hear was Shevi's rebuke.

"You see? Do you see? Now he comes out with it. Now we see what he truly is. But he did not show his madness to this poor girl. He coaxed her. He wooed her. A Dim, lusting after one of your Iron-clad women, one of your beautiful Ironclad women, like his father before him. Yes, indeed."

Something hard hit the back of Jackson's head. He heard his father grunt and knew that he was receiving the same treatment.

"Had he been so forthcoming with his blasphemy, with his idiotic, made-up nonsense, she would have never been fooled for a minute. Seduced by his flaunting some fictitious love of literature, or art. His sensitivity." Mr. Myrtle's voice dropped into a snarl. "Of his poor weakness, of his abuse of the very society that nurtured him—after his father seduced his mother and caused her to bear him—in contempt of our own president's grace and mercy."

The crowd behind them had turned into a mob. There was scuffling and fighting among them to get to Jackson. Hands clawed at the makeshift shroud, graciously relaxing the gag from his mouth. He leaned forward against the steady pulling. The mauling went on for only a few seconds before Mr. Myrtle graciously dispelled it with more of his soothing words. At first this surprised Jackson until he realized the little incarnation of Satan envisioned a more colorful means of their demise.

"Ladies. Gentlemen. Citizens of our great society. I beg you. Nay. I beseech you. Let this poor girl, who can go on, with proper guidance and direction, to become a productive—a beautiful— member of this great society, go."

Jackson listened in the new silence for Shevi to do something stupid and ruin her chance to get out of this mess. But she didn't, not right then.

"But for these two, especially that hateful little one there . . ."

Jackson leaned back now, wondering how close the two-pronged tip of the knocker rod walking stick might be to his throat.

"Let them suffer a punishment befitting of their crime. A sentence given to another seditionist just recently."

Jackson didn't know what the little creep was talking about, but apparently Shevi did. Now was when she decided she'd heard enough. Now she issued a single word, "No!" whispered really, barely audible. And before she could mess things up, before he could let her take another risk for him, despite the likelihood of a healthy bolt of energy awaiting him, he spat the gag from his mouth and rose again.

"BRING IT ON! I'LL KILL ALL OF YOU!"

◎

Shevi was sick with confusion. The events of the last few hours left her dizzy. She'd been whisked from the gutter of Wheel Three to a holding cell on the Civic Level where she sat and worried about the little boy. From there she was escorted back to the Hangar, the place where she and Cole had received their bids from the wheel bosses, for the most unlikely hearing that ever could be. And there poor Jackson was. (Why did he keep getting accused of stuff that wasn't his fault?) And then, instead of standing up for himself he had acted completely bug brains, which had only made things worse.

And all the false accusations! She hadn't kidnapped the boy; she'd rescued him. And she hadn't killed the man. No! He had gone the way of the great god, Randall Mann, the way all the big men and women would go in I Town. And now she was back in her new home, her room in the Turney Mansion on the Upper Crust of Wheel Six. She might be under house arrest, but Jackson would be put in the Duel Wheel. She had to save him and his dad.

The door belched open. The matriarch of the Turney family stood beyond it, her gentle giant husband right behind her. Again, Shevi had managed to invert his indelible smile. But this time it really wasn't her fault. She stood, ignoring the pain in her ankle, and launched into the presentation of her case.

"I saved that boy from—"

"Shut up," Mr. Turney growled, and Shevi did, chilled to her core by his tone and the darkness in his eyes. The walls of her defense crumbled around her leaving her feeling naked. The heads of the house marched into the room, their gazes fixed on her. "Young lady," he went on, "here are the new rules."

His wife took over. "You are, under no circumstances, to leave this house without either Cole or Leah by your side. You are not to leave their side until you return. Is this clear?"

She was about to respond in the affirmative, knowing very well that the question was at least mostly rhetorical, when Mr. Turney did something that froze her spirit inside her. He knotted up his left hand into a fist and grabbed his left arm with his right hand, massaging it slowly. His face paled, taking on that now too familiar yellow tinge. Sweat beaded on his brow like the jewels of a mighty king's crown.

She blurted, "You're going to die," and didn't even see the hand that slapped her. She couldn't see for several seconds afterward, not with as hard as the hit was. It made her ears ring and her nose and eyes burn with tears.

The matriarch went into such an overwhelming rant that Shevi could only sit back down on her bed and turn her stinging face away from the verbal thrashing. She was inconsiderate, selfish, wicked. "Marrying his cousin and having half-witted, deformed children couldn't be as bad for Cole as marrying you!"

"Come on, my love," Mr. Turney said, taking his wife by the shoulders and pulling her back. "Come along." He guided her out the door. He turned in the doorway and looked longingly at Shevi. "It's a shame. You want the best for your kids. But not everyone can have it as good as us, married to someone who is best for them. I pity Cole. I really do. But I still think that someday you'll turn around and be okay. I believe that about you." A tear rolled down the man's round cheek.

Behind him, his wife, the unyielding Mrs. Turney, began to sniffle. Shevi reached out to them. A rhythmic spasm had taken control of her chest. "Please, listen to me."

Mr. Turney only shook his head, grasped the doorknob in his large hand, and pulled it toward him until he was eclipsed and gone.

Maybe, Shevi hoped, he wouldn't die. Maybe he would only suffer a light attack and then they would believe her. She sat there on the bed, panting, too tired to cry, thinking of all she had to do. She had to save Jackson from the horrible man and his horrible wheel. She had to save Mr. Turney from his almost certain date with heart failure. She had to warn this town and all its Ironclads that they were doomed.

Someone was outside the door. She instantly knew who it was. "Mother! Mom!" She limped forward. "Mom, you were right to take the night shift. You were right not to eat like everyone else. That's why Dad died, wasn't it? You knew. You were right."

"Shevi, don't think about all that right now."

"We have to warn people. Mr. Turney. We have to warn him, Mom. He's going to die." She rattled the doorknob.

"They've locked you in, Shevi, and I don't have a key. Don't worry about all that other stuff right now. Just get through this. Then we'll deal with all the other problems as we can." She was silent for a moment and Shevi pressed close to the door. She could hear her mother's breathing through it. "That was close today, Shevi. I don't know what you did or what really happened, but . . ." Her words went high and soft—she was crying. "But I thought I'd lost you, too. I can't lose you, too, honey. Do you understand this?"

"Mom . . ." Shevi could at first only think of Jackson and Mr. Koss and Mr. Turney and the terrible fates that awaited them, but as she listened to her mother's sobs she decided that this wasn't the time to pursue solutions. "I love you," she said simply.

Her mother's reply was a strained whisper. "I love you, too."

And then she was gone and Shevi was alone again. She lay back on her bed and stared at the timbers and planking of the ceiling. The big house groaned around her, as if hungry. She felt her own insides empty now. She was more hungry for results than for food, and when the lock rattled and Cole appeared with a tray of food, she looked at the mound of fats and starches as the means of her execution.

She hopped from her bed. "Cole, thank goodness. We have to

warn your father. He's—"

"Do you love him?" He stood holding her supper between them.
"What?"

"This Dim. Do you love him?"

"Cole, please." Then her mind shifted gears again. "Do you know what they're going to do to him?"

"My dad?"

"No, the Di . . . the . . . Jackson."

Cole shook his head. He put the tray on the sidetable. Then he straightened, seeming very old. "I don't think I can do this. I love Cleo, but that's just not going to work out. I really thought you were a good second choice. And I still think you could be. You're beautiful, amazing really, but I just don't think we're going to work out."

He was at least talking to her, which gave her hope that a dialogue was possible. She had to take everything down a notch—explain things slowly and carefully.

She took his hands and pulled him toward the bed. "Cole, let me explain."

He shook his head. "I don't know, Shevi. You go out one day without your engagement rotor and you meet up with some Dim and you get a book from him and you get all wrapped up in a completely crazy idea." She stroked his cheek. He looked into her eyes. He leaned forward and kissed her. He leaned farther forward and kissed her harder. She allowed herself to lie back onto the bed. He kissed her deeper still.

The first chance she got, the instant her mouth was free, she whispered, "Your dad's going to die."

He launched himself off of her and off her bed screaming, "*What the hell?*"

"I'm sorry."

"You know . . ." He turned and began a short pace back and forth between her and the door. "Hester and Leah both said you should have come here right away after our engagement. They said girls could go off and do stupid things, get all confused—"

Shevi grabbed up the supper tray and hurled it at him. It banged against his face and chest as he turned, then the tray and dishes clattered to the floor, leaving thick gobs of mashed potatoes and gravy on his cheek and neck. He looked down at the mess on the floor and back up at her.

"I'm not marrying you. You're crazy. You're all out of round. I want my rotor back."

Said rotor was hanging by its heavy chain from the post at the head of the bed. Shevi ground her teeth together. Cole's eyes grew wide. She yanked the massive weight from the bedpost and reared back with it. He ran for the door, slamming it shut in time for the rotor to smash against it.

Shevi was done. He wasn't going to marry her? Ha! *She* wasn't going to marry *him*! They were all a bunch of idiots. Jackson was the only rational, intelligent person she had met in her whole life, it seemed, and this crazy, stupid bunch of people were going to kill him because . . . because . . . She really didn't even understand the first bit of that, but she knew she had to save him. She jumped over her ruined supper and rattled the doorknob. Despite his haste, Cole hadn't failed to lock it. She kicked the door and screamed at it. She screamed again at the world beyond, at their stupid nonsense.

Chapter

Twenty-six

Shevi opened her bedroom window and looked out. The Turney mansion was on the southeast corner of the Upper Crust of Wheel Six. Night had overtaken the sky except for a dusting of light along the horizon, like the scant opening of a sleeper's eye. There was one spot in the vastness between here and there, an exclamation point of light in what could have otherwise been a universal quiet. Shevi assumed it was some part of Agrarianna churning out fuel and death for the walkers below her. The Turney mansion was as complex as the structure of Wheel Six or of I Town. It was a cobbled together conglomerate of forms. There was a ledge two floors below. If Shevi could reach it she could crawl in a window and probably find a way out of the house.

She stripped the sheets from the bed and knotted one to another. She stretched the makeshift rope across her room and compared its length to the distance down to the roof. It might get her close enough to drop, but the landing would surely alert someone, and she didn't need to do more damage to her ankle. She began adding clothes: two pairs of pants, a shirt, and finally her bid day outfit. She pulled the knot in the last one hatefully tight.

The queue of fabrics unfurled downward with delightful grace when she cast it out the window, foreshadowing her pending freedom. She secured the upper end to the foot of her bedpost and crawled onto the window sill. The window was small, not quite big enough for her to fit through. She had to turn around and poke her feet out first then reverse snake the rest of her body into the vast openness six hundred feet above the makeshift shelters of Shack Town. She hung from the sill by her armpits, making one last appraisal of her knots, doing one more hopeful calculation of the weight of the bed compared to her own. She took one last big breath, let it out, then cast her fortune and destiny on the lanyard of bedding and clothes.

Something gave—the bedding or one of the knots—she wasn't sure which, but she didn't waste time waiting to find out. She followed the sheets, then the pants, the shirt, and finally that tight suit she'd modeled for the wheel bosses on bid night. She still had to drop a few inches onto the little roof, giving her good foot the brunt of the force. It thudded hard, but the noise was the least of her worries. From above, the roof had looked like a rough surface; standing on it she discovered it was metal and much steeper and slicker than she'd expected. Despite the pain in her sprained ankle, both feet arched inside her shoes and her toes curled into claws as her body tried to sure itself. She leaned her face and shoulders against the wall, looking back up at the dangling rope, wanting to reach for it but unable to risk her balance and sure it wouldn't help anyway. Her feet drifted down the slope of the roof another fraction of an inch and threatened full-bore migration to the unguttered edge, which seemed much closer to the wall now than it had from above. There was much more of nothing around her than something.

When her feet slipped again, she dove for the edge of the window, the only useful relief in the uncaring plane of the wall. Only when she was lying on her side and clinging to the window did she worry about the noise her body made in the process. She held her breath for a moment and looked up into the dark night sky. She listened for the maid or one of the Turneys to come around and check on the ruckus, but nothing happened.

She rolled onto her stomach and peeked in the lower corner of the window. The place was dark. Being on the outside edge of the Upper Crust, it was the servant's end of the house. (Who would want a view of Shack Town and the powerless Wilds out there? She'd heard Ironclads ask that question. More desirable views were inward, toward the central square and ordered streets.) It was dark in there; no waste of electric lights on the servants—an idea that had seemed quite practical only recently now agitated her. But it was good for her present intentions. She'd be able to sneak around better in the dark. She figured she'd need to bribe a guard or two to get to Jackson; that was as far as her current plan went. Get him safe, away from the evil little man with the horrific wardrobe and wheel, then worry about what to do next. So she had to get to Mr. Turney's office to borrow a little money.

She put her fingers to the edge of the window and pried. It held fast in its frame. High above her the improvised rope swayed in the breeze. Beyond the edge of the little lean-to roof darkness like the mouth of the behemoth gaped hungrily for her. She tugged the window again and got the certain sense that it was a molded part of the gritty wall. She made a fist and shoved it through the pane of glass, hating the singing noise it made on the floor below. She lay still for a moment to see if anyone would come to check it out. Inside the hole, the house was blessedly silent.

A dark spot on her knuckle showed that she had broken skin along with the glass. Pointed incisors of glass turned the hole she'd made into a screaming mouth. Carefully—with a bad ankle already, she couldn't afford an injured hand too—she reached inside and felt for a latch. In to her elbow, then farther in until her whole arm was inside the beast's mouth, she circled the sash and found no locking mechanics. This particular window was evidently intended only for natural light without the bother of fresh air. How inconsiderate—and inconvenient. Shevi gritted her teeth and slammed into the glass again, sending more shards and noise into the house.

She lay very still again, sure that someone would come and catch her. When nothing happened immediately, she quickly picked the triangular hunks of glass out of the bottom of the sash frame and pulled herself through the opening.

Then the ruckus started.

A horrific scream vibrated the interior of the Turney mansion.

311

Shevi's joints locked. She froze half in the window. There were stirs and footfalls here and there around her. She pulled back a few inches. A door swung open above her. The maid charged through it, rattling a knocker rod. The tip of the rod began to glow, opening up a view of the space below Shevi's intrusion. It was a staircase and the distance down to the uneven treads was several feet more than Shevi had anticipated. The maid screeched but not about the strangeness of a body poking in through the broken window.

"*The master's dead,*" she howled. "*Bernard, THE MASTER'S DEAD!*"

Shevi held perfectly still as the light of the maid's torch passed only a few inches below her. Glass crunched under the soles of the old woman's shoes and tinkled along after her, but she didn't notice. Shevi eased back out the window, remembering Mr. Turney rubbing his arm. It had happened. Her body went numb. He'd been a good man. No, he was a great man. Always smiling. Always happy. Only Shevi and her awkward ways seemed able to dampen his spirit.

The maid's induction torch lit a narrow hallway beyond the last tread of the stairs. Shevi could only see the hem of the woman's long dress. The light faded and she shook the torch to induce charge to the filament. "Bernard! Bernard!"

She banged on a door. It opened. Shevi contemplated getting down onto the stairs and going up to the second floor. She pulled herself back in the window almost to her waist as the door opened.

"What's the matter, woman?" the butler asked, sounding dazed.

"The master's dead," she repeated. "That awful girl has poisoned him."

Shevi, about to execute some sort of unarranged summersault through her violation of the Turney mansion perimeter, now froze. What had the woman just said? Mr. Turney had been poisoned? He hadn't died of a heart attack caused by the excessive Ironclad diet? And who was 'that awful girl'?

Shevi had missed her chance.

"Oh, for Scott's sake," Bernard gasped. He had pushed past the maid, up the stairs, his torch aimed right at Shevi who was sticking in the window like a figurehead carved into the prow of a ship. He halted, looking down at the path of glistening triangles decorating the way like Hansel's bread crumbs.

The maid shrieked, "There she is, that awful girl. She said she'd kill the master and she did."

She was stunned—Bernard, too. They stared into one another's eyes across the fading glow of the torch's filament.

"*Get her, Bernard!*" the maid screamed and pushed him.

Bernard woke from his paralysis of fright and confusion and swung the knocker rod at Shevi like swatting at a bug with a rolled up paper. Shevi, also jarred back to reality, yet another new reality, jerked back out the window and watched the bulb end of the torch shatter against the sash frame. The maid screamed, throwing up her hands and dancing around as if a rodent had scurried under the hem of her dress.

"She's here! She's here!" She whirled and ran down the hallway.

A door burst open and light flooded in from beyond it. The maid went on braying and tromping. When the sound of her footsteps had faded, others, larger and heavier, replaced them. The wall of the house vibrated with them. Shevi looked up at her open window. She crawled to the edge of the roof and looked out across the darkness. Back at the top, the butler was holding his sentry inside the window. Shevi worked her way across the top edge of the roof and found a roof below, the roof of a Terrace house. She looked back up and found a face staring down at her: Cole, holding a knocker rod torch in his hand.

"What did you do to him?" he wailed.

Shevi slung her legs over the sloping edge of the roof as another face poked through the open window above.

Leah shouted, "She's down there. She's getting away."

Shevi stretched out as far as she could down the corner of the house. She took a big breath, then another. The walls vibrated with excitement. Voices echoed around her. She let herself go, dropping down the rough surface of the wall, falling into darkness for what seemed like forever.

Chapter

Twenty-seven

Shevi hobbled through the streets of the Terraces of Wheel Six, dodging pools of light and stirrings in the dark places. Both ankles were banged up now, since she'd forced her good foot to take the bulk of abuse during her escape. She didn't have cab fare and wouldn't want to use one of the lifts anyway because the operators might already be warned that there was a murderer on the loose. Shevi couldn't believe it. She tried to warn them. And when the very thing she predicted happened, which should have been her testimonial, they turned it all around and used it against her. There was just no winning here. She knew how the lessers felt, those the ignorant people called Dims. They were being driven out of usefulness by a blockade of ideals.

She ducked into one of the service stairs and began a clumsy descent, thinking about everything she would need to rescue Jackson. She needed to rest, but that would take time. She had no time. She had no idea when the evil little man would put Jackson and his dad in that awful duel wheel, but she couldn't count on them wasting any time.

At Level 10 she heard a current of heavy footsteps on the stairs either above or below her; she couldn't tell which but she knew they were getting closer. And their voices were the low grumbles of men with dreadful intentions rather than the jocular songs of men whose intentions had been spent at the Club above or the Avenue below. She ducked into the counterpart of the place she had once called home in Wheel Three and found it alarmingly the same—the same long narrow corridors, the same ambient memory of food, the same muffled sounds of families settling into their little apartments after a long day on the wheel.

The north stair was quiet. She began her descent again. This time she made it all the way down to Electric Avenue and found it populated enough still this early in the evening that she could blend if she could manage to walk normally. This was easier now that both legs had approximately equal complaints, as long as she kept her going slow.

A bench in an alcove beside the entrance to Wheel Five offered a discrete place to rest. She rubbed her ankles and wondered if she could get more of the frozen veggies from the little man in the kitchen of Wheel Three—or maybe Wheel Four or one of the others. It seemed that if there was a funny little man in the kitchen of one wheel who liked her looks enough to share his stores with her, then there was probably one just like him in every other wheel. She'd never pondered just how engineered life was in I Town until now. Meeting Jackson had really messed up her world.

Out on the avenue a small man came by with an armload of posters. He scrubbed glue on a wanted poster of old King Ludd of the Wireless and slicked a new campaign ad over the crazy man's face, exchanging one of the flamboyant Richard Philbrook's photographs for another. This new one was even more chilling than the portrait of the mad chieftain of the Wilds. There it was. The Duel Wheel. Shevi remembered the man hopping about with his camera and knocker rod flash, snapping pictures of that event same as he had at the Stendahl wedding and at her own bid day festival.

In the photo at the center of the bright white poster the poor victim inside the barred wheel was still trying to compete against the Ironclad on the outside. The caption was an invitation to "The First Ever Public Display of Just Humiliation and Probable Execution of Terrorist and Seditionist Jackson Koss in the *Brand New!* DUEL WHEEL". The time was Thursday at 2:00 a.m., when demand was lowest and the fewest number of walkers were on the wheels. It didn't leave even as much time as she'd hoped, just over twenty-four hours to find him and figure out a way to free him. The place was the Hangar, where they had had the silly little hearing and the bid day festival. The price was an alarming three dollars, a full week's income for some people. Good. At that incredibly high price and ridiculous hour nobody would bother coming to see the abomination. The crazy little man could dance around the stage for . . . well, hopefully no one. But Jackson would be there—and enough Ironclads . . .

There was more, smaller text below, but Shevi had read enough. Disgusted, she turned sideways on the bench to ignore the repulsive image and propped the more aggravated of her two feet up on the seat to relieve the swelling. The skinny little man had moved on to put up another poster down the avenue when a pair of big voices interrupted Shevi's consideration that everything seemed to be pressing down on her.

"Ha ha ha. Gonna put them in the old spinner," one of them said.

"It's called the duel wheel," the other replied.

"Well, I like calling it the old spinner. You going?"

"Of course. I wouldn't miss it. You?"

"Oh, yeah. What a show that'll be."

"Look here. It says down here that Koss will be on public display from now until the event."

"Right here on the avenue under Wheel Three," the other chimed.

"Well, that's right down the way."

"Yeah. Let's go see him."

"Work up some spit along the way."

They both chuckled and stomped away. Shevi turned and watched them go. She stood up and felt suddenly sick from pain, not in her ankles but deep inside her. Everything around her seemed so putrid. She came out of the alcove and followed the pair of Ironclads down the avenue. They stopped before a small cage on wheels, exchanged jovial comments, and took turns gibing and hacking spit through the bars.

When they'd had their fun and moved on Shevi finally saw

Jackson. He was sitting in the middle of the cage, which wasn't much bigger than the crate he'd kept his books in, his knees pulled to his chest and his arms wrapped around them. Shevi's chin began to tremble until one of the black-and-whites guarding him looked her way curiously. At least she wasn't notorious yet. She drew in a deep breath and marched rigidly toward the cage.

As she passed the guard she asked, "Mind if I look at the pig?"

"That's what it's out here for, ma'am." When she walked right up to the bars, he said, "Careful, ma'am. It's highly dangerous."

"Looks like you've got him secured pretty well," she said, studying the shackles binding his hands and feet together and wondering how she would ever set him free.

"You can never be too careful with the likes of that," the guard said.

That? she thought. *It's.* He's not even a person anymore? But of course he wasn't; he was a Dim.

He glanced over at her and then turned away again.

She whispered, "I'll get you out of here."

"Get away from me," he whispered back.

"I've killed a man."

"You were acquitted."

"No. Since then. Another. Cole's dad died like everyone else is going to and they think I did it."

Behind her the guard said, "Ma'am, I'd really rather you didn't stand so close."

Inside the cage Jackson growled, "You'll be better off dealing with that than messing around with me. Haven't you learned that yet?"

"We've got to get out of this place," she pleaded.

His eyes cut suddenly and coldly toward her. "There is no *we* in B-Y-M-Y-S-E-elf." A maniacal grin spread across his lips. He snarled and crashed his face against the bars.

"*Ma'am!*" the guard shouted and pulled her back. "Did he hurt you?" He rattled his gigantic knocker rod and stepped between her and the cage.

"No," she screamed, not able to bear even the thought of the guard turning his weapon on Jackson. "He didn't hurt me. I'm fine. Please."

She pulled at the guard's arm until she heard a voice behind her shouting, "That's her. Seize her!"

It was Bernard, the Turneys' butler, and he had a mad posse behind him. Shevi ran past the guard who was still too intent on taking the excuse to shove his knocker rod through the bars and give his prisoner a good zapping to know what was going on behind him. She stole one more glance at Jackson as she fled.

Chapter Twenty-eight

Few things had satisfied Jackson as much as the moment when Shevi finally abandoned him, like a zit finally popping after days of festering or a sneeze finally exploding after minutes of nose burning and eyes watering.

She ran from him. Jackson appreciated this. Maybe, hopefully, she understood now that there was no *we* between them and never could be. No sins of the father for Jackson. She'd gone off and married Ward Stendahl—his mother, that was. He put his face back into his hands, seeing that another angry mob was coming to afflict him, and imagined her again, sitting at dinner in the Stendahl mansion. In his mind the Stendahl mansion had lots of vases with flowers in them. He was pretty sure that was only the case in his mind because cut flowers weren't the vogue in I Town. He adjusted the image to contain sculptures based on the Stendahl armorworks: figures made of crank- and camshafts, massive bouquets of leaf and coil springs, a pyramid of graduated engine blocks—a big old four-fifty V8 on the bottom and a tiny single cylinder four-cycle like the Carbon Nation used to mow their lawns way up on top. Flowers or engine blocks mattered not; the center of the vision was still the same: Jackson's mother laughing. She was always laughing and having the greatest time of her life, the way she had when he was little and Ava was still just a baby, before the weight minimums shot up and Dad lost his place on the wheel. She was happy again. She had moved on.

The realization hit him suddenly that the angry mob had moved on too. They ran past the cage in which Public Enemy #1 was being held and displayed for humiliation. They had no interest in the Dim boy who had defied and defiled all they held dear. They were chasing Shevi.

They were chasing *Shevi?!*

Jackson's shackles rattled as he grabbed the bars of his cage and peered through, watching the posse follow her into Wheel Three. The instant they had disappeared the bars bit into his fingers. A thousand tiny mouths all lined with pointed teeth had suddenly yawned open and snapped closed on his skin. His arms tensed and his shoulders drew together as voltage coursed through him. He and the bars released one another simultaneously and he turned to the guard who stood with his knocker rod still only an inch from the gridwork that separated them.

"No touching the bars, Dim," the black-and-white said.

"What was that all about?" he asked the guard.

The black-and-white shrugged.

"Did she really kill somebody?"

"I dunno."

"So, you might have just let a murderer escape?"

The guard looked around, confused or at least uncertain. "Shut up, Dim."

"You know," Jackson said, knowing he wasn't doing himself any favors, "if it weren't for that uniform, you'd be just another Dim yourself."

The guards nostrils flared and his eyes went horribly wide. He jacked his knocker rod about erratically. Jackson braced himself for the blow, but nothing could have prepared him for the depth of the charge. The black-and-white delivered the two-pronged end of the weapon to Jackson's ribcage. The tips themselves wounded his side. The voltage coursed through his muscle fiber. Behind all of this, he could feel not just his bladder but even his kidneys tighten and expel their contents into his crotch. His bowels did likewise.

As he slumped against the bars of the cage, back in the depths of his mind his mother, eating a chocolate bonbon, laughed at a joke someone had told while Ava crawled into her lap and hugged Heavie against her.

How many Dims does it take to turn on a light bulb?

Only one if he can get a ride on an Ironclad.

Chapter

Twenty-nine

Shevi's ankles kept quiet and let her run, at least until she was inside Wheel Three. But here the shouts of the angry mob outside were echoed by hisses and boos from people who recognized her. Here, the place that had been her home all her life, where people had known her dad and liked her and her family, she was now infamous for stealing a child, causing a man's death, aiding and abetting a terrorist, and, worst of all, standing idly by in her society's time of greatest need. Ty and Murray made rude gestures from her mom's favorite old gambling table. A manager left his post at the offramp platform and strolled unaffectionately her way.

She rushed for the service stair and began her ascent. That's when the agony in the lower legs trumped the flight response.

Every stair tread gave a ping to her tendons. She looked up the dimly lit shaft at the handrail twisting into infinity. Somewhere high above was Admin Level where the first exit from the tube would be. At the fifth, or perhaps it was only the fourth landing her own scuffing footfalls were joined by the sound of the door below bursting open and a herd of angry breathers entered the shaft. Now she was able to run again. She tried taking two stairs at a time but it was no good. After just a couple of strides she could tell it wouldn't help in the long run.

Glancing down, she saw flashes of hands and legs animated between the crissing and crossing of railings. Most were shuffling along behind old Bernard, but some had passed him and ran ahead, their feet pounding as they took maybe two, probably three stairs at a time. Above, the first opt out of the stair shaft dawned into view. Hope helped her manage a few two-riser strides—hope and the pounding of unfriendly feet behind her.

She shouldered open the door to Admin and ran in the only direction available, down a wide corridor with sparse options out of it. Instinct told her not to take the first one, but the second one led to the same place, the large control room that overlooked the walking zone of the wheel. Technicians glared at her. Down and across the hall was another door, smaller and dirty from use. She pushed against it, knowing it would be locked but getting a joyous surprise when it swung open and let her pass just as the door from the stairwell did the same for her pursuers at the other end of the long corridor.

More stairs waited behind this door. With a deep sigh, she commenced the climb, around another landing, farther up to a single exit option, some interstitial mezzanine within the administrative level. She made way for the door but drew back in shock when it opened automatically before her. Richard Philbrook came rushing through it toward her, too busy straightening his enormous bright orange bowtie to notice her until they were ready to collide. His eyeliner matched the color of his tie.

"Hello, lovely," he said, putting on a sudden and sincere smile. "Imagine meeting you here! There's been a murder. I'm off to get photos and the story."

"Hide me," Shevi said, "and I'll tell you what really happened."

"*You!?* Dear girl, what manner of god have you pissed off?" The door below burst open and Shevi's eyes hardly had time to widen before he hissed, "Come-come-come," and danced her around him and into whatever lay beyond.

He tucked her into a dark room filled with a nasty biting odor and closed the door behind them. When the tiny bulb sticking out of the wall by the door flashed on, Shevi found herself surrounded by hundreds of ghoulish faces, but as her eyes adjusted she found them to be only flat images on paper. She was in the photographer's darkroom. She found her own face among the crowd, staring back at herself with the eager anticipation of her bid day festival, her shock at hearing of Jackson's arrest at the Piedmont-Stendahl wedding reception, looking back at the insane crowd who watched her dance on the stage at Ward Stendahl's bachelor party. There was even one of her hugging Jackson's novel against her the day the president—or was he the king?—addressed the walkers of Wheel Three. It was like a history of the mountainous changes she'd been forced through.

"You're my favorite subject," Philbrook whispered, and she only then noticed that he'd moved in dangerously close to her and was looking at her with dangerous intensity. "I do believe you're the most beautiful creature I've ever had the good fortune of capturing." She jumped back, looking around frantically for the door. He grabbed her wrist and held it firmly. "On film, that is." He laughed but his eyes darted in their sockets as his gaze crawled around on her. "So—well-proportioned. You promised me a story." His tone went suddenly cold and serious. She glanced at the door again. The sound of the posse rumbled beyond it. "Don't worry about them," he said. "They wouldn't bother me."

So Shevi sat and told him all of her suspicions and suppositions about what had really happened to Mr. Turney and to her father and too many of the Ironclads. He listened with interest and intensity, nodding regularly in agreement with her arguments, eyes going wide when she declared the really radical ideas of the high calorie diet causing blockages in their circulatory systems. When she had finished he slapped his hands down on his knees with such vigor that it startled her.

Jumping to his feet, which scared her even more, he shouted, "What a story! What an amazing story." Shevi nodded. "I can't believe my luck of being here and happening to meet you and getting this from you."

"Right," Shevi said, finding herself perplexed that anyone actually believed her.

"I must write it up right away. But first I must go and get some pictures. Every story needs its visual component. Helps make it more believable."

"Yes," Shevi said.

"So you wait right here and I'll go get some pictures. Then I'll come back and we'll hammer it all out." He trotted toward the door. Shevi rose. "No, no, no. You just wait right here and I'll be back. You'll be perfectly safe here." He whirled out the door.

The instant the latch clicked, she noticed his camera and the knocker rod flash sitting on the table by the door. He's forgotten it, she thought at first. He'll come right back in any second, grab it, laugh at himself, and disappear again. His feet rattled down the stairs. She considered grabbing it and taking it to him, but then she remembered that she was a wanted girl. This was the only safe place for her, here where someone finally would listen to her and believe what she said.

She looked around the room at all the faces looking back at her, their eyes all focused directly on her. She knew that this was a trick, that each had only been looking at the camera when the photographer had 'captured' them, and that's why they all seemed now to look out of the photos directly at her. Their eyes would seem to shift if she moved around the room, never leaving her. The president was among them, and the princes: Tyler, Jasper and Hugh. Princess Sophia. Mayor Van Asche. Several of the wheel bosses. And there was a large collection of crazy Ludd, King of the Wireless of the Wilds. In one shot he sat contemplating something behind and beyond Philbrook's camera. It was one of the few photos in which the subject was not looking directly into the lens. What was interesting was that in the distance behind him a large round object interrupted the otherwise natural landscape—a tread-wheel. She couldn't tell how big it was because she wasn't sure how far away it was. But if she had to guess, she'd say it was about the same size as the duel wheel that Jackson would be forced into in a matter of hours, in which his sentence of death would be carried out.

Behind her the door popped open. She whirled and found Philbrook marching inside, past his camera where he'd left it on the table. No, he wasn't back for the camera, not exactly, because he hadn't come back alone. Mayor Van Asche came in behind him. Behind him was a crew of black-and-whites. Behind them, Bernard and members of his mob craned their necks to see what Philbrook had in his studio.

"Bind her," the mayor said.

Two of the black-and-whites rushed forward with the same thin straps that had secured Jackson's hands. One grabbed her while the other pulled her hands behind her and cinched them together. The mayor stepped forward and produced a dingy rag. Securing it across her mouth and tying it behind her neck, he said, "Mustn't allow that mouth to get you in any more trouble."

Philbrook stepped proudly up beside the mayor, his hands clasped nobly behind his back. "Quite a story, my lovely girl. But you didn't actually think that such a grand pronouncement against the very foundation of our society could be disseminated?" He and the mayor looked at each other and exchanged a mirthless laugh. Philbrook ran his eyes up and down her again, but this time it was with disgust. "Such a waste. Such a shame."

The mayor said, "I understand that in Agrarianna they must occasionally prune back some beautiful and healthy stock for the better of the whole crop. And so must we."

329

"And so we must," Philbrook said.

Jackson had drifted off sometime through the night when people became scarce enough to leave him alone. It was a blessing to finally get some rest; he of course wasn't surprised when it came to an end—all good things, as they say—when people began to pass by again to gibe him. He was however shocked at what he found when he woke completely: he wasn't taking all the abuse himself. Now he had a soul mate, a partner. Shevi sat huddled in a cage of her own, a match for the one he was in, shackled, facing him.

When the hecklers got tired of ridiculing the two of them and passed on, Jackson glared at Shevi and said, "You couldn't just leave it alone could you?"

Shevi raised her head out of the protective cover of her hands and looked at him. His heart melted. She was crying, as he had done after the first waves of assaults, before he settled into his own new status quo. He fought now to keep his defenses up. She was, after all, one of the lucky ones. She, after all, had the genes to rise up in this world. And she had sloughed it off like dead skin. He wanted to hate her for that. But looking at her . . . something about her reflected his irritation onto all others things around them: this place and its stupid needs. What if people could do or be or at least have the chance to be whatever they wanted to try to be? Self-willed individuals, as Christopher Bartlett had suggested. But that was crazy talk. That was Carbon Nation talk. And the species had almost destroyed itself and everything along with them because of it.

"You too, Jackson?" she begged, and he felt the place inside of him, that odd solid-void that made him feel like he could float upward and rise above the gravity that held him down.

"*Et tu, Brute?*" he said mockingly, fighting back that feeling that just shouldn't be, the feeling his dad had for the woman who rejected them. "I really didn't think they'd do this to one of their own. I figured the only way to get this treatment was to be born a *Dim.*" He sharpened this last word and thrust it at her to stab her with it.

And stab her it did.

She shot back like a wounded animal, all of her pride stripped away. "You're so pathetic," she blubbered and foamed. "Oh, poor me. Poor Dim me. Born too small to be put on a wheel and walked to death and fed poison and used and thrown away like a worn out shoe. Poor *pathetic YOU!*"

"Whoa." Jackson put up his hands as best he could in his shackles. "Easy does it, girlfriend. Are you actually suggesting . . ." Her eyes were torches and her lips were pursed with vehemence. "You're going to gripe about *your* state? Oh, please." He laughed.

She put her face back in her hands and began to sob harder still. Jackson watched her, trying to figure out what she was talking about. *She* could get a good job. *She* could provide for a family. *She* could have a family, for goodness sake. And she was *bitching*?

He wanted to hate her for that. But instead, he hated himself for the way he really felt: that she was special, that he wanted more than anything else to reach over and touch her, to feel his skin brushing against hers. How pathetic was that?

Her face rose again. He drew back best he could, putting what distance he could between him and another of her outbursts.

"They killed my daddy," she said.

"Well . . ." Jackson thought about that. He thought he remembered her saying that her dad had died of thrombosis or something. Lots of people died of that. And you couldn't say that anybody murdered any of them. They just died. Lots of them were Ironclads. Jackson considered this. What was this 'they' crap? THEY ran *his* dad off the wheel and out of work. Why? Because it was easier to feed one big guy than two little ones. It was more efficient to house one big guy than two little guys. It was easier . . . to . . . fatten . . .

"Wait," he said. "The Ironclad diet is *killing* them?"

They stared at each other.

"Like Randall Mann," she said.

"Who?"

"The guy in the book you gave me."

"*The Great God, Mann*?"

She nodded. "Like Mann."

Beyond her, on the wall of Wheel Three along Electric Avenue, Big Steve held out a big basket of vegetables and claimed to love them.

"How do you know?" he countered.

Beneath the poster of Big Steve and his plethora of veggies the doorway to the service stairwell of Wheel Three burst open. A pack of Ironclad kids gushed onto Electric Avenue. The leader yelled, "There they are." Another screeched, "They're still here." As they stormed toward them Jackson braced himself for more abuse. Kids were the worst. They didn't hold back, gave it their best, egged one another on, each trying to outdo the others, to be the best of the worst. The closer they came, the clearer it became that Shevi was their target. Jackson watched, horrified, as the pack swarmed around her like scavengers on carrion. He sat up straight, the crown of his head pressing against the top bars of his cage, and watched one of them jab at her with the gear end of a scepter. He knew that kid and that scepter from the beating he'd gotten for talking to Shevi the first time.

"Hey," he barked. "Leave her alone."

One of the boys looked over at him but the rest went right on. "You're dirt," one of them said. "Scum," said another. "Dim lover!" They spat and dumped rotten food through the top bars of her cage. Shevi tried to cover herself but her shackles were too short to allow her hands high enough. Watching this hurt Jackson much more than getting the abuse himself.

"*STOP IT!*" he shouted, his voice breaking as he felt the last of his dignifying control slip away. Then he felt something warm brushing the side of his face. The band ceased their torments to laugh and point. Jackson turned his head and got the full force of a stream of urine coming from the one who had acknowledged his first rebuke. He whipped his head back around then shook it wildly as the stream entered his ear.

The black-and-white watched with amusement, the big knocker rod slapping into one palm, and Jackson had a sudden wonderfully evil idea. He leaned all his weight left and then right, rocking the cage on its wheeled base. The guard stiffened. "Hey, Dim, quit that." He stepped forward as the first stream shot down the collar of Jackson's shirt for a second and another stream, this one from the boy with the scepter, came at Jackson's face.

"Make him be still," Scepter Boy told the black-and-white, and Jackson gleefully braced himself for the sickening thing that was about to happen.

The guard poked the two-pronged end of the knocker rod through the bars and into Jackson's shoulder. The point of contact was a severe, cutting pain but the payoff was more than worth it. The two peeing Ironclad boys shrieked and danced back from the cage, knocking over their friends like a bowling pins in a strike. Jackson rolled around to the extent his bonds would allow and laughed, howling when he saw the look on the black-and-white's face, terrified at having accidentally used his weapon on these kids of the elite. The streams of pee had shot around and the young mobsters who hadn't been bowled over danced disgustedly to get away from it.

Jackson cackled madly. "Piss on you," he sang. "Piss on all of you." Then he stopped, cut off in the midst of his outburst, his sudden sobriety borne by the guard who had recharged his knocker rod and was now sliding it through the bars of Shevi's cage, a wicked grin on his face as he watched Jackson.

Jackson tried to brace himself for the outcome, telling himself to keep what little upper ground he'd managed with his cleverness, but the way Shevi jerked against her shackles when the prongs touched her near the right kidney tore him apart. She snapped and whipped in the cage, her head banging against and scraping across the bars. Fingers bent in tormented angles as she reached in desperation for salvation and understanding. The mob stepped back and reorganized themselves as the guard recharged his weapon and went at her again. Some of the kids watched with delight, some in horror and disgust, as Shevi bounced and thrashed involuntarily.

Something flashed at the edge of Jackson's vision. He glanced away from Shevi's trial in time to see the geared end of the scepter shooting through the bars toward him. It collided with bone just above his eye. Bright spasms of light deposed his brain. And then darkness.

Chapter
Thirty

Jackson awoke to freedom, at least his shackles were gone and he was out in the open with no bars around him. He and Shevi weren't exactly free, only relatively so. The room was hard-surfaced, the floor sloping to a trench drain along one wall. His head throbbed. He remembered why. He had a goose egg on the side of it from Scepter Boy using it for a cue ball. His pants were full of piss and shit. Shevi sat against the opposite wall watching him—same basic condition. Now that he stirred, she crawled to him and stroked his cheek.

"I'm sorry," he said. When she looked puzzled, he explained, "You got the rod because of me."

"I wasn't the only one who got it," she said, choking on a sob.

She was about to say something else when the door burst open and Mr. Myrtle strolled in, swinging his knocker rod like a baton, leaving Jackson wishing all the more that he could hear what else Shevi had to say.

"Hello, kiddies," he sang. "Your public awaits."

Through the open door the sound of a crowd splashed in. Jackson looked into Shevi's eyes. She was afraid of the thing that awaited them. Two guards stepped over the raised threshold of the washroom door.

"Strip 'em and hose 'em down," Mr. Myrtle said. "I'll not present them in this pathetic state on *my* stage."

The two came forward and hauled Shevi to her feet. They sliced and tore the clothes off her entire body, leaving her completely bare before Jackson. Then they grabbed him up and did the same to him. One turned on a hose and sprayed them recklessly while the other and the imp watched with satisfaction. When he was done, Mr. Myrtle and the other guard came to Jackson and each grabbed an arm, pulling up and apart until they had him stretched out. The other turned Shevi to face Jackson. She looked at the floor, but the guard grabbed a handful of her hair and yanked her head back.

"Look at him," Mr. Myrtle hissed. "Look at this skinny, scrawny thing you traded a wonderful future for."

Shevi stared intently into Jackson's eyes, and he did the same, refusing to look at her body, disobeying as best they could.

Shevi's gaze suddenly darted sideways toward Mr. Myrtle. A quizzical expression crossed her face.

"What!?" the little man barked.

Shevi's chin quivered.

"*WHAT!?*" His voice rang in the slick and wet room.

"I know who you are."

"It's about *time*," Mr. Myrtle screamed.

"No," Shevi said. "I mean . . . you know the Prathers, don't you?"

He rushed across the floor, skipping as the soles of his boots slid on the water, and slapped her hard, sending the tails of his jacket flapping as he did. Then he spun to face Jackson, reaching back with a stiff arm to point at Shevi.

"You see this?" He yelled, his face red, his little round belly pumping with each heavy breath. "You see this? You know what she'll do? She'll use you. She'll play with you. Then she'll throw you away." He stopped right in front of Jackson. They were nose to nose, those green eyes on fire with rage, and Jackson saw what Shevi had recognized. He had known the girl that brought the thugs to the cinema looked familiar. It was Mr. Myrtle's eyes he had seen then, glaring angrily at him, wanting him dead. And that black stubble on her scalp would have grown out as thin and fine hair that dangled down the sides of her face just as his did. "*YOU KNOW!*" Now he was stabbing a finger at Jackson and screaming. "*YOU KNOW!* Your own mother did it to you." Stepping back, nostrils flaring, he said, "And after all I did for you, you go running after her." He pointed again at Shevi.

"What did you do for me?" Jackson asked coolly.

"*What did—*" The man jumped up and down and stomped his feet. "I gave you books and I gave you a place to be and I gave you a chance to be something more. And you threw it away for the first girl who came along and had a little meat on her bones."

338

"I earned—"

"*I GAVE IT TO YOU!*" He turned away and grabbed up his walking stick. Marching between his two prisoners, panting, grinning, he said, "I've got something else to give you, and you won't have a chance to refuse it. Dress them." He whirled and shot out of the washroom like a serpent.

One guard tied a thin string around Jackson's narrow waist and dropped a strip of white fabric down its front, pulled it between his legs and tucked it over the string at his back. The other guard tossed a big white sheet over Shevi and pulled her head through a hole cut in its center.

Jackson's dresser smirked and whispered in his ear, "White, so the blood will show up."

Jackson looked at Shevi and saw that edifice of fear again. Whatever was coming, she knew it well and dreaded it deeply.

They were marched out of the washroom where a band of guards surrounded them and led them at rod tip into the vast space of the Hangar, a temple dedicated to the great god Man from a time when he could fly. The enormity of the space was amazing, but more amazing was how full of people it was. Jackson guessed that ninety percent of the hundred thousand inhabitants of I Town had shown up for the event. He wondered how they were keeping the wheels turning. The crowd chanted and jeered. When someone raised a hand to throw something, one of the guards pointed his knocker rod that way and shook his head.

Protect the whiteness, Jackson thought, and almost smiled. Then he saw the main attraction: the stage and the big wheel on it, the goal of their march. He examined the thing, not quite believing what he was seeing.

He looked over at Shevi and found her blanched ghostly white. "That's it?" he asked. When she nodded he had to laugh.

◎

Shevi had dreaded the duel wheel from the first moment Mr. Myrtle had suggested it to the mayor. At first she hadn't really believed they would do such a thing, but sometime in the course of being shoved into that cage she began to believe, and sometime while Kyle and the others heckled them, she had repented her choices. She actually came to wish she was with Cole, getting married, getting on with life as a good Ironclad wife and mother, a matriarch and a dietitian who could carefully consider her family's output on the wheel and know how much of what foods they needed. That had been the worst of it: that she had reached the point of selling herself, of regretting ever meeting Jackson Koss. And it was mainly because of his friend Christopher Bartlett, because she had seen what had happened to him, how helplessly he'd been tossed around in that wheel, and feared the thought of it happening to her and to Jackson.

And now here it was, standing before them and they were being marched toward it—she and Jackson—and she felt the dread tighten its grip around her throat to the point that she could hardly breathe. She'd wanted to tell him it was worth it, there while she had huddled over him, when the little man and the guards had burst in. For that brief moment, after he had apologized for the sins of this insane society, she had forgotten her dread and fear and just wished to say that everything she had been through was worth it: worth knowing him and worth knowing the truth he'd shown her.

But now the wheel was there, and she could see the poor victim being tossed around inside it like a rag in a clothes dryer, and she didn't want to see that happen to Jackson and she didn't want it to happen to her. And the worst part of it all was that Jackson didn't know; he couldn't realize what they were facing, obviously, because he just looked at the monstrous wheel and laughed.

He was walking along beside her toward the instrument of their death and he didn't care. He was looking around at the enormous crowd—Shevi recalled believing that nobody would bother coming out at this hour and paying the outrageous admission, but how wrong she had been—and looking at the Hangar and the wheel like it was his first movie and it was all just too fascinating and awesome to believe.

He looked over at her, that twinkle of his burning brightly in his eye now, and whispered, "They're in for a big surprise."

"What are you talking about, Jackson?" she whispered.

"Well, look at it."

"I am. It's horrible."

"It's pathetic." He stared hard at her as if trying to understand something strange about her. "It's a bad design. It's all wrong. I don't know who came up with it but they don't know jack about physics and structure." Then the smile flashed again, and it thrilled her despite her fear and confusion. "But they're about to meet Jack."

They were mounting the stage now, the awful torture contraption looming above them. The crowd was cheering at Mr. Myrtle's prompting. Shevi and Jackson were made to stand on either side of him. The guards formed a semicircle behind them. It was all so mean. Poor Jackson stood there with the muscles of his thin arms and the taper of his torso to his narrow waist exposed shamefully. Shevi was draped in a tent that hid all of her natural assets. They were made to be the worst people they could be.

They could run. She could imagine doing it, just bolting and fleeing . . . but she looked around at the options and found none that would actually work. The crowd was so wide and so deep, arrayed against them. And Jackson, she feared, had finally gone completely insane; this whole thing delighted him. But he didn't know. He hadn't seen what they did with the horrible duel wheel. Shevi just wanted to reach around this little monster that stood between them and grab Jackson's hand and tug him along behind her as she ran . . . into the crowd . . . pushing their way through the crowd . . . it could—

Suddenly her hand had been grabbed and tugged upon. She gasped. The muscles in her legs jerked in preparation for the flight she'd been imagining. But it wasn't Jackson who had taken hold of her; it was Mr. Myrtle. He hoisted her hand and Jackson's into the air.

"*Our champions!*" he shouted. The microphone was tied around his neck and broadcast his words across the seemingly infinite space of the Hangar.

The crowd boiled around the stage.

"All of you know why we're here," he said, calming them. "Some of you know how the game works." He glanced at Shevi and flicked his eyebrows up and down. "But please bear with me and allow me to explain it to those who don't know what to expect." Now he had turned to Jackson and the two were exchanging a look of daring.

"Isn't he just a little spitfire, folks?" Mr. Myrtle said. He allowed the sound of utter hatred to sizzle across the sea of people.

He stepped out to the edge of the stage, leaving Shevi and Jackson alone together in front of the guards. Again, Shevi contemplated escape, looking for some way out. The little man explained how the condemned would be put inside the wheel and their challengers would be outside. Whichever could offer the greatest force to turn the wheel would win. Shevi met Jackson's eye. He winked at her. She sighed, hopeless.

The little devil man came back to them and retook his place between them. "Now, Shevi," he said casually, "I wonder if there is anything you'd like to say, any last words—regrets, perhaps." He faced her but was grinning wildly at the crowd who had gone dead silent.

Part of her wanted to say yes, that she was sorry she had ever met Jackson, to admit that she just wanted to go off and marry Cole and if he'd take her back right now she'd step down off this stage and go with him. But she put her mouth near the offered microphone and only said, "No."

Mr. Myrtle shrugged. "Well, I had to offer. It's only fair. And speaking of fair," he said to Jackson. "Do *you* have any last words?"

The crowd seethed. Jackson stared out across them, out toward where the huge door stood open like a yawning mouth to make room for more spectators than the vast building could hold.

Leaning over to get his mouth close to the microphone, he said, "Let's get started."

Chapter

Thirty-one

Its name was the only thing about the 'Duel Wheel' that anybody had bothered putting any mental effort into. In the Carbon Nation, trucks with *dual* wheels hauled freight back and forth across the country, and a duel was a fight between two opponents, so Jackson was willing to give one point for a good pun. But the design of the wheel was all wrong. It was about four times as tall as it was wide, yet it used an undercarriage support system, two pairs of wheels. The support wheels were small and each had a small lip like the lip on the wheel of a train car to hold the bigger wheel between them. It was similar to the design of the big broad induction generator treadwheels, but they were only about twice as tall as they were wide, weighed hundreds of tons, and had hundreds of big train car wheels as their undercarriage. This *duel wheel* was nothing more than a cage of bars, and probably not even solid bars but hollow tubes of metal; it probably didn't weigh much more than he and Shevi did together. This, and the fact that the undercarriage support system was way too small to guarantee stability, gave Jackson a wonderfully wicked idea.

At first it offered only an opportunity to show Mr. Myrtle and the rest of these people how stupid and pathetic they were. It was limited to toppling the wheel. But that would only postpone the inevitable fate of the two alleged seditionists while adjustments were made. And that would only make the whole affair of their execution harder on Shevi who was extremely intimidated by the wheel. Rightly so, Jackson was sure—she'd seen it in operation.

But then a second thought had hit Jackson like a rotor to the forehead. It happened the instant the little imp had explained how the Duel Wheel 'game' worked. Up to that point Jackson had to admit that a kind of fatalism had set in. He'd given up on life, had felt hopelessly alone, since now even Dad had abandoned and rejected him. Losing Dad had really broken his will to go on. But then he'd been paired back up with Shevi—ah, beautiful Shevi— and he wasn't alone anymore. It was a bittersweet reunion. He loved being with her but couldn't believe she'd messed up so badly that the good life had slipped from her fingers. So it wasn't just him anymore. And he had dragged her into this. He knew this. If he hadn't been there peddling his books, if he hadn't tried so hard to sell her, if he hadn't gone and stolen that book from Grandpa Piedmont's library . . . He felt like such an idiot now for doing that. He'd chased after her. No wonder Dad had gotten sick of him.

Jackson must have looked like the biggest idiot in the world. He had to try to get her out of this, if it was the last thing he did.

Then the demon Mulligan Myrtle had explained about having one walker inside the wheel and one outside and Jackson immediately saw a revolutionary new opportunity to double production output of the induction treadwheel generators.

Dual rotors!

The standard design for the electric generator had a stator and a rotor. The stator, or static part, was fixed and didn't turn while the rotor turned either inside or around the stator. One had the coils of wire in which the current of electricity was induced. The other held the magnetic field that did the inducing. It couldn't be a steady magnet field; only a changing field would induce current in a coil. The faster the rotor passed by the stator, the faster the coils experienced the changing magnetic field, the more current they produced.

A big problem with the induction treadwheel was that it turned very slowly. To get the frequency of sixty hertz of alternating current, which was necessary to keep light bulbs from appearing to flicker and to make the standard wired electric motor turn, the coils under the tread of the great wheels of I Town were very small and very close together. But if you turned the outer field shell at the same time you turned the inner coil tread in the opposite direction, you'd get twice the output, maybe more.

This idea gave Jackson something to live for. He actually looked around the crowd to see if Sec Elec was among them. This idea would get him an internship with the great man for sure. An internship with Sec Elec would put Jackson in a position to afford a wife and maybe even a family—if he could avoid the Piedmont Protocol that called for sterilization of Dims.

So mere mayhem wasn't enough. Jackson needed to reset the situation. He needed to find a way to get an audience with Sec Elec. At first he considered pleading for the chance, but begging would only delight and inspire the evil Mr. Myrtle, not to mention his hordes of constituents who were much more interested in seeing blood than improving I Town's output.

Escape was what Jackson needed, and that unstable wheel, paired with the fact that the huge door of the Hangar stood open, might—just might—offer that opportunity. He had to try, for Shevi and for himself. And for the corporation, he supposed.

Cole was there with two of his brothers and Leah and Hester. Shevi saw them off to the left of the stage just before she was grabbed and thrust into the Duel Wheel. The Myrtle man went on with his explanations and introductions as a big man was lowered from the high structure of the Hangar. He dangled from a harness just above the top of the wheel. Jackson dove readily through the open hatch into the belly of the wheel. But Shevi flinched and screamed at a loud bang just over her head as she was pushed through the hatch. The crowd roared, delighted, and she saw that a man inside had touched the end of his knocker rod to the bars.

Jackson glanced back at her and winked. He actually seemed to be enjoying all of this. Shevi was sure now that he'd gone mad. Maybe he'd just snapped and didn't care anymore if he lived or died and whatever weakness he claimed to see in the contraption was just a cover for his true apathy. But as soon as they were both inside, he crouched and made a subtle invitation for her to join him. She checked the manager. He was still reveling in the response he'd gotten from the audience, so she knelt on the cold steel rungs of the wheel's curved tread, not believing she had actually gotten herself into this kind of mess.

"What do they do for a warm-up?" he whispered, the most serious and intense look she had ever seen on his face.

"What do you mean?"

"Well, they're not going to get all the people out here and kill us in fifteen seconds. How do they draw it out?"

"I can't remember."

"Think," he hissed.

Shevi shook her head. Every time she thought about that horrible evening of the bloody bachelor party her mind would skip around the most gruesome aspects. It was like a book with some of the pages torn out.

"Come on," he said. "Help me out here."

"They'll have us turn it by ourselves," she said, straining as she relived the torture of Christopher Bartlett. "Then the one up there will join us and we'll all work togeth—" Her voice broke.

"Stay with me," Jackson said. His voice was stern but comforting.

"Hey," the manager barked. "Get busy."

His knocker rod arced off the bars just above Shevi's head again, and again she screamed. The audience laughed again as she and Jackson climbed the tread and set the wheel in motion. A wave of nausea threatened Shevi's balance. Jackson took her hand.

"Trust me," he said. "Please."

She stifled a sob and swiped at a tear with her free hand. "It was worth it," she whispered.

"What?"

"It was worth it. I wanted to tell you that back in the room where they washed us. The cage and the kids and all that. It was—"

"*Is*," he said. "And will be. Don't go condemning us to past tense before you see what I've got planned."

They were going at a pretty good pace now. Outside the cage, Mr. Myrtle offered sarcastic praise and prompted the audience to encourage them.

"I wish I could strangle him," Shevi whispered.

"How about making an ass out of him?" Jackson said. "Would that do—for now?"

Shevi nodded, wondering what he would do and wishing they'd just get on with it.

"When the big guy gets on," Jackson said, pointing upward, "and I say go, I want you to run as far as you can up the wheel. I mean grab the rungs up there and climb. It's going to be hard to do in that thing they've got you wearing. Can you tighten it up so it's not getting in your way?"

"How?"

The knocker rod arced beside them again and the manager barked, "Less talkin, more walkin."

"You tell 'em, George," Mr. Myrtle crooned. "Ray, I think they could use some help. Are you ready?"

Jackson grabbed the corner of the sheet and tore at it until he had a long strip free. He handed it to her and made a spinning gesture with his hand. She followed the suggestion and tied it around her waist. This made all the difference in the world. Now at least she'd die without being troubled by her wardrobe.

There was a bang above them as their opponent was set down onto the outer side of the wheel's tread. The smooth roll of the wheel jerked, nearly throwing Shevi off balance.

"Easy," Jackson whispered, then he yelped and ducked as the manager's rod shocked him.

"I said no talkin."

Jackson snarled. "*GO!*"

Shevi did what he'd told her to do. She lunged forward, as hard and as fast as she could. Jackson disappeared from her side. An instant later the manager shouted angrily then howled in pain.

Shevi scrambled up the rungs of the wheel's tread. The wheel rocked oddly as she glanced back to see what Jackson was doing, but he seemed to have disappeared. An instant later he descended from above, dangling by one hand, holding the manager's knocker rod in the other. He loped along beside her, using his free hand to pull himself up the revolving bars. Their opponent outside the wheel hollered with surprise as the wheel suddenly lunged forward and down. Shevi wasn't sure what was happening until she saw that the scenery outside the wheel was moving, an odd condition for a treadwheel. But it was no longer a treadwheel, set in a fixed location; it was in motion, moving across the stage. They had jumped it off its undercarriage!

"*No!*" Mr. Myrtle screeched. "That is not how it's done!"

Shevi glanced around as Jackson used the butt of George's knocker rod to gouge the man hard in the forehead. The manager slumped in his saddle, arms dangling over the center axle, head lulling.

"Keep it going," Jackson shouted. "Turn it. Toward the edge of the stage."

Jackson rode the side of the wheel upward, making it tilt the way he had ordered. When Shevi turned back to face the tread rungs she found herself almost nose to nose with a terrified Mr. Myrtle. His eyes bulged. He whirled and ran from the oncoming wheel, screaming like a frightened maid, waving his walking stick like a conductor's baton. He bailed off the edge of the stage. The crowd gave him room, then, with gasps and shouts, yielded even more of the floor as the Duel Wheel plunged into their midst with a crash and a shudder.

Jackson landed beside Shevi and gave a fierce war whoop. "*GO!*" he shouted. "*Out the door!*"

Mr. Myrtle ran ahead of them, parting the sea of astonished faces. Shevi's ankles throbbed again, but she charged ahead, gaining on the flashy coattails that flapped behind the little man. She gritted her teeth now, finally seeing the maniacal wonder in Jackson's plan. They were almost out, nearly at the big open door at the back of the Hangar, when the revolving rungs of the wheel began snapping at the tails of Mr. Myrtle's jacket.

He dodged to the right, but not fast enough. The wheel crawled up his back, shoving his face down into the dirty street. The wheel rolled over him, rising as it climbed the bulge of his middle. Jackson lunged up the side of the wheel again, but this time he didn't get high enough to make a difference. The wheel wobbled then pitched, teetering around like a dazed giant about to faint.

Jackson looked down at Shevi. "It seems we've lost our

351

momentum."

As the wheel began to fall. Mr. Myrtle screamed. He had managed to turn himself over just in time to see the side of his torture device falling toward him. He put a hand up as if to deflect the second attack or scare it off with the knocker rod he held. But the wheel didn't care for its master anymore than it cared for its victims. It fell on him with a jarring rattle.

Shevi and Jackson stood on the tilting side of the wheel. All around them faces stared through its bars. The handle of Mr. Myrtle's walking stick poked up through the bars beneath their feet.

"I'll take that back," Jackson said.

Chapter

Thirty-two

Jackson handed Shevi the manager's knocker rod and unlatched the door of the Duel Wheel, which now lay on its side like a flying saucer from an old sci-fi story. They climbed together out of the hatch. The crowd backed away and stared in wonder at the alien beings who had landed in their midst.

Shevi whispered, "What's the plan?"

The spectators out here were smaller than the ones up at the stage, Jackson's people, his size and class. He saw a familiar face. Mr. Lambert, the old man who guarded the entrance to the Upper Crust of Wheel Eight. For a moment Jackson thought he could find alliances among these people at the fringe, until the old man spoke up.

"What have you done, boy?"

An old woman shouted, "She killed the master. *Murderess!*"

Jackson pulled the rubber ball off the top of the walking stick and gave it a shake to charge it while he shook his head in amazement. "I guess we fight our way out."

He bailed off the wheel, giving the best predatory howl he could, his loincloth flapping between his legs. The crowd clamored and fell back. Behind him, Shevi descended gingerly, letting herself down onto the street by her arms. She joined him and faced the crowd with much less presence than he'd hoped for.

"Are you okay?" he asked.

"Yeah," she whispered. "My legs had a good beating, that's all."

"Stay with me. Shock them or club them with that thing. Whatever it takes. We've got to get someplace safe."

He jabbed the prongs of his knocker rod at the crowd and they obliged. Mr. Lambert stepped aside but shook his head.

They were almost out of the crowd when someone yelled, "Stop them."

Jackson didn't look back to see who it was; he grabbed Shevi's hand and ran, tugging her along behind him. Her knocker rod rattled as she sprinted past him.

"It's Cole," she said.

They ran to Electric Avenue, entering the broad street at about its midpoint. Wheel Eight was to their right, Wheel Three to their left. A murmur of voices coupled with the rumble of stamping feet swelled behind them. They crossed the avenue and ducked into the service hall between Wheels Six and Seven.

"Up?" Jackson asked. "Lots of places to hide."

The dread that had been on Shevi's face as they were led to their intended demise was there again. "I don't want to hide."

She went to the stair that led to the cellars and loading docks. He followed her down. They came out of the narrow cascading shaft to the smells of fresh breads and meats and the sight of open boxcars. The loading dock was as long as Electric Avenue, echoing its gentle curve along the plan of I Town. Scattered among the huge piers that supported the undercarriages of the wheels, workers pushed carts and pulled wagons full of food to fuel the walkers above. At the far end, down below Wheel One, couplings banged against one another as the train set out for Agrarianna where it would be reloaded for the evening run.

The door from the stair behind them burst open. Jackson grabbed Shevi's hand again and took off running.

"*Wait!*" It was a woman's voice.

"Mom?" Shevi said and yanked back on Jackson's hand.

Shevi ran toward her but the woman shook her head and waved at Shevi to stop.

"They're coming, Shevi. You have to go." She looked at Jackson. "Take her and go. Both of you."

"Go where?" Jackson shouted.

"Get on the train," Shevi's mother said. "It's the fastest way out of here."

Shevi said, "You come too."

"I—" The door behind her slammed open again. The guy who had cracked Jackson's head into the rotor ran out alone, the familiar rotor bouncing against his chest. Shevi's mom whirled. "Cole! *No!*" She grabbed him.

The engagement of the boxcars' couplings dominoed past them and the train began to move.

"I'm gonna kill you," Cole said, jabbing a finger at Shevi.

Jackson grabbed her arm and pulled her toward the train. "Come on."

They'd ride the train out of town, he figured. Just far enough away to be safe. Then he'd figure a way to get back to Sec Elec and tell him his new idea and redeem himself. He towed her until Cole got loose from the woman. Then, Shevi turned and ran. They jumped the narrow gap between the edge of the loading dock and the nearest open car, feeling the acceleration of the train beneath their feet. Jackson grabbed the big door and began hauling it shut. Fat hands latched on from the other side and pulled back. Cole's face loomed beyond the open door. Shevi rushed forward and smashed them with the manager's knocker rod. He gave an angry barking grunt and fell away. Jackson and Shevi watched as he stumbled and fell into the open door of the next car back.

On the loading dock, a mob ran toward the train. Jackson pushed the door shut as the engine sped up and the last pier at the end of I Town flashed by.

Jackson waited to see if the train would stop, but it went on, beginning the climb up to the farmlands of Agrarianna. There was a long open meadow just south of town that would be their first option to jump off the train. Jackson rolled the door open and looked out. The soft glow of moonlight illuminated a flurry of passing tall grass and bushes. The train wasn't moving fast; it had plenty of time to make the few miles up to Agrarianna.

He turned to Shevi. "We can get off now."

"What about Cole?"

Jackson stuck his head out the door and checked the next car. Cole stared back, his face twisted with rage. "Two of us, one of him," Jackson said, thinking of getting his hands on that rotor hanging from the big guy's neck, returning the arc-shaped scar.

Cole yelled, "I'll kill both of you."

"Yeah, we'll see about that," Jackson replied. To Shevi he said, "Ready?" As she took his hand to jump with him, he saw the flicker of torches across the open field. He halted. She bumped into him, pushing him out the door. He let go of her hand to grab the door and yank himself back inside.

"What?" she asked.

"Freaking Luddites," he said, pointing at the advancing dots of light. He could risk it. He could jump off right now and make a run for I Town, but she couldn't make it, especially if Cole jumped too and gave them trouble. He could go back, sneak in, find Sophia or Hugh and try to convince them of his innocence and worth. They had seemed to like him. They'd probably do everything they could to help him. He had a great idea to share, the kind of idea that can put a person at the top of society. But he turned and looked at Shevi, the glow of the moon on her face, lighting up her eyes.

Up ahead, the engine would be getting close to the narrow pass cut into the hills where they became too steep for the tracks to ascend. Jumping once they entered the pass would be suicide. He had to choose.

He shoved the door fully open and sat his half-bare butt down on the floor of the boxcar, letting his feet dangle in the breeze. He looked up at her and patted the threshold beside him. She sat. They gave one another a long look.

"It was worth it," he said.

"What?"

He nodded back toward I Town, which lay in the valley behind them like a huge concrete and metal caterpillar. "All that. Getting thrown out of home. Myrtle and his junk." He took her hand. "It was worth it to get to meet you."

Her eyes were bright now. And he was crazy. This proved it. He touched her cheek and coaxed her face over toward his and kissed her.

From the next car Cole yelled, "*Hey!*"

They laughed at him.

Jackson yelled back, "Hey, Cole. Guess what? Out here there aren't any Dims or Ironclads—just us and you."

The riders were closing in now, racing with the train to the narrow pass cut into the hill. There was a flash and a bang and splinters flew from the boxcar Cole rode in. He pulled back and disappeared.

"Those devils have guns," Shevi said.

Jackson started to get up, but the air changed and the scenery vanished behind a rising shear wall of broken rock. He settled back down and squeezed Shevi's hand.

He didn't know where they were going or what lay ahead, but, whatever it was, they were doing it together. And it would be worth it—worth being with her.

THE END

SPECIAL THANKS TO

All the people who read early drafts and guided this work to a much better place.

Hayley and Will for pointing out some special places to make improvements.

Sarah, Bekah, and Shirley for excellent and thorough proofing.

Dr. Iris G. Shephard for editing and providing valuable insights in teen dystopian fiction.

My family for carefully alternating between offering support and space as I Town grew from its foundations to final realization.

Joseph Looney for advice on structural options for those tricky floors that span the inside the revolving wheels.

Kevin Lewelling and Donald Hayes for directing and encouraging my investigation into the feasibility of an induction treadwheel generator.

And a very special thanks to Al Silano for his many hours of patiently navigating me into the mysterious physics of electricity. Without his efforts, this work would never have been possible.

www.InductionTown.com

About the Author

TIMOTHY KOCH lives in Fayetteville, Arkansas, where he does computer graphics, drafting, and web design. Learn more at:

www.timekoch.com

Agrarianna

by

Timothy Koch

Chapter One

As the train trundled up the pass to the plateau of Agrarianna Jackson tried to enjoy the moment, holding the hand of the most amazing girl he'd ever met, ignoring the fact that their chance to escape would be narrow. The fractured rock cliff beside the track diminished to open up a grand view of the starry sky. They sat in the open door of the boxcar, feet dangling above the passing rocky track bed. He leaned over to steal one more kiss from Shevi before whatever hell awaited had the chance to dawn on them, but he'd waited too long.

Shevi's eyelids just started to flutter closed in expectation when she saw something that made her gasp and draw back, eyes wide and worried. Jackson turned to see an infinite barrier rise into view. It was a patchwork of colors stretching out of sight in both directions. It appeared that someone had boarded up the entire horizon, like the future in that direction had been closed permanently. The Iron Curtain—a fence made of Carbon Nation road signs surrounding godless and godforsaken Agrarianna. It was on them already, so soon. A guard tower loomed beyond, another silhouetted in the light of the setting moon. The train began to brake.

"What do we do?" Shevi whispered.

They were on the flat now, out in the open. Nothing hiding them from view except the faint twilight. A barren field stretched away from the tracks.

Jackson hadn't escaped execution down in I Town to fall into a worse fate up here. "Can you jump?" he asked. Shevi's ankles had taken some pretty bad abuse over the last couple of days.

Her eyes went to the Iron Curtain, the fear in them transforming into resolve. She nodded, tugged him toward her and kissed him.

When they parted, he asked, "On three?"

"Three!" she yelled and bailed off the worn threshold of the boxcar.

Jackson plunged with her. The ground was unyielding. It jarred his teeth and bones and guts. Their momentum rolled them across it relentlessly. There were rocks and thrashing sticks and brittle grass. Jackson found himself on his hands and knees, his skin stinging from the abusive impact. The front flap of the loincloth Mr. Myrtle's goons had dressed him in for his execution dangled from the thin cord around his waist. He checked Shevi. She was on her side, her bulky white gown wadded around her. She coughed.

"You okay?" he shouted over the rumble of railcar wheels.

She opened her mouth to answer but a roar from above drowned out her words. Something big landed near Jackson and bowled into him, scrubbing his bare skin along more of the uncaring ground. It was Cole, the big lug Shevi had been betrothed to back in I Town. Jackson had already taken one beating from him and had no intention of taking another. The big sandy-haired guy jumped to his feet, fists ready, but didn't come for Jackson. He turned his ruddy face toward Shevi. Pure hatred contorted his fat features.

"YOU KILLED MY DAD!" The roar shamed the sound of the train wheels on the track. Somewhere ahead, one dog barked and set off a chorus of baying.

"Hey, big guy," Jackson hissed. "Keep it down." He rose to his hands and knees again and peered cautiously in the direction the train was going. Lights flashed up there.

In the other direction Shevi wrestled with the robe Mr. Myrtle had selected to hide her wonderfully round body. Cole advanced on her.

Jackson jumped up and ran to him. "Listen, I don't know what your deal is, but—"

Cole's fist blasted against the side of Jackson's head. "Stay out of this, Dim," the big boy shouted.

Jackson staggered. With as hard as the contact had been, it still didn't bother him as much as the noise the idiot was making. He found a big rock, an equalizer, and prepared an assault to silence the giant when the ground around them exploded with light. Gray turned to stark white. Black turned blacker. Colors went to extreme, washed out hues: green, brown and red. Cole's eyes were white-hot spots on his red face, his mouth a gaping hole. He looked above and beyond Jackson, and Jackson knew what he was seeing— the guard tower's beacon had come on and was shining right at them. Jackson ran to Shevi and grabbed her hand.

She looked up at him and shook her head. "I can't."

He tugged at her. "Yes, you can."

"No." It was a sigh, a surrender.

"Shevi, try."

"Go."

"To hell with that." Behind him, Cole drew in a long terrified breath. Jackson spun around. "Yeah, here we are. You get it now, genius? We've got to get out of here. You've got to help Shevi. Got it?"

Cole looked at them, wide-eyed and open-mouthed. For a couple of loud heartbeats Jackson thought it would work. Cole looked shocked enough to go along with anything other than getting captured by the heartless cannibals of Agrarianna. But then fear overcame any form of rational or irrational thought. Cole belted out a shocking infantile cry and blasted past Jackson and Shevi with speed that was impressive for a guy his size.

The dogs' barking ramped up in volume. They were coming.

"Go," Shevi begged.

"No," Jackson replied. He stood by her and watched as a pack of the biggest, fiercest four-legged creatures he had ever seen charged toward them.

He took her hand. She squeezed his. They drew together like

beads of water on the side of a glass, not necessarily of their own will, but of the imposition of their circumstance.

The dogs had teeth, big teeth bared in hunger or anger. The fur of their brown coats rippled in the draft born by the swiftness of their feet. They were yards then feet then inches away. Then they were gone. They charged by the pair in total ignorance or with complete lack of concern. Jackson and Shevi watched after them, watched another oval of light span across the open field. Cole was a brilliant pantomime flailing against a seemingly infinite blackness—until the dogs caught up with him.

Jackson flinched and cringed. Shevi whimpered. Then a new sound disturbed them. Coming up from behind them, from the direction the train had gone, a cacophony of rattles and squeaks. Together, they looked back. Little lights flickered and bounced toward them—fast.

Jackson looked into Shevi's eyes. "Are you sure you can't?"

"No," she said uncertainly. She took a couple of steps toward where the dogs had Cole and stopped. "Yes. Are you sure you won't?"

Jackson sighed and looked toward the jagged edge of the dark horizon.

"If you did," Shevi said, "you could come for me."

Jackson turned to the Iron Curtain, saw how the patterns along the bottom disappeared into the ground. No telling how far down they went. Along the top, silhouetted against the purple sky was a looped strand of barbed wire. Circular objects fastened it to the top of the curtain of steel signs. Insulators, Jackson knew—to keep the voltage in the wire from grounding to the signs. Once again, he was trapped between electric current and the ground, like he'd been when he vamped the connection to Wheel Three back in I Town for that nasty creature, Mr. Myrtle.

He gripped her hand tighter than he ever had held anything. "Whatever we do, we'll do together."

She leaned forward to kiss him, but again they were cut short. Two men on bicycles rattled past them, one on each side. Two more halted before them. Little lights on the handlebars died out when they stopped. Coils of wire on the struts and the magnets on the spokes of the front wheels induced the current for the lights. The two men drew long shafts from over their shoulders. Knocker rods. The two prongs ready to inflict a quick, painful stab of voltage. Shevi and Jackson parted and raised their hands in surrender—they'd both had enough of knocker rods over the last twenty-four hours.

Jackson suddenly saw an aspect of the situation that should have been obvious the instant the guards came into view. "Hey, you're free," he whispered and then laughed at himself—who was going to hear him out here in the middle of a field? "Come with us."

He reached out his hand in friendship to these poor souls who had managed to slip out of the relentless grip of the Iron Curtain. The results were grins, exchanged glances, and finally one of them lodging the prongs of his knocker rod into Jackson's bare chest.

It could be fatal. Jackson heard his own thought, as if one part of his psyche were conversing with another. So close to the heart. The voltage propelled him backward and onto the ground while, in some other universe far from the white hot pain he wondered what could have been wrong with his logic. No one ever escaped the maniacal regime of Agrarianna, and yet these guards had. Who wouldn't run from the oppression? Why hadn't they seen the huge advantages of his offer?

Questions crowded his mind until it was a black abyss.

Shevi gasped at the guard's unprovoked attack. Jackson was just trying to be nice. He just wanted to help them.

The other guard said, "Now he's not so smart." He pointed his knocker rod at Shevi. "You got any wise remarks to share?"

Shevi shook her head, stood perfectly still with her hands raised in surrender. She appreciated Jackson's forwardness and his desire to help these poor people, but in the last few hours she'd had all the knocker rod contact she wanted for the rest of her life. She wasn't as strong as Jackson, didn't have his willingness to take chances and risk everything. She guessed it was because she'd lived the good life back in I Town. Back there she was all but a queen—at least a princess—while Jackson had been little more than dirt.

The rhythmic beat of running footsteps approached, more people who had made it out of the hell of Agrarianna. Surely some of them would come to their senses and lead a permanent escape. Four men in the same camel brown uniforms ran up.

"What have we got?" one of them asked.

"Three," the guard who had zapped Jackson declared proudly.

"Excellent. Jasper and Lincoln, take these back. We'll go get the other." He and another guard ran on to where the dogs had taken Cole down.

The other two carelessly grabbed up Jackson's hands and feet and began hauling him in the direction the train had gone.

Shevi couldn't stand it anymore. She had to say something even if it meant taking another knocker rod charge. "You're not seriously going back, are you? After you got out?"

The guard who had stunned Jackson shook his staff to recharge it. The other said, "You contentionist scum. You're all the same. One more word and you'll be joining your pal in La-la Land." He motioned with the end of his staff.

Shevi drew herself in as small as she could to slip past the end of the man's weapon and follow Jackson's carted body toward the doom of Agrarianna. If he'd lasted a little longer, he would have figured a way out of this. The instance of the Duel Wheel coming off its undercarriage shone as brightly in her mind as the beam of the searchlight that followed her now. The audience that had gathered to witness her and Jackson's inevitable and unavoidable demise had witnessed Jackson's buoyancy instead—his resiliency. He would get them out of this when he came around.

She trudged forward. That one hope keeping her from falling down on the ground and giving up, digging like an animal into the dirt to escape, making them stun her and put her out of her conscious misery.

The rails of the train track disappeared under the hideous wall of signs. A guard tower rose above. Jackson was on his feet now, barely, staggering along between the two guards who had carried him. He didn't look back or seem to know where they were, still dazed from the pain of electric shock. One of the guards pounded on a big brown sign with KNOTS BAY BOAT ACCESS written sideways up it and an arrow pointing heavenward. The sign swung inward where the terrible place of Agrarianna waited to destroy them. Shevi watched Jackson, hoping to see him looking around, taking everything in in his methodical way, dissecting the environment and locating its weaknesses, but he just swung loosely between the guards as they took him into the gaping mouth of the beast.

Shevi's head swooned. The morning seemed suddenly very bright as she took the last few steps of freedom, before her life officially ended. Her resolve to trust in Jackson waned. What if they didn't get them out? Couldn't? What if this awful place was too much even for him? She couldn't do it. She couldn't pass through that horrible portal of doom.

"Miss?" one of the guards behind her said.

Her steps were small and unpredictable, the muscles in her legs trying to take charge of her destiny and save the rest of her from death.

A strong hand clutched her arm—squeezing, lifting and guiding.

"No," she panted, her head shaking side to side as if on a broken neck.

"Miss." The voice was stern now.

"No," she repeated. "No. Please. No."

The maw of the beast was right in front of her. It was so big now. Oh, it hadn't looked so huge and overwhelming from the distance when it opened. An iron pipe served as the threshold. She would have to step over it. Oh, God, how could she? It was the gate to Hell and she had to make the effort to lift her feet over that line on the ground.

She grabbed at the sides of the opening, wanting to hold herself back, but another hand took her other arm and forced her inside.

Everything around her was metal, all hard and cold. Rust and dirt everywhere. Dim light bulbs under metal overhangs. And the smell of death. The place reeked of death. On the loading platform beside a train that here seemed rustier and dirtier that it had back home, a man struggled. Two other men contended with him. They would kill him. That's what happened here. Everyone knew it. Everyone said it. It was a place of death and of damnation and of no return, of lost hope. They would kill this man right in front of her. Maybe it would be her initiation into this hell, to witness death firsthand and know its certainty.

Ahead of her Jackson straightened up and stiffened, halting between his captors. "Dad?" he said. "Dad!" He bolted forward.

One guard grabbed him. "Hold on, boy. That's none of your business."

Now recognizing that it was Levine Koss, Jackson's father, Shevi yelled, "It's his dad."

The guard said, "There is only one father of us all in Agrarianna, and that's not him."

Jackson looked over his shoulder at Shevi. He looked around, taking in where they were. His eyes bulged. "Oh." It was a hopeless sigh.

www.Agrarianna.com